The set-up is perfect: it's 1972, a bunch of hippies & misfits are living in and around a ramshackle hotel on the beach in tropical Africa. The counter-cultural detail is funny and deeply authentic - Jim Anderson was at the centre of London's sixties counter-culture. The story-telling is terrific: shades of Evelyn Waugh's Black Mischief *and Tom Sharpe. Makes you think too.* Barry Miles, author, definitive biographer of the beat/hippy generation and sixties counter culture.

Jim Anderson's new novel is an epic of rootlessness and the search for certainty – it has swung me round and flung me out of the window into a freakish, comedic free-fall. Its message seems to be: in the modern world the only anchor is truth to self – but I'm not sure. Duncan Fallowell, novelist, travel writer, critic.

An exuberant, rollicking narrative spiked with sex, drugs, and a thoroughly wicked wit. Graeme Aitken, author of *Vanity Fierce.*

Jim Anderson's Chipman's African Adventure *is the ideal gift for all those who lived through the sixties and seventies but can't remember anything about them. And an eye-opener for those who weren't there but wish they had been. A splendid psychedelic flashback of all that weird and wonderful sex and drugs and therapy and the rest of it, before the shades of political correctness rolled in and tried to shut it all down.* Michael Wilding, author and Emeritus Professor, English & Australian Literature, University of Sydney.

Jim Anderson has always been pulled towards both the literary and the visual arts. He graduated as a lawyer from Sydney University in 1961, but says he can't remember anything he learned. He discovered bohemia and frequented the Sydney Push in the late 1950's and was soon caught up in Sydney's counter culture. *Where Have All the Flowers Gone*, his *roman a clef* based on those experiences, remains unpublished.

He became Art Editor of Oz Magazine in the UK in time to be put in the dock as a conspirator in the famous 1971 Obscenity trial at London's Old Bailey. After the demise of Oz in 1973, he spent 20 years in the US where, as well as engaging in various hippie excesses, he edited the Monday edition of *The Bolinas Hearsay News*, for which he also designed front covers and wrote a column on the previous week's events. During that period he also worked as amanuensis for writer Charles Fox (*The Noble Enemy, Portrait in Oil*) and had a novel of his own published, *Billarooby* (1988) a wartime story set in the Australian outback.

Since returning to Sydney in 1993, Jim has continued his editing, writing and photo-artist careers and still plays an active role in the cultural activities of the GLBT community. Anti-establishment satire has remained a focus. Exhibitions of his art include a major retrospective, *Lampoon, an historical art trajectory 2011* at the University of Sydney's Tin Sheds Gallery.

It has been said that, of all the youthful Oz-related revolutionaries, 'it is only Jim Anderson and Martin Sharp who have apparently attained life membership of Bohemia.'

Chipman's African Adventure is Jim Anderson's second novel.

CHIPMAN'S AFRICAN ADVENTURE

Jim Anderson

Valentine Press

First published by Valentine Press 2015

Valentine Press
P.O. Box 527,
Bellingen NSW 2454
www.valentinepress.com.au

National Library of Australia Cataloguing-in-Publication entry:

Creator:	*Anderson, Jim, 1937-, author*
Title:	*Chipman's African Adventure/Jim Anderson*
ISBN:	*9780994224408 (paperback)*
Subjects:	*Satire*
	Gays-Travel-Africa-Humor
	Africa – Humor
Dewey Number:	*A823.3*

Printed and bound in Australia by Lightning Source Australia

Front Cover artwork, Jim Anderson
Interior drawings, Peter Kingston

When you have finished reading **Chipman's African Adventure**, Valentine Press and Jim Anderson would appreciate your feedback. There is a Reader's Comments page on the Valentine Press website: **http://valentinepress.com.au/?page_id=1866**

Characters in the Story

The International Travellers

Chipman Smith, a 30 something lawyer with the NSW Department of the Attorney General; on recovery leave, staying at the Hornbill Palace Hotel at Tlula Leisure Beach in Bomzawe, an imagined country in West Africa.
Dr. Starry Sanguini, an idealistic if disaffected Sydney psychotherapist, living in a customised bus near the hotel.
The Honourable Cerisia Twitchley, Sanguini's wife, daughter of Lord Wittering, former British Ambassador to Libya.
Zach Shaler, an aspiring but troubled Peace Corps worker from Nebraska, staying at the hotel.
Drift, a dropped-out Chicagoan zoologist, collecting mambas for an English private zoo.
Toffee, his transcendentally beautiful but disturbed girlfriend.
Lotus, Californian flower child and artist also travelling in the customised bus.
Stan Francisco, her boyfriend, a musician and acid casualty.
Floralee Bush, former Canberra political wife, now a globe-trotting Byron Bay grannie searching for naturally growing hallucinogens in the Bomzawe rainforests.
William Oates, Consular Attache at the British Embassy in Okidoki.
Wally Whitbread, Deputy Clerk of the Peace, Chipman Smith's boss back in Australia.
Seamus Shamrock, old friend of Starry Sanguini, saxophone player and courier for the Professor Adolf Siegfried Clinic in Switzerland.
Sundry hippie 'dreck', passing through.

The Locals

Sir Henry Kmango, a rich tycoon, owner of the Hornbill Palace Hotel at Tlula Leisure Beach. Convenor of the hotel's fabled Easter Carnival.
Lady Chompia Kmango, somewhat disillusioned wife of Sir Henry.
Ulysses Oratorio, exiled Great Liberator of Bomzawe. Suspected of absconding with the priceless Bomzawe Bronzes.
Ntank, Sir Henry's sexy if brutish chauffeur.
Attah Lalwani, from India, chef and manager of the Hornbill.
Qumqwat, schoolgirl who works part time at the Hornbill.
Qwesi Lanfal, bartender at the Hornbill.
Qojo Lanfal, his younger brother who cooks for Dr Sanguini on the beach.
Qofia, Lady Kmango's personal beautician. Cousin of Qojo.
Lilibet and Josiah Lanfal, parents of Qwesi and Qojo.
Qaddo, ganja grower and protector of Drift.
Blossom Rokoku, enemy of Sir Henry Kmango. She runs a local bar and chop-house.
Fangga, Snake Fetish Priest, friend of the mambas which infest the hotel grounds.
Kraka, the much feared Crocodile Fetish Priest.
Akwa, chief of Tlula village.
Samuel Ichoko, director of the National Museum in Okidoki, responsible for the Bomzawe Bronzes.
Bonnie & Clyde, two Hornbills, symbol of marital fidelity.
Old Idi, an Eared Vulture.
Sundry villagers.

CONTENTS

BOOK ONE
BUMPY LANDINGS
Thula Leisure Beach, The People's Democratic Republic of Bonzawe, West Africa

PART ONE
The Beautiful Afreakans

ONE: *A tide in the affairs of men*

The flight from Sydney had been long and arduous. Chipman was not looking his best and the woman at the Embassy front desk was flinty-eyed and uncommunicative. She handed him an envelope and disappeared into a back room

3rd February 1972
Dear Chipman Smith,

Awfully peeved about this. Going to miss you by an hour or more. Have had to whizz up north. Some of our citizenry caught in the tribal cross fire. Back in a day or two. Had digs lined up for you near the Embassy, but my advice is to clear out of Okidoki until everything has blown over. It might take a while but don't worry, it will. This is Bomzawe, not Biafra. I suggest you take a bus to Doggone, the provincial capital and then a trotro (a taxi truck) to Tlula Leisure Beach, a resort near the border. It's a way but you'll find a delightful old hotel right on the water called the Hornbill Palace. All the lobster and prawns you can eat. Relaxation. Fun. Ruined slave castle on the headland. Dutch, very romantic. Best beach in the whole of West Africa. No jelly fish, no undertow, no sharks, no robbers, no rubbish. It's something of a 'hippie' hangout in fact, but there's also a very decent psychotherapist chap I met briefly at a reception here,. His name escapes me but another 'Aussie' in fact. Charming blue blood English wife. Your impending arrival never came up, but I realise now he may be of some assistance in getting you through your little career crisis. I'll give you a tingle when I return to base and we will meet. You'll thank me for this. You're going to have a 'leisurely' time. Sink one for me in the hotel bar. I won't tell Wally. Ha ha!
Cheers, William Oates.
P.S. There's a bus at 11 am from Western Region Transport Hall.

"Psychotherapist?" Chipman queried to himself. What on earth had Wally Whitbread actually said to Oates?

"Everyone love Attah." Attah Lalwani, manager and chef at the Hornbill Palace Hotel, booked Chipman in, handed back his passport. Lalwani was an oleaginous, middle aged Sindhi with protuberant lips, a stringy moustache and no chin. In profile he looked like a catfish. "My pleasure to carry bag and escort you to your room."

They entered the first of four rows of slant-roofed bungalows, gaily painted in pastel shades, but dilapidated and under attack from rampaging tropical vegetation. Several gangly birds with bushy eyelashes and enormous ivory-coloured beaks, surmounted by a casque, were wandering unconcernedly about.

"These our famous hornbills," said Attah, deftly kicking a couple of them high in the air. ORK! ORK! they shrieked, urging themselves off with a creaky flapping of wings. "Those two called Bonnie & Clyde."

Chipman knew the reference but winced. Large birds made him nervous. He had yet to forgive two black swans who many years ago had attacked him and his best mate Tibor Radovan in their rowing boat on Narrabeen lagoon. Alfie (his father) had parried them away with an oar.

Attah bowed Chipman up some rickety wooden stairs and along a railed verandah which fronted a set of rooms at the back of the main hotel. "No bungalow but an airy repose is yours for the keeping, Mr Chipman Smith. My sorrow it is infinite but we is scrubbing up lovely bungalows for Easter Carnival. I put you next to poor Mr Shaler. Mr Zach." Half way along the verandah, Attah paused and peered through a jalousie. "He sleeping. I tell you he sleep a lot these last days." He tapped his temple. "Have a squint but cover your eyes. He has entirely nothing on."

A man with dark shoulder length hair lay on his back, head towards them on the pillow, one knee raised, concealing his nakedness. An arm dangled over the edge of the bed. He hadn't shaved for a while. Thirtyish, Chipman's age, his face presenting a sad and wearied look. There was a pale equatorial tan to his skin. A bandage with dried blood stains had been wound around his head. Even as Chipman gazed, the knee went down, Mr Zach's eyes opened and Chipman felt the strength of a wide-awake stare. Hastily, he moved back. He liked the look of the man, and felt there was a reason for that, but was unable to tell himself why. There came Attah's voice again.

"He American Peace Corps worker. Arrive hotel one day and lie around on beach very tragic. He fair to middling gentleman, he read books, but..."Attah twirled a finger above his ear. "There is talk he murder someone long time ago. Now that no good Mr Sanguini come and look after him." Attah let his nostrils flare and eyes to widen in disapproval. His eyeballs had purple discolourations.

The walls of Chipman's room were a faded mustardy colour, the ceiling lowered by being painted indigo. There was a large wardrobe, a small table, a single bed, a couple of frayed canvas chairs. A shower and a flush toilet in a tiled alcove occupied the far end. Attah set an overhead fan wobbling. Tiny dipterous insects were already making themselves at home. Through a gap in the lush foliage he glimpsed the promised 'best beach in all of West Africa' and the ocean, a murky blue under a hazy sky.

The wardrobe was actually a well-finished English rosewood period piece, with a substantial key, and the bed had a bright, Bomzawean patterned coverlet, but to Chipman's mind, the room was not exactly resort accommodations. He would certainly make a complaint when William Oates rang from the Embassy. The price was a bargain, but hot water would be extra and if he wanted Qumqwat or the other girls to clean, that would be extra also. A telephone was available in the hotel office but Attah warned it was difficult for guests to get through to "the infinitely faraway world." And watch out for mambas. "Mr Fangga, the Snake Fetish Priest he cause many to infest bungalow area. We call black mamba the two-step. First step on the snake, second step into the grave."

Chipman assumed that was an exaggeration. He gave Attah a grin, just to humour him. "Ah! I forgot." He handed over three letters from the satchel he had slung over his shoulder. "Josiah Lanfal, the trotro driver gave them to me. The hotel mail."

Attah sifted through them. "I not want this one. You give to Mr Sanguini your sweet self. He ignore my excellent dining room. He make insultations about me and my girls. I high morals professional man. He not even stay at hotel but he ablute here and pay no dues. That performer fellow, his group, they..."

"Where do I find him?"

"Heh heh!" Attah laughed nastily. "He find you beware, Mr Chipman."

The effort to appear sober in front of the manager had taken its toll. Chipman put the vivid coverlet away in the wardrobe and managed to sleep for an hour before rising to take a shower. A slug or two from the first of the bottles of Johnny Walker he had scored at the 'infinitely faraway' Okidoki International Airport, a valium, and he felt ready to face his destiny, or at least his immediate future. Grabbing his Camel Filters, he got himself down the rickety stairs and into the heat of the afternoon.

Almost immediately he was waylaid by a muscular, heavily bearded man. There was the suggestion of a jagged chest scar that disappeared under the beard. A wiry tangle of darkish brown hair stuck out from beneath a tattered baseball cap on which was embroidered in green lettering, ADOLF. A sleek, even gangster looking pair of sunglasses added to the concealing façade. Of average height, with swarthy skin, he was wearing only a pair of blue cotton shorts. His sturdy, nicely haired legs caused a small, unwanted desire to stir in Chipman.

"Dr Salvatore Sanguini. Call me Starry, if you like." There was a forward step and even the suggestion of a curtsy. A smell of seaweed and fresh underarm sweat came wafting

Chipman handed over the letter, feeling he should be giving it to someone who looked more like a real doctor. Italian heritage, he assumed, with a name like a pasta.

Sanguini was a man both impulsive and impatient. He stamped his feet like a brat, swirled theatrically about, sent a post card that was inside the envelope sailing into the shrubbery. What dipsomania had left of the sleuth in Chipman knew instantly that Sanguini was the therapist recommended by William Oates, even though there was nothing grave or distinguished, nothing remotely respectable about him. And what was on that card that required it to be concealed in an envelope?

The glasses had been repaired with gaffer tape and Chipman did wonder what Sanguini might look like behind the beard. He rather liked the man's hawkish nose which created a certain handsomeness, causing him to give his own nose a circumspect squeeze between thumb and forefinger. Chipman was in fact, rather pleased to be (for the first time since his plane touched down in Okidoki), conversing with someone comfortingly un-black. Pleased but also aware of Dr Sanguini giving him a hard once-over. Sanguini was in fact assessing him as a future patient, but Chipman took it as a look of envy of his summery, and not inexpensive, David Jones suit, the daring op-art tie he was wearing. Apeing Wally Whitbread, his fashion conscious boss at the Department of the Attorney General and of Justice, had Chipman keeping up with Sydney urban style, as in fact he did even in his drunkest, darkest days back home.

"So who are you?" Dr Sanguini queried, pulling his cap a little lower on his forehead. Not entirely seriously, he added, "I'm not particularly fond of taller men."

Chipman was tired and vulnerable. He handed over the missive he had been given that morning at the British Embassy reception desk. "Chipman? What sort of name is that? I bet I'll be calling you Chip."

"Please don't. It's an old family name. My father was proud of our Scottish American ancestry. After the Californian goldrush…"

Dr Sanguini interrupted. "Australia has no diplomatic representation here of course. Lets London do the dirty work." His voice, of which he was very fond, was a buttery baritone. In the ten years since Sanguini had left Australia, it had become more BBC than any kind of ANZAC. "That communication from Professor bloody Siegfried was the last straw." He rummaged in the shrubbery and retrieved the card. "Did Attah give you a tour of the dreaded bungalow area?"

"He told me about the mambas. The early grave."

"I feel your fear. OK, the bar it is. You want some suncream for that nose of yours? Or even something stronger?" Dr Sanguini snickered at the whisky and more, on Chipman's breath.

"Thank you but it's not burned, and I am not a drunk." After a moment's pause, he added, as he often did to ease his extreme self-consciousness about his nose in new situations. "It inexplicably turned this colour a few months ago. It's a rare condition."

"Still beyond the reach of medical science." Dr Sanguini smiled pleasantly as he pressed an advantage and took hold of Chipman by the elbow. "You are a little unsteady on your feet."

"I'm not. Well, maybe, I'm on leave from my job."

"Who does your hair?"

"It's natural."

"And so very blond."

From the trees above there came an eruption of cicada rattling. It caused Chipman's head to fill with a sublime childhood memory. "Imagine me thinking only Australia has cicadas."

"Couldn't get out of that dreary country quickly enough." Dr Sanguini's hand moved from elbow to a tousling of Chipman's neat little curls. "Let me shout you a cocktail. A Pink Lady perhaps?"

"I don't like cocktails." Privately, Chipman rather did, but he found Dr Sanguini's fingers intrusive and the inference that he was, like that, offensive.

"How could I have got it so wrong?"

The bar was in the main building which seemed unusual in its size for such a remote location, almost like a hangar for small aircraft. It had a wide gable, was lofty and open on all sides to catch the slightest breeze. The square wooden pillars which held up the corrugated iron roof had decorative capitals, picked out in purple and green, the colours bleached by salt and sun. Two magnificent poincianas overhung the building and there were several varieties of exotic palm in the forecourt. The hotel had been built right on the broad, white sand beach and had a solid feel to it, but like the bungalows, it was in danger of being devoured by the jungle advancing ominously from the hills behind. The national flag, vertical bands of yellow, black and white, a red star in the centre of the black, hung listlessly on a pole.

An early Beatles song was playing on a Dansette. *Love, love me do, You know I love you* ... The bartender, his hands cupped under his chin, elbows on the bar, was clearly asleep. Dr Sanguini de-propped him with a rough chop of the hand.

"Excuse me, suh, I forty wink."

"Two Red Star beer, Qwami. And a glass of whisky for the travel weary Mr Chipman Smith here. Your new customer. You don't get many. Take a good look at him."

Qwami was a plumpish youth, of pantherine blackness, like everyone Chipman had met since arriving in Bomzawe. The voluptuous market women who had shared the benches in the trotro from Doggone, had skin so black it was blue. Exotic people, neatly lipped, eared and nosed, pink palmed people crowding in on him from all sides; everyone was very dark – and shiny – indeed.

Qwami was taking his good look and grinning. Beautiful white teeth. Chipman refused to admit that a black person could be sexually attractive, and made himself look away. He was only aroused by the unavailable and older man anyway. As he – with increasing bitterness – was fond of musing.

"Put it on my bill, Qwami." The doctor pushed a coin across the counter. "No need to tip but dash him if you want coldies."

"Thank you, Dr Sanguini," said Chipman as the whisky was handed to him. He was not a man easily able to refuse a drink.

"Qwami is Lilibet Lanfal's eldest, aren't you Qwami? A lady of some substance. Qojo, his younger brother, cooks for us every night by the sand." Sanguini took a good pull on his beer. "The village girls are required to be virginal unfortunately, but there's accommodating widows, not to mention wives." He paused, eyed the newcomer over his bottle. "The young men are always available of course." Chipman was irritated by yet another lurid inference, but lit up and offered the doctor his pack.

"Tobacco? Don't smoke. You'll soon run out of those here."

The bar was less than busy. Four sunburned Scandinavian men – lank flaxen hair, baggy shorts and rubber thongs – were sprawled around a formica-topped table amid a haze of smoke. A torpid game of poker was in progress. They called for more margaritas. Scarlet the Harlot, a careworn, local 'fancy lady', bare midriff in a short stretch skirt, arrived, doing her nails. She demanded they buy her one too. Smiling sweetly she sat on a welcoming knee. Further off, a couple of teenage boys, licorice torsoes slick with sweat, were immersed in an unleisurely game of ping pong. A tall, slender man moving languidly about to The Beatles, and dressed in a turban, a cream coloured djellaba and red leather babouches, was Hamou, a watchman. An exiled Fulani from Chad, he was the one who would change Chipman's money into the local currency.

Dr Sanguini borrowed Qwami's damp bar rag and cooled his brow. Overhead fans swirled sluggishly in the dry air. A fly-specked mural of a large African gentleman fully occupied the area above Qwami's bottles. Splendid in a powder blue tuxedo and spotted bow-tie, he was portrayed with an oily, avuncular obesity, his right hand about to drop a centipede into the gaping mouth of a hornbill. Underneath was a poorly spaced caption:

BE   LOVED ULYSSES – FREE DOM FOR ALL BOMZA WEANS.

"Yes, Ulysses Oratorio, Bomzawe's Great Liberator. Close friend of Sylvanus Olimpio in Togo."

"I saw an overturned statue in Okidoki. Bigger than a Greyhound bus. Someone had tried to hack off its head."

"There's been madness in this country ever since the Liberator fled. Five years ago now. President Mguavas is finally doing the right thing and bringing the great man back from banishment. A misunderstood hero."

The doctor waggled his broad, high-arched feet. His legs were stretched out at right angles from his bar stool. He noticed Chipman's sudden interest and smiled. "Legs! My finest attribute." The bare limbs and shoeless feet had Chipman thinking of Wally Whitbread, and the fact that his ultimatum would have to be faced sooner rather than later. Until the shocking mention of a psychotherapist in William Oates' letter, he had not thought even once about therapy of any kind. In fact, he now found himself hating the idea of it as something entirely debasing. When Wally had confronted him back in Sydney, he had not used the term. Wally, fortunately, had allowed him to be neither a mental case nor – a queer. He was just a drunk.

"You must be surprised to find a hippie haven like this on your trip, Chipman. It's the Hornbill's cheap accommodation. Owned by a tycoon called Henry Kmango. Sir Henry, if you please. A mad Anglophile." The doctor downed more beer, ran a tongue around his somewhat thick lips. "The hotel's been falling apart ever since Ulysses Oratorio got axed. Telephone never works. Kmango subsidises the place from other enterprises, cacao and palm oil plantations, a gold mine, off-shore oil. Newspapers. He has lost interest in it but keeps it going with a skeleton staff. Locals, to keep Tlula village happy."

Qwami changed the music, turned up the volume. Chipman recognized *Sergeant Pepper's Lonely Hearts Club Band*, and didn't mind but Dr Sanguini clapped his hands over his ears for a moment and moved away. Chipman bought a couple more beers, downed another whisky (Qwami, he was pleased to note, made no use of a shot glass) and joined the doctor who indicated a thatched pavilion, one of several under the palms, close to the sand and well away from the loudspeakers. The hard-packed pale earth of the area was the domain of many large dozey lizards, grey-backed, sulphur yellow underneath, an orange knob at the end of a long tail. Dr Sanguini, to Chipman's amazement, started stalking one of them. The man lunged and the lizard was up a tree trunk. The doctor did some low, wide-legged movements in imitation of the fat lizard's waddle and laughed. Chipman, although a discreet and polite man, even when inebriated, let out a derisory exhalation before he could suppress it. "Sorry," he said, an apologetic hand going to his thorax.

"They expend the least effort but always get away!" The doctor smirked. "Like me."

To Chipman's ears, there was something less than inconsequent in the tone of this remark. The quizzical look the doctor then gave him produced the thought that this was a man with a dubious past. But there also came an unexpected determination to overcome any misgivings and take up William Oates' suggestion. He cleared his throat. "Dr Sanguini, about your therapy, I…"

"I have had love affairs with lizards. Australia has goannas and many other wonderful reptiles, as you must know. I've had trouble moving on." At this, there came a wide grin, a facial statement that Sanguini liked to impose in close encounters with others. It revealed that he had a couple of teeth too many, and that there was a snaggly one, protruding on the upper left. Sanguini felt it to be disarming, rather than lascivious which was how Chipman judged it. "Remind me about Australia. I hear koalas are in trouble."

"They've got a virus."

"Aborigines extinct yet?"

"They wish to walk with us. They don't want to walk alone."

"I'd give them a name change. You've got Chinese, Maltese, Portuguese. Call the poor buggers Aboriginese. That would give them a bit of a leg up. Ha ha! Opera House finished?"

"It's coming along."

"So suburban, the harbour. What Sydney needs is a truly spectacular feature – a Vesuvius instead of Parramatta or something. That would send whatever imagination's down there soaring."

The doctor stretched for the *Okidoki Post* – left on the pavilion table – and turned the pages. "Here, one of Kmango's rags. Read the editorial. Three days ago, President Mguavas sacked General

Kporpor, Minister for Internal Security and he's retreated to his pomegranate orchard at Larrikini in the Islamic north."

WHAT IS OUR BLACK PEARL OF A COUNTRY COMING TO
"...the palmy days are long gone, but fomentation of ethnic unrest and creation of armed militias is not the answer. Do we want to wind up with jackal packs scouring the streets of our treasured capital? More than any other West African country, perhaps to a fault, we have contrived that our reputation not be tarnished on the world stage, but what has happened to our British friends is an unpardonable crime against humanity and we have to come clean. With the International Committee of the Red Cross reconsidering its guidelines in the light of this outrage, it is time that Bomzawe..."

"A supply convoy on its way from Okidoki to Ouagadougou in Upper Volta was hijacked, medical supplies and 4000 sacks of grain seized, two British aid workers hacked to pieces and burned."

"Oh my God! No wonder William Oates is busy."

"Nothing's going to stop me being here for the big Carnival."

Chipman was relieved to have a change of subject. He had finished his second beer and barely managed to stop himself from taking a swig from the doctor's bottle. "Yes, what is this Carnival? Attah..."

"Sports and entertainment. Many Ye Olde English touches. Cultural detritus from colonial days. This year for some reason, Kmango is restoring the tradition. I'm looking forward to it. Cerisia and I are going to get Sir Henry to hire us both to dance. She can sing too."

Again Dr Sanguini was a surprise. The lizard waddle? Chipman gave way. That, he supposed, was a sort of dance.

"The Honourable Cerisia Twitchley. My wife. You might call our African trip our honeymoon. We were in the tabloids. *The People. The News of the World"*

"You're a dancer as well as a doctor?"

"Jung was yitterbugging way into his dotage."

"Who?"

"Oratorio, the Great Liberator was no wallflower. Most adept at the political polka but it was the sheerest luck he escaped with his life. There's a story."

"I read in the *Daily Telegraph* once, of an amusing scandal involving the Liberator. A dog."

"Yes, on his big visit to Buckingham Palace he sat on one of the Queen's corgis. Killed it. Ha ha! He requested asylum in England, the obvious place for him, but the British Government turned him down. The Queen had something to do with it."

"My taxi driver in Okidoki said that Oratorio looted the Treasury, lives high on the hog in Haiti of all places. Not only that but he stole the world famous Bomzawe Bronzes from the National Museum."

"The old bloke was welcomed there as a guest of Papa Doc Duvalier. Became President of some weird Cricket Club in Port-au-Prince. I hear he's still pissed off about the Westminster treatment and is homesick. Will do anything to be accepted back here. Anything. The Bronzes are still missing. I doubt the Liberator had anything to do with it."

A silence, the first, fell between the two men.

Why on earth had he not done some proper research on Bomzawe before allowing himself to be railroaded into this solution to his 'problem'? was Chipman's thought. He seemed to have walked into the beginnings of a civil war. And the Liberator sounded somewhat disreputable. A wave of paranoia came. Maybe Whitbread had cooked this up with Oates as a discreet means of getting rid of him. He hated to see it that way, but he supposed it had been a terrible thing, spying on Wally's naked sexual activities like that. Closing his eyes, he gave his head some physical attention. Chipman knew a dozen or more shakes and continuous hard massage with his fingers could do it.

Long before Chipman finished dealing with his crisis, Dr Sanguini had abandoned him. By the time the lawyer opened his eyes again, the largest of the lizards had moved close and was casting basilisk eyes at him. It began something that looked like press-ups, a pumping of itself for attack. Chipman was scared but could not bring himself to give it a good kick. Hastily retreating to the other side of the table he looked around in vain for the absent Sanguini. What the hell; he snatched the doctor's bottle of beer and drained it. It didn't help, and paranoia came engulfing once again.

TWO: *Between the devil and the deep blue sea*

"Argh!" Chipman let out a scream before he realised that it was a hand that was clamped firmly down on the top of his skull. Dr Sanguini's hand.

"You need to take a swim. Come on, get yourself up!"

Sanguini scattered the lizards and hurdled the low sea wall onto the sand even before Chipman was on his feet. The doctor's activity jolted something in Chipman. "Doctor, were you famous for anything in Sydney?"

Sanguini turned, took a second or two to reply. "No, not me. I was a nobody back then. Over here I snared the Honourable Cerisia Twitchley. Now I'm famous..."

Chipman made the mistake of dismissing any thought of familiarity from his mind. "I'll get my togs."

"Don't bother," Sanguini called as he hopped, skipped and jumped towards the water.

Chipman returned to his room, changed. A reflexive action had him tossing down more Johnny Walker. He reached for a towel, a fresh pack of Camels, and his camera, one he had specially bought for his big adventure.

Dr Sanguini had joined a knot of men and boys around a large canoe that had been hauled out fifty yards further down the wide beach. Heartburn and a hiccup or two caused Chipman to stop. He took a couple of pictures of what was going on ahead, resumed his trudge, and was surprised to see amid the group, Zach Shaler, the man with the pale equatorial tan from the room next door and still with his bandage – 'Poor Mr Zach.'

He was horrified to realise what it was that the fishermen, wiry limbs glistening in the late sun, were lifting from the canoe. His intestines crawled but he took a photograph of a bare-torsoed body, that of a young black man. The head was bashed and broken, the eyes partly detached, hanging out on stalks. There was a deep slash below the neck. The body had begun to bloat, as though it had been in the sea a day or so.

Horrified yes, but what really stopped Chipman in his stride, was what happened next. Zach shouted something, threw himself at the body, embraced it. The fishermen erupted with a chorus of dismay, and in a single joint effort, wrenched him aside. Dr Sanguini put an arm around Zach's shoulders but was forcefully rejected, with Zach instead, following when the dead man was carried away. But not before he turned and took a look at Chipman. What was it about those green, gold flecked eyes, was the thought, what kind of craziness lived in there? Well, Attah had already warned him.

Chipman Smith had never seen a corpse of any sort before, not even his Dad's and cringed at how his mind had been attracted to the sight. Did that confirm alcoholic poisoning? That his brain was diseased? He noticed his hands were trembling as he lit a cigarette.

"Mr Smith, I assure you there is nothing to be frightened of here." Dr Sanguini's matter of fact voice brought him back. "Your friend William Oates at the Embassy was right to recommend the Hornbill. Of all the places in Bomzawe at the moment, Tlula has to be the safest."

Chipman kept his eyes on Zach and the fishermen who were disappearing behind a row of beach shacks.

"They float in from time to time now. Kraka takes care of them. He's the Crocodile Fetish Priest. One of the local sorcerers."

"What on earth could that bloke have been up to?"

"Ah, yes, Zach Shaler. The Nebraskan cowboy with the Peace Corps dreams. His parents were Baptist missionaries, no less, before they settled down in Omaha. Cleans up in the village but spends a lot of time in Castle Vinkenoog. He is involved in some kind of pathological war with himself."

"He showed some anger towards you."

The doctor gave a dismissive grunt. "I'm looking forward to the challenge. I can only hazard a guess at this point what his problem is. Enjoys his food though. That's a hopeful sign."

Chipman had to turn away from the intensity of the doctor's gaze but he did wonder if Zach Shaler enjoyed a drink as well as his food.

The sound of tomtoms and chanting, heralding the approach of, of all things, a palanquin, was coming from further down the shore. Four Tlula youths were carrying it, each wearing a smart orange cap in the manner of a uniform. Reclining on the contraption's cushions was a bare-breasted woman, of generous proportions, with unruly red-dark hair. Cavorting around her were several people, festively if minimally clad. Very picturesque, the whole scene Chipman allowed, and clicked away. Were these the 'hippies'? Oates had mentioned, the hotel as a 'hippie haven'.

"Was your camera good enough to get Cerisia?" The lady in question was waving from the near distance. "My very own lady love and her Boys returning with tonight's lobster. Our band of outcasts live like kings and queens here." Dr Sanguini readied himself to introduce Chipman, but at the last minute changed his mind. "Let's dive in."

"Best swimming in the whole of West Africa," Oates had written. "No jelly fish, no undertow, no sharks…"

"I'm sorry, Dr Sanguini, the water is looking vile. That man Zach…" Deep down, there was also a resurfacing fear of drowning. Drunk (as he was now), Chipman had been close more than once.

The doctor was not one to put up with hesitation of any sort and dragged Chipman along. The blue shorts were dropped to the sand and as they waded through the wash and froth of a broken wave, Chipman noticed that the globes of Sanguini's buttocks were coated with a fuzz of downy hair. Ridiculously, there was a hint of memory about that too. Further proof his mind was going.

As they angled towards deeper water, Dr Sanguini said, "Visit our bus tonight. The big one parked on the other side of the hotel palisade. I'll tell you all about my new mission in life here at Tlula."

A bus? William Oates' recommended therapist was living in a bus?

"Dinner. Keeping on Attah's good side is advisable. Best to get it over and done with. To dine at the hotel twice is to realise once is more than enough." He gave a snuffle at his deft phrasing. "Come by after you've eaten."

Under the water, Dr Sanguini gave a rub to the lawyer's lower vertebrae. "But only if the head on those shoulders of yours tells you therapy is the dance for you, that is." He gave the elastic of Chipman's togs a snap.

THREE: *The cropdusters of desire*

Chipman was surprised at how quickly the equatorial night fell. Attah Lalwani's dining area was down a step from the bar and had a floor of beaten earth. Rattan blinds had been lowered, ageing plastic chandeliers threw a chintzy light. A faint chug came from the hotel's generator. Hamou the watchman sat smoking and expectorating at a table for two, but Chipman was the only diner, and a disappointed one. The evening meal was an inferior example of his mother's meat and two veg fare and it left him feeling hungry. "I'm in Bomzawe," he scribbled in his now shaky hand. "I mean, Africa has to be more than this". Attah hovered, clearly wanting praise. Infinitely concerned. "Best Mayfair style broil. Everyone love Attah's cooking."

Dessert was apple pie – *Auntie Kate's* from an individual box which Attah ripped open in front of him. Nestles tinned cream followed. Chipman finished his bottle of Bomzawean claret.

"Pretty cocktail for you now, Mr Chipman Smith? Qwami can make whatever you wish. The supreme knowledge here comes from a book of recipes for London's famous Savoy Hotel itself. Created during your sad wartime privations. Sir Henry, he…"

He ordered another bottle of claret.

The second bottle went down easily enough. Suitably emboldened and feeling the full lawyer once more, Chipman Smith found himself on the way to Dr and Mrs Sanguini's bus. With darkness, a sea breeze had risen, sending the black bamboos clacking. From the vegetation came a smell of deep decay. He had swallowed a couple more of his valium supply with the wine and didn't much care about the dangers of the night. He did stamp a foot at a hiss and slither or two but soon stumbled upon the palisade, a vine covered, almost non-existent barrier which separated the hotel grounds from the village coconut grove. The ocean, glittering under the waxing moon, opened up on his left. The surf crashed softly upon the sand, like the drugs he had ingested were acting upon his senses.

The bus, something less than a Greyhound in size, was painted lavender and was labyrinthinely muralled. He made out the words *THE BEAUTIFUL AFREAKANS* curling in discouraging fashion along one side. The palanquin, a conveyance linked in his mind to colonial privilege, stood nearby. It was sturdily constructed from tree bamboo, and was both rakish and elegant, the roof thatched with dried elephant grass.

A Turkish carpet had been spread in the sandy glade. By the light of a small fire and a hanging lamp, a skinny youth, squid ink black, was clearing up, picking as he did so at the remains of a feast – lobster claws, giant prawn shells, a smattering of beans and rice, vegetables, a fruit salad. Chipman began to feel hungry all over again.

It had to be Qojo. Dr Sanguini had mentioned him. So too had Lilibet Lanfal, one of the big market women in the back of the trotro, when she had introduced herself. "My udda son. He cuisine on de beach."

He caught the sound of low conversations and laughter and looked around. This partly cleared area of the coconut grove was studded with the glow of other fires on which fish and seafood were also being grilled; at a fraction of the price, he found out, charged by Attah for his ersatz English cooking. The sound of drumming came from the village.

"Good evening. I'm looking for Dr Sanguini."

Qojo's long-lashed eyes, big and lustrous, rested on Chipman with no great surprise. "Starry he and Missus Cerisia is nappin'. You dancin' wit us tonight?" His voice was still not broken. A source of sadness for him. He was already sixteen. "De drums is for Aqosua. My sister she sick."

Chipman shook his head.

"You like eat my fish?" Qojo bent down and picked up a platter on which lay a barbecued fish, bigger than a side of lamb. There was still plenty left. Close to Chipman there was a bite sized piece. He could not resist.

"That will cost you, Mr Whoever you are," came a woman's voice.

Mortified (Chipman had become an easy prey to mortification), he coughed out the morsel, concealed it in his fist for a split second then decided to swallow it.

Qojo ran off, a spindly silhouette on the moonlit sand. "I's comin'," he called back mysteriously. What Tlulans meant when they said, "I's comin'," was "I's goin' but I's comin' back." Not necessarily soon, but sometime.

The voice, rather posh, had shot from the palanquin like a directive from the Bench. A beringed hand had pulled back the curtains. Propped up on pillows was The Honourable Cerisia Twitchley. Amber beads were roped around her neck, coral bracelets adorned her arms. The light was dim, but she was wearing nothing at all where Chipman thought it mattered. Outsized, somewhat squashed and scarcely visible behind her, was the bearded Dr Sanguini. He was observing Chipman's discomfiture with amusement.

"I'm sorry, really sorry, I was so hungry. Attah..."

"Attah!"

"Eat up," said Dr Sanguini. "It's a whopper."

"Fuck you, it's a teensy lil' ting." The ample creature loosed a belch that kept rolling up.

"Dolling..." said the doctor, nuzzling her behind an ear.

"Mmm. Toots." She gave him a kiss and turned back to Chipman, smiling, suddenly gracious. "Hoick that platter over here and feed me, like a good chappie, then you can have a morsel or tree." She leaned forward, waggled her full red lips provocatively, parted them wide. There seemed no other response but to obey. There were no utensils so he tore off a chunk and pushed it into her mouth. "More." She indicated a gourd. "Now that." She guzzled and handed it back.

Reaching out, she ripped off another piece herself. "Open wide. Stand back!" Chipman actually managed to catch her poorly judged throw, not in his mouth, but catch it. "Wash it down. Tuna can be dry."

The liquid burned his throat, exploded like a bomb in his stomach. He gagged, precipitating from her a high-pitched, gleeful cackle. "Battery acid. Should have warned you." It was a gin made from a local palm and called akpeteshie. Chipman was drinking lots on a regular basis in no time at all.

Lost over the past months, even years, to such playfulness, he stood there completely at a loss. He had found the food exchange crude but strange to say, also a tad erotic. As had been her jokey diction. He adjusted himself slightly down there.

Cerisia went squirming back into Dr Sanguini's arms. She let out another cackle, gentler this time, smooched her face into the doctor's beard. Noticing Chipman's transfixed gaze she snapped, "Twiddle off." The curtain was within her reach. "I said beat it!"

"Chipman, I'll be with you soon enough," the doctor called. "Darling, hullo? Hullo in there? *Round and round I go, down and down I go, that old black magic called ...*" The doctor's voice was developing something of a warble, a warble that also contained a boast. "I'm having an after dinner mint here. Off you go, Chipman, the bus. Enjoy the books, the magazines."

The interior of *The Beautiful Afreakans* was lit by candles and smelled of frankincense. Chipman hesitated. "Ooo, papist decadence," Alfred Chipman Smith, his father, Alfie, as everyone called him, who in early life had turned his back on any kind of religion, would have made fun of the chapel-like ambience. Yes, the lawyer was given pause but on the other hand, everything was meticulously cared for, with none of the disorder he had expected from people living in a bus. Indeed, Matilda, his mother, kept the rectory nowhere near as tidy. A polished hardwood kitchen bench containing a small metal sink ran along one side. The ceiling was painted ultramarine with swirling clouds and stars. Moonlight streamed in. A central aisle led to gloom.

Votive lamps burned before a Tibetan Buddha. LOTUS = STAN read a gaudy heart-shaped plaque. Below the windows was what Chipman hoped was more than he needed to see, a shelf of serious looking books. He switched on his little torch. *The Primal Scream* by Arthur Janov. *In and Out of the Garbage Pail* by Fritz Perls. *The Mass Psychology of Fascism* by Wilhelm Reich... He let out an "Oh dear," of dismay.

A stack of comic books cheered him up until he realised they weren't exactly the Phantom or Donald Duck. An incursion into *Snatch* by one Robert Crumb, had him snapping his head away. Too reminiscent of sexual hallucinations that had started to come and go as they pleased in his head. The alcoholic heebie jeebies. Cerisia's gin bottle had definitely been a mistake. He gave his head a few warning bangs, belched, gulped air, gathered himself, moved on. An autobiography by one Mary Kingsley – that had to be safer; a well-bred Victorian English woman who had adventured in Africa. A signed copy. *'To my adored Nigel, with much love, Mary'*, was scrawled on the flyleaf.

He selected a magazine, sat down at an oak topped dining table and found something about alcohol, the liver, and the limbic brain. The humid air made it hard to concentrate. One of the table drawers was ajar. He pulled out an exercise book and flipped through. It seemed to be full of scribbled chemistry formulations, names, dates, equations, quantities, a colour coding. All rocket science to him, but certain sections of the *NSW Crimes Act 1900* as amended, did come to mind. He permitted himself a grim smile. A Tarot deck, a stout yellow backed book called *I Ching*, a half empty carton of Gitane cigarettes, a set of tiddlywinks – and then a revolver, the dark outline gleaming dully in the candlelight. His heart gave a couple of thumps. Dr Sanguini has been travelling through dangerous climes, he reminded himself quickly, but registered? He doubted.

Chipman should have made a quick exit. Instead, he fantasised himself as an Interpol operative for Wally Whitbread, going through Dr Sanguini's case files for ever more evidence of ill repute. FAST EDDIE & NIGGLING NANCY, a slim folder, LOTUS & STAN, a hefty one. DRIFT & TOFFEE, even heftier. A fourth had a passport and a stack of US$100 bills attached to it with a metal clip. The passport belonged to Zacchaeus Gabriel Shaler. The man in the hotel room next to his. The man who had followed the black-skinned corpse to the village; born the same year as Chipman, 1940. The photo was unflattering, like a police ID shot. STARRY & CERISIA, another manila folder. Perhaps it also held passports. He couldn't resist.

"Ah, my files." Chipman had just undone the string when the file was whisked away. Dr Sanguini had stolen up behind him. There was a rich and unfamiliar bodily smell. Maybe something on his clothes. Or even an unguent in his beard.

The doctor had dressed for the evening – a well-worn, calf-length tunic, brightly tie-dyed, loosely cinched at the waist and slit open at the sides. He looked younger than he did in the afternoon brightness. Mid-thirties was Chipman's accurate guess.

"I'm sorry Dr Sanguini, really sorry, to be such a nosy parker but I was interested in finding out something about Zach Shaler."

Sanguini was not in the least upset, made a mental note of the profusion of the apology; and of Chipman's continuing interest in the weightlifter-like solidity of his thighs.

"Ah, the Nebraskan, of course. Concussion is not pretty. Cerisia is handling his affairs. Somebody had to."

"Oh dear, concussion?"

"He was arguing over losing a game of warri in Blossom's. She settled it by whacking him over the head with the flat of a tomahawk. Blossom's a bull dyke who runs the Leisurely Chophouse and Bar. She tends to take things out on people who stay at the Hornbill. Zach's been discombobulated ever since so we took him on."

The doctor noticed the exposed gun and closed the drawer. The folders were pushed to the far side of the table.

"So you take people on?"

"And my clothes off ?" He gave Chipman a questioning look.

"I beg your pardon?"

"Never mind. What do you think of the bus?"

Chipman wondered about the look, and the speed with which the doctor changed the subject. He ran his hand along the front of the table drawer and said, "Nice cabinet detailing." By way of explanation he added, "Alfie's hobby."

"Alfie?"

"My father. It was his idea way back when, that we – my sisters and I – were to call them not Mum and Dad, but by their first names."

"Radical," said the doctor giving a chuckle.

"He taught me a lot. We made a Huon pine table for Matilda, that's my mother. With tapered legs. That wasn't easy. One year we made a swing sofa and chairs for the porch. Painted. My father would have liked your ceiling."

"We have Lotus and Stan Francisco to thank for that. I have come to love the bus. Her dear Stanford is finally getting the hang of driving it. He's even fixing the handbrake. Four wheel drive capability. Cerisia had the interior all fitted up no expense spared, before we shipped it to Dakar. Hidden recesses you would never ever find. If my born-again incarnation as a therapist goes up in flames I will try my hand at smuggling – diamonds, drugs. Teenage body slaves." He snickered. "If they're cute."

The lawyer in Chipman reared up at this. Human trafficking? He would have to apprise William Oates. But surely he was joking.

He cleared his throat to respond but was distracted by the unexpected arrival of Cerisia. She was wearing a flowing gown which concealed her considerable amplitude. Her hair was a wild Beethovian mop, dyed with henna, and greying at the roots. Seeing her in full view for the first time, Chipman found there to be something Tongan, even regal, about her bulk.

"My grande dame, my dowager doll," cried the doctor, his tone syrupy. He opened his arms in welcome.

"Toots, you forgot to pull it to. Again." She was smiling but a little snappish as she reached for a lever by the steering wheel and closed the door of the bus. "Mosquitoes." Sitting down heavily at the table beside Chipman she took a pack of cards from the drawer along with the pistol which she placed down beside her. She lit a Gitane. "Tootles, go talk the talk with your new gent here. Forty minutes. I'm laying out a game before we go." She started shuffling. "And I want you and Stan to stop pissing by that wheel."

"Darling…" The doctor had become nervous about the gun being in full sight. He took hold of a strand of her hair which had fallen over an eye, smoothed it back into her mop. "Cerisia's Saturday night special, Chipman. Second nature to her. Grouse shooting. Duels. The Ancien Regime! I stick to the clinical notes. Have to at least look like a pro. Ha ha!"

"I must confess to surprise that you have set up a practice here, Dr Sanguini. Your selection of books is intriguing though. Ah – is it classic New York type psychoanalysis that you do, Freud stuff or…?" He found himself attempting to sound more knowledgeable than he was and stopped. Cerisia arched back, gave Chipman a chilly stare and blew a jet of smoke at him.

The doctor was eager to get away. "Cerisia darling, we're moving into the operating theatre. Ha ha! We'll soon know if he is a suitable case for a lobotomy. Forty minutes."

FOUR: *Some enchanted evening*

A filtered moonlight lit the way through the darkness of the central corridor. Passing through a portiere painted with Matisse-like water lilies, Chipman found he had been led to the back of the vehicle. The doctor lit a paraffin lamp to reveal many plumped-up pillows on an outsize bed which occupied the entire width of the bus. Directly above and set in another starry starry night ceiling, rather low, was a large oval mirror. Beneath the bed was a cupboard with brass handles set into a fine grained wood. Chipman guessed a stained cedar. Coconut matting lined the walls and partially covered the windows, inducing in him a brief claustrophobia. Grotesque African masks stared intimidatingly at him. There were splashes of red and he noted a silky gold cushion, but mostly all was ochre and black. Fleshy odours, composting with a cleaning fluid residue, hung stranded in the fuggy air. On a shelf was what could only have been a phallus, poking up from a nest of raffia.

"You like?" Dr Sanguini queried. "One of the fine ebony jujus that Cerisia collected in the Sahel on our way down here. Cost an arm and a leg. Make her an offer." He lounged among the pillows, patted the gold cushion for Chipman, who hung back and sat on a stool. He was glad to have the doctor pull a bottle from the cupboard below the bed. "I'm starting on this Courvoisier just for you. It's the last, I'm afraid."

He picked up a magazine. "Cerisia and me." On the cover, holding hands, were two fearsome figures, both with wild flowing hair and naked but for sunglasses and nappies. It was not a reassuring look. *TWIDDLERS' MAVEN MOVES ON, Hoodlum's Moll Born Again, Weds Downunder Dude.* The magazine was called *Thug.*

"You've probably never been Thugged. Banned in Australia, of course."

"Never heard of it."

"Started off as *Hug* but too hippie-dippy, too *Gandalf's Garden*. Danny Dudgeon, London's latest publishing sensation took it over, decided on a more seditious approach." He flipped the pages. "Danny is a dear friend. You want to check out my credentials? Read the therapy clinic piece."

The doctor closed his eyes and began rotating his hands clownishly above his head, leaving Chipman to his drinking and just enough light to skim the article, *Lobes in Limboland*. It seemed to be built around an interview in Switzerland with Salvatore Sanguini and a Professor Adolf Siegfried. The same whose postcard had so upset him earlier.

"Adolf's born of an old Teutonic line," came the buttery Sanguini baritone. "One of the new breed of practitioners. Before he settled in Verbier, he lived in Vienna by the hawkers' market where they all seem to come from." He chuckled. "Impaled on my selfish theatrical ambitions, I crashed and burned. The Professor made me destroy my diaries, my hand written one-act plays, my correspondence with Julian Beck of *The Living Theatre*, even the 16 mm film of my unforgettable time with *Hermann Nitsch and the Viennese Actionists*. My rescuing angel was not a man for half-measures. For Adolf, successful treatments result in patients who are as helpless as babes. Communards whose conditioning he has so broken down they're in diapers, primed for reconstruction." He paused long enough to pierce Chipman with a look. "Every man deserves a second chance in life, does he not? And of course a third."

Chipman was not about to let the look and the remark entirely pass. "Dr Sanguini, I have to know. Where in Sydney did you practice? I mean as a therapist. Macquarie Street?"

The doctor was quick to give a dismissive flap. "I'm not a therapist. Don't be alarmed, mate, I have what the great Sigmund called the "furor sanandi."

"I beg your pardon?"

"The healing frenzy. For some time I was a new born, happy with a dummy in my mouth. Cerisia Twitchley, of all people, checked in shortly before I was ready to leave. *Twiddlers*, her London club venture had gone up her nose, her arm, her low-life gangster boy had been gunned down. He was her second husband. Sophie and Suki, her teenage tearaways were taken into protective custody. Fabulous *News of the World* stuff. Lord Wittering, her pious old dad, close friend of the Archbishop of York, wouldn't you know, stepped in and took the girls home to Wonkers, the stately pile in Derbyshire and she was forbidden to see them until she was cured. Wittering packed the Lady Cerisia off to Adolf's Verbier clinic. The place to go, naturally. Little did he know. Ha ha! Ever the heterodox rebel, she proved resistant to rehabilitation and Adolf asked me to stay and strengthen his hand with her detox. She fell in love with my fall from grace, and I fell in love with hers. Not to mention her family background. Her Mum swans around in a tiara and drinks gin and tonics with the Queen Mother." He contrived to look bashful. "I've always had a thing about the English aristocracy. Cerisia was born at home. Had a nanny. More than one, she's never been easy. Rides horses. If we ever get back to England, she's promised to take me hunting. Get my face smeared with a fox paw. 'Blooded' they call it." He gave a wriggle of anticipatory pleasure. "My kind of ritual. I still can't believe we're actually married. Despite appearances, Cerisia is a sweet old-fashioned girl and wanted a white wedding. So we compromised. A ceremony, but in diapers."

Chipman had trouble believing any of what the doctor said, but he dredged up a laugh and drained his cognac. Even as he did, he was reaching for more. It had been a long day.

The bottle was moved out of his reach and the doctor rattled on. "Cerisia is a sport who believes having a good time in life is paramount. She's spent decades defying her Dad and getting away with it, which endears her to me like nothing else. Parents are the problem. Generational abuse, generational incompatibility like never before, is the springboard these days, as you know. Or maybe you don't. Anyway, we've been on the road ever since. The revolutionary road."

"To ruin," Chipman added to himself, impatiently tapping his empty glass. Irritated also that Sanguini seemed more interested in talking about himself than he was with doctorly inquiry.

"Frankly, I would have been happy to stay in Europe, getting my act together again, even working on Wittering to back another club, but the new improved Cerisia wanted to lead a simple, drug free life. Nigel Wittering's a tough old bastard but he finally agreed that a period of extended travel would be rejuvenating, but not Afghanistan or Nepal. Too close to the hash and opium trade. Too associated with our alternative society's global trail. Ha ha! He is related to that Kingsley proto-feminist explorer woman and admired her 'pluck'. So, pluck, fuck, Africa it became. Cultural studies, anthropological note taking, all that. Whatever it took to keep old Witters happy and her substantial second favourite daughter allowance coming. I have to admit Africa has, unexpectedly, been a great move. We have been seizing every opportunity. At least I have." Dr Sanguini regarded Chipman with a reflective, even hopeful look. "Danny Dudgeon's expecting something equally inspiring will come out of this darkest Africa odyssey. Pays well, Danny, if he gets something that will send his circulation soaring. Something – sexy, if you don't mind my using that word again."

"Dr Sanguini, stop for just a moment. I knew there was something about the name Dudgeon that didn't ring right. He's in jail. Wanda, his American wife is missing. He killed her, didn't he?"

"Trust the dead hand of Australia to get in on the tabloid angle." The doctor's bonhomous tones had acquired a vexatious edge. "She was drunk. Did she fall off the barge on the Thames or was she throttled and thrown? Yackety yackety. No body found. Danny's out on bail and free to publish. All I care about. Dashing Danny, the dark prince of the new journalism. Passionate voice committed to the on-going orgasmic revival." He rolled out the cupboard again, and from a folder extracted an envelope. "Let Danny speak for himself. The letter I received only last week."

Chipman held it towards the lamp and read:

Sanguini, what the fuck are you up to? Hearing more about infamous Tlula Leisure Beach from the freaks coming in off the longhair streets than you. What's this ULYSSES RETURN, verge of CIVIL WAR crap? Your latest Siegfried INGESTIONS and cock-ups? Cerisia Twitchley's shock BLIMPOUT? Let's have a better look. Get her out of that MUMUU, into a BIKINI and go for SIMPATHI. I'm thinking peer's dissolute daughter COMEBACK TRIUMPH lead feature, SOCIAL PARIAH no longer. No more VICE, let's be NICE. Travel issue rescheduled, so plenty time for your EASTER CARNIVAL story. Bombard me with bare breasted ETHNIC and FULL FRONTAL vaginal ROOTY TOOT TOOT. Into the PSYCHODRAMA, the LUSTODRAMA. Generally more SEXFILTH and ATROCITIES, more LOTUS, much more TOFFEE, less STAN and DRIFT. Zero ZACH. No more environmental ENCHANTMENT crap. No more spiritual. Let's go CLITORAL. Think ENGORGED and ERECT. Think WET DREAMS, WET LIPS and SPREAD SHOTS. Think SENSATION and SHOCK. Let's rewrite the SUCK AND FUCK MANIFESTO, let's get LOOSE and LEISURELY!!! Do I have to descend time's greasy pole and JACK OFF for you? Best wishes in the name of back alley Fleet Street fodder, Danny thug-a-lug Dudgeon.

PS. Advance cabled to National Bank of Bomzawe in Doggone. Sorry so little but uncharted waters are always CHOPPY. If not SHITTY.

Chipman hated every word of what he had just read. He didn't bother to suppress his grunt of distaste as he handed the letter back.

"Danny can't help himself. Out it all comes. "Dissolute daughter, don't you love that alliteration? Listen, the high point of West Africa so far was the weeks we spent in Abomey. The voodoo capital of the former kingdom of Dahomey. Wild exorcistic dances. Had me making all sorts of fabulous connections between the therapeutic techniques I learned from my months with Professor Siegfried and the healing rituals African witchdoctors have been practising since time immemorial. Sexual healing!! Danny will go for it big time!"

The doctor adopted a more confidential, oozier tone. "This may be beyond your conventional comprehensions, Mr Chipman Smith, but a seed was sown for me in Abomey. The tribalists there have a dance for everything from birth to death. Fighting and fucking, flirting and fertility, marriage and offspring, success and failure, illness and ageing. Even dances to kill your enemy." He paused to remove with thumb and forefinger a little foam that had accumulated in his beard. "The enemy within, I mean."

William Oates' knowledge of Dr Sanguini probably stemmed from no more than a decorous conversation at an Embassy cocktail party. Chipman had seen enough B-movies to know that what the doctor was now saying was rubbish and would not have been touched upon with Oates. Danny Dudgeon would certainly not have been mentioned either. He looked at his watch. Surreptitiously, he thought. Forty minutes?

Starry took off his dark glasses and leaned forward. "Quite a timepiece. Swiss?"

"Present from Alfie. Girard Perregaux. Years ago, even before I left school."

"Ah, yes, your father. And what does this generous dad with the childish name do for a crust?"

"He taught English and Ancient History at Canterbury College." Chipman paused, took a deep breath. "Unfortunately, my dad is no longer with us. He died of a heart attack some years ago. It was very sad."

"Ah." The doctor was finally prompted to pour more cognac, a good measure. "Hold your hand still!" He did not speak for a while. And then "Which year was that, exactly?"

"The summer of 67," said Chipman, who had expected him to say how sorry he was to hear about that as most people did. He felt tears of a sort begin to surge, and supressed them, as he well knew how to do. Lighting a Camel, he watched the smoke rise and vanquish with its fragrance, the earlier odours loitering up there.

"I've heard of that College," the doctor said, breaking a silence. He waved at the smoke, pushed an ashtray forward. "So you were educated at a well-known citadel of the suitably proper. Not exactly la vie boheme, Chipman." He went to put his dark glasses back on, changed his mind, tossed them aside.

Chipman felt he had to correct him."Alfie preferred to send us kids to public schools."

"Did he now!" His grin came again, an undeniably amiable one.

The friendly teeth and the additional cognac suffused Chipman with a glow that released him into a verbal intimacy with this stranger who had taken upon himself the unlikely role of healer, accredited or not. So strong was the urge to speak, so loosened was the lawyer's usually tight tongue that for a fleeting paranoid moment, he believed that something more than cognac had been slipped into the glass. But it was time.

"He was a well loved and respected teacher. He umpired the cricket team to competition success, twice. Everyone at the school looked up to him. He was a wonderful father, always kind and gentle with us. It was a shocking thing, so unexpected. We were all devastated. Well, Matilda not so much. She married again not that long afterwards. A religious bloke, the Reverend Melville Motherwell. Very different to Alfie. Big and a bit daunting, Melville, but everyone calls him Melody because of his mellifluous voice. We live in the rectory now, a few streets away. He runs the Enfield Congregational Choir. Very popular the Choir."

"When did you turn into a – dipso?"

"When Matilda moved in with Melody." He said it as a joke but in fact the truth lay not far from there. "He immediately took over as my father and blamed Alfie for what he saw in my nature. He was constantly pushing girls in his congregation at me, ones he considered available. His not so subtle hints made it clear I was to seduce them or let them seduce me. "We're not going to let that side of Alfie develop in you, darling," Matilda said more than once. I gave in to the two of them, but they created a fear in me because I soon found that I did not have that sort of interest in girls. Melody kept redoubling his efforts to cure me. He even threatened to throw me out if I didn't get it together. That's when all the falsity started and the drinking to deal with that. One thing led to another and over the years to Wally Whitbread and…"

Chipman stopped abruptly as there had come a firestorm of embarrassment, his face burning like hot coals, not so much for being trapped into intimate confession by the doctor but at the memory of getting caught that night outside Wally's Waverton window. Chipman Smith of all people, in his mind, an ambitious, well-presented and respectable lawyer with a fine instinct for self-preservation.

Chipman closed his eyes. Idiotically, he could not help thinking his boiling face would make his nose seem less like a stop light. The thought produced from him a smile, thin but genuine and his temperature began to drop. He opened his eyes to the doctor's gravid ones and started again. "Alfie was OK with a son who wasn't your every day son. That I was ..." The word he never ever used about himself would not come. His head went down, there was a painful stiffening in Chipman's jaw.

In the semi-dark the doctor's face moved forward with consoling interest.

"Alfie told me about the Theban Band. Gave me things to read like Plato's *Symposium*. Andre Gide. Walt Whitman."

"Very boring, Andre Gide."

"He told me not to tell Matilda, he would do it himself."

"Easier for you that way?"

"Well, I don't know. Alfie always seemed younger, but he was actually quite a few years older than Matilda and she took all her cues from him. Later she said she knew it was a horrible mistake to let my father get so close to me."

"Look up!" came a stern command from the doctor. Chipman's hands were brusquely pulled away from his head.

Chipman did look up but was alarmed by the change in tone. He determined not to talk further about Alfie, certainly not about the unquestioning regard he still had for him despite Melody's ministrations. He was ready though, to tell the doctor about what he regarded as the more relevant trauma in his life; the Waverton windows. He feared the doctor might find this trivial compared to the death of his father, but there was no doubt it was the reason he was here in Bomzawe.

"I hope the forty minutes is not up."

"She'll definitely let us know."

Chipman gave a prim clearing of his throat. "I got caught outside Wally's bedroom window, spying on him having intercourse with Jeanette. His wife..."

Chipman noticed that the doctor was already smirking. "Please take me seriously."

The smirk became a grin. "You found Jeanette attractive?"

"Dr Sanguini, stop that. I'm obsessed with a man old enough to be my father and I've made a complete fool of myself. I became deluded into thinking that the display was all for me, that Wally desired me, loved me. He walked around naked and aroused in his bedroom and in full view of his side garden, had intercourse with her at least three nights a week under lights that could not be brighter. If not for me, who? Even now..." Chipman caught himself, changed tack. "I had been doing it regularly for months even though he lived way over on the lower North Shore. Their bathroom curtains were never drawn either. But his younger brother was over from Adelaide that week and urinating on the other side of a big camellia bush and noticed me up in my tree. He dragged me down, tried to tear off my balaclava but I kneed him in the testicles and managed to leap over the hedge into the street. I was parked a block away and escaped. I accept that I am a drunk, but I think the continuing agony of it all has triggered a – mental imbalance, a sickness even. I am no longer myself. My brain ..."

"You had better tell me who Wally actually is...?"

"Wallace Whitbread. My superior at the Department. My boss."

"Public servant. I thought so." There was a certain knowingness in the tone of his voice. "Which Department might I ask? Trade? Transport?" A slight pause. "Attorney General? "

Everything – *The Beautiful Afreakans*, the social pariah wife, her revolver on the table, the lawlessness in the air at Tlula Leisure Beach, the glimmerings of a memory associated with the doctor, that slight pause, the smirking – was telling Chipman to be careful. He recalled a French film he had seen some years before at the Paris Cinema in Liverpool Street, *The Heroes are Tired* with Yves Montand and Maria Felix. Shady people stranded in Liberia trying to smuggle gems. No one in that movie came to a good end. He certainly was not going to reveal that Wally was a senior prosecutor, in fact, Deputy Clerk of the Peace. "Ah – Education. Head office in Bridge Street."

"Hmm. Education. And the connection with William Oates at the Embassy?"

"Oates is his brother-in-law. Wally Whitbread had been invited to address an international conference on – ah – third world schooling and female disadvantage in Nigeria at Lagos University, less than two hundred miles from Bomzawe, in April, not that long after Easter. It was just a mad idea of his. Killing two birds with one stone sort of thing."

"He knew it was you spying on him?"

"No. I was wearing my balaclava. Well, yes. The way Wally acted afterwards towards me, I knew he must have twigged. Nothing was ever said but standing in front of him one day, the realisation came and it created such embarrassment in me that my colon twisted. It was agonising. 'Something the matter, Chipman,' he asked. 'No no, I'm fine' I gasped, all bent over and contorted. There were other things. Drunk on the job. Once, I was confused leaving his office and walked into the wall. Another time he came back unexpectedly and caught me wearing one of his jackets. I had removed it from his office wardrobe and was admiring myself in the full-length mirror. Smoking one of his Camels. My obsession with him took many forms. I..."

"So he was far-sighted enough, generous enough to get you rehabilitated with the help of a friend and a totally different environment?

"Yes. "

"Amazing."

"When I had enjoyed my adjustment or whatever in Okidoki with Oates, the master plan was that we would liaise at the Conference and return to Sydney together."

"The queer aspect was not an issue?"

It took Chipman a while to summon up an answer. "Well, there was my doe-eyed behaviour in his presence but things like that can never be acknowledged in a work situation like mine. It being illegal and everything. Ah, the education of children."

Suddenly Chipman had had enough of keeping up his lie and he wanted to get away from the doctor. He stood up but was firmly motioned down.

A deluge of new questions came quickly. Not probing about the long and winding road that led from the death of Alfie to Wally but about matters he regarded as entirely extraneous.

"Are you a virgin? You look like a virgin."

"No. Well, the last few years I have been virginal. Celibate I mean."

"No boyfriends?"

"I'm in love with Wally and no-one else."

"I detect you are a man with a strong libido. You jerk off as you watch?"

"I never do things like that."

"No shame?" The doctor was scribbling notes on a pad.

"With Melody it was always 'pureness', as he called it. The purity of my feelings for Wally had me affronted at being disturbed by that brother of his. I even went back one night a week or so later and Wally still had not drawn the curtains, the lights again full on. It was only when I realised that Wally knew it was me in the balaclava that my life began to fall apart. And even then it was more embarrassment than shame."

"How are you doing right now? Your balls loaded with spunk and pleading for release? Or do wet dreams do it for you?"

The doctor's crudity had to be intentional. It had Chipman's nose once more disappearing into the fiery sunset red that was heating up the rest of his face. "Spunk?" His pretence that he did not know what that was, indicated an attempt to slow the doctor down, slow himself down, even as he wanted to keep telling the truth, as much as he dared; not much. "I have started to have some malfunction down there lately. Like what's going wrong with my head, my physical state…" He glanced at his watch feeling he was saying too much, merely blabbing away, now wanting Cerisia to come and put a stop to it all.

"You mean a dysfunction? Can't get it up?"

"I – I find myself incredibly aroused all the time."

The doctor began to laugh, poured more liquor. "Here, let's drown that drinking problem again," and pressed on with even more scattershot questioning.

"No, I'm not neurotic about my nose. A little. Well, a lot. My skin otherwise being so very pale. I am envious of noses. I reject people with ugly ones."

"How's mine?"

"I like aquiline. It's fine."

The doctor took that as an invitation to come closer, to touch his nose. As Chipman was shrinking away, there came a summoning yell from along the corridor.

"Coming, my darling!" Jumping back like a jack-in-a-box, he bounced high enough on the bed's mattress to have his head hit the ceiling.

"Witchery calls." Sanguini gave a cooling swish or two with his tunic, revealing greater things than any professionalism dictated. But the deep set Italianate eyes, Chipman told himself despairingly, exuded integrity and a profound intelligence. It was the eyes and the extraordinary flow of ideas that was seducing him, not the goat-haired inner thighs and what had been displayed between.

The doctor blew out the lamp, was through the portiere and into the corridor. Chipman rose unsteadily from the stool, "Whoops," as he almost fell before following. "Dr Sanguini, I'll let you know in a week or so if I need to consult you. I'll lie around, swim every day. Watch my drinking. Away from where it all began, maybe I can deal with this loss of balance. Wally's idea was…"

"I'm telling you now, with your fucked-up family history, your transparent state of high anxiety, and the bunch of lies you have just told me about your sex life, you can't afford not to consult me." Dr Sanguini had stopped abruptly in the dark. Now he turned and brought his face to Chipman's. That smell again. "Or to wait. William Oates and your Wally will be expecting us to get started."

The corridor was narrow. The doctor squeezed close as he put an arm around Chipman's shoulders and moved him towards the living area. He raised his voice, the more for Cerisia to know they were finally on their way. "There's dancing in the village tonight. A healing in itself. Come along. The night is young and she will be delighted to hear that our new recruit is a Peeping Tom and all screwed up about it."

The room was dark and Cerisia had gone. But there was the gun and the pack of playing cards. With Sanguini already outside, Chipman lingered. Almost as though he wanted to deny its existence, he put the gun back in the drawer. The cards too.

"There's no mosquitoes in the dry season, but pull the door shut," said the doctor who was taking a leak by the already acrid area by the front wheel. As he gave some ostentatious shakes to his penis, Chipman could not help noticing that the disobeying of his wife had somewhat excited him.

"Ah, Cerisia! Africa has not been to her liking in the way it has been for me. She has indulged herself with the palanquin and taken to the uncontrolled consumption of food and drink. Basically she is staving off another bout of depression. We have to restore her buoyancy of old so she can wow 'em at the Easter Carnival with her belly dancing. Kmango will pay plenty for the sort of performance she can put on." Dr Sanguini adjusted his tunic and walked towards the palanquin and the little fire. "She loves to dance even more than I do. Let's finish off the tuna. Somehow she's managed not to eat it all. She'll be fuelling up on fufu in Tlula."

The moon had risen high above the coconut palms. The sea was a silvery black. As he crouched beside Dr Sanguini, Chipman found he was enjoying ripping apart the remains of the fish with him. Something primitive stirred in his mind. Images of Tibor Radovan went flashing by.

His mouth full, Sanguini was talking. "…and I don't think I told you. As a teenager, Cerisia learned belly dancing at the King Idris Academy for the Arts in Tripoli when Wittering had a Libyan ambassadorial posting there. How old do you think she is?"

"I have no idea. She looks younger than my mother."

The doctor's face creased up with pleasure at that. "I shouldn't even think of her in terms of age, what with all her energy but, as Lotus puts it, last year was the fiftieth time the earth went round the sun for her." He paused then went on affectionately. "Her sexual vitality sets a healthy example for us all. You too. In her debutante days, she was a great society beauty. The heart shaped face. The pert nose I am sure you have already noticed. Rosetti would have painted her. Now she's gone Rubens. Or Botero if you know him. I've always loved the biggies, but I'm not having this one get any bigger." He picked up a tambourine, gave it a flourish and a bang or two. "What a life she has led! Punched Timothy Leary for being out of control in her club. His minder and he were both on Purple Haze. All the more reason, she said, to beat the shit out of him." The doctor commenced a little shimmy to the clash of the tambourine.

"What was that about belly dancing?"

"Her Leicester Square club was a sixties sensation. The famous came flocking. Jagger and Marianne Faithful were both *Twiddlers'* regulars. Julie Christie. Terence Stamp. Paul McCartney. Lord Weymouth. Vivienne Westwood. Eric Clapton. You must know about Martin Sharp and Jennie Kee. Shall I go on? Trendies all of them. The artistic Kings Road not so intelligentsia if you like. Warhol arrived one night with Ultra Violet and Candy Darling, his chick with a dick. Cerisia has a photo of herself with Germaine Greer. At midnight she belly danced for everyone. With an anaconda."

"Anaconda? I don't think so."

"Listen to Qaddo's rhythms! My ballooning babe is already sweating it off." He thrust a pair of maracas at Chipman. "Here, shake and bake. When we get to the village you can get acquainted. I sense an affinity has already developed between the two of you."

The sound of the drums had the doctor escalating his nonchalant shimmy into a high kicking dance, and Chipman found a foot being waggled in front of his face. "Like my toe nails? Lotus does them." They glinted menacingly in the moonlight. Even at that moment, came an out of breath voice.

"Starry, Cerisia's sent me back for my dingdang massage oil. We're about to lose that loopy Gus."

"Loopy?"

"The ornithologist."

The gorgeous young woman who had appeared out of the palms was Lotus. "Well, hi there. It's Chipman, right?" She hesitated a fraction, then posed in languorous fashion against the palanquin. Her nose was fine with a slightly curved ridge, a gold stud on one side. Her cushiony lips were painted a pillar-box red. Her hair, an elaborate web of blond braids, was crowned with a circlet of fresh blooms. She unstuck from her skin the diaphanous chemise that clearly revealed she was wearing nothing underneath, no panties, nothing. Her breasts were tanned, the nipples rose-pink and pointing through the material. She smelled of sea and Neroli, an aromatic oil. The phrase "flower child" came to Chipman's mind. Not that he knew anything much about flower children. She was probably in her early twenties.

"My Californian pedicurist herself. The lovely Lotus. In her baby-doll attire."

"You dig the job I did on the bus? All wooshed up for you. An hour ago Starry had me on my knees with a scrubbing brush. He likes the back view. Hee hee."

"When you go, my Luscious One, take Stan's metronome for him."

"Ugh! The mould! The millipedes! Cerisia's been letting everything slide since arriving here. That scorpion." She brightened. "Did Starry illuminate my ceilings for you? Van Gogh night sky, Chagallian angels. I couldn't have done it at all without my poor darling Stan's help. Inspired by you of course, Starry," Lotus added quickly. She leaped into the bus, returning thirty seconds later with a bottle of oil. And the metronome.

"Just a moment, Lotus," Chipman asked. "What sort of help is it that Dr Sanguini gives here to people?" He gave the doctor a reproving glance. "He's refusing to tell me."

"Dr! That's a new one. Hey, anything for a buck. It's all loony tunes, as far as I'm concerned." She tossed her braids, sending her ceramic teapot earrings jiggling. "Stan needs a bit of character beaten back into him, but I'm not letting Starry beat mine out of me." She snuggled up, ran a hand through the hair of Dr Sanguini's broad chest, tugged a nipple, patted his little paunch, moved her hand lower.

"Sweet Lotus. You know what happens when you go down there."

She gave a mischievous snort and turned to leave. The doctor was quicker. A single terpsichorean movement had his fist and wrist under her wisp of a chemise and between her thighs. From behind, Lotus found herself lifted up on the beam of his outstretched arm. She squealed as his fingers tickled her. "Dr Kinsey!! Please!" She was carried like this to the other side of the embers and dropped to the sand. "Put something on." He grabbed a sarong from a washing line strung between two palms and threw it at her. "We're in enough trouble with the village as it is."

He came back, smiling broadly. Chipman stopped himself thinking in terms of violation. It was more like play. Of course it was play.

"What would I do without Lotus? Think she's sexy? Thousand petalled?"

"Oh, yes. Very!"

"Really? Great titties. The sweetest of pussies." He caressed his beard. "I have Lotus to thank for adding to my knowledge of the world of art."

Chipman had agreed automatically, even as he suspected his survival habit of exhibiting heterosexual credentials could now be dispensed with. It had been scary, but in the bus he had managed to reveal something of his true self to Sanguini, and now, after the doctor's display of inventive heterosexuality with Lotus, he felt a parallel freedom to perhaps give his own sexuality free rein at Tlula Leisure Beach. A quiver of excitement at the very thought, ran through him.

Chipman realised he had unwittingly given a few shakes of the maracas and began to feel foolish. He put them down and knew he had not the slightest desire to go dancing. It was not late, but the sounds of festivity from the village were inducing in him not just a travel related weariness but an intense fear of Africa itself. The solution was a nightcap from his own trusted bottles, and for sedatives from his own medicine case.

The doctor's continuing chatter about other 'patients' was being lost on the sea breeze and to Chipman's own indifference – Drift, 'draft dodger', Toffee, 'intoxicatingly beautiful'…

Finally he managed a departure. The doctor's raised voice came clearly to his ears as the palm fronds creaked above.

"Two concerns, Chipman Smith. Just two – your virginity and your job. If you don't lose the former, you're bound to lose the latter. Department of Education. Bridge Street! Ha ha ha!" The laugh was derisive. "You won't regret putting yourself in the hands of Starry Starry Night Sanguini."

Starry Starry Night Sanguini. No, he wasn't. Whatever happened to him during the course of any coming ministrations, Chipman knew for certain that he was going to get to the bottom of who the doctor really was – behind all that hair and beard. And the gangster glasses.

FIVE: *If luck is the hero chance is no villain*

Next morning Chipman found a note under his door.

"Take Attah's 'Full Breakfast' with Drift and Toffee. They will bring you to the palm shelter. Get those layabouts moving. It get hots, and I do mean hots/ You must drink water. Lots and lots. Thank you for those 'confidences' last night. Candour, my dear Mr Chipman, not concealment, is the first step in everybody's journey.

Starry Sanguini, your Doctor Feel Good."

Showered and shaved, attired in a linen safari suit (bought in a last minute panic that he had nothing suitable to wear for Wally Whitbread's Conference), he took his place for breakfast. A broad brimmed panama from Strand Hatters and sunglasses to hide his still drugged eyes, his leather satchel (with a flask of whisky inside), completed his ensemble. Roman sandals.

The breakfast area had no walls, only a low whitewashed parapet. It looked through palms to the ocean, coruscating palely out there in the early morning sun. A sign read: *GENTLEMEN TO WEAR CLOTHES WHILE SEATED. FOOTWEAR, UNDER WARE PLEASE YOURSELF*. On a central table stood a vase with huge trumpet shaped flowers. A pungent odour came wafting over.

The Scandinavian foursome had just finished their breakfast, were moving away, as were a few casually clad others, and Chipman was the only customer remaining. Well, not quite. Zach Shaler sat at a beachfront table, a gourd (which Chipman knew from the night before had to contain the local gin) in front of him. He was bare chested, and wearing baggy black and white striped shorts. A battered cowboy hat covered his head bandage. Long, darkly haired legs. Bare feet. A couple of coloured plastic bangles on his left arm. There was a frangipani flower behind an ear, and the phrase 'bit of a hippie' came to mind. He was smoking a cigarette, reading a book. Chipman imagined something novelettish. Something corny, like the cowboy hat. He could not help being amused when Zach poured some of the gin into what looked like a heaped bowl of cereal and fruit. The low sun was illuminating his face which was half turned towards the sea at which he would stare from time to time. He seemed melancholy, but hardly "discombobulated" as Dr Sanguini had put it in the bus. His outlandish behaviour with that floating body had been disgusting, but had also aroused a curiosity. Was it because, like Chipman, Zach was a man who had in some way gone a bit off the rails? Chipman had already set up his day with a drink or two, but a slug of that gin would not hurt. Even as he took a step towards joining Zach he changed his mind. He was far from home. It was best to think twice about whom he associated with. Sanguini and his wife on their honeymoon, of all things, were proving more than enough. A lilting voice from behind confirmed his decision.

"Good morning, Mr Chipman Smith." Half-concealed by a bank of philodendrons, was Attah Lalwani, the manager chef. Hamou, who seemed to be both day and night watch, squatted next to him, his robe hiked high, exposing his black legs, skeletal and hairless. Attah was holding up the head of a greenish grey monkey. Its dead eyes stared at him through a lace of flies. In front of Attah was an enamel bowl filled with body parts; behind him, the embers of a fire. Charred pieces of smoked flesh on racks dried in the sun. The hunter himself, a lemon-eyed old coot in a fatigue cap, leaned nearby on a musket. Attah squeezed the cheeks until the head grinned. A chop across the mouth with a cutlass sent the teeth flying. Chipman flinched as though he had been struck himself. Attah hacked off the top of the skull, removed the brain, then tossed what was left towards a flock of turkey-like birds clustered a few feet away: so frightful, they made the ubiquitous hornbills look almost lovable. The huge birds were Eared Vultures, the big boss one called Old Idi. At night they roosted on the hotel roof. As the raw-necked creatures made a raggedy-winged rush and began tearing at the monkey's eyes and tongue, Chipman took a snap, and felt a small dissipation of the alcohol related violence and disarray in his head for so doing.

"Qumqwat," Attah shouted. A village girl appeared. Her coiffure was a complex interchange of plaited loops, woven with ribbons and beads. She was dressed like a six year old in a green and cream checkered mini-dress with a Peter Pan collar and puffed sleeves, clothes she was bursting out of. "Why are you neglecting your customer. One full breakfast here for Mr Chipman." The manager chef reached for another monkey and raised his cutlass.

Chipman could no longer watch. Taking out his journal, he made a note to ring the Embassy; a reminder for William Oates that he was going to make contact the minute he returned. Chipman noticed with a slight shock that his calligraphy was no more than a scribble, close to illegible. What had so suddenly happened to his copperplate abilities? With the bar not yet open, he took a quick drink from his flask. He opened up the latest *Australian and New Zealand Journal of Criminology*. Wally's lead article.

…measurements of one's cheek bones or hairline, or a cleft palate, considered to be throwbacks to Neanderthal man, were indicative of 'atavistic'- criminal tendencies. This approach has been superseded…

As he read, nothing made any sense and there came agitation and then a terror that he had already lost touch with his life as a lawyer and the Sydney legal world. He took panicky gulps of the cool air, even as second by second, the coolness, like his sanity and skills, was leaching away. He wondered if he had over-dressed for breakfast.

"Hi. You must be Chipman. We're joining you."
Rescue had come in the form of a tall moustachioed man in his late twenties who had approached. A body lithe and lanky, his torso deeply tanned, a canvas shoulder bag. He was wearing threadbare Bermudas, greyish-pink with a pineapple print, worn low on his hips. Introducing himself as Bob Drift, he gave Chipman a warm shake with a big hand.
"Call me Drift. Sanguini told me all about you in the village last night."

There came a wink and a knowing double thumbs up. "Way to go, man." Drift had rescued Chipman from his panic, but received only a cold stare. Dr Sanguini must have broken client confidentiality.

Drift lowered his voice. "I have a proposition for you. We have to talk. Seriously talk." He looked about shiftily, saw Zach Shaler and said, "Later."

The man had luxuriant hair, long and dark, parted in the centre. Scooping it back from his forehead with both hands, he sat down. As the doctor had indicated, Drift was photogenic, with blokey, well-travelled good looks. The moustache was a modified General Custer, his sideburns were long and neatly trimmed. Chipman did not notice the revolver tucked into the waist band of his shorts until he transferred it into his shoulder bag.

"Snakes," he said, giving a laugh. "They reckon they own the place, but they're sitting ducks. I shot a couple more this morning."

What happened next caused Chipman to momentarily forget about Drift and his revolver. Coming at a leisurely pace from the direction of the bar was a young woman who could only have been Drift's stripper girlfriend also mentioned, he vaguely recalled, by Dr Sanguini the night before. Her skin had a deep caramelised colouration that put Chipman in mind of the décor of an Ashfield milk bar he frequented before he came to regard himself as persona non grata in the area. Her outfit was one of ice cream tones – a pistachio halter-top blouse, raspberry hot pants. The blouse more than half revealed taut and lovely breasts. The main impression was of someone who was indeed, as the doctor had intimated, 'intoxicatingly beautiful'. Fortunately, Melody Motherwell's focus on sexual achievement with women, had not destroyed Chipman's ability to adjudge them beautiful to his eyes. In fact, he encouraged himself to gaze and gaze upon such women, hoping that he would one day discover the secret of their sexual attraction which always seemed so entirely unavailable to him.

"Ah, our most bountiful Toffee, our beauty queen," Attah cried, flashing her a look before returning to his bloody task at the bowl. His tone was strangely mocking.

She had a little monkey on her shoulder. Its goggly leathered face was surrounded by a picturesque corona of russet fur. The black tail swung about, as active as a conductor's baton. As Toffee sat down next to Drift, the pretty creature reached out a long arm and fingered Chipman's own corona, of which he was rather vain.

"He's not dangerous?" Chipman showed the monkey a warning palm and shrank back, not wanting a curl messed up or even yanked out.

"It's a lady," Drift sneered. "Mucho dangeroso. Red Colobus. Dumb idea of mine."

Toffee's lush mulberry lips parted. "Honey, I'm warning you. Like Starry says, jealousy is so history." Drift gave an exasperated exhalation. She laughed in response, revealing teeth of china white perfection. Her voice was nicely pitched, with a musical ring, quite a match for the rest of her attributes.

Qumqwat crashed her breakfast tray on the table, miscalculating the distance by a couple of inches. Steaming tea from the teapot spout spilled, white china cups rattled in their saucers. She flung down napkins, green-checked like her dress, clunked cutlery and plates into place. The teapot was a Victorian relic. Fruit salad in a large bowl, a basket of toast, butter in a dish, carnation milk in a jug, jam in a Fortnum & Mason jar. "Sausage an' chip is comin'." Drift reached out for her bottom, but she was much too agile, banging him on the head with her tray. 'You very bad man, white man."

"Right on, sister," said Toffee exchanging a matey look with Qumqwat.

"I's tellin' you again, Toffee, I's not your sister." Qumqwat stormed away.

Drift's ogling had indicated clear bewitchment. "Would you believe she's only twelve? Attah has a whole bunch working for the hotel. They rush off to school if they get their chores here done in time. Hand picks them."

The chips were plantain. Not bad at all.

"Qumqwat is Qaddo's daughter. Qaddo, my massive friend."

"Massive?"

"Shoulders. Barrel chest. Big for here, six feet. He's my guardian angel," Drift said, attempting to push a piece of poached egg into Toffee's mouth. She showed him her profile in sweet annoyance. It only made Drift try again. She flapped at him delicately with her left hand.

"Qumqwat's the hottest thing around. Kmango will be recruiting her for the Carnival. The English maypole dance."

"Black people dancing a maypole? You must be joking."

"What would you know, you're from Australia," Toffee put in. "I bet it originated someplace in Africa."

"Qumqwat and her age group haven't done it, of course, but they've all heard about it from their mothers and older sisters. I don't think any are yet disqualified by loss of virginity. Although I wouldn't mind disqualifying a few of them."

"Honey..." Toffee's tone was so resigned it was obvious that his remarks were typical. Chipman looked from one to the other. Little spats were part of the give and take of a relationship? A surge of romantic longing almost overwhelmed him. He too wanted to be one of a loving couple. He made Toffee an offering of the toast. "Wah, thenk youuu!" Her accent, Chipman then recognized (from the movies), was American southern.

Chipman watched her nibbling away. Maybe, he thought wildly, she might grant some of her beauty to him. He had already scrutinised her for nasal flaws and had found none, but later when she removed her oversized sunglasses, she revealed a rubble topped wart above where the left nostril joined her cheek. She gave the wart a touch with her forefinger but did not seem self-conscious about it. The glasses had also concealed her eyes which were a forget-me-not or cornflower bluish. An extraordinary colour juxtaposed with the caramel.

"...yeah it's nuts," Drift was continuing. "All part of Kmango's love affair with British cultural traditions. Beatles' Sing-a-longs. Egg and Spoon, Thread the Needle. Sack Races. You'd think the colonial era had all been a bed of roses. There's a glowing account with photos from an *Okidoki Post* up on Attah's wall, covering the last Carnival five years ago. The Liberator was present of course.

His swansong. Ulysses Oratorio, the guy that ripped off the Bomzawe Bronzes. As you probably know, the Bronzes..."

Chipman found his attention shifting back to Toffee as she fed the Red Colobus pieces of papaya. She used the monkey's neckerchief to dab its mouth. With the two of them gazing at each other in solemn adoration, Chipman, rescued from his personal angst, was entranced. Madonna and Baby Jesus, he thought. Stepping back, he took a quick shot. Drift growled, "I don't want that photo going anywhere."

Qumqwat pulsed up with another pot of tea. With one hand she poured, with the other she thrust hard into Toffee's hair. As her arm disappeared almost up to her elbow she gave a giggle. "Nice lady, I keep tellin' you, come to salon, my aunt she cut yo' silly hair, do nice rows for you. Some good grease and shine."

Toffee's hair was large and fuzzy, beach ball round. There were apricot highlights, subtle hints perhaps of her mixed race origins.

"I love my afro, Qumqwat, it's called a natural. All the sisters in the States have them. We're discovering the traditional loveliness of the African woman. Black is so beautiful."

Qumqwat guffawed and tripped over to Zach in front of whom she plonked a plate of sausage, chips and egg. It wasn't until the man was cutting into the sausages, that Chipman realised that Zach was quietly crying.

Drift had moved on to his snake catching venture. A deal with an Englishman whom he described deprecatingly as 'an old port swiller', who had, with the help of an entrepreneurial daughter, turned the acres around his stately home into an amusement park. His latest added attraction was a zoo entitled *The World's Most Dangerous Creatures*. The African carnivores of course, lions, leopards and hyenas, with rhinos and Cape Buffalo representing the herbivores, but Drift's speciality being reptiles, he had been hired to collect the two snakes, the black and the green mamba, that the forests of western Bomzawe were famous for. Drift had all his permits together. Made sure of that. He and Toffee had a booking on a cargo ship, the *Star of Casablanca*, a couple of days after Easter.

Drift caressed Toffee's bare arm. "Do we really have to wait for this stupid Carnival? Your wish is my command, but honeypot, every day we wait, the risk gets greater. And it costs me dough."

Southampton! Casablanca! Carnival! Risk! Everything had such a thrilling, adventurous ring to it. Their American accents and diction, made Chipman feel his life up to that point had been totally deprived of excitement and experience. Was he really having breakfast with such a glamorous globetrotting duo? This couple who thought nothing of having a miscegenetic affair, who did not seem to notice his nose, or that he was an alcoholic mess who was about to undergo – treatment. Should he let them know what they were getting into by befriending a disaster area such as him? How far did their sophistication and tolerance extend? Would it be a good idea to let them know he had a prestigious job with the Public Service back in Sydney? Would they reject him if he told them he was – gay? That new word for Chipman. And why on earth would Drift want to discuss a 'serious' something with him? He gave his troubled head a shaking and a bang.

"…lounging on the beach psyching ourselves up for the mambas. Toffee wanted to check out all the ethnic shit, so I leased a Range Rover and we did a month up in Mali, the Dogon people, got chased by a hippo on the Niger, saw the mud minarets of Timbuktu, came back and found the infamous Cerisia here. Talk about a small world. Talk about bad luck. And hooked up with Sanguini. Cerisia helped me get a start in London but I hadn't seen her in yonks. I had a run-in with her back then. Nothing much, but that isn't the way she sees it."

"A run-in?"

Drift did not reply immediately. He ate a plantain chip, did the two-handed flick-back of his hair. Chipman noticed there was a silver stud set with turquoise in each of his ear lobes.

"Hey, I organised a bucks' party in *Twiddlers*, her swinging Leicester Square club, one night and we all split without paying the bill. Perfect timing, right at the climax of her floor show. The after-midnight belly dancing with her under-age daughters, '*The Girlie-Whirlies*. Dopey thing to do, but we were out of our skulls. You know what it was like back then. The Summer of Love and all that great Owsley acid. Anyway, I've no intention of coughing up. Cerisia's some dancer, I'll give her that but let's face it, she's off the planet. First husband jumped out a window. Coroner brought in suicide, but who knows. Her second was gunned down in an East End slaying." Playing with one of his studded earlobes, he continued. "Wittering set her up in that club."

"The titled gentleman?"

"Yeah, Nigel, her dad. You know where the Twitchleys got all their money? Sugar and slaves, where else." He clamped a hand down on Toffee's wrist. "My beautiful soul sister slave chick."

"Your slave chick gotta relocate." Toffee indicated the vultures. Avid for scraps, the dirty scavenging birds had come close, their naked necks bobbing over the low parapet right by their table. Toffee's body had begun a severe shaking. Beads of perspiration were breaking out on her forehead. Her nose wart had changed colour.

Chipman's sympathy being aroused by that in particular, he rose and ran at the vultures, waving his arms. "Shoo!" The birds stared at him, stood their ground. Old Idi made a threatening flap onto the low parapet and with Chipman backing away in a panic, his bravado was revealed for what it was – skin deep.

"Drift, relocate me!" Toffee's voice had risen an octave. Qumquat made another appearance as though ready for something like this and within seconds, breakfast had been transferred to the central table with the trumpet flowers, a table inaccessible to Old Idi and his flock of horrors. "Floripondio," said Drift shoving his nose into one of them. "I like these, they smell like a bordello."

Toffee drained her teacup. Drift poured some more. Facing away from the now distant vultures, she made a quick recovery.

"You might be allergic to the droppings, Toffee." Chipman found he was keen to give advice. "You could press charges against the management. It could not possibly be legal that creatures like…"

Toffee opened her mouth but Drift spoke for her. "Don't start mouthing off like an attorney. It's Attah's cutlass as much as the vultures that Toffee reacts to. She won't talk about it." He gazed concernedly at his love. "You saw that palsy? Every few days this nervous condition comes tormenting her. A little brain lesion, whatever, search me. She calls it her tormies and it scares the shit out of her. Me too. Began right here at Tlula. Sanguini says it's psychological, something to do with childhood memories, the family turkey farm. He's hot to cure her, and that was cool by me but now I'm thinking it was one of his dumb massages that triggered the torments in the first place. I'm not letting him do to her what happened with Niggling Nancy. Sanguini's beat-ups just wipe my plumcake out. And she hasn't had her period for months."

"Honey!" Her cornflower eyes were flashing cold iron. "Quit it! You don't have a fucking clue about modern psychology."

"They ran some neurological tests at the British Hospital in Okidoki last week. The Tropical Diseases Unit too. All negative. She's had fevers. I thought she might have been bitten by a tsetse fly or something." He glanced at Lobelia, now perched within the top of Toffee's afro, lowered his voice. "Even a virus from you know who."

"I said quit it! We're here on a fabulous beach. It's a whole new African life for me. My homeland. That's all I care about." The colobus who had been preoccupied with picking out minute bits of salt or detritus from deep in the afro, suddenly took a swipe at Drift, got his bare shoulder and drew blood.

"Fucker!" Drift, just as swift, grabbed the creature and threw it over Toffee's head. Lobelia landed on a table and scarpered, with shrill cries, for the kitchen, her long lead trailing behind.

"Oh no, no! Attah will..! Honey!" Toffee stood up, started screaming and didn't stop.

Drift was all over the dining room recapturing the colobus. Chipman made attempts to stamp his foot down on the flying lead. Attah had grabbed his cutlass but kept his distance. Qumqwat, arms wide, blocked an exit. Qaddo, who was in charge of the hotel gardens, made an appearance. For the few minutes it took, Toffee was manic and unhelpful, her eyes stricken until Lobelia swerved suddenly and leapt back into her arms. "Mmm! My babywaby. Mmmmmm!" Smothering it with kisses, she delivered a well-aimed kick at Drift.

"Oh, sugarpot, pardon, pardon. Look at you! So drained. Your face needs some colour," Drift got his hair back into shape then made to gently pinch Toffee's cheekbones. "Jellybabe, I'm going to get you on the cover of *Vogue* I swear." Drift started poking at an unhealthy puffiness which seemed to have erupted below those eyes.

Toffee shoved his hand away, put on her sunglasses, grabbed the end of Lobelia's lead, and was off at a run along the beach. Drift watched her until she arched Lobelia through the air to the sand. The graceful, long-striding Toffee and the scampering Lobelia with her neckerchief, were like performers primed for a Palladium turn.

SIX: *River deep, mountain high*

"Toffee's a trip isn't she?" Drift sighed and turned to Chipman. "She was awkward as a kid, her Dad said, but beautified as a teenager. She was Miss Deep South Turkey Farms Association. Colonel Dawson, her Dad, began promoting her like crazy and next year she was runner up to Miss Georgia Peach. Almost the big time. She was the first black babe ever to enter. If she had been white she would have won for sure. Her dad's Irish, her mom's swamp black. She came out that carob colour. I love it. Wanna know her real name?"

"Not really."

"Minerva Jane. Minnie. She and her sister grew out of chopping the heads off turkeys for the Colonel and developed a talent for stripping. They went north. Worked their way up to Rosarita's Candy Bar in Chicago's Spanish Quarter. One of my hang-outs. That's where I met her. A high class joint, specialising in chocolate chickadees. Rosarita had put together a show called *The Sweetest Thangs – Toffee, Fudge and Licorice go Uptown*. Minnie was Toffee. She found the name really cool and Rosarita said it was more African so she has kept it ever since. We fell in love, said to hell with our careers. I quit my job with the Chicago City Zoo. We started listening to Aretha Franklin, Ike and Tina Turner, even Miriam Makeba. She grew her afro and we hit the hippie trails with the international freaks. Like everyone else back then. It's been perfecto ever since." Drift gave another sigh. "Tits to fucking die for. Keep your hands off. I saw you drooling."

"No, no! Well, yes (Chipman added appeasingly) what man wouldn't. I mean…"

"I hate to say it, Chipman, but I'm at the end of my rope. If Starry's new age paycho bullshit doesn't have the answers and frankly, it doesn't, well – he's a joke. Doctor! Figured he'd get to shack up with the aristocracy by marrying Dame Cerisia. He's supposed to be a revolutionary socialist, get rid of the Monarchy, the House of Lords, up the workers guy. Turns out he's a brown-nosing social climber. You into participating? His Love Rituals as he calls them?"

"He assumes, quite wrongly, that I have committed myself, but…"

"Couple hours each morning. Rest of the day you can suck on a bong and a beer under a palm tree. Work on the leisure. Just like all the freaky dreck hanging out here. Some of them are eating the Angel's Trumpet seeds and going batshit. You won't find many of them buying into Sanguini's trip. Except the chicks. They seem to find him attractive. By the way, don't hand over your entire fortune to Cerisia Twitchley. A month into their African odyssey, Wittering found out the truth behind that Professor Siegfried clinic in Switzerland and cut her off without a cent. It was the last straw as far as he was concerned. He hadn't known about her after midnight high jinks with her fifteen year old daughters in the club either. That's why the honeymooning doctor and his wife are stuck here. She's not too adjusted to living below the poverty line."

"Cerisia seems charming. I mean, quite a character."

"Don't be fooled by the baby talk. She's as tough as a $2 T-bone."

Chipman stubbed out his cigarette, threw it hard at Old Idi for his bad behaviour and as he did so, came Drift's threatened talk. "Starry told me in Tlula last night that you work for the Department of Education in Sydney. Turn on, tune in, drop out, is the mantra – but I still respect someone like you wanting to hang on to their job." There came a pregnant pause. "What do you know about cabinet making? Chiffoniers, kitchen drawers, things like that? Excuse me, but I'm asking everyone."

Chipman had blinked acceptance of the Education lie he had told Sanguini but now he said. "Why me?"

"Starry said you have an eye for a bit of wood."

"It was my Dad's spare time activity. School holidays. He turned his shed in the back yard into a workshop and got me interested. Anything for Dad, and we knocked up some nice things for Mum. Bookshelves, an oak dining table..."

"My hunch was right. I noticed your piano player fingers. Craftsman's hands. Hey, way cool!" He tapped Chipman approvingly on the back, took a misshapen, hand rolled cigarette from his bag, lit up. A sweet, unfamiliar aroma came wafting.

"Toke? First of the season. Oven dried. Massive Qaddo's finest." He gestured with it again. "Maryjane. Set you up for the day."

"Good heavens, no. Absolutely not!" Chipman stepped back, reached for his cigarettes as though to divorce himself from disrepute.

"Your loss, amigo. But mosey on over here. Last night I handed it to Hamou who said he could fix it but he's el pathetico. Worse than me."

In the open passageway to the bar, Hamou had left a gimcrack cage, built out of what might have been a couple of old packing cases. Inside was one of the silvery black mambas. Drift tapped the wire mesh. The snake lunged and spat a pale liquid. A drop oozed through. He wiped it off with a forefinger which he then sucked. In an invitation to admire such reckless macho behaviour, he sparkled his small, wide spaced eyes at Chipman, who had backed up against the wall.

"They come around for eggs. Nestlings. The bush rats. The mice. The hornbills give 'em hell, but they still come." He paused, gave the waxed ends of his Custer moustache a twirl. "I'm not much of a handyman. Loose board at the back. Needs a nail or two. Couple days ago, this baby got out in our bungalow. A close thing."

"You and Hamou can't even bang in a few nails?"

"You're definitely the one to build my cages. I need sixteen. Pronto."

"I'm on holiday, Drift. I'm having a – a breakdown. I mean, I'm trying to quit drinking. Look, my hands are shaking. I don't even trust myself to drive any more. I've become paranoid lately about things. At night..." Chipman noticed Drift's eyes glazing over and stopped. "Why don't you hire someone in the village? Dr Sanguini said they built Cerisia's palanquin."

"Ha! Palanquin. Just because a scorpion stung her toe."

"Oh dear. Do I have to worry about those too?"

"Nah, she was unlucky. Off-colour for coupla days. Scorpions rare here. Yeah, palanquin, lording it over the locals, who does she think she is, and not paid for yet. And won't ever be if you ask me. Those bearers of hers are lucky they still get their pittance. I would say the differences between Nigel Wittering and Cerisia are irreconcilable."

"You speak as though you know this Wittering."

The shifty look came over Drift again and he turned the conversation back to cabinetry. "It's complicated. I mean, complicated." He saw Attah passing nearby, continued *sotto voce*. "Too complicated for anyone at the hotel. Or the village." He moved closer, pivoting slightly, almost as though he was presenting himself as a product for inspection. Drift's troublesome hair had once again fallen over his forehead, a rather low one. To Chipman, he didn't look at all like a natural scientist, but then again, he had never met a drop-out before. He rejected another offer of a toke. In response, Drift changed tack. He gave himself a scratching. Chipman's eyes went to what he had already checked out. Yes, there was more than a suggestion of actual scrotal visibility. The raggedness of the Bermudas must have been intentional, for the rest of him was immaculate; the chest hair certainly was, exquisite even, in its patterning and particularly in the way it descended in a fine line all the way to the low slung shorts, where it expanded prettily into what was the beginning of his pubic hair.

The snake catcher engaged Chipman's eyes, began a slow rubbing. Chipman took a step back, pressing a hand to his sudden thickening as he shyly turned away. Well aware by now that something had become overactive down there, something with a mind of its own, he should have been pleased but as many times before, he just felt tawdry.

Chipman's mind raced. How could Drift be so sure he would be susceptible to seduction? He liked to think he passed for a regular bloke. Back home it was absolutely essential to be so. He sighed. Sanguini's loose lips! Or was that being unfair to the doctor. Was it the safari suit? Too neat, too smart? The Roman sandals? He took great care with the ordinariness of his clothes, thus camouflaging suggestion of anything other than conventionality of desire. After Sanguini's illuminating monologue the previous evening, he was telling himself his current difficulties were not that he was attracted to men rather than to women, but that within the confines of that attraction, he had problems.

Drift had an enviable nose, one that was the same colour and grain as the rest of his face. The ridge was straight and the nostrils so refined Chipman hoped he was getting enough air for himself through them. And under that moustache, his lips were full and wide. Chipman added another hand to the coverage of his crotch.

"Massive Qaddo might know where we can get the right sort of building materials. Give it some thought, Chipman. This is a surefire thing." Drift rested a hand on his shoulder. "Let's talk again after Starry's morning session. About the – complications." There came that wink again.

The man was a winker. Drift left the less-than-adequate cage where it was and zoomed off towards Dr Sanguini's palm hut in pursuit of his Toffee.

SEVEN: *Poor poor pitiful me*

Hammer and nails were supplied by Hamou who came along to watch. Chipman became aware of the snake's increasing irritation, but pressed on and in no more than a minute or two, had repaired and strengthened the cage, so inappropriately left there. In fact, Chipman's hands had steadied, and he enjoyed having something on which to focus while he fretted about Drift's wink and its implications. Taking out his mother of pearl-backed hand mirror he applied a coating of zinc cream to his nose. For once he did not mind that someone saw him doing it. "It makes me look like a clown," he said to the uncomprehending Hamou who bowed and moved away. Yes, something acceptable to cover up its red sheen. Zinc wasn't make-up, it was protection against the sun. It had a strong surfer thing about it, an everyday masculine association. As he put his mirror and cream away, he gave an all-encompassing groan of self-pity.

Chipman became aware of Zach approaching even before he turned towards him. The Nebraskan was clutching his book with its no doubt lurid cover. Perhaps it was just the book that had made him cry. The man took in the cage with its angry occupant, and glug-a-glugged some gin from the flagon he was carrying. His eyes searched Chipman with an inscrutable not necessarily unfriendly stare.

Zach had heard his groan. Chipman could have stuck out his hand and introduced himself like any man might but then again Zach didn't either. Chipman's returning gaze had a memory of his old mate Tibor Radovan looming again; childhood recollections, happy high school days really, with Tibor back in the late fifties. The lump that rose in his throat as he suppressed an emotion, was accompanied by the tightening in his larynx that could turn his voice into something of a squeak. Simultaneously, the hotel's early morning cacophony decibelled upwards – the hornbills' klaxon hoots, the chorus of lesser songsters, but most of all, the cicadas revving up in the poincianas.

"Chipman, right? You cool?"

He nodded.

"What's that white stuff on your nose?"

Chipman gave his throat a thorough clearing. His voice when it came out was still something of a childish piping. "Ah – what are you reading?"

The book was held up. "Rimbaud. Derangement of the senses. Ever read him?"

"Oh. Well, no. Not really…" Chipman was right about the lurid cover but lowered his gaze. Rimbaud was a name he was vaguely familiar with, but Chipman was more of a prose reader and not of a particularly literary bent either. Raymond Chandler and Agatha Christie both came to mind. So did Melody Motherwell's burning of Mary Renault's *Last of the Wine* when he realised what it was all about. The flames brought to an end an early attempt at escape.

"*The Drunken Boat. Illuminations*. A big influence on Kerouac. On Bob Dylan too. Meant a lot to me when we, when I, was younger. Now I'm re-reading him, for Chrissake. Not the same. In fact, I now find his later life in Abyssinia more interesting." Zach shrugged dismissively, gave his dark stubble a rub and moved on a step or two. "Dylan is my new Rimbaud." He gave a brief laugh. "Can't imagine Arthur Rimbaud singing."

Chipman kept looking at him out of the corner of an eye; there came more infirmity, a reaching for the wall in support, that need for a drink. Damn. Yes, Zach had the look of Tibor. The profile particularly echoed it. And the dark green eyes with a gold fleck. Even the stubble. Something Slavic.

Tibor Radovan was a boy that Chipman had loved and adored like no other. It was Alfie who told him, after all the thievery came to light, that Tibor would lead him astray, but it was Melody Motherwell much later who told him to forget Tibor, to grow up and become a man,

"You coming to Dr Sanguini's palm shelter?" he managed to ask.

"That fuckwit! Wild horses couldn't drag me. He's desperate to augment his Afreakans. Fast Eddie was on the run and had to move on. Pity, he was a great drummer. Trained dancer. He may have ripped Starry off in some way as well."

"Who is Niggling Nancy?"

"Fast Eddie's squeeze. Bit of a pest, poor girl. Played the mandolin and sang, but the therapies exacerbated her mental problems and last week an aunt came to the rescue. Took her back to England." Zach paused. "Well, I'm off to Mbutu with a work party. The next village along the coast. There's an old colonial guardhouse being refurbished as a kindergarten. Come along if you want. Chief Akwa responds to offers of help." He paused again and Chipman detected a moment of uncertainty. "There's bad feeling between the hotel and the village. I'm working on it. Kmango destroyed over 500 trees to build this so-called resort. Tlula's wonderful coconut grove was decimated. Cut in two. The villagers have to detour around the hotel to work the eastern section."

"Oh dear, but I'd better find out what Dr Sanguini has in mind for me. I'm beginning to accept I might need refurbishment myself."

"I've been through some therapy stuff. I could help if you're looking for something more genuine."

"Ah, did you know the dead man that the fishermen brought in yesterday?"

The Nebraskan offered his gourd.

Chipman drank greedily, started spluttering, hung onto it. Zach might well be sympathetic as stated, but after the utterly mad behaviour on the beach the previous day, the lawyer in him was not ready to reveal his detour to *delirium tremens* to such a man.

"I get deluded." Zach reached for his gourd, began walking away. "Sorry about that. Pathetic really. I'm back on my meds now."

Chipman supposed he was grateful for the gin, but Zach's resemblance to Tibor was something he resented. He experienced it as a sullying of the uniqueness of his one and only boyhood beloved, his brash little bad news Tibor Radovan. Fourteen long years before. Yes, a sullying – and by such a man as Shaler. The choking emotion came again and this time it was impossible for Chipman to stop a self-pitying gush of tears.

PART TWO
The Palm Shelter On The Far Beach

EIGHT: *All this every day*

With the traumatic events of breakfast behind him, and the big slug of Zach's local gin lubricating the capillaries of his mind, Chipman found himself finally able to appreciate what had been so recommended by William Oates – the beach itself. Fringed by dense lines of coconut palms, its band of sand (as white as that of Jervis Bay) stretched in a wide and most harmonious curve into the far distance. Starry and his group were out there somewhere, but not a soul could be seen on its entire length. A quarter mile out to sea, there was a small palm clad island, more correctly perhaps an islet, with a sharp promontory rising like a miniature Matterhorn at the eastern end. In the sea lane beyond the islet, a freighter was passing by. The gentle surf and turquoise water were inviting, but somehow the swim he had intended to take before submitting to any alcohol recovery session (if he could so typify what Dr Starry Sanguini was up to), was beyond him.

The shelter (only one of several locations at Tlula, it turned out, at which Dr Sanguini was pursuing his 'new mission in life') had been erected towards the end of the beach, a fifteen minute walk from the hotel. Brooding over the sand was an undulating ridge thickly draped with jungle, the deep greens of the canopy punctuated by the pink and purple of flowering tree tops. Hornbills honked from the wild hibiscus trees. Monkeys shrieked in the distance. Rusting on the rocks below the headland where the sand and coconut palms ended, lay a long-wrecked oil tanker, the *Accra Queen*.

The doctor had been right about the heat. At eight in the morning the temperature was up in the nineties. Half way along the curve of the sand, Chipman took off his safari jacket. Debris swirling from a nearby patch of dried up swamp land behind the beach made the trek particularly unpleasant. The hotel was protected, but out on the far beach, the harmattan, a hot seasonal wind from the desert north, was blowing hard.

The shelter, larger than his bedroom in the rectory, had a thatch of dead palm fronds. Lengths of faded sail cloth, stitched together, had been stretched between bamboo uprights to deflect the wind. Immediately behind, in the shadows and shelter of a huge banyan, stood the palanquin. Cerisia, wearing nothing but a pair of sunglasses (identical to those worn by Dr Sanguini), was munching her way through a truckload of breakfast. One of her four orange capped Boys, kneeling on the cushions, was just finishing oiling her back. Another village youth was wielding a hornbill feather fan on a polished black stick.

Lotus was there to wipe Cerisia's mouth, and feed her further. Even as he watched, Mrs Sanguini's chin hit her chest. She had nodded off or was even sound asleep, a gob of deep-fried fufu still clutched in her hand. Near naked, her skin tanned but weathered, she seemed vulnerable and almost endearing. Not something she had been in the circumstance of the previous evening. Nor was she simply fat. She had a lot of shape. He began to doubt it was the same woman.

Lotus gave a sigh. "Poor baby, she danced til dawn."

"If only," Dr Sanguini commented, also transformed that morning, now a vaudevillian figure in a Balinese sarong and tall wizard's hat woven from raffia with a topknot of coloured ribbons, his hair scraped back into a bunch at the back. He was swirling about, also eating. "You got that camera of yours, Chipman? Move in on that marvellous unreconstructed bosom, the beautifully turned ankles. Capture the dignity of form that comes from years of selective breeding. The aristocratic milk-white skin. Well…" He paused. "Make up for all those missed opportunities outside Wally's windows. Become the photo voyeur you were born to be."

He let out a laugh and Chipman turned away from him. Unprofessional was the word. 'Malice aforethought' also came to his forensically oriented mind.

There were quite a few people lounging about, others returning from a swim, none of whom Chipman had seen before, and none looking like they needed therapy. But why else would they be here, waiting for the Sanguinis to finish breakfast?

It became obvious to Chipman that apart from Dr Sanguini, he was the only one wearing clothes. And the only one with a white zinked nose. The bronzed group, skins glistening, were giving off a strong smell of coconut oil, and seemed composed almost entirely of heterosexual couples. Melody Motherwell would approve was his first thought. "Am I really welcome here, a – homosexual man?" he half-whispered to himself. It hurt him to even use the word. But even as these doubts surfaced, Starry introduced him to Thierry and Jean-Claude who had dropped in on their way to Yamoussoukro in Cote d'Ivoire. From them, both long-haired and bearded, came wafting that sweetly unpleasant smell of marijuana. "Have a kiss for Chipman, here. Show him what it's all about." They laughed and obliged. Chipman's distress at the sight of two men kissing was acute. Jean-Claude offered his joint and Chipman backed away – from the open gayness more than the marijuana.

Chipman's mind whirred crazily inwards. The internal furnace of embarrassment at being in this alien situation soon more than matched the heat coming from the corrosive glare of the climbing sun. He walked away into deep shade of the grove, where he was able to regain his composure. The nerveless doctor was soon yelling for him to get back. Slowly, resistingly, he took off all his clothes and re-joined the group.

Drift and Toffee appeared from beyond the big banyan. Lobelia, still on her long lead, was travelling behind, chewing a piece of coconut.

"Peppermint, Chipman?" inquired Lotus, pouring cool tea from a thermos. Stan Francisco was an intent watcher of her servicing. Stan, Lotus's stripling of a boyfriend, had thick chestnut hair in a Prince Valiant cut and facial fuzz that was more down than beard.

His pubic hair was much the same. His amber eyes were as large and bright as a goat's. Chipman's legal mind had him definitely wondering about age of consent, musing about indictment possibilities, crossing US state lines, statutory rape. Lotus second guessed him. "Stop that. He's not as young as he looks." Both Lotus and Stan were wearing an ADOLF cap.

Dr Sanguini threw aside his sarong and hat but retained his dark glasses. As he bobbed around, he outlined the Siegfried approach for newcomers like Chipman, Jean-Claude and Thierry. Stan Francisco beat haphazardly at a frame drum and from time to time, dinged a triangle. "Rhythm, Stan," shouted the doctor helpfully. "Rhythm!"

Adolf/Sanguini PSP (Primal Scream Plus), a fast track, hands-on, psychoanalysis, combining Arthur Janov's Primal Scream techniques with Wilhelm Reich's non-verbal deep tissue massages. Apparently regarded as a 'revolutionary' in psychiatry, Reich says sexual repression, usually at the behest of the monotheistic religions, is the most perverse force in the western world. All the unhappiness, all the violence, every war can be traced to it. Hitler was a known homosexual in WW1. If he had given rein to his natural sexuality there would have been no Nazis, no WW2, no Holocaust. Reich says sexuality is fundamental to our well-being, and yet for centuries, a sense of shame about sex has been drummed into us. Sex has the power to heal us if only we would let it.

Chipman scribbled away, determined to keep a record of all this. For his sanity if nothing else. And Wally, he was sure, would be fascinated by any criminal aspects he was able to uncover...

Sanguini emphasises the tribal ritual mumbo jumbo he talked about last night. Rhythm apparently very important. Rhythm enhances access to memories locked up in the human musculature. Has repression really produced the paranoid state that has developed since getting caught outside Wally's window? Well, it was Melody's repressions which initially drove me to the booze. Look where that has got me. I'm an addict, drinking just to stay afloat. What is he talking about now? What are visualisations? What is meditation? Surely renegade to say these techniques bring release from 'absurdly punitive' Western societal codes...

"Drift, we will demonstrate for Chipman with your darling Toffee. Yes?"

She lay down and the group began what Adolf Siegfried called, and whose pronunciation everyone merrily imitated, "dizgonnegtion of ze zinking prozzezez." This seemed to involve beating Toffee about the head with some vigour. Cerisia had come alive and was in there, banging away.

With Toffee's thinking thoroughly disconnected – Chipman feared she may have been knocked unconscious – the group was directed to search for tensions locked up in the musculature of various parts of her body. "Deeper," cried the doctor. "The thighs, the calves!"

The group's screaming escalated empathetically with Toffee's. "Flip her over."

"They've got me, the tormies have got me," Toffee moaned, all in a sweat and shiver as the group, tiring in the heat, geared down to a slower rhythm. Soon she was quiet with everyone gently resting their hands on her body.

'Healing rituals.' Destruction of 'body armouring', apparently essential for 'exorcism' of negative childhood memories, in particular sexual abuse. I have never been sexually abused. But what about Melody's Old Testamental stuff? He is a charmer and popular with everyone, I certainly never thought of his restructurings as abuse until too late. Alfie had taught us kids how to avoid sanctimony but I embraced the Rector's. It was always the voice with Melody. His big asset. His weapon I would call it now. It got to me. Wally encouraged me to join the Waverton Theatrical Society but Melody forbade it. Instead he let me sing in his Congregational Choir, the men in it usually restricted to those who were married. There is a Green Hill Far Away, Abide with Me…yes, all too late. Here I am.

Cerisia rocked Toffee gently in her arms, like a mother would an unhappy, crying child. "What a splendid girl," she cooed. "Did we recover something? It was your Papa wasn't it? The turkey sheds?" Toffee nodded. "Unburden yourself, sweetiekins. Tell Mama." With silence the only response, Cerisia put her cheek to Toffee's only to have the girl throw herself at Drift. She clung to him as he covered her face with kisses. "My poor pumpkin," he murmured. "Mi amor."

"Trauma resulting from the father's possessiveness has become chronic." Dr Sanguini announced portentously. After twenty minutes of leaping about, he was aflow with perspiration but still more energised than anyone. "Relax, Chipman. Stop that crazy scowling. You too, Drift. The only way out for Toffee is further in, towards the heart of her dilemma. Until we illuminate the darkness in her past, every time you have sex with her, you're lighting a gunpowder trail."

"What fucking darkness?" demanded Drift irritably.

Chipman, in his final journal note that morning wrote, *I may be a 'fucked-up alcoholic' (quoting the doctor), but I'm not 'fucked-up' enough to need anything as extreme as Primal Scream Plus.*

NINE: *I'm ready for my close-up Mr deMille*

The morning's harmattan had been ferocious enough for Starry to move his group from the beach into the coconut grove itself. When Chipman came to, he was lying on his back, a piece of rattan beneath him. A Tlulan work party was standing on the path through the centre of the grove looking over at him. Chief Akwa, a tall man with distinguished mien and a craggy, deeply cicatriced face, hair like a steel wire scrubber, stepped forward. His regal robe exposed a shoulder on which was hoisted a blunderbuss. When Chipman realised he himself was not only naked but engorged if not erect, he grabbed for a dead palm frond.

Behind Chief Akwa, were farmers with scratch hoes and other implements, women in dazzling cotton print ntamas, poised with enamel bowls filled with cassava roots and cocoyams on their heads, one with twin babies in a back sling.

Standing to one side was Fangga, the Snake Fetish Priest, a truculent little man with grey hair neatly corkscrewing out from under a faded corduroy cap. A short tasselled smock revealed a withered leg, and he was leaning on a stave. Feathered leather bands decorated his wrists and a pair of shiny custom-made ankle boots graced his feet. There was a dandified effect.

"Why you killin' this poor fellow man here?"

"Not at all, Chief…" began Starry

Cerisia snapped an order. "Let go of the silly twank, Stan."

Dr Starry Sanguini had had his way after all and Chipman had agreed to a preliminary series of 're-birthings'. His change of mind had come after being scraped off the floor of the hotel bar one lonely and extended lunchtime. A faintly contemptuous Attah had given him a mop and a bucket to clean up the vomit. He had also passed out on the far beach one night, waking at dawn not only with a hangover but covered in unsightly sand flea bites which had given him a forty-eight hour fever. Once bitten twice shy he told himself, not wanting to succumb to any more liquid attempts to find the health and happiness promised by the paradise that was Tlula Leisure Beach. He had disgraced himself. Even the 'leisure' had proved beyond him.

"Yes, yes, yes," Dr Sanguini had shouted. "Let it out, let it out," the group chorused. Chipman eventually complied by spewing not so much his "full breakfast" as the alcoholic accompaniment to it. He was still woozy despite the release.

"You is all immodest in the extreme." Chief Akwa's voice rang with moral authority. "I am requestin' that you all gain more attire this very minute."

"I'm sorry if we have upset you and your people." Starry made an intimidating leap forward. "You have to admit, though, you don't come along this way very often." He snapped his fingers. "Lotus, gimme."

Lotus danced over with Dr Sanguini's sarong and wound it about him nimbly as he talked. "Chief, for the purposes of our therapies it is necessary to be open to all the elemental forces." Indicating both sky and sea, he coughed. "You have just now seen our very respectable new educator friend Mr Chipman Smith here, for example, spit out some of his self-induced psychotic madness and misery. Lotus, wipe his chin. He was telling us about how he spied night after night on Wally Whitbread, that's his boss, waving his dick around and having sex with his wife in their bedroom. And bathroom apparently. Chipman got caught. And then escaped."

Chief Akwa put a cupped hand to his ear. The doctor raised his voice. "He was telling us a story about how demons have possessed him, causing voyeuristic behaviour, something which our intolerant mainstream society forbids." Chief Akwa began looking around at his entourage, a scowl of puzzlement on his face. "Well, maybe your society too for that matter. We both know about demons, Chief. For us they are bad chemicals in the head. Neural pathways that have become blocked on the way to the frontal lobe. For Africans, for you, they are still all creeping around in the bush. The animal spirits, the night witches and bugaboos who make you do bad things. Your old fetish priest here would know what I am talking about. The blood sacrifices you have to make."

Chief Akwa exchanged a glance with Fangga. "We is a strong Christian community here in Tlula. You unwholesome white peoples getting to be big, big nuisance. This is not first time I catch you with these heathen savageries. I am accord with Fangga on this point. It safer if you all leave Tlula very soon. I am definitely advisin' you now."

"We've fallen in love with your simple village, Chief Akwa. Mr Fangga is not our enemy. He has much to teach me. Witchdoctorwise. While I have got you here, could you ask him for me if..."

"Our heads is hurtin' with your shriekin' and misbehavin' and no clothes. Lady Cerisia, you too fat. You come visit one day soon and my wife she sell you proper garments for your figure." He unslung his blunderbuss, aimed it skyward and let off a blast. "All of you take heed!" He walked off, the women following, silent and self-contained. Chief Akwa made a final turn. "You do better to have example of your Mr Zach."

Chipman had not even noticed that Zach was at the back of the work party. His shoulders were yoked with a couple of buckets. They were filled with some kind of meal and obviously heavy. Zach did not even look over as he passed by.

"Peace Corps," Lotus said, also eyeing his retreating figure. "So last year. But what Zach's really interested in is the crocodile ponds. He says it's a King Tut pharaoh thing. Is that cool or what?"

A final shout came from Chief Akwa. "I am advisin' Sir Henry Kmango." The antique gun was shaken as he disappeared into the trees.

"He may be the Tlula bigwig, but he's a compromised figure," the doctor pronounced, loosening his sarong, throwing it back to Lotus.

"Boozes in Blossom's but kowtows to Kmango," said Cerisia.

Dr Sanguini's fresh nakedness and the disparaging remarks made Chipman wish he was with Zach and the work party. A surge of dislike and more, a hatred, for whatever he – and Cerisia – were up to, swept through him.

"I'm finding it all utterly pointless, Dr Sanguini."

Chipman was bruised, crumpled, humiliated and after three days without alcohol, feeling utterly wretched. The group's gentler hands during the post-brutality "recovery session" had helped, and the 'cradling' by Cerisia had even briefly transported him back to his early childhood and Matilda's loving arms; but one of her Boys, Chipman noticed, was wearing the underpants which had been removed from his person at the beginning of the session.

"Hey!" he yelled, stumbling over to the young man and grabbing for them. Another ebony youth was sashaying by in his safari jacket. "Hey!" he yelled again. That jacket had to be in good shape for Wally's conference in Lagos. "Cerisia, I appreciate you are doing something for the local economy by employing them, but your bearers are nothing but louts. And light-fingered at that!"

"You don't need that stupid jacket," she responded. "Let it go."

"If Primal Scream is good enough for John and Yoko, PSP is more than good enough for you," the doctor intoned, settling the matter.

Chipman knew he had screamed out intimate information about Melody's inflexible *modus operandi* and many other things he could not now recall.

"Gerontophilia, I love it," the doctor had cried in glee. "And you have a taste for the trashy. We were all most entertained. Old Mr Duffy, the flasher? What a character!"

"You exaggerate as usual. He was an orchardist. Dr Sanguini, and I give you your phony title only out of kindness, but what you are up to has no chance of ever achieving official psychotherapeutic or legal recognition. Being a law unto yourself is called vigilantism"

"Chipman, I like it. We are all vigilantes."

"Democratic freedom," Cerisia put in.

"Any number of third world despots would love to have you around. You're like a medievalist. Torture never works. It's pointless." Sure of his ground, Chipman spat out some of the bile in his mouth, looked for support. There was none.

"The Spanish Inquisition wasn't pointless, my pet." Cerisia expelled smoke from a Gitane into his face and let out a cackle. "We all need role models."

A cackle he could not relate to. Had alcoholic excess completely deprived him of any sense of humour? He felt like tearing off her Al Capone glasses. Why had they never pummelled her? Or Sanguini for that matter?

"Charlatans," he said to Lotus later when she was plying him with water. "Both of them." He drank and drank, finding it almost an intoxicant. He had been, he realised, close to dehydration. It wasn't the first time it had happened in the equatorial heat of Tlula.

"Chipman, you have to stop analysing and surrender to the guru. To the Starry Starry Night." Prone to the delicate giggle, Lotus was clearly enjoying his plight. She watched him take one last swallow. "You're not letting yourself get your money's worth."

"Lotus, I'm a drunken sot, and I accept now I'm an unhappy homosexual, but this is definitely not the way to get my money's worth."

The wizard's hat was flung high into the air. Lotus made an eager catch as though it were a bride's bouquet. Cerisia was unlacing the pair of red canvas bootees she had put on when she had climbed out of the palanquin. Starry gave his beard and chest a scratching with both hands. Chipman noted again some kind of nasty scar, half-hidden by both beard and chest hair. "Warriors all, together here, closing in on the climax and the constellations!" he trumpeted as his right arm shot up in a gesture which had his open palm flattened against the sky and waggling. "Do you think Zach's friend, Chief Akwa, would understand the Pink Panther salute?"

Starry could not stop his gleeful laughing. Secure in his feelings of goodness, he enjoyed his provocations, his wicked taunting self. It was all part of his master plan.

"Would Angela Davis, Toffee? Kathleen Cleaver? Can you handle it? Can we handle you? Are we all ready for the rocky road to unrestrained sexual and spiritual joy, to universal love?"

"Yes!" shouted the others (about a dozen of them that day), taking their assent as a permit to swim, and off they all dashed. Dr Sanguini showed the tip of his tongue and was mugging, in a most overtly sexual fashion, in a vain attempt to cheer Chipman out of his sulk.

Chipman felt victimised. Who was this evil monster? Was this another Melody come into his life? There surely had to be someone behind the façade to remember and recognize. That Starry had been up to something illegal, something despicable in his past, he was now half-convinced but as they suddenly locked eyes with each other, he had to confess that foxing out one such as Starry was no easy task. Like the fox in the fields for the hounds themselves. And there was that destabilising feeling that Starry was foxing him out in return.

It was with a sneering curl of the lip that Chipman watched Starry hold out one hand to Cerisia (his slightly taller fellow monster) and the other to Lotus, his all-weather acolyte. Out into the scorching wind and across the sun-seared surface of the wide white beach the three graces floated, following the others in a tiptoey gallivant of a dance.

"Water torture!" came Starry's mocking voice. That downy black haired bum of his. Had he once seen a newspaper photograph of such buttocks? Even in his departmental files? Impossible. The absence of alcohol had him imagining things. He remembered suddenly that Wally himself had a similarly attractive downy coating on his lower back and bum, one of course, that he had seen many times; and with binoculars. Chipman let out an "Ah!" of recognition and relief.

Stan Francisco was lost to his drumming, his eyes closed. "Lotus gone, Stan," said Drift, giving a kick which caused him to jump up and run.

"Lotie, wait," he cried.

"Stan panics if she gets too far away."

"He's not all there, is he? Did Sanguini, I mean Starry, do this to him? Like Niggling Nancy."

"Hey, you've got a point. To be fair, Stan's one of those cases. A long distance truck driver or something. He and Lotus were the numero uno Summer of Love poster couple, Grateful Dead groupies, into the whole hippie fiesta thing. Lotus concocted super-cocktails for both of them at one of Ken Kesey's Acid Tests, changed her name from Rebecca to Thousand Petalled Lotus overnight. But Stan totally flipped. Morphed into a state of cosmic identification with the Haight-Ashbury, climbing the lamp posts, kissing the street dividers, decorating police officers with flowers and eventually making signs of the cross with his own shit, sacred and all that."

"Oh, my God!"

"He never really came down and the name stuck. Fucked-up but cutesy. Lotus had a nice thing going with the Przinkowski Design Studios in Berkeley, but when she realised that Stan was going to need serious day-care she began a new life. She's dealing with a lot of guilt. They spent three months in an ashram with the Maharishi, meditating and doing yoga, then wound up in Swinging London. Lotus got a gig painting sets for Cerisia in *Twiddlers*. They went with her to that therapy clinic in Verbier. Stan thinks he's a musician now, all that yoga and crap, but he has no sense of rhythm or melody. I wouldn't mind betting he's tone deaf."

"He doesn't seem able to talk much."

"You get on Stan's wavelength, he can be quite chirpy." Drift threw a stone in the direction of the canoodling Toffee and Lobelia. "Ouch!" as the colobus zipped round and threw it back. Toffee laughed.

Drift changed the subject. "So now we're all psyched up for a Peeping Tom in our midst. Way to go, buddy!"

Having the Wally Whitbread stakeouts aired publicly in front of a bunch of strangers during an everything-but-the-kitchen sink therapy session may have been helpful in some way, but Starry's embellishments and distortions were the symptoms of an out of control personality. Chipman had come to feel that Starry was a virus incarnate, infecting his life and lawyerly being. Even swimming with him had been turned into therapy. Chipman bowed his head and forgetting that Drift was there, he fell to the sand and cringed foetally, overwhelmed by feelings of defeat. It would have been better if he had stayed home and joined Alcoholics Anonymous.

"Hey, leisurez vous." Drift reached down and squeezed his shoulder. "Fruit cakes, frotteurs, things like that, queers, what's the difference. Everybody's got to be something. You're a gay stalker."

"Voyeur," he put in faintly.

"Whatever. I even made out with Stan one night. Man, was Lotus pissed off. During my army physical I ticked the box asking if I had tendencies." Drift gave a limp wristed flap. "That's what got me out of Nam. Ha!" Checking that Toffee wasn't watching, he lifted Chipman up, turned him round and began a kneading of his neck and back. "You've seen her state when she's in the therapy. Cuddlefuck and all that afterwards, but she's always back kissy kissy with the imbecile monkey. The bitch! They're both bitches. I'm not putting up with it much longer."

Still unused to any man touching him after so many years of Melody's insistences that it was sinful, Chipman made a leap of faith, and allowed himself to appreciate the intimate caress of Drift's hands.

"I'm taking Toffee back to England. London has the best neuro-surgeons in the world. Ever heard of Harley Street?" Drift let his naked body rest against Chipman's back, pressed his extending penis against the flesh of the lawyer's behind. A wriggle followed. "About those complications with the cages. It's high time we..."

"Off you go, honey. Starry is waiting." Toffee and Lobelia were suddenly there.

"Come on, Chipman, baby, it's schemes and dreams time. In the water."

"Drifty, I have a few things to say to Chipman myself."

"Pumpkin pie…"

"Piss off!" Off he slunk, a picture of subservience. "Yeah, he's a hunk and all that," Toffee said, following Chipman's gaze, "but believe me, he can be a lousy lay and not as liberated as he thinks he is."

"Oh, you're getting it all wrong. You mustn't think that I…"

"Oh, get him wasted. He'll accept a blow job. Jerks like him always will. Not the sort of thing he likes from me. With my teeth." She laughed a carefree laugh. "He's always got it up for me. Mmmmm! You getting a good look at those nuts of his? I shave them for him sometimes."

How could a woman so beautiful talk like this?

"I can take a big dick. Can you?"

"Ah, well, yes." Chipman was shocked that he had confessed to that before quite realising what she was saying. "Oh, you mean…" he paused. "I have never had a dick, I mean penis, up my…" He stopped, too embarrassed to continue. Not only that but he was again sensing disturbing malfunction down there. It was definitely tacky and unfair that his alcohol induced brainial aberrations, while decreasing his usual intelligence, had actually increased his libido. And in the presence of a woman.

"Toffee, I'm not a practising sort of person. I mean – I mean, since falling in love with – ah, Mr Whitbread, I've been, ah – celibate. I think the unrequited thing is preferable really, more hygienic. Safer emotionally. Nobler."

"Screw that. You're just scared shitless. That story you told about wanting to feel up your Wally asleep in the airplane home was the dumbest thing I ever heard. Guys like you can't handle the fact that you want to have sex with other guys, so you fall in love with straights and get your kicks concealing the sexual side of things." She paused and with a glint in her eyes said, "It would be better if you just made a pass and got beaten up for once."

Chipman couldn't bear to hear her parroting Dr Sanguini and, like him, getting it all so wrong. "I'm not denying anything. Well, maybe. Wally is not just a crush. It's complex. And confusing beyond understanding." Chipman's throat was becoming constricted, his voice thinner. As usual he directed a curse at this chronic problem, that throat of his, under stress, becoming a war zone. When he spoke again there came the squeak and the hiss. "It's my – nose. The ugly colour. The cause of my celibacy, I mean."

"Oh, please! What's ugly?" She thrust her face sideways at Chipman. "See my wart? It bothers Drift but it doesn't bother me. It will go in its own sweet time. I bet you deliberately developed the nose in those lonesome days with that Melody asshole you go on about. Reich says it all." She began to laugh. "The head of your dick's a bit red too." She gave the head a squeeze. There was a blood response down there, more stirring. "Another stop light to keep the guys away. Hey good looking, go for Drifty boy. Maybe he'll give you the tormies like he gave me. The asshole can sleep for nine hours straight. Even those bedbugs in Bamako didn't wake him. I had to scream. And as you know, I can scream." She drew Chipman towards her. "Drift wants me to check into a psychiatric clinic. Like, psycho surgery stuff, immediately. I know I'm having these attacks, but I feel the winner in all this. He's the loser. Saggy butt!" she yelled at the distant Drift, about to dive into a wave. "I didn't mean that. He's got a great butt. It's just that I've decided to give Dr Sanguini his big chance so fuck him!"

Chipman could not help but melt as she held him close to her breasts, her nakedness. When Toffee's 'tormies' were gone, they were really gone. Her skin was silky and warm, and smelled so good, not just because it was freshly perfumed with a drop or two of petunia, one of Lotus's essential oils. "Dig, we're all doing this shit with Starry because brainwise, we're all fucked up, your mad gay voyeur window thing, but lemme remind you it's not the only reason I'm here. Bomzawe is where my family comes from. I'm a Qhatan. My tribe. I'm a proud Afro-American." Toffee gave Chipman a kiss on the forehead and let him go. Entranced, he watched as she began a fluffing up of her big hair and took the chance to change the subject.

"Toffee, the cages. Your boyfriend is being very mysterious. "I can't..."

"Oh, climb aboard. You'll find out soon enough. But don't sweat it. I yell at him about the dumb chillums he smokes but baby, I'm cool now. Anything to slow the fuse." Her beautiful blue eyes rested on him as though she was really seeing him for the first time. The talk was tough, but there was a tenderness and she gave that smile which had, on and off, been taking Chipman's breath away ever since he met her. There was another, even more roiling sensation in his penis. First Drift, now his girlfriend. He even jutted his pelvis so she might notice the rather attractive arousal.

Toffee hauled in the monkey, kissed it again and again. Lowering it deftly to the sand she murmured, "Wait here for me, my precious." Lobelia surged to the end of her lead and back again. The creature began to whimper at impending separation, her tail flicking about restlessly until Toffee handed her a banana and Lotus' thermos. The monkey knew how to drink from it. Her lead was securely tied to a solid piece of driftwood but Chipman couldn't help wanting the sad eyed waif to make a break for the jungle and the other monkeys not so far away.

"The sea is always gentle at Tlula. It's a healing in itself. There's no way Drift is going to talk me into splitting before the Carnival. That means there's time to do whatever you two dorks work out with the cages. There's plenty bucks involved. Make sure you nail down a proper deal. He can be one flaky son of a bitch. Ask Cerisia." She reached out and ruffled Chipman's own 'big hair' in the friendliest possible way. "Come on, race you in."

Dr Sanguini had them all on their backs beyond the breakers, holding hands, feet touching. "Sense our bodies all connecting." His voice floated soothingly over the dappled glass of the water's surface. "Breathe into your groin and send the connective focus all the way down into the soles of your feet, then on the exhale, legs in the air, flush it out into the cosmos. You too, Chipman." Ever the wordsmith, Starry had given the name, *The Esther Williamsicals* to this exercise. "...and now, on the inhale, bring it back to mother ocean. Imagine The Beautiful Afreakans are all one single living organism..."

The water was turquoise, the sand beneath fine and white, clear of weed or stones. A shoal of small silvery fish was slipping by. The waves curled over in benign slow motion, softly kissing the shore. At an immense height, the mendacious frigate birds hung, always alert, always waiting. Their lengthy forked tails trailed in the windless air.

PART THREE
Hotel de Schemes if not Screams

TEN: *Tell-tale signs and other initiatives and inebriations*

Attempting to avoid anything further to do with Starry, Chipman found himself back on a drinking binge. Mostly alone, but one night he had caroused with some passing travellers until Qwami with the help of Hamid had thrown them all out and closed the bar. Stumbling up the rickety stairs to his room, he had lurched against the verandah rail which had given way. Fortunately for him, his fall was tempered by the shrubbery below. Scratched and bruised, he made it back up to his room, but only as far as the floor, not his bed.

In the late morning, Chipman managed to put a call through to the British Embassy. Oates was 'in conference.' "There's no point shouting at me, my good Mr Smith," snapped the receptionist. "Conditions are as critical as they can be in Okidoki. There are people being disembowelled in the street here. You should just stay put." For a psychotic second or two he thought that it was Cerisia on the end of the line. But through the window of Attah's office, he could see the disinherited daughter thirty yards away on the palanquin's cushions, luxuriating in a floral patterned bikini. Kept cool by a vigorous fanning from one of her attendants, her substantial midriff was being oiled and rubbed by another. The receptionist's similar born-to-rule uppity English voice had confused him. He apologised profusely for his ill temper – and his hangover. Would she mind requesting William Oates to ring as soon as he had a free moment?

"May I ask why?" The voice was icy.

"He's supposed to be looking after my welfare. Regulating my alcoholic intake. I got drunk again and had a nasty fall. He promised to ring. Days ago now."

"Really!"

"It may not be safe in Okidoki, but I don't feel safe here either. A body washed up on the beach and the therapist that Mr Oates recommended is a quack. We have to take off our clothes in front of the villagers and …" Click!

Mid-afternoon, a Silver Cloud Rolls Royce convertible slid silently through the palm grove. Burgundy coloured, it pulled up outside the yellow painted Bungalow One. A chauffeur with a neck as thick as his skull went round and opened the passenger door. Sir Henry Kmango accepted a hand and eased himself out. Oxblood toe-peeper shoes, cream linen trousers, a fitted short-sleeved pink shirt. His skin was mauve-ish, his lips carmine; his platinum-grey hair was glossy with grease, straightened and brushed back. A pencil moustache. "Duke Ellington," said Lotus. "I like. Totally chic."

Both men were a stocky 5′ 8″.

"Look at him," crowed Starry. "Because Kmango's got 15% English blood in him he's allowed to identify as Caucasian. He's a member of a powerful mulatto elite here in Bomzawe. English and Dutch colonialists often married local women."

"How do you know all this?"

"Your William Oates slipped me a lot of information about him." Starry's snaggle-toothed grin erupted. "Oh, haven't I told you? I met Kmango at that Embassy cocktail party. He apologised for a 'touch of the tarbrush', as he himself called it." Starry gave Chipman a smirk, a stare and a soothing stroke of the hand. "My poor Mr Smith, your bruisings. I also have to tell you that Sir Henry Kmango and William Oates seemed to be the best of pals. Welcome back into the fold."

Attah Lalwani had given Starry little warning. He was infinitely sorry, but not only was Sir Henry Kmango arriving later that day to supervise preparations for the Easter Carnival, but in light of the fact that all the bungalows would be required for his many prestigious guests and the grounds for parking their motor vehicles, everybody would have to find accommodations elsewhere over the Christian holy period. Nor would he look kindly upon the fact that Starry was making use of the Hornbill's facilities but evading payment of dues. "Mr Starry, you bus people have not eaten one evening meal in my dining room since that first time. I tell you, everybody enjoy my international cuisine except you."

Attah also delivered Dr Sanguini's mail. Professor Adolf Siegfried's letter produced a "Bugger!" The second was from Danny Dudgeon.

Shortly after Attah's warning, Starry had bounded up the unstable stairs, eased past Jimmy Carpenter, one of Sir Henry's workmen who was replacing the rotted section of the verandah rail, and invaded Chipman's indigo and mustard retreat in the back wing of the crumbling hotel. "I cannot allow Attah to throw us out before the Carnival. Kmango's a zillionaire, he's going to hire us, and that's that. *Thug* demands nothing less." He waved the Dudgeon letter. "This dump loses Kmango a ton of money. We list twenty ways he can upgrade and start turning a profit. *Thug* will produce a series of touristic brochures. While Kmango is basking in the glow of entrepreneurial possibilities, we hit him with our ideas for entertainment at the Carnival."

Starry had brought his Olivetti Lettera 22 portable. "Cerisia and I are illiterate."

"Get out. I'm ill. I have a hangover. I need peace and quiet."

"Lotus is bringing around a bucket of the delightful gin. Hair of the dog. I'll let you have a glass. Or tree!"

Perspiration dripped from Chipman's fingertips onto the typewriter keys while Starry dictated under the blades of the creaking fan. The sounds of Jimmy Carpenter's hammer and saw were coming through the louvres as were the waves of drilling from the cicadas. There had been an explosion in their population and the hornbills were waxing fat. Cerisia too, had no trouble getting quantities of them down. Deep-fried in batter.

"Gassing the cicadas, Starry, no! They're making my head ache, but definitely no. They are so beautiful. Organised hornbill hunts, I can understand, the sooner the better, but..." When it came to Starry's Carnival proposals – choreographing for the stage, various aspects of his daily sessions out by the palm hut – he expressed the strongest misgivings. Starry listened for a moment or two before shutting Chipman up.

The Beautiful Afreakans' dream is hanging by a thread and you hit me with all this antipodean shit. But of course, I forgot, you've never allowed yourself a dream. You tell me you're a two bit pen pusher toiling for some Government department in something or other street, that you not only vote, but vote for the bloody Liberal Party. You demean the memory of your Dad by lusting after your boss and every other unavailable father figure within cooee and doing nothing about it. Do you realise how truly perverse you have become?"

It was the usual tirade, but with laughter (Starry always made sure he laughed frequently), which made it bearable enough, despite the occasional spray of spittle that went with the speed it was delivered. Inevitably, Chipman was soon working on aspects of Starry's *curriculum vitae.*

"My participation in Otto's *Neo-Artaudian Theatre* will impress Kmango. It was a highlight of the Amsterdam *Wet Dream Festival* but for Sir Henry, such an Anglophile, let's say it was part of cultural programming at the Victoria and Albert Museum. What would he know."

"*The Humouristic Bodily Functions Revue,*" Chipman typed. "In homage to magical mavericks Julian and Malina Beck of *The Living Theatre...*"

"Starry, I'm desperate for a drink. Where's Lotus with that gin?"

"I've got something for you better than any gin." The latest Danny Dudgeon missive was thrust at Chipman.

28th February

Dear Starry Eyes, just a note and another bank draft, small but enough I hope to keep your hands on the wheel. Of LIFE. Who said it was going to be easy? Thanks for introducing the GAY LIBERATION angle. Can we make a quid out of it? Have we got an updated HOMOSEXUAL HANDBOOK to rip off? Would BACK DOOR MAN issues sell out? TLULA BANKHEAD HOMO HEAVEN. BIG BLACK BUTTOCKS. PEDOPHILE RINGS. Another QUEEN in the PALACE? Tangier REVISITED? Has PAUL BOWLES come through? TENNESSEE? TRUMAN? GORE? GINSBERG? Who the hell is CHIPMAN SMITH anyway? He may be a FUCK ME JESUS buttplug but is he a NAME? Has he slept with TROY DONAHUE? DANNY LA RUE? JOE ORTON? Designed candelabras for LIBERACE? What does SMITH have to say on the SAVIOUR as SODOMITE theory? Did he and the DISCIPLES ever go to PISS PARTIES? Any FISTING in Bomzawe? RUBBER? LEATHER? MARY MAGDALENE as MADAM LASH? What about that possum, the big bad BLOSSOM and the LESBIAN angle? Let's smoke out the DIESEL DYKES. Remember the testosteroneod Cerisia Twitchley rumours? Can we work those in? Whatever. QUEER it UP, QUEER it DOWN. Give your imagination a CURDLE, give old Cerisia a CUDDLE from me!

Love or what you will, your Danny HIGH de HO Dudgeon.

Chipman's head sank into his hands. He closed his eyes. "What is a buttplug?"

"Danny's our big chance, Chipman. Now that I'm curing you of voyeuristic tendencies, leave those to me, preparing you for life as a regular gay bloke, a multi-monogamous serial sex life, you'll stop voting for conservative Menzies' clones, your creative juices will start flowing. We can write *The Leisure Beach Chronicles* together. Exploit the shit out of Cerisia's celebrity before it leaves memory and fades into history. Get the sixties counter-culture subversion stuff back in the headlines. Push Danny's circulation up there with *Playboy*."

"This letter confirms my worst fears about Dudgeon. It's demeaning. *Thug* would never pass the censors in Australia. I have no wish to associate with the obscene. The barbarous."

"There's a couple of big words for a nonentity like you, it's his best riff yet."

"You even told Danny my name. If my boss ever..." Until his binge, Chipman had been drinking less, feeling more sane with each day at Tlula, less fearful of the wide world, his physical body cleansing, becoming more balanced, more honest with himself, but now he was back to anxiety and uncertainty. "I'm not much of a writer, Starry. Certainly not about to become a Dudgeon pornographer."

"Or allow yourself to learn anything in the Starry & Cerisia School of Life. You can't still be planning to return to that dingbatty desk job. The office pecking order. Working on policy for the school kids of New South Wales. All that organised classroom crap makes for a wasted life!"

What was it about Sanguini that made him so vitriolic about public service? Helpless in the face of ebullience, Chipman lit a cigarette, hunched once more over the Olivetti, clenched his teeth, squeezed his eyes shut. In vain.

"Blow me down, you're crying again." A hand went to the nape of Chipman's neck, a regular gesture, and his tone softened. "Chipman you have been the prince of patients. Enough of this despair! I think it has actually been your presence that has begun to turn things around. Cerisia is coming out of her swan dive into obesity and depression. Unlike you, she has cut down on her boozing, she's paying her Boys, the village louts as you call them, more than just cigarette money. You're too scared to attend her erotic workshops but they are attracting the sex-starved Foreign Aid workers and the lonely lepidopterists, who turn out to be generous to a fault. The lovely Lotus has got her tarot readings together. The *Ching* if she needs a second opinion. Stan Francisco's mother sent a couple hundred dollars. I'd be flogging the new generation Siegfriediana if only Adolf had the nerve to post it. He's written that Seamus Shamrock will be delivering it personally instead."

"Siegfriediana?" Chipman had tried to get to the bottom of this before.

"Drugs, you dummy, superdrugs. The psychedelic Holy Grail!" cried a g-stringed Lotus, a garland of flowers around her head, wafting up in a cloud of lily of the valley. She had a tray of toasted peanut butter and banana sandwiches, coconut cupcakes from the Kmango subsidized *Devonshire Tea Shoppe* in the village, and a calabash of palm wine. "Sorry, too early for gin."

"Finally you get here. Thank you Lotus and get lost. "Starry patted her affectionately on a buttock. "*Starry starry night,*" she was singing as she went down the stairs, "My idea, *Flaming flowers that brightly blaze/Swirling clouds of violet haze…*"

"I might as well tell you now before that silly servant girl gives you the wrong idea. Professor Siegfried works with Sandoz, the very reputable Swiss pharmaceuticals firm. Their neurological research division. As a renowned bioethicist, Adolf has authorised access to certain chemicals. During my devolving days in his Swiss clinic, I volunteered as a guinea pig for various combinations of hallucinogens. I suffered no ill effects so have continued as one of his most trusted lieutenants. It's tricky work but beggars like me can't be choosers. Adolf is generous with his supplies and I know he does not blame me for making a little profit from the extra."

"It's best I remain ignorant of all this."

"Oh sit down! We are not talking drugs here, but cognitive enhancement, the frontiers of human intelligence. A little tweak to the formulas and it's all legal. Every one of your damned schools should have a regular supply, let it become an essential element of the education system. Introduce the children of the world to the company of the godlike and the great – Huxley, Burroughs, Owsley, Timothy Leary, Ram Dass, Terence McKenna, Albert Hoffman…" The messianic strain in his nature, that Starry was fond of giving rein to from time to time, came to an abrupt slump.

"Oh, why do I waste my time?" he seethed, giving the top of Chipman's head a flip. "I'm taking a dump. Let your tight little alcoholic arsehole loosen at the thought. Help yourself. One glass."

The wine was freshly made, frothy and a whitish green; more a soft drink unfortunately, the fermentation process scarcely begun. Chipman quickly added a measure from a bottle of Fundador brandy he had Zach purchase for him in Blossom's. Swallowed some aspirin.

Starry had made a half-hearted effort to lower the lawyer's level of drinking, but he did not care (nor was fully aware) that his indiscriminate one-size-fits-all ministrations had made some problems worse for Chipman, even as they made others better. The creepy-crawly feeling, for example, that was, even at that moment, making its insidious way along Chipman's limbs (a feeling that could turn into an explosive nervous spasm affecting his right elbow, but sometimes the left, and depending on circumstances, could occur as often as twice in the space of an hour), was something that merely amused him, an innocuous something, like persiflage, that did not disturb the wider canvas of his curative vision. It was one of the reasons Chipman had started drinking again. The toilet flushed and he made haste to put the brandy bottle back in the wardrobe.

"A new name has just been granted to me," came a shout as Chipman turned the key. For the Easter Carnival we will become *"The Eighth Chakra Evolutionary Dancers."*

"Shark...?"

"Simple, unpretentious. Says it all." Starry came bouncing back, his good humour restored. "There are only seven, you see. Lotus is the one who knows all about them. The eighth is the one beyond enlightenment. The only one I'm interested in. You'll be an Eighth Chakra Dancer for me at the festivities."

Starry picked up Chipman's hand mirror, plucked a premature grey hair or two out of his beard and made other adjustments to his appearance. "Your performance will symbolise a stake through the heart of your degenerate behaviour, in fact, a ritual coming-out. Your very own Gay Liberation Full-Frontal. Ha ha! In a puff of lavender smoke, your shameful redneckery will melt away. Let me take the neurosis out of those arousals of yours. The happy hard-on. What a story for Danny!"

"Starry, you're getting it hopelessly wrong. I..."

"All right, you loved your father. I didn't love mine but I understand. But somehow, his untimely death set you thirsting for the thighs of a daisy chain of Daddy doubles. With the ultimate booby trap being your ungovernable, unrequited obsession with that bloody Whitbread! I'm getting it wrong? I don't think so but I need to know more. The Tibor story, the Alfie story. And the real nigger in the woodpile, the Reverend Melody Motherfucker. You are still in love with life as a victim in the rectory! That is at the heart of your problem."

To Chipman's eyes, Starry had never looked more demonic. And then, alarmingly, the man threw himself down on the bed, pulled back his tunic and started examining the base of his penis. At this, Chipman's crawly feeling gathered force, and with the sudden eruption of the spasmic tic he feared, the entire contents of his glass spilled over Starry. "I'm sorry, I didn't mean to …"

"Chipman, I didn't know you cared! I smell brandy." Starry patted the coverlet. "Lie down with me, have a good look. My exceptional unit. Available. On your very own bed."

"Starry, I have no medical knowledge."

"I said available, right here!" Starry gave a snicker. He was tumescing rapidly. " Heal thyself! Pretend I'm a Wally you can actually get your hands on."

Chipman found it hard to look away from the thing, expanding and curving up as it was out of its dark bramble like a rare toadstool. He had to admit it had a beauty all of its own and foolishly took a step closer. Then another.

Invitations to inspect Starry's verruca had been going on for a while. Out in the palm shelter, Toffee, Stan, passing strangers and even a couple of Cerisia's barely articulate Boys had given an opinion. Zach had been asked and had refused. Lotus was the one applying the salve.

"It's a gift for all of us," she had said. "It's me who's going to snip it off if all else fails. Love it away so I won't have to use the surgical scissors."

Chipman recognized Starry's request for what it was, one of the omnivorous power games that he played with everyone, male or female. He could not, however, deny that he had become vulnerable to the affectionate rufflings of his blond hair, the gazings into his "Saxon grey" eyes, the intimate gestures that indicated Starry was enamoured of the firm contours of Chipman's "rump." Versifications, designed to be comforting, about Chipman's colourful facial 'curse', had been slipped under his door late at night. Set like a flower amid a shower of fetching freckles, it was *"A beet red rose of a nose, nose, nose/ Wanna suck it all night like a school girl's toes. Brings out my pederast and also my poet/ I want you, my sweet, not to blow it but glow it (even brighter)."*

"That Zach bastard is not the only one with poetry in his soul, my boy. Let the queer Bojangles in us sing and dance. One two three, kick two three."

Something about being on the bed had made Starry overly elated. The staid lawyer's earlobe was grabbed and he found himself being pulled downwards with some force. "'Starry's the straight fags love to hate/Before they've learned to 'jaculate...' Come on, baby, give me the next line."

"In my mind I'm wed to Wally Whitbread, Starry. I'm not going to allow myself to be seduced by you. I…"

"My exceptional thighs no longer attract?" The grip on his earlobe tightened. "You create a lot of affection in me, Chipman. Chippo. I'm going to call you Chippodeo of the Rodeo."

"Ow, Starry, stop." His nose was in Starry's pubic hair.

The creak of the stairs outside signalled an unexpected arrival. Starry released the earlobe, gave a push away. Chipman was surprised to realise that the imperturbable doctor was acting as though he had been caught *in flagrante delicto.*

Clad in a clingy counterpane, tucked cleverly into her cleavage for support, Cerisia commanded the doorway. A straw hat with silk flowers held her wild mop of hennaed hair in place. She had brought lunch from Attah's kitchen. On a tray there was a mound of fried plantain laid out on banana leaves and a deep enamel dish containing Shepherd's Pie. "It's chimp. The one in the cage yesterday. Bismarcks are coming." A fretful wave with her free hand momentarily scattered the swarm of little sweat bees she had brought with her. She hiccupped.

"My dear Cerisie Wiesie, you're drunk."

"Toots, ah ain't. Ahm jes drinkin'. An eatin'. "

"An' lookin' dat slendah dis mo'nin'. Darling, I think I am taking on Toffee's wart. As hers shrinks, mine grows. Put that shit down and help Chipman verify."

"The boudoir of Mr Smith!' Cerisia gave a twitch of her nose as she advanced.

The room had become way too crowded. It wasn't just the sweat bees that warned Chipman to give Cerisia a wide berth. It was the severe goosing she gave him as she leaned forward to verify. He backed out quickly – never never would he get talked into one of her 'touchy feely' workshops – and ran into Qumqwat on the way up with the Bismarcks. Chipman had tried the Bismarcks – half Guinness and half champagne, served in what passed in Bomzawe for beer steins. Cerisia had become addicted to the cocktail when 'de-toxing' in the Verbier clinic and had shown Qwami how to make them.

"Wagging school today, Qumqwat?" he asked brightly, so happy to have engineered an escape.

She delivered a swift kick to his ankle.

ELEVEN: *Imagination will thrive upon a kiss*

Rubbing an earlobe and an ankle, and almost immediately below his room, Chipman ran into Zach Shaler. He was bare chested, a white t-shirt dangled from a back pocket of his shorts. Starry had confirmed that the Nebraskan was interested only in girls. Straight, that new word. This man was not going to find him sexually alluring but he went to cover his nose with his fingers anyway. The Tibor Radovan echoes that the man's appearance aroused, kept his feelings about him ambiguous. Chipman knew the Peace Corps aspirant had been busy working with the villagers and he had not seen him for days, nor wanted to.

A cicada, newly emerged from its shell, and resting on the trunk of a dominant datura, had engaged Zach's attention. It was almost ready to fly. Chipman joined him.

"Starry mentioned you know everything about cicadas. Had some kind of transcendent experience?"

"Transcendent? Ah – there was a kiss."

Zach smiled and sang, "*Give me, a kiss to build a dream on.*"

"Bob Dylan?"

"Louis Armstrong. Great old song." Zach was looking expectant. "So tell me about the kiss."

Chipman was still sexually charged up by his clinical encounter with the doctor's wart. He was always charged up to some extent, 'neurotically' according to Starry, but the combination of the frothy wine and the Spanish brandy had exacerbated it. He knew that it was going to be for Zach, not Starry and Cerisia that he was going to talk about Tibor. Besides, it was a happy story, not one filled with the traumas that the doctor liked to ferret out. And with Zach, he felt he would be taken seriously, in a way that somehow, Starry and Cerisia never did.

"As a lawyer for the crown, I've always assumed I would be a prosecutor or even a judge one day. I..." He stopped, aghast, felt himself turning crimson at his gaffe, but his stupidity found him a truer tongue in compensation and his Tibor tale came tumbling out. "There was an efflorescence that summer, so many of them that everyone was going deaf. Billions in the eucalypts and coastal scrub. Green Grocers and Orange Mondays, Black Princes, Red Princes, Floury Bakers, Double Drummers, Cherrynoses..."

"Wow! Cute names. What's this one?"

Chipman needed to move closer to Zach to inspect, and it wasn't until they were actually hot skin pressed to hot skin that he realised he had seized a chance to be in physical contact with him. Zach stepped back abruptly. "Sorry," Chipman said. "It looks like a Cherrynose. My favourite actually."

"Hmm. Cool." Zach remained a length away but kept looking at Chipman in a way that indicated continuing interest.

"Only girls were supposed to take biology back then. Tibor Radovan and I, the only boys in the class at school, swatted up on cicadas. We found out they were not a plague like locusts, they just suck a little juice from the leaves. The noise is all courtship cries, males attracting partners."

"What about that kiss?"

"It's a long story."

"Long is good." Zach smiled again, to ease Chipman's obvious nervousness. "We've got all day every day."

Chipman had not experienced Zach in a happy mood before and was momentarily fixated on the newly revealed upward curve of his lips, the slowly revealed grin. The fact he had freshly shaved was also unusual. He decided that Zach must have found a girlfriend in Tlula. That didn't stop him from grinning back. As Chipman did, he felt both headache and hangover melting away. Like his shyness.

"It was a best mate thing I had at high school that rescued me from problems that my parents couldn't do much about. Out of the blue one day, everything changed. It was a big family picnic up on a ridge in the Kuringai Chase. Tibor and I scooted away from Alfie and Matilda and the others…"

"Who"

"Sorry, that's my Dad and Mum, we scooted away from all of them to go for a walk, just the two of us. The cicadas were everywhere. Tibor rescued one, a Green Grocer drowning in a natural sink hole filled with water. He held it in the palm of his hand while its wings dried. It was during the time we watched, that in an unthinking surge of feeling, we both looked up from the cicada, leaned forward and kissed each other. He still had the cicada in his hand. We had known each other for almost a year before this happened."

Chipman became aware only then of the current parallel. He felt a fresh blush suffusing his face, more heat rising in his shorts, and tried to suppress both by focussing on the drying cicada but again it was in contradictory fashion, that embarrassment had him rushing recklessly on. "We took a leak and got hard-ons before we had finished. I didn't know whether to touch him or not. But he took hold of me and that was it. I reached out too. An unbelievably beautiful feeling. A rapturous feeling."

"Kid stuff," said Zach giving a half laugh. "Nice."

Was the word 'rapturous' too much? Chipman had a fleeting thought that for Zach he should have pretended Tibor was a girl, used a girl's name. Back in Sydney he was well used to employing that sort of evasion. Too late for that now, and he ploughed on.

"The cicadas were singing all around us. It was illegal to pick the wild flowers, but in between giggling and wrestling, we picked two huge bunches of them, oblivious to any world other than our own. A ranger cruised by in a truck on a fire trail, almost catching us red handed. It was incredibly exciting, not only crouched down together so closely, but hiding from authority as well…"

"Tibor?" Zach had moved away again, kicking at a snake slithering by as he did so – not a mamba but the smaller bush viper. "Where was he from?"

"Yugoslavia. His family came to Australia after the War. Matilda said I should not associate with him because of that but Alfie did not mind. He liked Tibor. I got a bit jealous of all the attention he gave him." Chipman looked tentatively over at him. "Am I boring you?"

"You've got me thinking about my own father and the different universe parents inhabit. The one thing I agree with Sanguini on."

"It all ended badly. One day, long after the cold weather had claimed the cicadas, Tibor did something with me they said was 'beyond the pale'. To me it wasn't, we just ran away together for a few days. But there had also been some burglaries about which I knew nothing. He was kicked out of Manly Boys High and sent briefly to reform school. We came together again, but a few months later the Radovan family moved down to the Riverina round about the same time we moved from Narrabeen to Ashfield. Dad enrolled me in Ashfield Boys High School. My two older sisters both married early and were long gone. Tibor sent a letter telling me I had to run away again, come see him in the next school holidays. Mum found the letter and crumpled it up in front of me. Even Dad said that Tibor was a delinquent influence, that it was best I end my friendship with him. I hadn't noted the address. There was never another letter, until..."

An emotion overwhelmed Chipman and when he continued, his voice was slightly strangled. As often.

"With Tibor no longer around, that cicada summer began to assume epic proportions. If only I could find Tibor, we would kiss again. The cicadas would sing, we would be together again, defying the travails of being thieves and sexual outcasts, never suffering loneliness. We would live in a delirium of love, be soulmates forever."

"You said 'until'. Until what?"

"Yes. Years later something from him did arrive. A forwarded envelope with a short letter and a photograph of him inside that said: *'Hullo Chipman. This is Tibor Radovan. Remember me? Congratulations on your University degree. Good bye. Tibor.'* I burst into tears. It made me frantic, the finality of it, but there was nothing I could do. The postal stamp was so faint I could not even read it."

"Nothing's final. He might come back into your life one day. I wouldn't tell Starry. He will think it best to obliterate it for you."

"I'm telling the doctor as little as possible. But Alfie realised how deeply I missed Tibor and made it his business to make himself my best friend instead. I started spending a lot more time in his workshop, learning how to be a cabinet maker. I fell in love with him in a way I had not before. I mean, attracted even."

"Sexually?"

Chipman wasn't about to tell Zach what happened between him and Alfie. It was something he wasn't able to tell anyone. A small thing that was also a big thing. "Alfie realised that whatever Tibor did, I was not capable of blaming him, that condemnations just made me love Tibor the more. After he came out of reform school, the first thing Tibor did was come round with a bunch of snapdragons and we kissed in front of Alfie who put his arms around both of us. He could be a schoolboy, just like us."

"Good story, Chipman. Sounds like you became grateful to your Dad for accepting your yobbo klepto reffo no-good boyfriend." Zach let out a laugh, even as he was indicating he had heard enough.

Chipman had kept his eyes on the cicada almost the whole time he had been talking. But now, with his breath – and voice – coming more easily, he looked straight into Zach's laughing eyes, realising he didn't mind any more, not at all, that the man reminded him of Tibor. Those eyes which were similar in colour, greenish, with a bit of a gold fleck.

"Zach, is there Slavic blood or something, in your family?"

Zach's eyes lost their dance. He stared at Chipman coolly. "Well, not quite. My great grandparents were Coptic Christians. They came from Alexandria. You don't want to know about my family any more than I do."

The Cherrynose suddenly took flight and they followed it with their eyes for a second before it disappeared.

"Sanguini's at me to tell my sad story too," said Zach. "I'm not going to either, but it's reached the point where I have to tell someone." Zach's flecked eyes beamed once more. "Are you allowed to have a drink? Blossom's will be open by now." Chipman experienced an almost nerve-wracking thrill at this invitation. Still, he hesitated. "Come on, she's got some Jack Daniels in. How about that?"

Came a voice. "Of all the gin joints in all the fucking world…"

They looked up. From behind the repaired verandah rail, stood Starry who had a piece of Shepherd's pie in one hand, a Bismarck in the other. He grinned down then disappeared back into Chipman's room. Watching for a while, and listening, Starry had made good use of his well-attuned ears.

"Screw him! What's he doing in your room anyway? You don't want someone like him going through your stuff. Which he will."

"It's in the wardrobe. He's not going to go into that old period piece."

"If he knows you are keeping secrets, nothing will stop him."

Chipman knew Starry might turn that key, but the last thing he wanted to do was go up and check on Mr and Mrs Sanguini. "They're just eating, Zach. And drinking. Maybe – ah – fucking."

"She's up there too?" Zach gave a smile, enigmatic this time. "Oh, Mr Chipman, the price you'll pay."

TWELVE: *Springtime in the Rockies*

A crop-haired black Amazon in a shimmery, summery jumpsuit appeared in the doorway of the Leisurely Chop House carrying a zinc tub. She bared her teeth at them, revealing gold incisors. The contents of the tub were sloshed in Chipman's direction. He looked down with disgust as the greasy water and food scraps went all over his sandals. "Hi, Blossom, no hard feelings," said Zach. He indicated his head, well free of its bandage, and followed her into the Chophouse.

Chipman picked muck off his fancy footwear, thinking it was long past time for him to change to the flip flops everyone else was wearing. And there was nothing wrong with bare feet at Tlula either. He lingered a moment or two to gather himself. The need to keep his intake down was only one reason that had him avoiding the heavy drinking Chop House. Another was the intensity of the therapies which had detected the artificiality in the carapace of self-confidence he had developed over the years. Now he was vulnerable, exposed to new fears that had him scared not only of the Chophouse but the village beyond. Nor had he ventured to Doggone or even Kassini Junction, just a few miles away. Shame at his recurring spasm was an additional factor.

He gazed at Tlula's huddled, sun-bleached dwellings, at the narrow laneways angling away. There was a cubistic painterly quality he had not expected. There was no harmattan, just heat and stillness, the sound of surf, fainter here by the looming hillside which stretched to the north towards a local landmark, the Tlula Escarpment. It was where Josiah Lanfal, his trotro driver had made a sharp final turn down to the village. To the west, dominating the place, was the pinnacle on which perched the ruined slave castle that William Oates, the Consular Attache had mentioned. Attah had told him the 'fort' had been there since 1665.

He absorbed all this for the first time, brought out his little camera and took a shot or two. In the air was a pervasive smell of dried fish and that of Tlula's sole petrol bowser, across the road from the Chophouse. Gulls and Pharaoh's Chickens appeared and began squabbling with a village dog over Blossom's slops. Chipman shooed at them before going in after Zach.

The Chophouse was a rough barn of a building, high-ceilinged and dim enough to create the illusion of coolness. Along the walls were many intimate nooks and alcoves furnished with sturdy chairs and benches. Further in, there was a red-earthed courtyard with cocopalms, a spreading fetish tree, the odoom, and a couple of open sheds, their roofs, of tin or thatch, held up by pickled coconut wood poles.

They were the only customers. Blossom sloshed the whisky into enamel mugs, turned on some Bomzawean High Life. They sat silently for a while in one of the alcoves, looking away from each other and listening to the shriek of parrots, the cluck of wandering guinea fowl and other sounds of mid-day equatorial Africa. Out in the sun were a few of the same big lizards that lived at the hotel.

"Peace Corpse?" queried Chipman. Zach had put on his t-shirt. Beneath that phrase was, *'Don't ask what you can do for your country, ask what your country can do for you.'* "Official t-shirt, of course," he added, making an attempt at a joke.

"Yeah, that's me," Zach said abruptly. "Peace Corpse. I've tried to join a couple of times. They won't have me." Belatedly he gave a sad half-smile which slowly widened into a bit of a grin, but still Chipman wished he had not made the joke. Perhaps it was even a flirtation. Oh dear. He became self-conscious about his nose. The fresh silence that fell between them had Chipman holding a hand to his profile while he watched the lizards out in the courtyard.

Scarlet the Harlot and a couple of her girls walked in and Blossom turned the High Life up to a deafening level.

Zach got to his feet, drained his mug. "Let's get outta here."

Chipman's longing eyes on the bourbon bottle on Blossom's counter had him buying a few beers to take with them. Even before he was out the door, the women were giggling, shouting and dancing together. He smelled marijuana.

Castle Vinkenoog's vertiginous pinnacle above the Wawa River had many steps and they were both breathing heavily by the time they reached the top. The battlements were connected to the jungle slopes behind by a narrow saddle of land from where came the squeals and chatter of socialising monkeys. Above, long tailed hawks wheeled in a thermal. Below, fishing shacks stretched along the beach towards the river mouth, where the Wawa flowed through sandbars to the sea. Clustered on its closer bank, were the trees and tin roofs of the whitewashed village, with more substantial houses around a central square. Flowering treetops and clumps of vivid green were almost as numerous as the rusty roofs. No-one was to be seen, noonday shade having claimed them all.

"Fishing nets drying in the sun. I've been learning how to do some of the repairs. That's the old animist house, the one with the spirit poles and bones. There's still magic in these coastal areas, Chipman, despite the fucking Christians. Look, there's someone that has to be Kmango arriving. Checking out the latrine. Showing solidarity with the simple folks." Zach's tone was derisive. "When I got here I noticed it wasn't being properly looked after. Blossom told me to take charge. I have, with Qaddo, but it still stinks."

"Zach, I have to ask, are you still taking your medications?"

There came a rueful laugh. "Yeah, I'm taking them. They dumb me down some, but I keep up the work with the village and I feel I have a life. I'm making you nervous? Thinking I might throw myself onto you? Or over the parapet? "

"Perhaps I'm uneasy at finding myself a bit outside the healing zone that's Starry's declared."

Zach laughed dismissively. "Couple of mad dogs we are, out in the midday sun."

The harmattan up there was at its worst, causing dust and debris to swirl about. Zach's cowboy hat was almost caught so he anchored it on the ground with a chunk of masonry. The t-shirt went once more into a back pocket of his shorts. Chipman dared to take off his own shirt. They both got stuck into their Red Stars.

Zach paced back and forth as he drank. There was a loose-limbed roll to his gait, a bit off-kilter, like that of Tibor Radovan's dad and the other Yugoslav tomato farmers Chipman used to watch intently as a teenager. He felt a rare happiness zip through him at the realisation that he had found a friend at Tlula. Zach being straight did not seem to matter at all.

Zach stopped his pacing the better to dwell on the palm clad islet. Chipman's eyes followed his. It looked idyllic, and it was always in his mind to find out how to get out there one day. When he had the courage. It was being lashed by heavy surf on its Atlantic-facing southern side. The islet's location was clearly the reason, along with the gradual nature of slope of the beach into the sea, why the waves that rolled onto the Tlula shore were so benign.

Zach was choking up. Tears coursed down his cheeks. Embarrassed for him, as before, Chipman did not want to be drawn in. He did the manly thing, finished his beer, uncapped another and looking away, sat on a stone and waited.

"I was here long ago, Chipman. No hotel then, just a simple travellers' lodge back from the beach. Monkey heaven. And the snakes, I swear to God, like you wouldn't believe. Zoe got bitten but we saved her. A single bite."

"Zoe?" Shyly, Chipman looked up at him. Zach was standing too close for comfort."

"Twin sister. Bit of a tomboy. We used to come here to get away from the heat. Mom and Pop took up a missionary assignment with a parish in the hills north of Doggone. First Baptist Church of America. They worshipped in that church down there. It was Baptist then. They wanted to get us away from the American Beast, cure Zoe and me of our godless teenage inclinations. A weird teacher at school who knew Kenneth Rexroth, introduced us to all that beatnik Dharma Bums stuff. He liked Rimbaud and Baudelaire, but basically we were a pair of nihilistic jerks in duffle coats who didn't wash enough. In Bomzawe we got into the akpeteshie and whatever else we could get our hands on. Plenty of that grown here. One day we paddled out to the island on our surfboards. Drunk and stoned, we dared each other to bodysurf in the waves on the south side. The sea was way more treacherous than we bargained for. Sucked under almost immediately. Zoe got bashed against a rock. I tried to reach her but got slammed against that same rock. I remembered nothing until I regained consciousness half out of the water right where we had dived in. I don't know how long I had been out of it. I had a concussion, a gash on my head and a lot of bleeding. Zoe wasn't there. An undertow must have dragged her down, floated her away. The canoes were out for three days, my Dad and I with them, calling and searching. It was one of those catastrophic things. When someone disappears, you can't ever really believe they're gone. I wanted to find her so much. To say we were close was an understatement. A seaplane came from Okidoki, did an aerial search. Maybe a shark got her. Mum and Dad gave up their Ministry and we split for the States and home. They always blamed me for what happened and I agreed they had a point. I was the man, the stronger. The local pastor, the shithead, started those rumours about a deliberate drowning. Murdering her."

Zach, rubbing a temple, looked down at Chipman, still seated on his stone, unaware that the lawyer was struggling with a temptation to reach out with both hands and close them around one of his bare thighs. "Sometimes," said Zach, his gaze moving seawards, "I convince myself that Zoe was washed up on the beach or the fishermen found her floating in the water somewhere out there and handed her over to Kraka."

Zach looked down at Chipman once more. "Well, your first afternoon here, you saw what happened with me. Those bodies are taken up to the crocodile ponds. It's some African sorcerer thing that we will never understand. I heard old Kraka attributes more sacrifice value to white folks. He's been running things around here for decades. I should not be pestering Chief Akwa and the village elders but ..." He stopped.

The monkey's chatter filled the silence.

"Cerisia has my wallet and passport but they didn't get this." Zach brought out a black and white photograph, cracked but protected by a hard plastic coating. A close-up of him and Zoe, laughing, arms loosely around each other's shoulders.

Zach's hair in the photo was a brush cut. To Chipman's eyes, she didn't look much like the twin in front of him. Maybe it was her long hair, but something about Zach's story did not add up. As he handed the photo back he took a harder look at the Nebraskan, a look of suspicion this time, not desire. The lean almost thin body was still there to admire, but now it was things like the strain reflected in the facial ageing that drew his attention. Slyly, he checked if it was a scar on his temple that he had been rubbing

He was torn. Zach's grief made him want to reach out and give a healing embrace. The sort of thing that Starry encouraged. But he knew that if he did so, he would use the embrace to also give in to his temptation to stroke the man's thighs. And disastrously, even more than that, he would be committing a hands-on version of voyeurism, not necessarily criminal, but certainly an invasion of privacy, a molestation. Zach wasn't a father figure like Wally Whitbread, but the same sort of obsessive libidinous itch was involved.

What was that new word? Empathy. That's what he wanted. Was that too much to aspire to? He discreetly adjusted himself, stood up and offered his pack of Camels. Perhaps, albeit reluctantly, but thanks to Starry, he was moving on. He was a friend not a predator.

Zach lit his Camel, took a drag. "Bit like Cerisia's Gitanes. Nice. I managed to beg one out of her yesterday."

"How long have you been here in Tlula?"

"'I'm on leave from Alpine House, a mental institution in Idaho. Mom and Pop signed me in years ago." He palmed his hands over his eyes and kept them there, moving them about with some agitation. The cigarette remained between the fingers of his left hand. Ash fell.

So Zach was officially mad. A lunatic! Chipman's mood swung wildly. If he had embraced him in any way at all, some of his madness would have been transmitted. Zach was after all, in a room next to his. Those back room walls at the Hornbill were flimsy. His craziness would seep through. "I will have to ask for a different room, I will," he insisted to himself. He moved away from Zach and leaned up against one of the crumbling battlements.

"Thing was (came his voice), there were rattlers in the rocks there at Alpine House." Zach took another drag on the Camel and coughed. "Tempting. I mean, a rattler can do it for you. Just like the mambas in this snake pit here." He gave a little yelp. "I admit I've had big trouble coping with Zoe's death. The ache I can't get rid of even after all these years. It's lonely. Mom and Pop, particularly Pop, have always treated me as if I was a basket case. I've been in and out of therapy so many times I've lost count. Stable for eighteen months though and the mad monks let me out on supervised work. Looking after sheep, even some goats, on their ranch further along in the valley. So it being wintertime back home and with me promising solemnly to keep taking my meds, Mom pushed Pop to pay my way here for the 15th anniversary. Hoping I will vanish like Zoe and no longer be a stain on the family name," he added bitterly. He hurled his empty beer bottle over the parapet, cleared his throat and spat.

"Hey!" came a familiar voice, then a singsongy, "April showers have come my way!"

"You again!" Zach hastily, almost in a panic, shoved the photo of him and Zoe back into his pocket. Starry, barefooted, in his same low-slung sarong, shades and old ADOLF cap, was standing on a platform just below,

"More sheltered down here." He vaulted up and stood himself close, his garment blowing wildly in the wind. He belched and Chipman, already irritated at now having to share Zach with him, smelled the Bismarck and the heavy lunch he had no doubt wolfed down with Cerisia.

"You and Zoe were twins?"

"Yes, if you have to know. Zoe was the younger by twenty minutes. We were best friends. More, like one person. Wore the same clothes. When the snake bit they gave me the antivenin also. Just in case. You believe that?"

"I would if you had been identical twins, not just fraternal. Why did you use that word 'stain' a while ago?"

"Don't stir me up with your Freudian shit, Starry. I came back to Tlula to commune with Zoe for a spell. It's obvious that solitude is anathema to you. Not to mention virtue. Get a life, Starry, trashing everyone you can get your hands on. Just for the fun of it. Yeah, fuck you."

"I'm going to trash you if it's the last thing I do. Trust me."

Zach's flare of anger subsided. He picked up his cowboy hat, brushed off the dust and jammed it down on his head. "I've conspired with my parents to ruin my life. I don't want to see either of them ever again. Starry, if you can work out how to do that for me, I'm yours."

"First thing, Zach, is to stop taking your medication. As for you, Chipman bloody Smith, our proposals are on your table. Cerisia's added a photograph of herself dancing with her daughters in *Twiddlers*. All ready for you to present to Sir Henry Kmango. Make an appointment for the group."

"Starry, why me?"

"Treat it as a continuation of that therapy session you ran away from this morning. Don't forget to introduce yourself as a friend of his chum William Oates. Dress up in your fatuous Somerset Maugham ensemble if that's what you still need to give you confidence. Get moving!"

He gave a typical sideways swish of his sarong, revealing for Zach and Chipman a band aid at the base of his dick where his verruca had been. "She offed it, no thanks to either of you." The withering nature of the glare the doctor gave him, sunglasses notwithstanding, made Chipman wonder if Zach had been correct about Starry and Cerisia going through his papers. It had to be his lie about his profession, his work with the Attorney General and Office of Clerk of the Peace. He succumbed to fear and wished he had not left the key to the wardrobe in the door.

THIRTEEN: *Land of hope and glory*

The door of Bungalow One was pulled open violently.

"Who is you?" From heavy sockets, unfriendly eyes were glaring up into Chipman's. Built like his name and close up, Ntank, minus his chauffeur's cap, was shaven headed, all menace and intended to be. Fat witchetty grub cicatrices angled across each of his cheeks. He was wearing tartan shorts, tight on callipygian buttocks, and had his shirt off, revealing a powerful chest covered in tight whorls of hair, which funnelled down to his navel. A film of perspiration gave his prize fighter shoulders the gleam of highly buffed black vinyl. Under his left armpit, there was a holster with a pearl handled pistol. There had clearly once been a bone through his septum.

"I'm staying at the hotel and, ahh… Is Sir Henry in?" Easily intimidated, Chipman stepped back.

"I'm over here," came a voice. "Don't mind Ntank, his disposition is sweet in the extreme. He has been my loyal retainer for many years now." At this, Ntank grunted agreeably and ushered Chipman in.

Sir Henry Kmango was seated in a cushioned cane armchair on the far side of the bungalow. He motioned to another such chair and began smiling as he flicked daintily through Starry's submissions. Ntank put on a pair of pink tinted glasses and picked up a magazine which he held close to his face.

On a coffee table was a framed photograph of a younger Sir Henry, debonair in a morning suit. Tails, striped trousers, a grey topper in his left hand. On his arm, a smiling woman in a cream jacket and skirt, broad brimmed hat adorned with ostrich feathers. It looked like a wedding photo.

"Ascot. In the Royal Enclosure. One of the great days for Lady Chompia and me." Sir Henry's voice was high-pitched if at the same time, a little husky, the English precise and perfectly modulated, the plumminess the result of elocution lessons at too early an age. "Shortly after my investiture as a Knight of the Realm."

Ntank peered at Chipman over the top of his glasses. Flattered by the interest, Chipman adjusted himself through his shorts, fluffed his fair curls. Then losing confidence, he shielded his nose with his knuckles and looked out to sea through the picture window. "We can discuss Dr Sanguini's suggestions tomorrow morning," came Sir Henry's voice. He tossed the pages aside, stood up and moved towards his bathroom. "After breakfast. Ntank will arrange for some drinks by the seawall."

Chipman had been in the bungalow less than five minutes. Now more myopic than menacing, Ntank showed him out, one palm pressed firmly against Chipman's right buttock. A scuttle away in timorous fashion was Mr Smith's intent, but instead he turned. Ntank was all grin, his teeth a dazzling display, each one filed to a point.

Chipman arrived at Sir Henry Kmango's post-breakfast 'reception' late and rather inebriated, with no memory of much until he had his spasm and spilled Sir Henry's Chivas Regal not only over the damask table cloth but over another framed memento – Sir Henry and Lady Kmango in the foyer of the London Palladium; a Royal Command Performance featuring The Beatles. The hotelier had invited Starry and his *Beautiful Afreakans* to help themselves to the Chivas or Beefeater Gin. There was also Red Star and Fanta cooling in a tub of ice.

That morning, seated with his newly befriended Zach and following his example, Chipman had poured a large quantity of akpeteshe over his fruit and breakfast cereal; already well drunk, he had been unable to resist the whisky.

"My precious photograph! My Chivas!" Sir Henry cried, and in a tiny fury, the hotelier slapped and slapped again at Chipman's wrist with a horsehair fly whisk. Qumqwat darted forward and had the photo wiped and the mess cleaned up in a twinkling. The power of public humiliation had the consternated Chipman going from tosspot to teetotaller – also in a twinkling.

"Never mind Mr Smith's nervous disability, Sir Henry. He works on policy for the New South Wales Department of Education," Starry shouted, in the best of his adopted English accent. Gesturing ostentatiously towards a tape recorder as prop that Stan was now attempting to set up for the alcoholic public servant, he added, "Mr Chipman Smith is also a feature writer for *Thug*, the famous monthly. *Thug* is at the high end of the market. Sells tens of thousands of copies. More than *The London Illustrated News*."

"Ah! I am not familiar with it. Do you have a copy, Dr Sanguini, that perchance I might – peruse?" With a pair of tongs, Sir Henry delicately dropped an ice cube into a glass and poured himself some white wine. He held it up to the light. "A riesling. From my vineyard to the north in the Nwalabi Ranges." With a forgiving wave from a manicured hand, he invited Chipman to once more help himself.

They were all at a table in the serrated shade of one of the giant poincianas. Nearby, workmen, press-ganged from the village, were breaking up an old concrete path with sledgehammers. Billy Carpenter, muscled and wiry, and other employees seconded from Sir Henry's mansion on the Okidoki Ring Road, were marking with chalk and string where the foundations for a new bungalow would be dug. There was a pile of cinder blocks and a cement mixer.

The Rolls had been covered with a tarpaulin to protect it from the cicadas and the ever inquisitive and disrespectful hornbills. The cicadas were now so numerous a fine spray of their liquid wastes filled the air. Ill-directed flyers, they frequently collided with each other as they flew from tree to tree, and would come crashing down. The beauteous Qumqwat and the farouche Ntank were kept busy picking them off the table cloth and hurling them back into flight. The hornbills on the limbs above them, were at work reducing the population. They tossed the creatures to each other with greedy abandon.

"Excuse the racket," Sir Henry shouted. "We always have the insects here in the dry season, but never before like this. Never! I will get Billy Carpenter to spray! We have the wonderful DDT!"

"Oh, don't use that!" Chipman exclaimed, with a fresh drink and more than fully recovered from his *non compos mentis*. "It's dangerous. In fact, don't use anything! They are so pretty," he added, letting out a tiny whimper of distress at a remembrance of the lovely Tibor and his play with them.

"What's with this new construction, Kmango?" Drift shouted boldly across the table where he sat with the disintegrating Toffee. She was in the throes of a torments attack and had been on a downward slide for days. Her face was a waxen grey, but somehow, the beauty maintained. Lobelia, togged out like a toddler, lay asleep and sedated (like Toffee) in her arms. "Some special guest?"

"Sir Henry, if you please," he admonished, giving Drift the wag of a forefinger. After resting his gaze on Toffee for a moment or two, the hotelier lowered his eyes to the pages in front of him. "Let us say, an old man's folly." He cleared his throat. "I am delighted that you all take an interest in my obscure establishment. Alas, it is difficult to accomplish anything in this climate. Even simple things such as a new bungalow are like building The Great Wall of China. I am beginning to feel it is time for me to retire. To Mother England, of course. Chompia and I will be able to attend The Proms every year and join in those rousing choruses of Rule Britannia." He paused. "Naturally, the Cotswolds are where we would settle. I picture myself gathering lilacs in the spring, picking the whortleberries, listening to the nightingale and the skylark." He paused again. "And not just the birds. I must confess to tears when I hear your marvellous Tom Jones sing *Green Green Grass of Home.*"

Sir Henry seemed merely amused by Starry's proposals for things like air conditioning and parasailing. A suggestion that Vinkenoog Castle be remodelled, the top reached by a funicular, fared no better. "A restaurant with those old instruments of torture as décor was always part of Ulysses' Master Plan for the South Western Region. I wanted to feature the embrasures from which the dreary Dutch threw the bodies of the useless into the Wawa. Now foolish Mguavas has built that white elephant of a hotel above Doggone Bay instead."

The Sir Henry Q. Kmango International Healing Centre – gatherings of illustrious psychotherapists, spiritual leaders, multi-national business executives interested in improving their humanistic image; retreats and workshops, the bungalows occupied all year round, also failed to fly.

"A magnificent concept of course, Dr Sanguini. A Christian centre, I trust. We could get the Archbishop of Canterbury down here for the opening ceremonies. I have partaken of afternoon tea with him, you know." Sir Henry smiled modestly at the memory. "The weather is pleasant enough during the dry season, but for eight months of the year the humidity is impossible and it rains. The tidal swamps, the mosquitoes, the crocodiles. I don't think..."

Gourmet dining on the island. Seafood barbecues. Snorkelling? Scuba diving?

"Ah, Oratorio Island. At the Carnival regatta, the intrepid fishermen from the villages along the coast do a circuit. The waves are extremely dangerous on the south side. Many years ago, there was a most unfortunate incident that has gone down in local lore. Some Yankee Baptist group from up-country holidaying. I have always wanted to connect it to the shore with a causeway."

"A causeway?" Even Dr Sanguini, up against fantasies even more absurd than his own, looked amazed.

"I already have the timber concession." Sir Henry waved with his glasses towards the virgin headland across the Wawa River. "Mahogany, teak, silk cotton, camwood. My architect will design it in a picturesque style along the lines of Brighton Pier. With gambling and other English seaside attractions." He sighed. "So many opportunities. There were the Gucci representatives who wanted to turn the sacred crocodile ponds into a commercial venture. I have not forgiven Kraka for what happened to those gentlemen. An appalling – accident. Gucci will never be back." Sir Henry got a cigar going. "Regressive elements in the village derive solace from Kraka and his sincerely held traditional beliefs, but to all of us here at the Hornbill, he is as much a danger as the crocodiles themselves. If I anger him in some way, he is capable of imbuing the antediluvian creatures with his bilious spirit, and sending them on a rampage in the direction of the hotel."

"I hear he can be useful," said Drift. "Cadavers washing up."

Sir Henry chose not to answer. His cigar smoke wafted over them. "The question of oil drilling is also promising. The Hornbill Palace could come into its own as a recreational centre for the riggers. I have been pressuring President Mguavas about it."

"Sacrifices always have to be made to progress," Starry shouted as a fresh wave of cicada serenading erupted.

"It would be marvellous to settle on something. The coastal villages are dying. Few of the young men want to fish or farm any more. Only the riff-raff remain." His eyes fell with disdain on Cerisia's Boys, sprawled nearby on the sand, giggling and smoking. "The best and the brightest pin their hopes on the capital. But what is there for them? Venereal disease. Violence. Civil unrest. Certainly no jobs. Our poor country is once more in the throes of economic collapse. Inflation will soon be rampant. It is disgraceful that the National Congress puts obstacles in the way of the President's democratic reforms." There was a pursing of the carmine lips. "I long for the good old days of Ulysses Oratorio."

"I heard they weren't so good," Drift put in. "He neglected..."

"Ah, but you are American. Your perspective, excuse me, is skewed. Do not forget he was Chairman for many years of the Organisation of African Unity. That glorious speech in Addis Ababa in 1963. He was, and is, an African hero, a man of charisma in the tradition of our continent. Your government and the International Monetary Fund had much to answer for in his untimely fall. Like Lumumba, Ulysses was a victim of his own vision."

"The Mussolini of Africa is what I read. In 1965, he..."

Sir Henry raised a plump hand for Drift to desist. "Before his exile, The Great Liberator was planning a palace beyond the Tlula Escarpment, on a hill high above the Wawa with magnificent ocean and river views. Near his birth place. Oh, such a site! It would have been the beginning of his dream of unification – a Presidential home in all eight of our tribal areas. I pictured a hydrofoil that would take my guests up the wonderful Wawa to view it. It would have brought so many tourists. After the Carnival, Ulysses will..." He stopped abruptly, glanced at the workmen labouring in the rising heat and sighed.

"Well, I seem to have let the cat out of the bag, as Shakespeare wrote. *Much Ado About Nothing*, was it? Yes, my special guest is none other than my dearest friend Ulysses Oratorio, The Great Liberator himself. Wounded heart of the Bomzawean people. After six months of delicate negotiations, President Mguavas is about to sign the necessary permissions for his return from exile. Restoration of his good name is finally being achieved." Sir Henry motioned to Ntank who came forward and gently wiped at his tear-filled eyes with a cambric hanky. "The National Rehabilitation Committee, of which I am Chairman, can congratulate itself. It is not easy for a government to make a humanitarian gesture of this magnitude."

"Like if Napoleon had been welcomed back from St Helena," said Drift. The cicadas' siren song had been reaching even higher notes of longing for consummation. Sir Henry cupped an ear. "Trujillo from Spain," Drift shouted. "Trotsky from Mexico."

"Exactly!" Sir Henry bellowed. "The Duke of Windsor from Monaco. I have met them you know. Charming couple." He paused to let that sink in. "It was Ulysses' failing health that did the trick. I'm afraid the dear chap won't be with us much longer." He plied his flywhisk and after a glance at the tape recorder added, "Sadly, my carnival will be a valedictory one."

Into the relative silence that followed came the sound of a motley group of village women singing as they scythed. Among them was Qojo's mother, Lilibet Lanfal, the laughing mammy in the back of the trotro that had brought Chipman to Tlula. They had been hired to get rid of the huge tussocks of elephant grass and the rampant underbrush which, long neglected, had made itself at home in the hotel grounds. A flight of screeching African Grey parrots went skittering across the tree tops.

Toffee let out a pretty snort and slumped sideways, allowing one incomparable breast to slip from her blouse. The eyes of Sir Henry and Ntank were captured. Drift frowned, quickly popped it back in. He re-attached a loop. Lobelia woke up and bared her teeth.

"Beauty and the Beast," said Sir Henry with a knowing smile.

"Yeah, right. Fay Wray and King Kong," Drift muttered.

Sir Henry was puzzled, but laughed. Glancing at his Rolex, he stood up. "Qumqwat!" he shouted, indicating for her to clear the table. "What a fine English rose you are maturing into, my sweet." She glowered. "Dr Sanguini, I am sorry I am unable to assist you. But I am very glad to have met some of the estimable people staying at my beloved hotel." He cast a significant look at Starry and added, "Or in the vicinity."

Starry rose to the occasion. "I have been discussing with Chef Lalwani an arrangement we could make for our use of the Hornbill's facilities."

"Five guineas a day per person would be very satisfactory. You have four people in your fancy conveyance. Let's say a round twenty." Starry gave an obeisance. "And something for past usage. Attah has already made the computations. I am sorry to insist you all leave over the Easter period. Traditionally the Carnival is a closed affair. But there is an excellent camping ground on Doggone Bay. I am sure you will have no problem driving that far."

"I don't know if you read all of our submission, Sir Henry, but my *Eighth Chakra Evolutionary Dancers* could put on a wonderful spectacle for you."

"Ah, yes..." Sir Henry assessed them all with a swift look, hotashed his cigar on an unwary hornbill, turned once more to the pages in his left hand, "Your resume. I must say we are privileged to have such a refined performing group here at Tlula." He paused.

"*Humouristic Bodily Functions Revue* indeed. And at the beginning of a major Pan-African Tour."

As impresario, Starry brought his hands together in a prayerful gesture, bowed his head. Lotus had made an effort with his appearance. She had trimmed a couple of inches from his beard, and gathered it in with a red ribbon. Chipman saw for the first time the full extent of the jagged scar that ran across his ribs where chest hair refused to grow. The self-styled doctor was feeling magisterial in an open cotton coat, ankle-length and vertically striped, one of many items Cerisia had bought (when her allowance was still flowing) from the Wodaabe, a nomadic tribe of the Sahel they had encountered on The Beautiful Afreakans travels east and south from Senegal and Mali to the Gulf of Guinea. Starry's hair was scraped back into a chignon, and stuck with two plastic chopsticks, red like the ribbon tying his beard.

"Let me be frank. There will be no theatre of any kind at the Carnival this time. It was only with the greatest difficulty I was able to persuade dear President Mguavas to agree to the Carnival at all. I do not mind telling you that more than a small fortune passed hands."

"There has been no problem caused by the disappearance of your country's famous Bronzes?" Chipman asked, his boldness proof to himself that he was getting back to his old lawyerly self. He downed the last of his Chivas. He poured himself a touch more.

Sir Henry made a pretence of not hearing.

"I was informed in Okidoki," Chipman shouted above the shrilling, "that many people are convinced the Liberator stole them from the National Museum."

"Those scandalous accusations!" Sir Henry's annoyance flared swiftly. "Mr Chipman Smith, let me correct you. There is a small but quality collection of the Bomzawe Bronzes in the Metropolitan Museum in New York. Sold, I might say, by Ulysses' predecessor for a pittance. It is only recently that the immense value of the Bronzes has been realised. They date from the days of the Warrior Kings of Bomzawe. In the face of a flat refusal by the Metropolitan to return the Bronzes to their rightful home, Ulysses devoted much time during his Presidency to the rescue of many exquisite pieces from private hands. Shortly before his overthrow, there were rumblings in the air, and he was prescient enough to remove these new acquisitions from our National Museum for safe keeping." Sir Henry paused. "In the course of his telephonic communications with President Mguavas, Ulysses gave his solemn promise that the Bronzes would accompany him on his return to Bomzawe. The last and greatest stumbling block to his rehabilitation was finally removed. The Committee and President were overcome with joy."

"So the Liberator says the Bronzes will be coming back with him from Haiti." Drift's tone was so peculiar Chipman gave a sharp intake of breath. The 'complications'? The Bronzes? No, no, no, it was impossible.

"A vow on the withered breast of his centenarian mother," replied Sir Henry in a tone almost as peculiar as that of Drift. "Sometimes I can scarcely believe our battle against the forces of darkness has actually been won. It has indeed been a stressful time." He took a hanky held out to him by Ntank. "More than stressful."

"Ah!" Starry cried, seizing an opportunity and jumping in the air. "Our entertainment is the epitome of stress reduction. It's an artistic show, with singing and continuous movement in a melange of ethnic styles. Stan here, as you see, plays the thumb piano, is learning the art of the tin whistle. I have studied the dance with Robert Helpmann at Covent Garden. The beautiful Toffee and her circus trained monkey are already proficient. Our gay Mr Chipman Smith here is a budding Fred Astaire The lovely Lotus of Hollywood fame and my Lady Cerisia the former toast of London café society, third daughter and second favourite of Lord Wittering, dance the Libyan baladi. No mere belly dance, but a sacred feminist tradition."

Sir Henry reeled back in amazement. "Lord Wittering! My goodness! He is a Knight of the Garter! I have read all about him in my copy of Debrett."

Like Starry, Cerisia had dressed for the occasion, and was gowned in a gold-threaded cream caftan. Lotus had stuffed her unruly hennaed hair into a snood. Stuck into the frizz above her forehead there was a lacey silver clasp which could have been mistaken for a tiara. Lotus had pan-sticked her face, and applied to her lips a generous smearing of Cerisia's favourite colour, grenadine. Throughout the discussion with the hotelier, she had maintained a regal silence, her Gitane stuck into the end of a long ivory holder.

A star-struck Sir Henry could not resist making a light-footed move towards the palanquin. Cerisia held out her hand and he kissed it. "Ulysses and I are very partial to your British traditions, Lady Cerisia. As eager young men, our colonial masters spirited us away to Oxford's prestigious Brasenose College, and I am glad to say we became entirely corrupted by the culture of your green and sceptred land. Out there in the antipodes, Mr Chipman Smith, you enjoy the same happy fate. As you may know, we used to have the exquisite Maypole Dance at the Carnival. A great favourite of Ulysses. As I am sure it is of Lord Wittering, Lady Cerisia. At Wonkers his ravishing county seat." Sir Henry Kmango inclined his head and moved back a step. "We have been permitted to honour Ulysses by performing it once again. It is quite complex. Qumqwat and her young friends will need many rehearsals."

"Surely the powers in Okidoki would be honoured if we regaled him with English adaptations of your Bomzaweian ritual dances."

"I see you don't take no for an answer, Dr Sanguini."

"We are building on the work of an extremely famous Englishman, Professor Arthur Janov. We encourage audience participation."

"Stop! You are breaking my heart. Ulysses loved to participate. Myself also. One year we had an interpretation of *A Midsummer Night's Dream*. I was Bottom. Ulysses enjoyed himself immensely as Puck." Sir Henry gazed mournfully out to sea. "There would have been a part for me in your no doubt lavish production, Dr Sanguini?"

"Well, of course, Sir Henry. With your permission, we will rehearse Toffee's *Angel Baby Rotations* for you right here by the hotel. You will see immediately how a key role for you would be possible."

Drift and Chipman both raised their eyes to the sky. The *Rotations* was the first of the therapy to theatre crossover pieces that Starry was devising for the Carnival.

"Ah, the extraordinary Toffee. I am already bewitched." Sir Henry put his glasses away. "Ulysses' Public Expression of Remorse and other ceremonial abasements in Okidoki will be a healing experience for the nation. Health permitting, there will be a triumphal tour of the provinces, and finally a Grand Journey upriver here to his birthplace where his ancient mother still dwells. There the Statesman will expire in the bosom of his family. I am dedicated to making the Hornbill Palace Easter Carnival a fitting farewell to one of the finest gentlemen I have ever known." Sir Henry was once more overcome with emotion. "Repairing the road will alone cost me a fortune." Composing himself, he puffed out his chest. "Dr Sanguini and my dear Lady Cerisia, why don't you let me walk you around the grounds where it will be somewhat quieter, and share with you my plans for the festivities?"

FOURTEEN: *Death comes as the end*

Seventy yards beyond the palisade beside which *The Beautiful Afreakans* bus was parked, were the half dozen or so tents, makeshift dwellings and vans of those who, like Starry, often used the facilities but did not rent; the scene of tireless hand drumming and chanting, of parties that could rave into the midnight air and occasionally involved altercations in the hazardous Chophouse and Bar. There was much morning activity under the trees, the hot air filled with laughter, the clink of bottles being shared. The smells of marijuana and stale urine came drifting by. Pigs from the village were rooting in that particular part of the sand. There were many bared bottoms and breasts.

"This I detest," Sir Henry with sudden vehemence. "Lowering the tone of my entrance."

"I agree," said Starry. "Poisoning their own well. The parentless and peripatetic generation doesn't realise the turn on, tune in, drop out sixties space-out is over."

"They will all go. Hippies as you call them. Your gaudy bus too, Dr Sanguini. I have plans for this area. The Polynesian Long House through there by the hillside, tumbledown as it might be, will be renovated and used as a Cocoa Room and Watering Hole. One day I will build a rest house for these itinerants under my imported coral trees, and well out of the way. They are parasites, but I am not a hard man. Sometimes you westerners forget that we too are Christian."

Sir Henry made a prayerful gesture before moving on. "Are you still there with your tape recorder, Mr Chipman Smith?" A more rotund tone had entered his voice. "Lady Chompia and I have ushered Tlula into the twentieth century. I assume, as an educator, you have already inspected my exemplary school up on the headland?"

"He is already preparing a portfolio of photographs for you," Starry interjected quickly.

"Well well, that will be most appreciated Mr Chipman Smith. My pupils sing the national anthem every day, as well as the traditional Qahatan songs, and they no longer have to endure the old tribal scarring. The school has always had one of the best-kept cricket pitches in the country. Ulysses will be pleased to discover that despite his five years of exile it has been maintained as before. There is my state of the art Medical Clinic and Dispensary once a week."

Sir Henry put a hand on his heart in a self-affirming motion. "This afternoon I am donating a set of ceramic spittoons and ashtrays to the insalubrious Chophouse. The muscle-bound Efua Rokoku, whom we call Blossom, is aunt to the regressive faction in the village. You do yourselves no favours by patronising her greasy spoon. Many years ago now, her father went missing and she took over the running of the Chophouse, giving up Olympic Games prospects as a shot-putter. Somehow she came to blame poor Ulysses for her cantankerous father's disappearance. That woman was behind an attempt to assassinate the Liberator right here in Tlula."

At this, Chipman made doubly sure that the tape recorder was working.

"In the teeth of her generally hostile attitude, drains were cleared of rubbish and fluorescent street lighting was installed. The community has ever since been drawn like moths to a flame and even as I speak one of my workmen is now fitting new double strength bars. Powered I might say, like Blossom's juke box, by a generator provided and maintained by me. And who do you think gave the village its petrol bowser, right outside her entrance?"

Sir Henry paused for breath. "You must have noticed in the square an architect-designed public latrine I had dug some years ago. Many people use it by preference now, including your hippie friends. I am also encouraging the villagers to properly pen their pigs. There will be a second latrine in my projected Botanical Garden and Arboretum. If you visit the villages along the coast, you will immediately notice the difference. Mbutu to the east has neither clinic nor church. You will still see deformed children, women with bare breasts, men with swollen testicles and elephantiasis. They are scowling places, rife with the old superstitions. But here, the fetishes are used less and less. Reverend Adomako is already hauling the old witchdoctors into line. Even the terrible Kraka."

The stroll had brought them to within sight of St Bede's Anglican, which was halfway along the track to Tlula and Castle Vinkenoog. Nestled amid multi-coloured bougainvilleas and wreathed in vines, the church was a simple whitewashed building which provided a buffer between the hotel and the village.

"A sort of de-militarised zone," Chipman had noted in his journal. As a reluctant nod to Matilda (Mrs Melville Motherwell as she now preferred to be typified), he had attended a couple of Wednesday Prayer Meetings with the bespectacled Reverend Adomako, whom he found darkly attractive in his middle age, partly because his horn rims were reminiscent of those worn by his dear Wally. Unlike Starry (and Sir Henry), Adomako was refreshingly meek and modest. He had a wife and four children housed around the corner from Blossom's and didn't mind a drink with her in the Chophouse, but like Chief Akwa, was regarded as a Kmango lackey.

"You have been attending Sunday services, of course."

"Never miss," said Starry. "Chipman and Reverend Adomako get along like a house on fire. Singing the Psalms. When the Lord's Prayer comes up, down they go."

"Splendid. Let me show you some of the headstones in our cemetery. We have some particularly fine angels and broken columns."

The cemetery was beside a creek bed, no flow but with stretches of shallow, muddy water still left from the wet. In the near distance there was a crudely lettered sign.

BEWARE CROCODILES.
PLEASE NO SWIM ANY TIME.
SURVIVORS FACE RIGOURS OF THE BRITISH LAW
HQM

"Ach!" exclaimed Sir Henry, jolting to a stop. "What have we here?"

Zach Shaler and two men from the village were working hard with shovels to bury a large pile of bones which had become exposed by a collapse of the creek bank. They paused in their labour at their approach. Many skulls could be seen, several with shattered craniums, along with the tattered remains of clothing. There was no wind in that place and the heat seemed to be rising from the long dead and the mud itself. A mephitic emanation of rot and decay was all around. Chipman Smith put the back of his hand to his nostrils. But there was a diversion – a huge estuarine crocodile half-submerged in the lee of the collapsed bank was moving almost imperceptively in their direction. Everyone backed away, Chipman more hastily than anyone.

"One of Kraka's co-conspirators! What did I tell you about that odious man?" Showing scant respect for the dead, Sir Henry heaved a skull. Then another. "All of you, assist me here." Ntank's hand went to his shoulder holster. "No," said Sir Henry, perhaps losing his nerve, "the whip." Ntank cracked it several times. An expert flick got the creature on an eyelid, causing its jaws to open and close with a snap. A second flick had it levering itself back into the stagnant water.

"I know that particular beast," said Sir Henry as Ntank wiped his sweating temples for him. "Many believe it is Kraka himself in another shape."

"I had no idea crocodiles could get so big," Chipman announced by way of apology for his overly hasty retreat.

"You seem a Nervous Nellie, Mr Smith," said Sir Henry, giving a little giggle. "That is the term we English use is it not?"

"That's enough, Mister, he's not that well in the head," said Drift abruptly. "It's a psychotherapy group that's sucking up to you right now, in case you haven't cottoned-on. Something horrible has been going on here."

"Sir Henry, if you please, Mr Drift." There was a glance at the tape recorder, then at Ntank. "Well, yes. Many years ago, before the days of my clinic, I might say, there was an outbreak of – meningitis. It came on the wings of the harmattan. It was bad that year. The dust took the disease, a meningococcal virus I believe, into the brain. So many villagers died, a mass grave was dug. Yes, a sad time."

"Chief Akwa ordered the clean-up yesterday when it was discovered," said Zach.

"And who are you, may I ask?"

"I'm Zach Shaler. Staying at your hotel."

"Ah, so you are Mr Shaler. The Peace Corps cleaner man." Sir Henry made a little bow of his head. "Chef Lalwani tells me you are fond of poetry. I too. Keats is my all-time favourite. *'Season of mists and mellow fruitfulness, close bosomed friend of the maturing sun...'* So Arcadian! Have I got it right ?" He did not wait for a response. "I strongly advise you to heed that sign, Mr Shaler. Perhaps our arrival has saved you from a gruesome death. Crocodiles always see you before you see them."

"Chief Akwa informed me they are descendants of the even bigger denizens of the Nile," said Zach.

"*Crocodylus niloticus.*" Drift put in.

"Thank you for the science, Mr Drift. Yes, the ancient Egyptians worshipped Sobek, the crocodile god, reviled as well as revered and the sacred ponds upriver arouse in me feelings of extreme ambivalence." Sir Henry wheeled round and headed back towards his hotel. "They do draw the tourists, but on the whole I do not like to see chickens being thrown in merely for the drama of it. Incidentally, what is Kraka charging these days?"

"Three guineas a chicken," said Cerisia, who was now regretting having spent thirty guineas for ten minutes of blood-soaked thrills. It had been shortly after their arrival.

"Really!" Skidding slightly on some overripe fallen fruit, Sir Henry kicked at a hornbill family chortling imbecilically on the path. The big casqued birds swished off into the trees. ORK! HONK! CRASH! "How does the old fool get away with those prices? When we were boys, the Tlulans made real sacrifices. A child once, from a rival tribe. It made an indelible impression on Ulysses." His eyes darted about, almost as though he sensed disapproval. "There was a time when it was believed the sacrifice of a foreigner would bring about the greatest good. Now, of course, we make simple offerings to our Almighty Father instead. We have a bounteous Harvest Festival, for example, when the wet is over."

A breeze brought the unpleasant smell of an incinerator to their nostrils. Sir Henry plucked a flower from a half-collapsed trellis, and buried his nose in its perfume. Concealed behind the trellis was the hotel's refuse pit, roughly dug out of the thick jungle. The hard-working village women were making many trips with the slashed undergrowth, but really the pit was full to overflowing with plastic, old tin cans and other garbage, making for an insalubrious scene. A thin line of smoke curled upwards from the centre of the mound. When Old Idi and the vultures were not hanging about the kitchen, they were scavenging here, or, like harbingers of death, were perched in the overhanging trees. The hotel's suspect septic tank system was on a slope not far away. The Beautiful Afreakans were sped past.

Sir Henry's tour brought them back to the village women who were now, with the sharp escalation of the day's heat, beginning to wilt. Even as he indicated for Ntank to ply the whip, Lilibet Lanfal began to shriek. Others took up her cries. Abandoning their cutlasses and sickles, they came running, gesticulating wildly. An older man had collapsed. A woman kneeling beside him had began to weep. Billy Carpenter and the men who had been busy on the new bungalow or 'chalet' (as it was to be called) came rushing up, and amidst great hubbub, converged on a single coconut palm. Hamou the watchman had also appeared. (Or was it Hamid?

Chipman had only recently realised there were two of them, brothers, one older than the other but impossible to tell apart.)

"A mamba. It has fled to the treetop," said Sir Henry. "Old Kofu will die."

"No, I've got antivenom in Attah's refrigerator." Drift took a look at Old Kofu. "Where's the bite?" There was pandemonium. The workmen were throwing stones up into the top of the palm causing dead fronds to fall. "No, no! I have a noose and bag. I'll climb the tree. It'll be a green one. They are rare. I want it alive." Drift appealed to Sir Henry.

"Well, if you must, Mr Drift, your serum is perhaps a chance. My clinic is well equipped, but..." Drift dashed off. The hotelier made a helpless gesture.

Fangga, the Snake Fetish Priest, in smart cream-coloured leather boots, emerged from the jungle. "Go away!" Sir Henry shouted. "You evil little man." Fangga pushed aside the women and began sucking at Old Kofu's ankle. Ntank gave him a lash across the back with the whip and would have given another, but from behind them came a frenzied outcry as the snake's bright green head appeared. The snake began what seemed to be an orderly descent, but it was injured and when a final stone reached its mark, it plummeted. It was soon hacked into pieces, some of which were impaled and held aloft. The hacking revealed embryos on the point of birthing. Wriggling, they too were all dispatched. Some of the women went forward and spat. Old Idi and the vultures came rocketing over from the dump.

Foam had appeared at the sides of Old Kofu's mouth. Sir Henry and Fangga continued to exchange words, the hotelier indicating that Drift would be returning with medicine. In reply the Priest chucked something from his pouch. It hit Sir Henry on the forehead. A foul smelling liquid dribbled down and in a sudden rage, the hotelier seized the whip from under his chauffeur's arm and cracked it furiously at Fangga, who ducked and lolloped off in the direction of the village. The stricken man was hoisted up and carried at a run after him. Sir Henry spun round, cracking the whip at random. His workmen fled back to the new chalet.

As Ntank wiped his face for him with a handkerchief, Sir Henry's composure returned. "There's an old superstition that evil ancestor spirits will plague the family if he does not die in his own bed. Forgive me if it seems I am doubting the value of that – belief, but I do wish that Mr Fangga would not reject modern medicine with such indecent disregard." He kicked disdainfully at the grisly object that had been thrown.

"This is most unfortunate. Fangga! He will conduct a ritual that will have the spirit of the snake come back to haunt me. One labours so hard to keep matters running smoothly. Ten minutes ago the villagers were honoured to be clearing the tangle for Ulysses' homecoming. Now nothing will bring them back. I will send a recompense to Old Kofu's family, but it will make no difference. My hotel will get the blame."

At this he was accosted by Mrs Lanfal who had remained behind with Qojo. "Excuse me, Mr Kmango, your school it bad bad school. Aqosua, my young jewel, she learn notting dese days. You do notting fo' us five year now. I work your Dispensary ebery Wednesday. It no good. De shelves empty. Attah supply van no bring. You no care no more. De doctor he come only at two week."

"My dear Mrs Lanfal – we have all been in limbo since our Great Liberator's untimely departure. But now, I am once more in residence. The Carnival is nigh. Supplies are on order. All will be shipshape and Bristol fashion. My personal electrician is upgrading your street lights."

"We no like dose neons!" cried Lilibet Lanfal passionately. "Mr Kmango, we no want dat damn Carnival back. We no like dat colony ting no more. De maypole. De Shakespeare. Tings like dat. We is independent African long time now. I beg you, stop dis ting."

"Please, dear lady." Sir Henry's eyes were darting around. Ntank made a step towards her. "My people's carnival. My paramount gift to Tlula and our beloved Ulysses Oratorio."

"De Hornbill bad, bad influence. Qwami drink all de time. He lush."

Qojo laughed. "Qwami make plenty cocktail at de Carnival. Make plenty dollar."

Mrs Lanfal smacked Qojo with the back of her hand. "De blood and killin' days at hotel come again you not laugh."

"What do you mean?" Chipman had been following the exchange with increasing alarm. He had a flash of Wally Whitbread when he was making a decision as to whether to prosecute, hands behind his back, wrestling with his fingers. "Blood and killing?"

Lilibet Lanfal was silent. The big mammy bowed herself away as though she had said far too much. "Excuse me, Mr Kmango. De old days." She was gone.

"Mr Kmango! They refuse to give me my correct appellation." Sir Henry gave a contemptuous gesture. "Ungrateful wretches."

Chipman was about to put a question of his own to Sir Henry when a panting Drift arrived with the antivenom. Sir Henry dissuaded him from sprinting off to the village. "Too late. Fangga won't let you near him. Old Kofu will be sacrificed to the politics of the situation." His eyes rested on each of them in turn, a gaze so very amiable, Chipman decided to put his question about the "blood and killing" aside for the moment. "Next time, it might well be one of you. Wear boots when you are in the far bungalow area. A danger with those pretty sandals of yours, Mr Chipman Smith – particularly if they are Gucci." He gave a sly smile. "Mr Drift, since everyone is apprising me of your abilities as a marksman, bang, bang, bang, talk to me."

Drift became very much the herpetologist. The green tree mamba, he said, was a close relative of the cobra, nervous and obstreperous, particularly in the dry season. They mated for life, growing to twelve feet, with poison that attacked the central nervous system. If they struck, paralysis and death in a few minutes. The black mambas were the more common and just as bad...

"Spare us the grisly details. I just want them out of here before my Carnival."

"Your worries are over. When I've filled the legal quota for the cages I'm constructing," (Drift's eyes again caught Chipman's) "I'll kill every snake on sight."

"If you let us stay for the Carnival, Sir Henry," Starry put in quickly, "Drift's collection will be a wonderful attraction for your guests. A menagerie. You've got a lot of other stuff around here that could be displayed. Monkeys, chimpanzees, baboons. Holding pens for those big rodents they stew up. Grasscutters. Your hornbills are certainly showstoppers."

Sir Henry laughed. "My court jesters. Yes, we have a population problem. If only Kraka would sacrifice them instead of chickens at the ponds, but to the villagers the hornbills are symbols of marital fidelity. Ulysses loves them like children but until he arrives, I would have no objection if you discreetly help yourself to eggs and feathers. And they barbecue quite nicely."

"Look, we're not all angling to stay for the Carnival," said Drift testily. "I can get onto the snakes pronto, but once that is done, I intend to be outta here." Toffee glared at him. "Chipman and I are looking for building materials. Do you know where we can get hold of some local wood to make my cages?"

Sir Henry continued to be evasive. "It is unfortunate that in the village, the infirm Fangga, like the strapping Blossom, still wields influence. The clearing will help, of course, but while Fannga continues to inhabit this world, the snakes will continue to proliferate. There is a pernicious black magic involved here. I will be giving strict instructions that Fangga be kept out of the grounds." He cast a glance around at Hamou. "The village clique in league with the old rogue hopes the snakes will drive me away. There was once an attempt to burn my precious Hornbill down, but I refuse to be intimidated. Strange as it may seem, Fangga has tentacles far outside Tlula. I have secure information that he wheels and deals with powerful opposition figures in Okidoki. He is a dangerous opponent, for all of you as much as for me. Unlike myself, the fancily dressed feticheur has no warmth for our country's foreign guests."

"The sooner I'm gone the better, believe you me. Just make an offer."

Sir Henry Kmango, finally, engaged fully with Drift. "If we could find some way of dealing with the Fetish Priest –

permanently – the mambas might disappear of their own accord." His eyes widened and he let out something between a laugh and a growl. "If only your skills might extend to that! I'm joking of course, but let us talk together soon Mr Drift, and we will get down to tin tacks, as you Yankee Doodle Dandies say. You mentioned building materials?"

Sir Henry moved off. "My word! What a morning this has been. I am sorry to have been so discouraging towards your theatrical aspirations, Dr Sanguini, but it is out of my hands. Your proposal had considerable merit, and I will certainly honour you with my presence at some of your performances on the beach before you leave. Toffee's *Angel Baby Rotations*, was it? Attah Lalwani, and indeed, Chief Akwa, have already given me vivid descriptions of your thrust." Sir Henry paused and looked almost demure. "I think I am free to tell you that dear Ulysses would not have been entirely bored by your – activities."

FIFTEEN: *Pranks, postures and*
Pandora's Box

Chipman walked boldly to the village and booked a seat on Josiah Lanfal's trotro for the following morning. "You sure dis, Mr Chipman? In Doggone yesterday, de people very angry wit sticks. There is barricades, tyres burnin' in de streets. Not good place for nice blue-eye man like you."

It seemed that everyone knew immediately that Chipman was leaving Tlula Leisure Beach. In the shade outside St Bede's he sat down with a couple of beers and waited for Starry to hunt him down. His mind was soon in a meditative state, pretty much free of turbulence and anxieties. Right above him, beaming benevolently in green and magenta on black, was the faded church sign.

ANGLICAN CHURCH OF BOMZAWE
ST BEDE'S.
REVEREND Q. ADOMAKO. SUNDAY SERVICES 8am 5pm
Wednesday Prayer Meeting 10am

His thoughts returned to the events of the morning. Two hacked and decomposing bodies had drifted in and been ferried up the Wawa to the crocodile ponds; bodies washed south-west by the Doggone Current, said Zach, who had done some research on local ocean movement in the provincial capital's Public Library.

Doggone, increasingly riven by murderous factional and tribal discontent was only twelve miles east along the coast. The situation was enough to have Chipman putting a distress call through to the British Embassy. Since the arrival of the dubious Sir Henry there had been a slight improvement in service. William Oates had flown with the Ambassador to Whitehall for urgent consultations with the Foreign Office. No message had been left for a Chipman Smith. "Mr Oates won't be back any time soon."

"Oh no!" he cried, but really, he didn't believe her. It was that same woman and there was an even more intemperate tone to her voice. Somewhat desperately he thought he might even call Wally Whitbread, just for the comfort of his voice if nothing else, but Attah pushed him out of his office. "No international calls here, Mr Chipman. Ever! You go to Doggone."

Equally distressing had been the *Angel Baby Rotations* outside the hotel. Sir Henry and Ntank, seated in canvas chairs with their cocktails, had watched from the verandah of Bungalow One as the *Eighth Chakra Evolutionary Dancers* transcendentalising 'theatre' began. Watched as everything went wrong, as heaven had turned to hell. Toffee had accused Drift of rape and had run naked and screaming along the back row of bungalows. Mambas slithered away, hornbills blinked, honked and flapped for cover. She seized a workman's cutlass and subjected Drift to a double handed attack with it. Drift had managed to disarm her, but only with great difficulty. Some blood had flowed. "No wonder she wants to kill you," Cerisia had shouted at the Chicagoan snake catcher.

Starry chided Cerisia for her attribution of blame or at least for the tone of it. Rather, Toffee's 'freak-out' indicated she was now close to revealing what her Dad did to her in the turkey sheds. "Darling, there was nothing random about that cutlass."

"You're creating this story, Starry," Drift had said as he staunched the oozing blood. "Filling her head with false memories. She's a rural southern girl, chopping off the heads of her Dad's turkeys was no big deal." He wrapped Toffee and Lobelia together in a ntama, "Mi amor, cielito," he murmured, and moved towards his back bungalow. The monkey did not seem to mind for once as Toffee pressed kisses to Drift's face and nibbled at his formidable moustache. Starry had preened at the sight, already taking credit for the conjugal bliss that was to follow.

Starry in his shades and cap, came leaping up from the surf. Like a dog shaking itself after swimming, he gave Chipman a brisk spray from his naked body. "My pre-Makeover gathering has started. What are you doing here?"

"Sir Henry Kmango was the last straw, Starry. The man has a way about him, but I can't get mixed up with someone like that, no matter how much of a friend he is with William Oates. Wally would be horrified. I will certainly apprise him of things that were revealed."

"We have scarcely scratched the surface of your malaise. Leave now and you'll be back outside Wally's window before you know it. You're still drinking like an unhappy marriage and you have that puzzled look upon your face as though you're trying to remember some terrible thing I did back in Australia. I haven't done any terrible thing." Starry paused. "You have never shown any real interest in my past. Quiz me now!" Starry raised his beard, to fully reveal the scar that disfigured his hairy chest. "You have never even asked me about my grievous wound. A Manhattan mugger, Central Park, a year ago. It has come to symbolise for me the dedication I have made to the betterment of humanity. Our activities here have opened up everyone's Pandora's Box. Toffee's, Zach's, yours. You have already begun your surrender to the exploration of the Dionysian aspects in our natures. Interrupt it now and I repeat, you'll again be that silly superficial creature watching Wally and Janette at play in the bath tub."

Chippo chose to ignore Starry's heartfelt dissertation. "Well, OK, but for a start I don't believe your real name is Sanguini."

"If you want to change your life, and I did, bored shitless in Sydney, start by changing your name. Salvatore Sanguini was what I came up with."

"But changed from what?"

Starry looked around sharply as though someone was approaching, adjusted his dark glasses. "My mother has Italian ancestry so that influenced me. As did my Roman Catholic upbringing, my license to thrill. Sexually, if you like. Quite fond of my mother actually, if not of my father. He's a brain surgeon. Very lofty, rather dry. The one who sent me to St Ignatius. Her family came from Sicily originally. Palermo. Stopped there on my way over. Looking for my roots, like Toffee. Lovely Lotus came up with the idea of 'Starry' recently. Named me after her ceilings in the bus. Ha ha! Euphonious don't you think?"

"You avoided my question."

"What do you mean?" He raised his arms high and in a slow rotational gesture that encompassed both the sea and the shore's jungled slopes, he asserted some higher, more worldly-wise, moral ground for himself. "Chipman, you still have no idea where you have so fortuitously landed, have you? Let me give you some perspective. Tlula is one of those power points into which the new paradigm has been plugged. It's a node on the universal circuitry of the counter-cultural circus. A small but enlightened one. Professor Siegfried himself is excited that I have set up at Tlula. It's a life-enhancing opportunity to be in Africa at this morphogenetic moment in time. You'll be a fool to blow it!"

"Maybe I'm a fool." Chipman was already tired of the turn the discussion had taken, but asked, "Why do you and Cerisia wear these same unflattering sunglasses? Other people around you have them too."

"It's the French Foreign Legion here. Everyone's on the run. Zach for example, haunted by his past. Drift the draft dodger. Not long ago, the famous Fast Eddie was a member of The Beautiful Afreakans. You, a sexual refugee, fleeing antiquated homophobic laws. Consensual sex between men as indecent assault." He turned away slightly, removed the sunglasses, checked them against the sky, gave a polish with spit and sarong. "Shades is the hip word. Or was once. Siegfried had them designed, and insisted everyone in the Verbier clinic wear them. Like my provocative ADOLF cap. A few of those still around too."

"What was that big word you used earlier?"

"Morphogenetic? In the ether. Macaques washing potatoes in Japan soon have baboons doing it in Bomzawe. Butterflies fluttering wings in Brazil create tsunamis in Ceylon. A simultaneous happening all over the world. Esalen. Auroville. Marrakech, Kathmandu. Goa. Kuta Beach. Even in bloody Sydney. Although I wouldn't bet the farm on that."

He gave an 'ach' of frustration. Grabbing Chipman's hand he guided it into a tracing of the Sanguini chest scar. A seduction into staying but it only made the lawyer cringe; once again a much too intimate and inappropriate gesture from someone whose therapies – and body – he had never been able to fully accommodate himself to.

"Fascinating, wasn't it, Chipman. That session with Shaler, our would-be Peace Corps worker up there in that monument to Mammon. Zach the Knife. There must be something in those murder rumours, whatever that devious man says. I can only hope. We all have stories about the traumas that replay in our brain's circuitry. You have managed to confess to that night in Wally's garden, but I am still waiting for the rest of the picture. And how it was possible for a man like the melodious Motherwell to manipulate you into years of emotional and sexual deprivation, a time lost that brought you eventually to your lovely turns at the Whitbread windows. As I have already intimated, you can't leave before we get those wasted years fully exorcised."

Chipman flicked away his cigarette stub. Wally's Bomzawean solution had not worked out as he might have hoped but there was no doubt that it had been an act of unparalleled generosity on his boss's part. A compassionate solution to an unfortunate situation. Particularly in face of the fact that Wally had twigged the voyeur in the tree outside his window was Chipman, his long favoured doe-eyed protégé.

Whatever Chipman thought of Starry's cauterisations, his state of mind had been calmed. He preferred to think that the sublime nature of the remote beach and its benign waters had been the sole cause but he had to admit that without Starry and the constant attention he had his Afreakans lavish upon him, however bizarre, he would not have come to realise why he had fallen 'in love' with his boss; and why in the years before Wally, he had swooned over other fatherly gents (mostly members of Melody's Congregational Choir), lusted after their body parts, longed for the slightest sign of physical affection, something only occasionally, drunkenly given. Maybe he did owe Starry the full Chipman Smith confessional that he so wanted to hear – that trajectory from summer night origin with Alfie, to winter night dénouement outside that damn bedroom window.

Sanguini in his talking had not noticed that Chipman's mind had drifted elsewhere.

"… and that's when I discovered the freedom of being conspicuous! The smell of the greasepaint, the roar of the crowd. No more stage fright. Now that I am a celebrated performer on the world stage, my motto is never look back. My goal, Chipman, is education of the populace, raising the consciousness of the masses. Something of which you, and even your boss would have to approve." He gave an antelopean leap or two towards the water. "Come on. It's humid today. The wet season is on its way."

"I already swam. I'll see you at your pre-Makeover."

Starry increased his momentum, ran into the sea. Chipman lit another Camel Filter and watched him, in cap and shades, splash through the breakers then freestyle in the direction of the hotel. Starry was a powerful swimmer, he had to admit. Those arms. Not to mention the legs.

Legs or not, his decision had been made. Starry was never going to hear the story that meant too much to Chipman to ever reveal it to such a man as Starry, a man with no discretion or respect for privacy. After all, the story was of a somewhat illicit nature and respectable lawyers should not release such facts into the public arena. He was now regretting even having told Starry about Wally Whitbread and the window. He had finally come back to his senses.

Chipman leaned against a palm trunk, drank his beer, closed his eyes. A picture of his family's annual camping holiday at Booti Booti State Recreation Area on the mid-north coast came effortlessly to his mind.

The interior of Alfie and Matilda's big tent was set up with an inflatable double mattress. After his own little hiking tent had collapsed one night in the wind and rain and then, disastrously, blown into the rushing creek, it was Matilda who had suggested he sleep with them. Yes, once the big summer storm had blown over, there he was, sleeping beside Alfie. He felt his body against his own as his father did some arranging of the sheet over them. He was sixteen and had not slept with his parents since he was a little boy, nor wanted to. Tibor had been gone for over two years and Alfie's lessons in carpentry and cabinet making were well under way. He loved his Dad but could not help but feel awkward about being in a bed with him. Well, there was no alternative really. And he had always liked his smell. Alfie said to get some sleep and turned away, but Chipman remained wide awake. His Dad's breathing deepened. The downpour was over but light rain persisted, thrumming gently on the canvas. Despite the storm, it remained a hot January night. He liked to sleep naked and had pushed down his boxers the minute his father had turned away but he didn't know that Alfie also liked to sleep with his clothes off. His thoughts drifted in loving manner to Tibor.

He began to lose any sense of time passing. It was probably after midnight. His father turned towards him, his breathing light, his body moving closer. An arm seemed to drift and rest on Chipman's chest. He could scarcely breathe for his sudden excitement, feelings of both shock and pleasure. Matilda was sound asleep on his father's other side. What could this mean? Alfie kissed him on the neck, and then on the lips, things which he had done before with him and Tibor, but not lying down at night and naked in bed. He did not resist, even eased himself closer, much roused by the warmth and affection. Alfie's hand moved slowly, ever so slowly down his body until it rested in his pubic hair, then on one thigh, then the other. His dick was grasped, the length and shape of it assessed, confirming the fact of erection perhaps. Then the shape and size of his testicles. When the hand moved back up the shaft and closed around the head, Chipman ejaculated spontaneously. "Oh Alfie," he whispered. The hand squeezed gently, was then withdrawn. The body moved away slightly. Many minutes passed. His father's breathing steadied. Chipman wanted to continue what had occurred. He turned on his side and rested his hand on his father's thigh, just above his knee. Ever so slowly Chipman's hand moved upwards. A hand with a life of its own.

There was no movement from his father, no response of any kind. He rested his hand at the top of his father's thigh for a long time. He had to hold his dick. He had to. Hold it like Alfie had held his. Out of nowhere came a wonder if Alfie had also held Tibor and that made him even more aroused. Closer ever closer, then his father turned and eased further away. Forever after, Chipman relived that occasion, as one of the most beautiful and thrilling sexual moments in his life, one that needed completion. And honouring.

It was a year later, the following summer that Alfie died. He had gone with some teacher friends on a bush walk in the lower Blue Mountains to the beautiful Paradise Pool, not that far from Linden. The temperature that day had soared to over 90 degrees Fahrenheit. Walking back up a steep and rocky slope, he had a massive heart attack and could not be revived. He was 55.

Within six months of the death, Matilda married the Reverend Motherwell and Chipman moved with her into the rectory. The Ashfield house was sold. She had felt the need for the support of a man of the cloth, a man blessed with moral rectitude, devoted to the control of appetites, not necessarily with her. Alfie was an atheist and had never given the church any more than the most token interest required of him, and as the years had gone by, he had given scarcely more than what was required of him as a husband to Matilda. In her comparative neglect, she had taken to spying upon Alfie. There had been no other woman, but she began to notice particularly, the affection between Alfie, Chipman and Tibor. She had secretly witnessed the last night that Tibor had stayed over with Chipman. Noticed the way that Alfie kissed them and gave a long held farewell hug. It confirmed her worst imaginings. Her unhappiness was exacerbated by an envy of the closeness of her husband's mentor relationship with Chipman in the workshop in the back garden. Apart from a few sly remarks of which neither Alfie nor Chipman had any comprehension, she said nothing, but to her friend Melody, of the Congregational Choir in which she joyfully sang solo soprano, she told everything. He advised her to keep busy with her unstinting charity work.

After the stormy camping trip at Booti Booti, there had been no real change in the relationship between Alfie and Chipman. The young man felt that the never-talked-about, one-off intimate adventure that night, merely added some kind of patina that both father and son were blissfully aware of.

Shortly after Melody had married Matilda, he went to the local police and requested an investigation into the sexual habits of Alfred Smith. It helped that the local police chief sang in the Congregational Choir. Under pressure from Melody, there was a polite visit to Canterbury College and the questioning of staff and several senior boys, questioning which garnered no criticisms of any kind. Only gratitude and sorrow. At Ashfield Boys, Chipman was asked if he had been 'interfered with' and he said no. That was the end of the matter in many ways, but not with Motherwell whose focus on Chipman's re-structuring became an obsession.

Over sherry (Matilda's favourite tipple) one evening, Melody told his new wife and Chipman, that if the weak-hearted, incestuous atheist had not escaped conviction, he would have been glad to see him not only jailed, but put in the stocks as well. "I know we are no longer living in 19th Century England, but it would have been an appropriate punishment."

Yes, the end of the age of innocence for Chipman; the slump into utter revulsion with himself, into a crippling awareness of how society viewed his sexuality. Melody Motherwell's well-intentioned cures for Chipman's Alfie-groomed 'contagion' were in fact, not only a descent into the quicksand of obedience that went with religious sermons and servitude, but one into fear and friendless isolation. Not to mention boozing, binoculars, balaclavas and a bay window or two. There was no honouring of his father's memory in that. No completion, no completion at all.

Chipman looked in on Starry's gathering, but after a disagreement with Cerisia who made it clear she was glad to have him leave Tlula, he preferred to settle down with a drink at the bar.

He dashed Qwami well and the bartender showed him his beautiful salmon pink tongue. Pity he had not taken him up on his frequent offers. Never had Glen Fiddich and a splash of soda tasted so good. He fired up a Camel Filter, just about the last of his supply – another reason to leave – and settled down to seriously flirt. But Attah had sent Qumqwat running. "Telephone for you, Mr Chipman, suh." As he jumped up, he moued a kiss at Qwami who responded in kind. The day was long, there would still be time.

It was William Oates. Finally. A clipped English voice, calm and reassuring. Wally Whitbread had rung him from Sydney to check on the welfare of his protégé. Things had quietened down in the capital. It seemed the troubles had moved to the provinces. "Don't hang around Doggone longer than you can help. Look forward to seeing you when you arrive. I'll get you settled."

"That psychotherapist you mentioned, Mr Oates. He stopped my sink into alcoholism and Wally will be happy, but he thinks I am in deep denial about my sexuality. Really, I am much better, no longer worrying myself to death about emotional matters any more and I…"

"Sorry, Chipman, young fellow, not to fret. Must dash. Time for my iced cocoa break, ha ha! Toodle-oo, pip pip and all that!"

Well, it was upsetting to be cut so short, but Chipman gave a sigh of satisfaction. Everything was getting back to normal.

In a newly steady hand, he wrote a card to his mother. *Dear Matilda, he began, sorry to not have written sooner…* He knew using that appellation would irritate Melody no end, but after gaining new perspectives on the Reverend from Starry, he did not care. *Having a wonderful time, hot and windy but good safe swimming. No mozzies. I have become friends with the pastor of St Bede's here. You would be pleased. Missing your good old home cooking. Say hullo to Mr Melville. And stand up for yourself.*

Starry waylaid him as he was on his way to leave the cards with Attah for posting. His supply van was making a run to Kassini Junction that afternoon. Chipman had never before encountered Sanguini in a state so agitated.

"You OK?"

"It's nothing. Bloody Cerisia! She didn't mean that. She wants you to stay as much as I do," he lied, snatching the card from Chipman's hand, along with one he had written to Wally. "That women has depths I am only beginning to plumb. Marry in haste, repent at Leisure Beach. Ha ha!" He started to read, warning Chipman back with a hand. "Just checking!"

Dear Wally

Feeling remarkably recovered after relaxing here at beautiful Tlula. Hotel on beach recommended to me by William Oates has been most suitable. And sobering. William has been busy but he rang just now and I will be seeing him tomorrow in Okidoki. I had a little 'therapy' while here. I hope you will be pleased. Nothing drastic, but it has done the trick. Another of William's excellent suggestions, for which I am truly grateful. Looking forward to seeing you in Lagos after Easter as planned. Intend to do some travelling on the way. Have a peep at more of Africa. Ghana certainly. Togo. Dahomey.

Telephonic communication virtually impossible from here but will ring from the Embassy tomorrow.

Sincerely Chipman Smith

Starry calmed down, but still gave Chipman a blast. "I'm desolate at the enormity of my failure with you. DESOLATE! You know why? Because you're still a fucked-up faggot, a classic closet case, and you never gave me the chance to make an authentic human being out of you."

He held both cards out of reach, and before handing them back, made a smirky pretence of ripping them in two. Fortunately Chipman had addressed the card to Wally's home address, not to the Office of the Clerk of the Peace. Not that it mattered any more. If it had ever mattered.

"Starry, every day there are new arrivals who get interested in your techniques. As you keep saying, Tlula is a node on an international circuitry of people all looking for all manners of enlightenment. And healing."

"Yes, but none like you," he responded, in a tone so strange, even threatening, that a trickle of terror went through Chipman. He felt his spasm about to activate again.

BOOK TWO
QUE SERA, SERA

PART ONE
A Turning in the World

SIXTEEN: *Oh, island in the sun*

The dawn sky was an antique white, the sea immobile, the horizon as if cut by a scalpel. Luggage in hand, Chipman had left the Hornbill for good that morning, only to find that Josiah Winful's trotro, the only one operational in the village, had been tampered with overnight and would be out of action for days. He tried to ring William Oates back to let him know he would be delayed. He also wanted to convey his serious misgivings about the true nature of Sir Henry Kmango's Easter Carnival. Oates hadn't given him the chance the day before. The phone was once more out of order. He accused Attah of accepting a bribe. "Who dashed you? Did my cards get posted yesterday?"

"Mr Chipman, my sorrow is infinite, but please, my phone he dead sometime almost every day. No one cut wires. You try again next week."

"Next week?" Chipman shouted. "Why are there no police around here?"

"Tomorrow. You calm your hysteric self."

He was suspicious of everyone. Drift, for one, was clearly glad his departure had been interrupted. Toffee briefly held out Lobelia for him to pet. "He didn't do it, Chipman. He was zombied out all night long." Drift shook his head. "Drifty, yes you were." The monkey jumped back onto her shoulder, then her head and they moved away.

"Hey, be flattered," said Drift, following her with his eyes, but, ceding to the monkey for once, made no attempt to go with them. "Flattered that Sanguini wants you enough as a Family member to resort to vandalism."

"I was never going to build them, Drift. I'm getting out of here one way or the other. You're a crook."

Lotus stoked the fires by saying that Starry and Cerisia, "almost had a divorce over you last night. Starry won the battle, but check out his shiner. Hey, let's face it, she wants you twiddled. She says you're a corrupting influence, that Starry is paying you the wrong sort of attention. If you know what I mean. Since she caught you giving him a blow job in your room."

Chipman continued to fume. Of course the vandal was Starry; that passionate intensity, that irrationality, that egocentricity, that unjustified importance he attached to his failure as a therapist with him. There was neurosis there. An insecurity. It was as though by disabling the trotro he was making an attempt at a kidnap. Was Lotus correct? Jealousy? Cerisia thinks that Starry has fallen in love? With Chipman? With his unsightly Rudolph the Reindeer nose? If he had had the nerve, he would have told her that even if the doctor had fallen in love, Chipman certainly had not. And never would.

In the bar, a sleepy Qwami was still setting up, but poured him his first drink of the morning. He sat there feeling ill at ease, even paranoid, a reversion to the state he had been in during his first weeks at Tlula. He told himself to shake off those feelings. One more day in 'paradise' and more time to spend with Zach (and even the sexy bartender), what could be wrong with that? Earlier, he had wanted to consult the Nebraskan about the trotro. Restraining himself from entering his room, he had, once more through the louvres, voyeured upon his somnolent nakedness.

Starry approached. His Siegfried shades concealed any shiner but he did have a bruised lip and there was a swelling on a cheekbone. "No, I didn't nobble the trotro."

"I've alerted the Embassy that my travel plans have been jeopardised," Chipman lied. "Anyway, Blossom Rokoku is driving to Doggone tomorrow at noon. I have arranged a lift in the back of her truck. Not cheap, and if that does not eventuate, I can travel in Attah's supply van on Thursday."

Starry called to Qwami (polishing cocktail glasses, his glistening back to them), for two Red Star. And fresh peanuts.

"Chipman, you're leaving with Blossom tomorrow, but that is no reason to miss the Makeover today, the unique opportunity to visit our very own little Fiji, which by the way, I am renaming

Cerisie Wiesie Island in honour of my darling wife." He fingered his lip, rubbed an eye under his shades. "To keep her happy. Even as I speak, Lotus is knocking up a special plaque. Like a Dirk Hartog pewter plate." He gobbled some peanuts, drank some beer. "Zach's island. Do I have to tell you he's decided to come on the Makeover?"

Well, by the time the sea-going pirogues hired from the village had arrived to take everyone out, Chipman's better judgment had been neutered, his fears assuaged. Starry's offer of a position of honour in the prow of the lead canoe had been accepted.

"We will turn the Makeover into a Farewell Celebration for you." The doctor put an arm around Chipman's shoulders. "That's a promise."

Wading ashore, like Columbus or someone, General MacArthur? Chipman found himself suffused with an exhilarating sense of adventure. On approach across the dappled green and turquoise sea, the island did indeed look like a South Pacific idyll and even after exploration revealed much of it as an odorous rookery, he still felt he had undertaken something audacious. With the breeding season over, most of the birds had dispersed, leaving behind an air of dilapidation. In the salty, tough leafed boskage growing at the sand's edge or in the central clumps of pisonias which flourished in concert with the palms, there were hundreds of their untidy, boxy nests. Wheeling on the wind was a squad of black terns. The ever-present frigate birds soared high above.

Noticing Zach heading along a path that led to the south side, Chipman followed excitedly. Dirty white chinos half-rolled up, flip-flops, cowboy hat, a threadbare metal studded checked shirt, Zach had made no effort to dress up for the Makeover. Chipman hadn't either. Zach welcomed his presence. With his departure rescheduled for the following day, Chipman's head was full of 'nothing to lose' thoughts and he surrendered to a free-wheeling, non-platonic feeling of togetherness as they stood close to each other contemplating the crash of the Gulf of Guinea waters on the stony south side that had accounted for Zoe.

The waves were indeed chaotic. "I've been scared to come out here alone, Chipman. It's always there in my head, banging away. Why else would I have come back to Tlula? Where else do I have to go to? This is the last place for me." There was a pleading look in his eyes, almost as though it was up to Chipman to convince him otherwise. He had been going on like this a few days before in Blossom's. By now, Chipman was used to the morbid moods that came and went, the moods that he was not averse to jollying him out of. It was not only a way of intimately relating to him but also a way of dealing with his own glooms and confusions.

"Do you believe in a spirit force, Chipman? A force that can have an actual visual presence? An after-life of some kind. Sometimes I see one out there."

"Zach, there's no such thing, except in your head. Zoe is gone. Drowned a long time ago. I mean..." To cover for possible insensitivity, and to stop Zach from taking a flying leap into those treacherous, crashing waves, Chipman put an arm firmly around Zach's back, another on his forearm and tried to draw him away. "It's unbelievably hot, Zach. Let's take a dip before Starry gets started on us." Zach's body stiffened, moved even nearer to the edge. Angry spray splattered against them. "Oh God, Zach! I mean back on the north side, the safe side. No, no, not here, of course not. That's craziness! An accident, Zach! No need for guilt."

Zach's eyes searched Chipman's. "It's real." His voice was so low and throaty that it was hard to catch. "It's something beyond any sort of desire or temptation." He clutched Chipman's hands. "Why should I fear doing what Z-zzoe beckons me to do? Join her. Do what is right." He had begun stammering.

"Like one of sirens of Odysseus calling?"

He came even closer and Chipman smelled his breath, not a pleasant one for once, indicative perhaps of his degree of distress. It was as though Zach wanted to drag him into the water, as though they had already sealed a pact to die together. With the Nebraskan pulling at his shoulders, Chipman's fear gave way to a yielding to this wish, a yielding accompanied by a fierce sexual arousal, an arousal beyond anything he had experienced with Whitbread. It was as if Zach was saying he loved him – unto the end. As Chipman realised how tightly the two of them were clinging together, he was shocked at how love or even desire could so easily lead lovers into danger. There was indeed a seductive force in the next wave that crashed over their legs but there came also a regret that he was not in the Lanfal trotro, trundling along the dirt road to Doggone. He wrenched himself free.

A shout came loud on the briny air, calling for celebrants to "get back here, all you wankers!" Yes, a resonant voice, rescuing them from a temptation neither Zach nor Chipman had the power to fully dispel. But it was the same voice that had talked Zach into discontinuing his medication.

"This healing journey, this Full Moon Makeover is the formal initiation of everyone as members of the *Eighth Chakra Evolutionary Dancers*. A ritual cleansing preparatory to rehearsals for the Carnival. An overture to the Aida of Easter! Sir Henry's refusal is a spur not an impediment. I vow to you today, we will be here and we will be on stage, kicking up our heels, smelling the greasepaint."

"Until Starry signals the release, you are committed to the group process," Cerisia intoned, stubbing the last of a Gitane out in the sand. She gave a world weary yawn. "Personal difficulties are not a reason to leave, but a reason to stay."

"Until the bitter end," came a giggle.

"Thank you, Lotus, for that."

"Location is significant, both in terms of personal conviction and connection with the elemental forces. Look around and place yourself."

Around the 'energy core', Lotus and Stan had traced in the sand an outer circle with the four directions indicated by bamboo poles flying banderoles – green for north (the mainland and the Hornbill), blue for south (the Atlantic emptiness), yellow for east (the headland by which was the wreck of the *Accra Queen*) and red for west (the pinnacle on which stood Castle Vinkenoog).

One person not being made over was Toffee who was spending "yet another day in monkey world" with Lobelia and that was that. To Drift, "Get lost and fuck you!" He had taken advantage of her again after her freak-out and she and her adored Lobelia were not to be disturbed until after dark. If then. If ever!

Starry regretted that his old friend Seamus Shamrock, the long awaited courier from the Swiss clinic, had not turned up, but he had saved enough of his old cache of Siegfriediana for just this occasion. "A telescope into the inner workings of the mind. Adolf guarantees this one gets a conversation going between your aromatic amygdala and your ever malleable pre-frontal lobes."

Starry had attracted a crowd for once. Fourteen others had joined the expedition and as instructed, had brought along musical instruments or something with which to make rhythm and noise. And a contribution towards the Siegfriediana.

Floralee Bush voiced qualms. 'Everybody's favourite grannie', she was an old Aussie mate of Starry's who had turned up unexpectedly, early the previous evening.

Starry had contrived to stop Chipman from interrogating the woman, but after Cerisia had claimed the doctor for their usual tryst in the palanquin, it was easy enough to approach her, only to have Floralee excusing herself with a transparent evasiveness the minute he mentioned Sydney and Salvatore Sanguini.

Floralee was 73 years 'young' and based in Byron Bay, a voyager on a global search for plants with psychedelic properties and on her way to Gabon where the magical iboga root was used in the Bwiti Cult. She was taking a course of a psychotropic sex drug called yohimbine which came from the bark of a tree in the Bomzawe rain forests. With great pride, she informed everyone she was on Day 5 and her erogenous zones were on fire. From behind silver rimmed glasses, her eyes burned with pullulating desire.

Now Chipman tackled her again. "You knew Starry back in Australia?"

"You betcha I knew him. Articulate sort of kid back then, that's what I liked about him, right on the ball. Someone put him onto me and I helped him."

"He could not have been called Starry back then."

"I'll come clean, kiddo. He had never left Australia before and he needed a passport quicksticks. For reasons I am going to keep to myself, he could not get an official one so that's where I came in. A little sideline of mine."

"He must have told you his real name."

"Let's say he didn't. I had a nice selection at the time. He chose Salvatore Piero Sanguini. I put him in a wig and beard for the new photo, but you're right, there was no Starry back then."

"Forged passports?"

"Some dead Italian guy from Melbourne. Similar age." She gave Chipman a stare, in the heat of the day, frigid. "That's about it, baby face. What's it to you? You don't exactly look like Interpol."

"No no, I'm just a little shocked. Sanguini's – ah – an intriguing man who has been assisting me here. I was merely curious." He mustered up a laugh. "About what he used to be before he grew all that hair and beard. The dark glasses."

Floralee warmed a little, put a gnarled hand on his. "You don't want to know, kiddo. He's a good bloke. He won't mind me saying just this. Ten years ago, he was a clean-shaven toughie, looked a bit like a young James Cagney, giving a complacent society a few wake-up calls. All the University students were. A rethink of the whole Australian charade was long overdue. Still is. He did what he did, and Sanguini and I have been a mutual admiration society ever since. He wasn't expecting me to turn up here, and I'm not going to put him in the shitola with you or anyone, and that's that." She gave a snort of finality. "If you ever need a passport…"

Starry had overheard every word that was said between the two of them. "The sacred passport business" came his voice from the other side of the circle. "Everything and nothing is sacred, Chipman. You'll realise that before the day is over."

Chipman's conversation with Floralee had aroused his original wonderings about Sanguini. But, he reassured himself, beard or not, he would definitely have recognized anyone of interest to Wally, the Department of the Attorney General and its Office of the

Clerk of the Peace. There was no-one behind the silly gangster shades for him to be concerned about.

"This Siegfriediana crapola, Starry," Floralee called out. "It's not exactly a naturally growing hallucinogen."

"Floralee, *The Sound of Music* is the most radical of Adolf's famous Rocket and Boosters. The rickety-rackety Rocket will have you playing in the fields beyond Nirvana on a continuous basis for the rest of the day. The boogie-woogie Booster not only operates as a truth serum, but will stimulate the septal nucleus area of your brain. You will have multiple orgasms with everything including your DNA coding."

Floralee ingested.

"The Full Moon Makeover is dedicated to our friend, Chipman Smith. We will miss the benign oil of queerdom he has poured on the choppy waters of our sexualities. In return, we could have given Chipman the thing I'm sure his heart desires most of all – a true and loving life companion. As it is, this will be a farewell party he will never forget." So saying, Starry had his participants hold hands and lean back at full stretch, a test of the tensility of the energy circle.

Chipman had absolutely no intention of ingesting anything. Turning his back on the whole Mad Hatter's Tea Party thing, he moved away and dangled his feet in a coralline pool near the sheltered inlet where the Tlula fishermen had landed them. The pool's deeper crevices were thick with anemones, mauve fronds gently waving. Sea slugs in shades of umber and chocolate lay like sausages on slivers of pink sand. Tiny multi-coloured fish nibbled at his toes.

The thrill of being on new terrain, of being at the very lip of a continent, had worn off. A fierce renegade wind arrived, turning the island into a furnace. The palms began to groan and creak under its blast. Flying debris caught by his suntan oil turned his skin into sandpaper. He'd forgotten a hat. The thick guano underfoot was sickly and sweet, cloying to the nostrils.

He looked back to the Chakrans to see how they were faring. The north-facing beach was the only open area and it was not big enough for the occasion. Mad Oslo, a surly man with a mass of hair encased in a crocheted sack – he had arrived at Tlula in Floralee's Kombi van – was complaining about the lack of depth to the 'thand'. He was missing teeth, had a pronounced double lisp and tended to spit. A veteran of the pre-hippie international trails, he was known from Kabul to Kuta, apparently, as Lunch. His speciality was getting 'rooted' or back to the 'thourthe', which meant he liked being buried vertically up to the neck for hours, even days at a time.

"Thanks, Lotus." Helpful and considerate as ever, always smelling so nice, a melange of tantalising perfumes from her various phials, and clad, sylphlike, in an almost non-existent frill of chiffon, she had popped over with a thermos containing one of her cool teas. "Mmm, spearmint my favourite. Thanks Lotus, just what I needed." He gave her a kiss on the cheek as she crouched in front of him.

"Hey, feel free. I've made gallons. I'm not letting anyone get dehydrated on this special day. The name was my idea." She smiled, sparkled her eyes at him as he imbibed lots more. "Why don't you move into the shade over there. It'll be more out of the wind."

The shade was closer to the ritual circle but he focussed on the view back across the sea to the forested shore. He realised he was enjoying himself finally and downed a celebratory dose of Johnny Walker from the big canteen which he had thoughtfully brought along.

He yawned. And yawned again. Turning once more to the circle he met the eyes of Jean-Claude and Thierry, the Parisians who had returned from Yamoussoukro the night before, with a travelling companion, Veronique. "They're chic, they're still gay, they've got a triad going. Educate yourself," Starry had said, dancing away while eating a turtle steak at the barbecue outside the bus the previous evening. "Je suis desolee pour toi. 'ere, try zis Elizabeth Arden Matte Finish on eet," Veronique had breathed at him, tossing iridescent streaks of violet hair away from her eyes. "What do you think of Starry?" Chipman had asked, allowing her to treat his nose with the Finish. "Thierry, 'e zink 'e is too big narcissist, but I zink 'e is a good one."

Now, in the harsh morning sunlight on the island, the sight of them created only a queasiness in him. Thierry had an untreated tropical ulcer on his leg and the slim brass bolt freshly set through Jean-Claude's clavicle was not only suppurating but surely indicated self-mutilation rather than simple decoration. Their bodies were thin to the point of emaciation. Those had to be puncture marks on their arms. Chipman's jaw locked down tight in disapproval. It was not long before he realised he was slipping into a mindless void, and that there was nothing he could do about it.

Chipman sat up. A considerable time must have passed. His vision was distorted. He rubbed his eyes, shook his head to no avail. He put it down to waves of heat rising from the sand. The hot blasts of wind seemed to have subsided. The ritual circle had disintegrated. A great deal of activity was taking place, and the word 'carnal' came to mind, not a word he had ever used except in the legal context of 'carnal knowledge.' The slender Parisian boys with their well-trimmed beards were doing synchronised swimming. The Norwegian rooting freak seemed to be hiccoughing as he humped the sand. Stan was having his chest hair explored by Cerisia for Ouidah nits, a curse of the White Man's Grave coast. Like all of them, Starry had everything off even the Siegfried glasses usually cemented to his face, and was blowing bubbles with a coven of hippie chicks including lovely Lotus, Veronique and Floralee with her inflamed labia. Yes, Starry Sanguini; about to explore his favourite female body parts, the erotic mysteries of which Starry had, more than once, earnestly if pointlessly explained for him. And there was the recently melancholy and suicidal Zach, smiling now at the attention being given him by Heather and Fiona, two freckled Glasgow girls, also recent arrivals. Sluts both of them, Chipman muttered. Him too, he added, and forced himself to look more closely at what they were up to. Now they were lying on their backs and Zach had been persuaded to rub oil all over the both of them.

Chipman was in a most dyspeptic mood. In desperation, he opened up his journal only to have it melt in his hands. Or seem to, until he got control of his biro. His mind was in a free-falling daze. "Oh my God!" he cried aloud. His penis, a part of his body that Melody (whose favourite book after *The Bible* was Baden Powell's *Rovering to Success*) had trained him not to look at or touch inappropriately, erect or not, was multi-coloured and extending like a snake to a length he never knew it could.

The penny finally dropped. "Floralee's yohimbinied my Johnny Walker," he silently screamed. His next thought shocked him even more. Starry has Siegfriedianaed me. How dare he do such a thing. Was there after all, something in the man's past that the Attorney General's Department might want to know about? A man he should have recognized? But so unlikely that this tinpot little egomaniac would be deserving of attention by someone like the prestigious Wally Whitbread. Why had he not suspected that Lotus would have been acting under orders? The glee in the glint of her eyes should have told him that there was mayhem afoot. Now he was trapped at an illegal drug party with a gang of addicts and layabouts, Floralee Bush a collector and forger of passports. The dregs of society. Criminals. How embarrassing. Wally must never hear of this. "My legal career will be over. My judicial aspirations. I will be struck off."

There came an urgent whisper in his ear. "Let's split the funny farm. I want to show you something before you leave Tlula. There's a canoe." It was the cavalry coming to his rescue. Drift's hair was pulled back for the big day out, and tied with a ribbon. Chipman stood up. Under duress, his mind had become razor sharp, but he found it was almost impossible to keep on his feet.

"Hey, thit here with Othlo. Thelethtial Thpathe-Out ith juth the thacred tholution for you, red nothe man."

"Nobody leaves the circle, Drift. Rule One." Starry was blocking their departure. "He's mine for the day. Chipman has to embrace his horror." He gave his chest a King Kong thumping. His left eye was blackened and half-closed. He was wobbling on his feet and dripping with Ambre Solaire. Drift had no trouble sending him sprawling and they dodged past. The last voice they heard was Cerisia's. "I'm willing the canoe to capsize. The drunk will drown. With luck we'll be rid of both of them." She let out a cackle. "Come back here, my darling tootsie, and have fun fun fun."

Chipman overbalanced getting into the canoe. Yes, he had been Siegfriedianaed. Rogers and Hammersteined. The Rocket and Booster.

SEVENTEEN: *The hills are alive (with the sound of music)*

Back on the mainland, Chipman found himself on the central path through the coconut grove. How had Drift gotten so far ahead? His terror at being left behind was acute. Where was Julie Andrews when she was needed? Was this what they called a "bad trip"?

He began running and experienced a rushing, cathartic momentum. The central row of tall Atlantic palms transformed into a white, frost-coated cathedral nave so coolly and unexpectedly beautiful, it produced in him a rapture. He felt himself being lofted high and raised his arms. Holy he was, numinous, heaven bound, but no St Peter materialized to welcome him through pearly gates into a celestial paradise. Instead, the frosted palms collapsed on him like an alpine avalanche and he had to fight from being smothered. Creepers clawed at his ankles. The carpet of leaves was undulating then sliding from under him. He staggered, crashed to the ground.

Flat on his back, he realised for the first time he was naked. How had that happened? Was he an Adam back in Eden? He covered himself with his hands, got to his feet. "Where are my shorts? My shirt? My shoes? I want to go home! Drift!!" Yes, back to his secure, ordered and responsible existence with the Department. Back with the measure of his beloved mentor, urbane, witty Wally! He didn't have to wait until tomorrow. He could go now. Telephone Wally. NOW! NOW!

He ran straight into the mouth of one of the Tlulan jungle devils. Aaargh! Its jaws crunched down. Chomp! "Drift, help!" He writhed, struggled, then realised it was Fangga the Fetish Priest. His features were half obscured by a raffia masklet. He had him by the arms, and was giving him a good shake, a fatherly talking to.

Many things happened with Fangga before Drift returned and drove the old man off with a kick and harsh words.

"No, no..." Chipman told Drift how he had been mesmerised by Fangga's craqueleured eyes, been taken to a sacred altar deep in the jungle. How the fetisheur captured for him a cinnamon and pink butterfly, big as a dinner plate, showed him a cauldron of writhing mambas. How he had linked him to the complex healing powers of the primeval forest, dissipated all his terror, sent it coursing down his spinal canal and out out out, deep into the soil of healing Mother Earth.

"All that in five minutes?" Drift sniffed the rotting rag and snake guts fetish Fangga had tied to Chipman's genitals. "Yuck! Another warning. He lets my snakes out, I'll pop him!" Drift ripped off the fetish. "Steer clear of Fangga. I..." His voice trailed off. "Don't worry. I'm one of the good guys. I'm no Kmango hitman."

Drift led him high up a side track. Chipman marvelled at the sublimity of the view. The long wide arc of the Tlula sand seemed to be covered in some sugary white dessert he wanted to eat. The ocean, suspended between forested headlands to east and west, was a rippling blue membrane. The fishermen who had taken Starry's party out, were laying nets and lobster pots off the island's coral reefs and further out, a yellow hulled cargo ship was passing by. In the nearer distance, the gables of the Hornbill peeked through the dancing fronds of the poinciana canopy. At that moment, courtesy no doubt, of the Professor Siegfried way with a cocktail, he felt that this was the most wondrous place in the world. He no longer wanted to go back home. He was at home right here.

A plunge into the penumbra of deep climax jungle; buttressed silk cottons, giant mahoganies, his feet sinking silently into moist humus – had him in vapours of delight. Where a grand old tree had fallen, there was sunshine, and he stopped to watch hirsute vines exploding into bloom just for him. There were intricate displays by attendant insects. Humming birds hovered and darted. Drift, speeding away in front once more, called back for him to get it together, that Chipman was on his first Siegfriediana and he was looking after him.

He was in a cleared area, protected by netting. In the surrounding cashew and cassia trees, cicadas were singing their never-ending mating song. Young pineapples, pink and purple, were pulsing in and out of their encasing spikes. A zephyr brought a strong odour, redolent of childhood. It was tomatoes, lying in tangled clusters, red and ripe for the eating. Through a little bogan gate, he lay down on his side and began to eat one straight from the stalk. Briefly, he was back in Narrabeen, so thrilling to be sitting on a wood and wire packing case, sipping sweet tea with Tibor and his migrant father, Jarek, with his big moustache, his stubbled cheeks and pointy chin always in need of a shave: his two mates, both men without wives, their alabaster-chested bodies, fingers stained darkly with their pickings from the pungent greenhouse growings.

Into Chipman's narrow focus came two canvas boots, bare, Lobelia-lacerated legs, a bandage oozing ampicillin, a pair of ragged shorts. Stuck into the waistband was that .38 revolver of his. Stamped Chicago Police Department, which had been shown for his admiration more than once.

Drift bent down and wiped Chipman's chin. "Babe, we're here."

'Here' turned out to be the marijuana crop of Drift's drummer friend, the massive Qaddo. Hidden in a fold in the hillside on the other side of an abandoned banana grove, open to the sky, it was no hobby farm nodding sedately in a pocket backyard, but a tangled forest, each plant well over twelve feet high. Drift was a fount of more information than Chipman could absorb; the difference between cannabis sativa and cannabis indica; the patina on the buds was crystallised resin; sensimilla meant seedless, a sophisticated technique, unknown in Bomzawe until recently, a technique which substantially increased both potency and yield.

"They've got their own rhythm, their own solar show. Qaddo had never heard of sensimilla until some freaks from Humboldt county in northern California came through. They taught him everything. And he had never grown in the dry season. Watering, fertilising. He knows he's got something going here. He offered me the whole crop. Out of the question, unfortunately, but I couldn't go wrong with a few kilos. Third world prices."

"How would you get it out of the country?"

"It's time we had that talk I've been promising. You are special, as you know."

Maybe it was the flattery that made Chipman conscious of how much he was luxuriating in the flooded moment, his whole body aglow, shimmering along with the plant matter all around them. He checked his audial world; nothing but the cicadas. Their voices were like everything else at that moment; angelic, rising on an anthemic tide.

He and Drift had reached the far side of the marijuana garden. Immediately in front of them was a sturdy shed built out of overlapping sheets of rusting, corrugated iron. Drift unlocked a large padlock on the door. Inside, piled up in the shadows, wrapped in a dark green plastic, were a great many bundles.

Drift brought one out into the sunshine. By the door, he peeled away the plastic to reveal two strange artefacts, the first a blackish circular plaque in high relief, about 18 inches in diameter, two inches deep. It depicted male figures in chainmail armour drumming on human skulls. It was studded with precious stones. "Beating out a tocsin," said Drift, uncovering another. "How cool is this one!" He explained; soldiers with winged helmets and breastplates but otherwise naked, penises erect and flattened on the abdomen. "Rejuvenation and fertility juju. I know all about them. Toffee and I spent a day in the Okidoki Public Library."

Chipman could not resist reaching out to touch, but he was sobering up with a rush. The Bomzawe Bronzes.

"I found out more about The Great Liberator from Qaddo. The coup against him was bloodless at first. Ulysses Oratorio agreed to leave the country but was given permission to first say good bye to his mother upriver here at Tlula. Beyond the crocodile ponds. Within forty eight hours it all turned nasty. The Bronzes were one of the many reasons that it all turned against him. Mguavas the coup leader found out that the Bronzes were not in the Museum where they were supposed to be. Realising what the Liberator was up to he dispatched soldiers to Tlula to arrest him and get the Bronzes back. They missed him by seconds. He had his seaplane parked by his little marina below his palace and took off down the river and flew across the border to Togo where his dictator buddy Sylvanus Olimpio gave him asylum before he went to Haiti.

Chipman was mystified. "If he went off to Haiti with the Bronzes, how…?"

"A big fat lie on his part that he took them with him to Haiti."

"So where did you find them?"

"Castle Vinkenoog dungeons. Carefully placed in a chamber within a chamber accessible only by an aperture that Toffee crawled through for me. Easy enough. They were not even wrapped. Not only were the Bronzes in an adjunct to one of the deepest, darkest cells of all, but even with my high powered torch, they were almost invisible at the bottom of a trench, covered in five years of batshit. You don't even want to think of the original use made of such a place."

"What on earth were you doing up there?"

"Toffee wanted to investigate the incarceration conditions of her ancestors while they waited for the slave ships. And I was trying to find out how deep down the bats liked to roost. We snuck the Bronzes out late at night when everyone in the village was asleep. They're a very credulous people here. After the sun goes, they believe bush devils will get them. The villagers never went into the dark of the dungeons. Nor anybody else for that matter. It was disgusting down there. Vinkenoog's a forgotten ruin, small, not a rebuilt tourist attraction like Cape Coast or Elmina in Ghana."

"This is superb workmanship, Drift."

"You can see how old they are. The armour. Some of the costuming is European. 17th Century, Dutch or Portuguese from the early days of contact. Even some Chinese influence. Before slavery, before colonialism. When they were just traders and Bomzawe was still an independent kingdom. I've seen Benin bronzes in museums. These have to be of similar quality, but they are also set with these gems or whatever they are as well. Toffee and I started to clean them up then realised the bat shit keeps them looking a bit more like junk."

"Even third world countries must have strict laws about national treasures."

"We have a little time to smuggle them out. Here's where you come in. I've lined up this totally legitimate snake deal. I just make the cages bigger. Each one with a secret compartment. No one is going to look too closely at a cage with a couple of mambas in it."

"Does Qaddo know?"

"He doesn't use his shed any more. He dries and processes his crop in his compound in the village. It's not particularly illegal here in Bomzawe. Initially I asked if I could store some stuff here that Attah and Kmango wouldn't let me keep in my bungalow. He works for Kmango but has no loyalty towards him. Yes, he knew immediately what I was talking about. Let me tell you about Qaddo. What a piece of work he turns out to be. The Bronzes..."

"I'm not interested, Drift. Anything to do with contraband and illegality is off the agenda. I don't even like to see snakes in cages, permits or not. I'm on my way tomorrow."

Drift had his arms folded, his pelvis thrust forwards, his half hidden cock a deliberate distraction. "Chipman, I'm not the luckiest guy in life. For me this is the first big break I've ever had." Drift motioned for him to sit. "I'll be frank. Trouble with the sort of life I lead now, I never meet anyone I can trust. But I've been watching you ever since you arrived. I know integrity when I see it. You're a reliable, diplomatic guy. Civil servant, all that shit. Well mannered. Naïve, but cool. I can throw together something for the snakes, pretty rough as you know, but false floors, compartments, invisible to the eye, are beyond me."

"Manageable size," Chipman said, playing for time, seated and enjoying the view of the groin Drift had granted him. His brain was settling down. Perhaps by now he could handle going back to the island.

"That's the beauty of my scheme. Nothing big. Less than life-size busts of kings and tribal chiefs, dishes for food offerings, hip ornaments, figurines of court musicians and dancers. Most of them are actually palace plaques like this one. Or flat ceremonial masks. Everything's easily transportable."

"You absolutely must put them back before Sir Henry finds out. This is Africa. You'll be sentenced to death and disembowelled or something. Shot. I don't know how they do it here."

"No way. This is my Toffee Project. Chipman, I confess I've done a bit of this sort of thing before. But this is big time. No problemo once I get through customs. I have a primo connection in England. Toffee and I will be on easy street. I know just where we are going to settle. Above the Kona Coast on the big island of Hawaii, there's a place called Waimea, where it's all sunshine and showers. Rainbows every day. Snow capped volcano in the distance. We'll grow coffee, dope, have kids. Perfectimento."

"Drift, you have the wrong man. Why not get Qaddo to help you?"

"He's an honourable man, but he's no cabinet maker." Drift unwrapped another bundle. "I'll make it worth your while." He revealed a small male head, maybe a child's, covered in the same black substance, but with enough of it scraped off to reveal the alloy. The face was serene, with closed eyes and lips, but Chipman's attention went immediately to the skull, not to the emerald set in the forehead but the hair, which was intricately coiffured into row upon row of insects, insects in fact which looked very much like the cicadas sawing away in the branches above. And even as he gazed, it seemed the head's little bronze cicadas were vibrating and sawing away as well; not only that but doing it especially for him. He began a shaking of his own head in case it was all delusion.

"Quit that! Feel the weight." Drift was lifting the cicada bust towards him to hold. Chipman shrank back. "Ah, it's alive!"

"I'm already putting your name on this baby. And that's just for starters."

Chipman recovered. The bronze was a lifeless artefact after all. But even so, the collector in him would not be denied. He found himself drawn powerfully to that exquisite little bronze, but even as he was, ruinous headlines in the *Sydney Morning Herald* flashed through his mind. He couldn't possibly. The ignominy. "I'm not the adventurous type, Drift. I'm a law abiding citizen, a humble public servant. And intend to stay that way."

"Yeah, right! Low paid civic servitude. If you could only see your face. You're into it. Hey, rise up, buddy. I'll pay you by the hour as well. Once I get my quota of snakes, load up the Bronzes, we're outta here. The way things are going in Bomzawe, the sooner the better."

A conversation with Cerisia came back into Chipman's head, voice and all, as though she had time-travelled and phenomenally, was right there with them.

"No doubt Drift has gloated about him running out of my club. Guilty as only a draft dodger could be about it. As if I could give a twiddly. Although I won't deny it would help right now if he squired up with the lolly. I'm not racist but a septic tank Yank is a septic tank twank. Don't get me wrong, Drift has his qualities and I adore Toffee. He named the first snake he caught here in honour of me. Charming, but it doesn't change the fact he's a skinflint and a deviant who doesn't honour his debts. If you are thinking of building those cages for him, you have been warned. He didn't tell you who's bankrolling this snake catching stupidity, I'll be bound. He's too embarrassed to admit it. My father. Nigel Twitchley. Lord Wittering. Ironic isn't it. The senile beast cuts me off for no good reason and gives a lowbrow twit like Drift a fat deal. And I was the one who introduced them. Daddy knows I hate his brainless animal park idea. I'm not exactly a vegetarian, but I can't stand to see creatures in cages. Unless they're destined for dinner that is...."

"You OK," Drift was giving Chipman's shoulder a shake.

"If you're caught you'll bring disgrace on Wittering."

"Ha! Cerisia told you about old Nigel and me, did she? I don't care, he's a man who can sure look after himself. He sits in the House of Lords. He's got immunity from everything. But there's no way I'm going to get caught. Me?"

Drift clasped Chipman's forearms with both hands. "You're going to listen to this whether you like it or not. You heard Sir Henry tell about Blossom trying to kill the Liberator?"

Chipman nodded.

"Well, I got the full story from Qaddo. The night before Ulysses fled to Togo, she sent one of her guys up the river to kill Oratorio. She finally had the chance to get her revenge on him for disappearing her Dad. The guy did shoot him, twice, in the back and left him for dead but there were the Bronzes, all around ready to be packed up and taken to Haiti. A simple copra cutter, greed got the better of him. Forced the servants to load up his pirogue. Downriver and up to the castle with them. Not easy as you must know, didn't tell Blossom. After stashing them he fell down those steep steps and broke his neck. I don't know what Qaddo was doing out there at that time of night, but he found the guy at the foot of the steps, still alive. Before he died, he confessed to Qaddo what he had done and where he had hidden the Bronzes. First thing Qaddo did was carry the dead man and dump him outside Blossom's. By the bowser. Later he took a look at the Bronzes but did not touch them. He knew they carried a long time curse. Unbelievable to me that he just let them rot away in that trench. He's let me use the shed but says they will bring me bad luck. I don't think he cares that they are worth a lot of money."

"How badly was the Liberator hurt?"

"Pretty bad, but there was a medical team stationed at the palace because of his old mum. They fixed him up enough to travel, I guess. Qaddo was a bit vague about all that."

In that instance, they heard voices coming from the trail. African, in spirited discussion. The voices grew closer. Soon they had diverged into the marijuana plantation itself.

"Shit a brick! It's Yaw. He must have been at his farm further up." Drift was throwing the Bronzes and the packaging back. He pulled the shed door to. There was a dull clank. No time to do the padlock.

"Ah. Mr Drift. Mr Smith." Ntank, in singlet and Bombay bloomers, emerged and came to a stop no more than a few yards away. He gave his saw-toothed grin, gazed about greedily. "So this is Mr Qaddo's garden I hear about. A power drummer, the long tall Mr Qaddo. He muscled like me, but he stoop. It many years since I see him." Behind Ntank was Yaw, peering round a clump of plants, and further back was the old monkey hunter, with his musket and sack. Drift had drawn his revolver from his waist band, and Ntank's eyes took it in. He commented on how much better

Qaddo's crop looked than anyone else's and approached. "Is that Mr Qaddo's shed he use to dry? I think I will have some smoke."

"He hasn't started the cut yet," said Drift. "Pick some green"

Ntank keep coming. "The cut it well started, Mr Drift." He had a soft and sibilant voice, one at odds with his appearance.

Drift smacked at several large ants, big as bulljoes, that were crawling up through the hairs on his leg. "Look at the size of these things" He held out his palm to Chipman and Ntank for inspection. There was a searing smell.

"The green it big nuisance. Let me by."

Drift ever so slightly shifted the angle of his revolver.

Ntank paused, his barrelled nostrils dilated hugely. "Ah, this aroma." Ntank paused a couple of yards from the shed, moved back down the rows. "Maybe I take the green." Ntank found some maturing heads, broke off half a dozen of the best and brightest, deliberately taking his time.

"You tell Mr Qaddo I pay for these some time soon. You make a very excellent guard man for him. I compliment you." Ntank's glare was combative. He raised an arm in farewell and went on his way. Yaw and the monkey hunter followed.

"There's no reason he would suspect. None! Why would he? Like everyone else, he thinks the Bronzes went to Haiti." Drift was fizzing, distraught, waving the revolver around. "Chipman, answer me! What's the matter with you?"

The answer was that as the tensions of the encounter with Ntank drained away, the deeper aspects of the Siegfriediana were getting to Chipman again. Perhaps it was the Booster kicking in. "Sex," he said aloud, with a significance that must have indicated that somehow, in all his life to that point, he had scarcely ever managed to use the word. He could not take his eyes off Drift, the lithe bare torso, that outline in his threadbare Bermudas. "How marvellous that you are not like my colleagues back at the Department," he said, his voice barely more than a burble.

Drift tucked away his gun. "Excuse me, I never thought to use it. Shit, how was I to know Ntank was friends with Yaw. Fuck this acid or whatever it is. Making me paranoid."

Those colleagues, principally Wally of course, that Chipman had compulsively and serially fallen in love with over the years, married to women, all certifiably heterosexual (whether they were or not), had children and were unavailable. Unavailability had been the entire point.

Chipman's sublimated sexual behaviour had become an homage to happier days and his filial love for Alfie, but yes, Starry was right. Celibacy had driven him to perversity, to the nadirs of Peeping Tom and alcoholism, at least something akin to a nervous breakdown. Now, layers of denial and deceit were peeling away with psychedelised rapidity. What an absurdity self-inflicted disease was! He now slammed the door on the disgust with himself he had been living with for so long. Slammed the door on shame. "My goodness!" he exclaimed, as with the door closing he found himself on a slide and a glide along a Ganges, riverside temples floating by in a panoplied array. He was lying back, cushioned in luxury on a gilded bier, as it skimmed the water, skimming, skimming… Thoughts took form – Starry's potion means I am going to fall in love with the first person I see when I open them. Like Titania in *A Midsummer Night's Dream*. Chipman felt himself swooning into a delight that it would be Drift, a man who, by his own admission, was not entirely straight. There would be a niche into which he would fit. Starry would definitely approve. Drift could even be the 'love of your life', that phrase celebrated in song and legend, repeated often by Starry. A man to marry. A man to die for. A man who would die for Chipman. It was most unlikely Toffee was going to survive. In any case, she had fallen in love with a monkey. This stoned herpetologist would be free, he would be mine. We would be as one…

"Well, what do you say, Chipman?" came Drift's voice. Chipman opened his eyes. Drift's face was close. He could smell his cannabis breath, his luxuriant moustache, his skin, all so impregnated with the stuff. There was a slick of sweat and oil on his pleasing proboscis, an attractive insect grotesquery to his features. Chipman felt their bodies were about to merge. The singing of cicadas was growing louder and louder, a Mormon Tabernacle Choir of supernality. His mouth was open, tongue ready, milliseconds away from a kiss, from being bent back in a pair of manly arms, from consummation. "Drift, tell me about that time of yours with Stan. Do it to me."

But a gawky grin had spread across Drift's face and he was drawing away. He gestured and Chipman looked down at himself. Engorged, the cap a flower of purple fit to burst, the shaft alive and exhibiting a serpentine sinuosity even more extravagantly than it had behaved earlier, on the island.

"See, the rejuvenation juju's sending it into overdrive." Drift gave the penis a dismissive bat with the back of his fingers. "You gotta be with me now."

Chipman scarcely heard Drift. He had already moved on, spreading his arms wide and making slow and triumphant rotations. His balance was perfection itself. The Tabernacle cicadas were chorusing deep inside his head. Not since his boyhood days with Tibor Radovan had he felt so liberated, so happy.

"Well, tango on, dude. No shorts, no shoes, nothing."

"I don't need anything like that anymore."

"You say that now, but what about tomorrow."

"Or tomorrow either."

"You're double dosed." Drift turned the key in the padlock. "You're out there, buddy. That fucking Makeover is not my idea of a party, but I'm escorting you back to the island. Otherwise that hard-on will be bitten off by a hungry crocodile."

"Yes. Otherwise you might go and interrupt Toffee's honeymoon day with Lobelia."

Drift gave a rueful laugh. "I guess we've got a marriage of convenience going here."

As they walked along the jungle aisle, with Drift's loving arm around Chipman's bare shoulders, the singing in his head swelled to a crescendo. A soft implosion and there came a blissful vision – he was strolling hand in hand with Tibor after raiding Granddad Duffy's apple orchard on the slopes above the family home on Warraba Road. They were both enthralled by the joyful noise from the cicada participants in that grandest of all efflorescences. Tibor put one in his mouth and it still kept making its noise. Tibor was so excited he crunched down, swallowed it. Chipman screamed at him with both distaste and excitement.

"Chipman, I'll do it for you." Tibor said, his eyes shining.

"Listen!" Ever the mimic, he opened his mouth and forced out a strange high-pitched rattling. "They make it with their legs but I can make it like this. I'm a cicada." Yes, he sounded like a cicada. Chipman tried to do for Tibor in return, but failed. "It's a knack," Tibor said, and Chipman loved him all the more for his having the ability. They held each other tight. Distaste was replaced by desire. He nuzzled and smelled Tibor's unwashed neck while his friend made that shrilling vibration for him again and again.

The cicadas. Wherever they went those summer holidays, the whole district was the same; billions of the creatures, congregating the eucalypts, the angophoras, the golden wattles and she-oaks, the dry coastal banksia scrub, delivering a chorale that rolled so gloriously, irrepressibly and maddeningly on, all season long, that it was the sound of Australia itself, and Tibor and Chipman, running together, were that glorious sound.

EIGHTEEN: *O that my keel would break!*
O that I would go to the sea

Hours had gone by. Never before had the water looked so blue, the rocks so glossy, the rust of the *Accra Queen* so – rusty.

In the early afternoon, Starry had signalled the fishermen. The inhospitable island had been abandoned, with the party regrouping on the far beach. There were two striped canvas canopies, red and white, looking splendid in the late afternoon light. A wisp of smoke came from a fire, and a knot of village children were a short way off, watching. As they drew nearer, Chipman began to laugh. Gingery, metal grey seals. On Boxing Day one year, Matilda and Alfie had taken their children to see a colony of them on Montague Island, off Narooma on the south coast; blurting and blarping, they were heaped together, sliding awkwardly over each other, or sleeping in furry body piles.

Starry set up a welcome chant.

"You say a word about the Bronzes I'll kill you," said Drift, squeezing the back of Chipman's neck until he cried out.

His ecstatic state had subsided. "I'm sorry I missed the Full Moon Makeover, Starry."

"We're still Making Over." Starry was lying back between Cerisia's thighs. "And so are you. We can make up for lost time right now." Starry reached up from where they lay on a cotton bedspread, and Chipman didn't have to be coerced. This fleshy, tactile world was where he wanted to be. He was at one with Starry's doglike pleasure in body parts, odours and emanations, at one with Cerisia's tongue when she put it in his mouth, at one with her legs, soft and cellulited, when she wrapped them round his waist.

He told everyone about Fangga the Fetisheur, about Ntank pilfering massive Qaddo's crop, about his wonderful Drift fantasies, how Cerisia had paid a magical visitation, told how he had gone back in time, the thrilling crescendos of noise, about Tibor's mimicking, told about everything; everything except the Bronzes.

"We had all that here – and more!" Starry swept a hand around the group, laying claim to their experiences as well as his own. "If two can connect, how about twenty? One mind, Chipman, one heart. Imagine a whole people. A world. The power. No religions, a planet utopia, a better, more intelligent, more compassionate humanity emerging!"

"I was seeing it more in terms of the love of my life. A love that never sleeps, Starry. Like you always say." Chipman gazed into his eyes as if for the very first time, eyes that were blazing like black opals, eyes filled with a knowingness, with much to teach, one of them bruised and half-closed nevertheless. All that despite the fact that according to Floralee, he had some student peccadillos way back in his past in Australia. "How marvellous to be melded with another person. Emotionally. Physically."

"Well, thank you, Chipman. Finally."

"I mean Drift."

Starry frowned then gave a grunt in the direction of Drift who was charging for the water. "You've become a fool for a moustache and a Roman nose? What about your little crush on Zach? Has the Siegfriediana taught you nothing at all?"

"This *Sound of Music* is totally organic," said Floralee, snuggling up. "Up there with the Byron gold tops. It feels like forever when you're on it, so why can't it be forever forever?"

"One day, Floralee," said Starry, "with the help of the Adolf Siegfrieds of this world, we will be able to choose not to come back, we will dispense with this everyday reality altogether, body and consciousness both."

"Are you trying to make sense out of things?" Lotus was shimmying in front of them, her lovely, lilac scented, copper toned bosom bobbling like a blancmange. She rattled her maracas, one in each of Chipman's ears, the noise blending effortlessly with the homophonic choir already resident in his head. "Let's all be Mary Kingsley, our West African heroine."

"We don't make sense," said Starry, "but on this stuff, at least we're original. Chipman here, says he has been singing like a cicada."

From a coconut, Lotus poured milk intended for Chipman's mouth but it went all over his curls. Qojo, who had come by with sweet green-skinned mandarins and other snacks, held a pineapple upright on his left palm and with swift strokes of his cutlass, separated it into twelve even sections. It was beyond mere expertise. Floralee Bush and Chipman applauded. Qojo began on another.

Floralee looked like an apple, long ripened and shrivelled on the ground. Red lips, russet cheeks and a frieze of freckles on her bony shoulders. Her hair was the colour of pink champagne, and held in place by a wide mauve ribbon. "Always beaut to run into another Aussie," she said in her broad, cracked Australian twang. "I'm disappointed with Starry. He's let that high-faluting English feedbag he married rub his accent out." She held her cheek against Chipman's, licked his hair and then an ear. Her granny glasses were hanging between her breasts from a beaded string. "I'm hot to trot, kid, but don't worry. I can be a faghag, but I'm no rapist." A liverspotted hand was held to Chipman's chest and he tickled it.

Floralee's confidences continued as they sat eating Qojo's succulent pineapple. "I know all about the cicadas. We had a bumper year in Canberra, about 1946 I think. Back then I was what they called a political wife. I was going to poison the slug, but unfortunately Senator Bush karked it before I could stir in the weedkiller. Suddenly my boring bridge and Mt Buffalo ski lodge days were over. I joined Sgt. Pepper's Lonely Hearts' Club Band and started living by my wits. I moved in with my eldest son who has a house in the hills above Byron. Made a name for myself in the town as a pompon dancer with the *Totem Sutra Theatre*. Changed my name. Never did like Enid." She giggled nymphettishly. "Now I'm a tough hippie sheila with a washboard stomach, nipple rings, wrinkles and the pharmacology bug."

It took a while for Chipman to notice what had happened to Zach. He had been immobilised, his ankles and wrists tightly wrapped with a couple of discarded sarongs. Starry's work.

"Floralee, Chipman, get these off me," the would-be Peace Corps worker said grumpily. "While he's not looking." Starry was busy with Cerisia, snuffling in the hennaed thickets of her armpits and her 'curly triangle of pleasure' as he was calling it, like one of the pigs that rooted in the sand each day near the village.

"This bloke tried to re-enter the food chain," said Floralee. "We mounted a rescue party."

"It's not like that." Zach's head was down, but his voice was a defiant shout.

"Get over it, kid. Life is a one-time-only opportunity. At the rate you're going, you're gonna miss it." Floralee had her glasses back on, was deftly loosening knots. "Starry was the one who noticed what Zach was up to. He ran across the island, jumped into the surf on that south side. Got sucked out to Kingdom Come. Had definitely gone down for the last time by the time we reached him. I pumped him out on my surfboard. Said he wasn't coming back if it was the last place on earth. The stupid drongo rolled off the board and started swimming again. But the fishermen were there by then. Had to knock him about a bit. Took all of us to get him back in. Starry organised a binding ceremony, to lighten things up. It was bloody hilarious. Except for Zach, it seems. He's one cuckoo kid."

"Oh, Zach." Chipman's undoubted desires that afternoon had been directed entirely at Drift. It came as a shock to realise this. A mighty, emotional surge of tenderness for Zach washed through him. There came a need to look after the man, to care for his welfare. He rested a hand on his forehead, smoothed a throbbing in his temple. He had never felt more sane, never felt such an affinity. "Mad Zach. It's right that you were saved from yourself. I'm relieved no end."

"Our Makeover turns out to be the same day as the fifteenth anniversary of Zoe's drowning," said Lotus. "How were we to know? So now we're going to cure him with granma Floralee's pygmy dance."

"Whoopee! When I was in the Ituri with the Bambuti pygmies I joined in their communal rituals. After the calabash has gone by a few times, the men dance shoulder to shoulder forming a circle around the drummers with the women in another circle outside. Each man has a one tone nose flute and together they lower their heads and..."

"Hey, that's what I call group grope," Lotus said, with her little giggle, interrupting Floralee. "Starry's inspired. He's already calling it *The Pygmy Head Rushes*."

"Reckon it'll be bloody aye for your Easter Carnival. My contribution."

"Okay for the tiny pygmies," growled Zach, shaking himself back into life. He gave his ankles a rub, put on his cowboy hat, and sat close to Chipman. "Zoe," he demanded, giving Chipman's nose an affectionate tweak, "what you do with our smokes?"

"Zoe?" Chipman had completely forgotten who Zoe was. Zach's naked thigh pressed into his. Chipman had had a hard-on fit to bursting for some time but he did not associate it with Zach at whom he kept gazing, like the brother he had never had.

That sun and drug-drenched day, he scarcely noticed his own engorgement. It was just something there, a natural part of him that seemed to make him popular with the previously aloof Thierry and Jean-Claude. He didn't mind at all that Veronique and some of the other girls, like Zach's laughing Fiona and Heather, played with it as well.

Starry drew Chipman aside, suggesting they walk to the wreck of the *Accra Queen*. As the guru strolled with his arm around Chipman's shoulders, he began questioning him closely about his daring exploits, particularly the aural ecstasy he had experienced when he went back to the long hot cicada days of his Tibor summer, but Chipman, no longer interested, found he had turned into an inquisitor himself. "Why did you leave Australia on a forged passport?"

Starry removed his arm and managed a carefree laugh. "O.K. I'm on the run. As I've told you before, we're all fugitives here. That's a reason for you to stay, not desert."

"Floralee was pretty tight-lipped about you."

"There's nothing to tell. A few student political stunts. No Rum Rebellion, no Eureka Stockade. No cutting of any Harbour Bridge ribbon. Just the joy of being young and alive. Not that you appreciate that. Calcified in – was it Bridge Street you asserted - with Wally? Come on, Chipman, you don't have to line up with the wowsers any more. You had your silly voyeur period. You've moved on, getting a second chance.

"Yes, I've moved on. And I'm going back."

"Going back to the Office of the Clerk of the Peace, my dear Mr Chipman?" Starry had his snaggle tooth grin going. "The Attorney General's Department?"

Chipman stopped dead. Zach had been right. Starry had gone into his wardrobe, into his papers. "Sorry about that. I found Tlula scary at first. Lawless. The lie made me feel safer. I'm not much of a liar."

"It's nothing. Back then I was drunk and out of my mind most of the time. It was stifling in those days. Shocking the shit out of the buggers was the only way to feel alive. I broke a few taboos! Any student worth his salt was doing the same."

"All right, you've gone on enough." Chipman paused, wanting to pay him back for uncovering his little white lie, about typifying his 'voyeur period' as silly. "Just one thing worries me, Starry. What was your name before Floralee's passport turned you into Salvatore Sanguini?"

"I was glad to get rid of it. A totally boring moniker. Look me up in Debrett." Starry's grin made a reappearance. "But seriously, Barry Wilson was my name. Barry Howard Wilson, from Dover Heights, born fourteenth September 1936. Almost the same day as Salvatore Sanguini. Now are you happy?"

"I'll have to check it out, but it doesn't ring any bells. I suppose that's good."

"Okay, let's shake on that." They shook hands and Chipman smiled at the gesture which seemed to have acquired an old-fashioned quality to it on this kissing-and-hugging, transformative day. Musing on the changes that still seemed to be taking place, Chipman realised he was having trouble remembering he was leaving all this behind in the morning. And really, his bonding for life and love on the hillside with Drift was beginning to seem somewhat ludicrous, his concern over Zach, however deep, completely pointless.

"You've got me hopelessly and happily stoned on something or other, Starry, it's not like me to forgive easily, but I forgive you for having Lotus dose me." He could not stop grinning back at Starry's snaggle tooth. Good humour had come as part of Professor Siegfried's sound of music package.

"...and now that Starry Sanguini is about to become an even more celebrated performer on the world stage, I remind you once more of my motto; never look back. Educate the populace, raise their consciousness. Something which even Wally Whitbread, awaiting news from you, would approve of."

"All very vague, Starry. Why did you start calling yourself 'doctor'? Even Lotus doesn't take your title seriously."

"Neither do I. But, as I have said before, my months in Professor Siegfried's clinic were more than the equivalent of any bloody academic degree, more than years of training in some over-funded educational institution. It's a young man's duty to throw it all away. The university system is for the toilers and the also-rans. The brave joyfully grab whatever comes. *Brightness falls from the air...'* John Paine wrote that. I would have written it if he hadn't beaten me to it."

They reached the *Accra Queen*, turned and began to walk back.

"Cerisia and I have not been able to persuade you to stay, Chipman. But who knows. Maybe my path will take me back to Sydney one day. You have indicated that Australia is emerging from the past, joining the rest of the world."

"Lotus said you had a fight with Cerisia."

"Love bites, Chipman, we are on our honeymoon."

Chipman allowed an arm to go around Starry's bare back. Nagging feelings about the man had not evaporated, but really, he was past caring. He would be gone by the morning, leaving forever this backwater, this Leisure Beach, all this nonsense and madness. By tomorrow evening he would be in the real world, ensconced in Okidoki with William Oates, ringing Wally Whitbread with reassuring news about his new well-being, the success of his boss's bold plan. His departmental credit would be once more sky high. His future career secure. And he would certainly run that name Barry Howard Wilson past Wally at the same time.

Yes, this was his farewell, Starry had dedicated it to his welfare and he was determined to keep enjoying the freedoms and delights the Siegfried concoctions had granted him. He was still a lawyer, perhaps old-fashioned, like that handshake he had just shared with Starry, but he congratulated himself on managing, throughout a whole day, to go with Starry's 'be here now.'

Rock tribal it was. Tambourines and maracas were shaken. The bammity bam bam of the timbales and conga drums were an endless rhythmic, even symphonic loop. Food was consumed, the Parisian junkies shot up their smack; Cerisia was a marshmallow, overweight but shapely and perfectly toasted, "old money" as Starry so admiringly called her, plopping around with a video recorder. Many hands helped Oslo Lunch exhume from the hole in the sand in which he had spent the previous hours. Lotus helped him release his hair from the crocheted octopus sac. Tied high and back in a tentacled top knot, the bleached Rastafarian locks hung down stiffly like a display of loofas in a chemist shop. Chipman found it a wildly attractive feature.

"I abthorb the thoil'th eththenth through my rootth, now I am thelethtial thun tholdier theithing the thword of thpathe and thanity."

Cerisia put Lunch to work recreating Castle Vinkenoog in wet sand. She tried to get the village children to join in, but they were not into such child play. Starry said the reason for their attendance that afternoon was a wish to study Western behaviour patterns. "We are the kids today and they are the adults."

"Zey are ze tourists," Veronique intoned, "and we are ze natives. We put zem all in a big pot and cook zem up."

Apart from Qojo, the children and teenagers around that day were girls, among them, Aqosua, Qojo's younger sister. She brought ripe fruit every morning for Toffee's little Lobelia. Cerisia, having no success with the sandcastle, organised a workshop and was soon answering questions on menstrual and other gynaecological matters of importance to them. Veronique displayed the gold rings inserted into her labia majora. Inspection and much serious discussion ensued. "Girls, zere is beaucoup need to 'ang on to – 'ow you say – ze pretty clitoris. I 'ave 'eard zat 'ere in northern Bomzawe where ze animist and ze Islam ees..."

Despite Chipman's state of expanded awareness, and his joy at the on-going collapse of many of the boundaries he had been brought up with, certainly those imposed on him by Reverend Melody Motherwell, he soon realised he had less interest in vulvas than in the opium suppositories that handsome, if junked-out Jean-Claude, Thierry's equally handsome, if pierced, partner had brought to share. It was Starry who submitted to the first ritual insertion. He lifted his legs in the air and Jean-Claude with the aid of some vaseline ("Watch that sand!") shoved one into Starry's rectum. Jean-Claude or Starry performed the same service for everyone who wanted to indulge, Chipman included. Much jokery ensued. He found himself giggling uncontrollably.

"How much bloody pleasure can the nervous system stand?" shrieked Floralee as she danced by, scrawny body gyrating, knobbly knees quivering.

"Let'th do tantric, my girly," cried Oslo Lunch. "Let'th do yab yam in my thand hole."

"Bugger that spiritual shit." Floralee flung her tambourine high and making a leap, wrapped her sinewy legs around his waist. "Lunch, maate, let's do dinner!" Floralee hauled Lunch up by his equipment into the giant banyan tree and he did it to her up against the main trunk while he balanced on a lateral.

"Yohimbine, your name is fuck!" cried Floralee. She clung to Lunch and he swung the two of them on the knotted rope to another branch. She sang snatches from *Nature Boy*. *...the greatest thing you will ever learn is just to love and be loved in return...*

"Oh, Floralee," Chipman cried, "those are the most beautiful words in the whole wide world." That was the last sentence he was able to utter for some considerable time.

Chipman no longer had any idea where he was. He could hear only voices.

"Is Chipman OK?" he heard Lotus ask. "Starry, I saw you sneak them up his asshole. Adolf said never to follow a red and black capsule with a blue and grey."

"As a neuropsychologist, Professor Siegfried knows of course about quality and quantity control, Lotus, but he's wrong about mix and match. That grey and blue was one of his psilocybic Site Specifics, as accurate as the surgeon's scalpel. The atrophies of the left hand brain will be overcome, and the untapped creative potential in Chipman will be tapped."

"Insectiwecti heaven for the little bastard." Cerisia's voice.

"He doesn't look well."

"Tough nuts to crack sometimes need the Hammer of God, sister Lotus," said Starry.

Chipman lay helpless, cooking in the afternoon sun. To his eyes, Starry, basting him with coconut oil, was a cordon bleu chef, a Boddhisatva grease ball, ballooning in the sky above him. "You're peaking, Chipman. We're taking you out of the frying pan, and dropping you into the fire."

Everyone gathered round. Cerisia had great fun disconnecting his thinking processes, what was left of them. He squirmed, he experienced for the first time Starry's much touted Total Collapse, and then like Alice down the rabbit hole, he went backtracking in time, revisiting on the way every single one of the life traumas he had explored, albeit cursorily, albeit drunkenly, in the fast track Primal Scream Plus sessions at Tlula Leisure Beach: of the night grabbed outside Wally Whitbread's window in his balaclava, the hair-raising escape to his Volkswagen around the corner; a detailed reliving of the sexual incident in the tent with Alfie. It was all a falling that bottomed out into the lonely, barren plain of his lustful but sexless years in the thrall of Reverend Motherwell. He felt a scouring, a slowing in momentum, a dying that never came. Instead, a releasing, a preparation for the future, which, as Starry rightly guessed had already been presaged on the hillside with Drift. The cicada sirens were now luring Chipman to his destiny. He was lulled by the primeval clangour of their song, afloat in it, imbibing its warm amniotic intimacy.

He opened his eyes, found faces close above him. A rich odour filled the air, familiar but unidentifiable.

"Good boy," came a victorious cry from Starry.

"You just took a dump, kid." Floralee's voice. "Granma spank!"

The sun was approaching the headland at the western end of the beach. Castle Vinkenoog and tall kapok trees stood out in silhouetted beauty. He gazed out over the Gulf of Guinea, where the satellite moon had risen just for him, full and pale in the still daylit sky. He lay there absorbed in his infantile grace, filled with feelings of great and unconditional love. He tried to express these feelings in words, but no words came. Instead he expelled a shrill and vibrant humming.

"For fuck's sake, Starry," Drift shouted. "It's a Niggling Nancy disaster all over again."

"On the contrary, mission accomplished," was Starry's response.

"Nothing a good throttle won't fix," Cerisia snarled, getting her hands around Chipman's neck.

"Darling, darling!!! Stop!"

She settled for a backhanded flip across Chipman's mouth. "That shut him up."

Ritually, they smeared him with a mixture of ground nut oil and all the other sacred exudations expelled from his body in the course of his crisis – or whatever it was. His re-birthing. After being rolled about in the sand like a piece of dough, he was tossed boneless and rubbery into the sea. Then he was carried aloft to the cistern where he had had his encounter with Fangga the Fetish Priest another lifetime before, and scrubbed with a detergent. Finally he was doused with patchouli oil, and left in a nappy to kick and gurgle and burp coconut milk bubbles to his heart's content. And when the ecstasy cup flowed over, would come again that shrilling trill.

"You've left the infernal regions, Chipman," Starry sang. "Let your divine comedy begin."

Qojo was shouting urgently at the village children, driving them into the grove. Aqosua got a whack with his stick. "Everyone smoked too much proper," he piped. "Mr Kmango and Chief Akwa, dey come." In the distance, the Silver Cloud was slowly proceeding towards them along the beach by the water's edge.

"Starry, if he sees us like this," cried Lotus, "the Chakra Dancers will get shitcanned long before Easter."

"I might already be in big, big trouble," muttered Drift. "Fucking Ntank's on to me. I'll kill him."

Chipman didn't care whether the Dancers got shitcanned or Drift got busted. He lay back, looking intensely into the eyes of Stan Francisco. There was a serenity there, a depth and a warmth. How could he have seen only vacancy before? "Hello dear Stan," he attempted to say but instead out again came that chirring hum.

"Here you go, bro." Stan, the former long distance teenage truck driver, embraced him, handed over a rattle, put his own pacifier in Chipman's mouth. Yes, he had broken on through to the other side, as the some-time poet sang, inter-species communication was taking place. Stan rested his hands, his feet, and then his opiated anus on the infant's throbbing forehead, in a complex set of blessings.

It was strange how all the sounds seemed to float bodiless, somewhere in the ether. It took him a while to pin the voices to their source. It was Starry of course who was saying, "Cerisia's fabulous cunt is an artwork. More beautiful than his Rolls Royce. Sir Henry is about to appreciate our theatrical genius, will understand the revolutionary nature of our show."

It was low tide. The burgundy convertible was now close, a splendid sight on the wide glistening belt of firm sand at the water's edge, the islet with its peak, and the ultramarine depths of the Gulf beyond. Sir Henry sat in panana hat and white suit, Chief Akwa beside him in a sky blue robe stamped with symbols of local significance. Ntank, shirtless but wearing his chauffeur's cap, was, to Chipman's new eyes, even more his usual shark-toothed, bare armpitted, sexy self.

By the time that the Rolls, mirrored in the glistening sand of the still retreating water, was level, the *Eighth Chakra Evolutionary Dancers* were in a semi-circle facing the sea, all at their drums and gongs. Jean-Claude played a clarinet. Stan, in tarboosh, tie-dyed jock-strap and silk-flowered waistcoat (Lotus's regular outfit for him), danced in front, blowing his latest musical gizmo, the ghaita, a strident Moroccan flute. Chipman whirled mindlessly in his nappy, sucking Stan's dummy, arms outstretched, one palm to the sky, one to the sand, attempting the dervish ritual that Starry and Cerisia had learned from the Gnaoua dancers in Goulimine. It was an exercise Starry considered essential for restoration of the balance, and the nearest Chipman got to ballet at Tlula. As he slowly spun around, discovering for the first time the mantric rhythms of Stan's music, hitherto hidden, there came from his mouth, that wordless, laryngeal Tibor Radovan inspired vibrato.

The Rolls slowed to a crawl, no more than twenty yards distant. Sir Henry put away a telescope and made whirling movements with his hands in response to the performances. Chief Akwa stared morosely ahead. Partially hidden behind the drummers, Starry and Cerisia were defiantly fucking. They were making an inordinate amount of noise. The sand shook under their tonnage. At the last minute, noticing Sir Henry's telescope focussing again, Lotus panicked, and collapsed the central canopy over them. The Rolls never came to a full stop. It continued past, a tyre going over the cotton blanket on which Chipman had spilled his stomach and emptied his bowels, and glided to the rocks which marked the end of the beach. Sir Henry and Chief Akwa debouched and walked to the wreck of the *Accra Queen*, possible at low tide. They seemed to confer briefly before disappearing into the trees which grew in serried rows all over the lower slopes of the headland. Sir Henry Kmango was making a late afternoon inspection of his oil palm plantation.

NINETEEN: *The missionary and other positions*

The portcullis of the equatorial night came down. The stars and moon shone benignly over a silvered, almost silent sea, as a gradual move back towards the Hornbill Palace began. Constellations of fireflies whirled and wheeled, their looping flights sometimes having them crash into the wet sand. "Spittle of the gods, the Mayans called them," said Floralee who had harvested and ingested wild peyote in Mexico. Bip bip! Bip bip! went their fallen electric lights in some antique code.

The Eighth Chakrans dashed in and out of the waves of the on-coming tide. The water was full of phosphorescent algae. It was like playing in surges of glitter, with electric sparks exploding away from their fingers in pyroquatic display.

Chipman found himself the subject of attentions from Lotus. "Hey, it's way cool you're now one of us!" She put her arms around him in the water, gave a glutinous kiss. "You have a free ticket to Lotusland any time," she giggled. "Stanford," she yelled the next second, "I'm over here." She apologised. "Stan gets loopy if he can't see me."

Starry's voice came from the shore, reminding them of the commitment to stay the distance. They gathered around him for a final ceremony which consisted of a lot of more or less organised shuffling around in the moonlight, a communal rite designed to have every participant touch with a hand, without fear or favour, every part of the body, emphasising the forehead, the heart and genitals, of every other participant. Chipman was officially given the name Chippo Cherrynose. After his very favourite Tibor cicada, and virtually identical to those thronging the trees at Tlula. He was ineffably moved. Starry asked him if he would say a few words about how he was feeling but words again refused to come. Instead that sound of utter bliss and contentment manifested. As the lovely 'mmmmm' streamed out, he closed his eyes and experienced a dreamy vision of Tibor, Alfie and himself on a summer's day swimming in the pools along Kangaroo Creek in the Royal National Park. He could not help but feel they were both there inside him, chorusing that sound with him, making love.

"Dawn tomorrow, we will have your Confirmation Ceremony," said Starry, and taking a cue from Cerisia, he unceremoniously shut him up with, not the throttle, but the backhander across the mouth

"I'm dragging her out of monkey world whether she's ready or not," said Drift who had taken charge, even possession, of Chippo.

The bungalow area was crowded with unfamiliar vehicles, one of which was a large white bus labelled *FIRST BAPTIST CHURCH OF AMERICA*.

It was a surprise to find Sir Henry Kmango standing under the dim verandah light outside Drift's isolated bungalow. The rafters above were thick with gecko lizards, alert to the capture of fluttering moths and other unwary insects. Ntank was nearby, leaning on Drift's Range Rover.

The bungalow door was wide open. Affecting unconcern, Drift untied his sea-soaked ribbon, shook out his bedraggled hair. Maintaining his suavity, Sir Henry led Drift inside. Chippo meekly followed. Drift's not insubstantial supply of buds from Qaddo's crop had been chewed and spat out. The walls were smeared with the pap as if someone had made a crude attempt at graffiti. The tape from Drift's cassettes, his Allman Brothers and Janis Joplin compilations, his Pink Floyd, were all torn and tangled. His not necessarily cherished copies of *Penthouse*, *Screw* and *Suck* were ripped and scattered. The standard lamp lay athwart the queen size and bloody paw prints patterned the pillows. Two mambas were coiling around furiously in another poorly constructed cage.

With a crocodile-skinned shoe, Sir Henry delicately pushed aside shards of glass fallen from one of the louvered windows.

"Lobelia's gone loco," said Drift, sniffing at some of the chewed marijuana. "Monkeys hate this stuff." Suddenly he remembered

Toffee, looked around. "Hey, where is she?" Drift rushed for the door. Ntank, an obsidian mass, blocked his path.

"We were sauntering under the moon, drinking in the musky perfumes of the Angel's Trumpets, dear Ulysses favourite flower I don't mind telling you, when we heard unwelcome noises." Sir Henry smoothed the back of his pomaded head with both hands, smelled his palms. "There was the sound of our sad beauty crying for help, and glass shattering. The monkey came leaping through a broken window and headed in the direction of the bar. The door was flung open and Miss Toffee dashed past, hotfoot in pursuit, as one says. As usual, rather scantily clad."

Ntank snickered at this. His boss lit a Benson & Hedges, swept a hand accusingly around the devastation. "I adamantly urge you to get rid of that monkey."

"Good idea. Sorry about this, Kmango. I'll throw any dope left into the mangroves."

"Sir Henry, if you please. There is no need to be so drastic. Just smoke it discreetly. Like they do in Blossom's. I have no wish to start up any ganja wars." Sir Henry made his way to the door. "I want you out of this bungalow immediately. Attah will find you a room in the back wing with your friend Mr Chipman here and Mr Shaler. We will discuss the matter of reparations in due course." He cast a glance at the agitated mambas. "Please concentrate on eliminating the snakes for me, would you, my dear Mr Drift. And speedily." He paused. "And as I said before, we can discuss the future of Mr Fangga anytime you are so inclined."

"Dig! They have no idea I've got the Bronzes. I'm going ahead with the false floors. So good they will be invisibo. Are you with me this time round? The cages." Drift snapped his fingers in Chippo's face. "Hey! Get with the program!"

He sat down to pack a chillum. "That fucking monkey got at my hash brownies stash too. I brought them all the way from London." He wrapped the chillum in a piece of rag, held it to his cheek, got it going with his Zippo lighter, sucked hard. The room filled with pungent smoke. Coughing and gasping, he fell comatose to the bed. Chippo wandered outside, sat down on the verandah edge and drank in the perfume of the pink and white trumpet flowers. Nearby, a horde of bats was flapping in one of the fruit trees. He listened to the creatures screeching and tinkling, smacking their lips; a continuous shower of pits and juice poured down. He remained there, entranced, until he heard Drift calling.

"You can fake those cage floors so we can squeeze in plenty of this fabulous sensimilla as well, can't you, Chipman? Chippo. That couldn't be hard. Pack it around the Bronzes. Am I being greedy here?" The whites of his eyes were pink and watery. "We're in this together from now on. Buddies, right?" He stuck out his hand and involved Chippo in a complicated set of hand clasps.

Chipman Smith had shown he had scruples when the plan had been presented earlier, but of course, it was Chippo Cherrynose now, a man who found no vice, only virtue in everything, a man yet without ethics, guile or doubt, re-wired, re-named, a nature boy yet to be nurtured, following only barely-formed instincts and desires. A prey, basically, to anything. He found himself nodding, electrified by the forceful, even abusive tone. Yes, he had become a man extremely eager to be part of Drift's outrageous scheme. The lovely mmmmm noise started. Drift put his hands over his ears.

"You've joined the fucking Aerospace Industry."

"Chirrchirrchirr!"

Drift drew him into the light, and with finger and thumb he opened Chippo's mouth. Peering in, he noted the wildly vibrating vocal cords. "Ye cats! Doesn't it hurt?"

There came a smack across Chippo's mouth, and a pouring of palm wine down his throat. "There! Have a gargle. Beats me what's going wrong, some kind of glottal malfunction, but cicadan mutation? I don't think so. You'll be talking again in the morning." He gazed intently at Chippo. "Hey, I'm not getting you into this just for me. It's for my Toffee, my monkeywunky sugar baby. We might have to carry the can for her from now on. You're the one going to keep your eyes open and your ears pricked. And your stupid mouth shut. Kapiche? Comprende?" Drift correctly took Chippo's silence for agreement. There followed an even more complex handshaking. Finally, Drift closed his eyes and held Chipman's hand to his heart. "My buddy." From the intimacy of the bonding, from the use of that emotive American word, 'buddy', Chippo experienced surge after surge of pure and honest lust.

"How about you come in on this on a more substantial basis?" As Drift shampooed and showered away the detritus of the day, he outlined some deal which Chippo scarcely heard, distracted as he was by the workings of his libido. One thing he did hear clearly was that Drift wanted to move the Bronzes away from Qaddo's shed (and from Ntank's possible interest) into the big wardrobe in Chippo's hotel room. Attah's girls would no longer be doing the cleaning. He would be saving money. Someone further along the nurturing road might have wondered, "Why my room, Drift, why not yours," but he shut his eyes, picturing the two of them amorously entwined on his bed, the Bronzes piled up around them like some Aladdin's treasure trove. Years of frustrated desires, unleashed by the Total Collapse, confirmed by Starry's final ritual on the moonlit sand, rose from molten core, seethed dementedly on his surface, for Drift and all the universe to see. And to hear – when his ecstatic pot boiled over. "Crmmmmmmm"

"I'm running short. You lend me enough to invest in Qaddo's crop, Chippo, I'll repay you with interest. Big interest. If you know what I mean. The fabulous little cicada head will be yours of course. It's your totem."

Chippo wasn't sure what a 'totem' was, but knew his head was nodding in vigorous assent.

"Hey, that's my buddy. My buddy in crime."

Chippo walked into the shower and put his arms around Drift, his cheek against his chest. "Chirr chirr chirr…"

"I'm not going to fuck you, no way. I keep that for my honey pot. But hey, this Siegfriediana shit makes me horny as a jack rabbit."

Chippo wanted them to kiss like Tibor and he used to kiss, but found his head being pushed firmly downwards. The cool water cascaded over their bodies. "Ah. That shut you up. Watch those teeth, buddy. Both hands. Give my nuts a squeeze. Great, tickle, tickle, now you've got it."

Chippo did what came naturally. Drift was no premature ejaculator but even so it was all over much too soon. Drift came in Chippo's mouth with a mighty rush ("Ah! Ah! Ah ! Coupla pints, buddy, my gift for you") and detached himself without ceremony. He turned off the shower and was shouting, "My old lady. Holy Toledo, I forgot my beautiful old lady."

Within seconds it seemed, with Drift pausing only to towel off and brush his hair, they were out of the bungalow. Hamid (or Hamou) blocked their way, his hand out.

"Piss off," snapped Drift, and then was paranoid. He signalled to Chipman, who held out a palmful of change, Drift helped himself, handed it over.

"Just in case." As they ran for the bar Drift added, "That's all you have to remember in this business. Every man has his price."

Attah Lalwani, the manager chef with the catfish profile and discoloured purple eyeballs, sat alone in the dining room, eating cold Toad in the Hole. Attah put the last of a sausage in his mouth, pushed away his plate. "Mr Drift, we are all very upset here. Tonight my dining room is good capacity for first time this season. We are serving sixteen English Classic dinners, and monkey come and jump all over. Miss Toffee she here and chase her monkey. Everything spill. Seven dessert plate broken. Three cup. I am infinitely sorry, but my guests they are very high class people. First Baptist Church of America. Missionaries on way to Christian conference in Monrovia. They are friends of Mr Zach who come by and have much shouting with Pastor Swingle."

Attah stood up. "I tell you, I have enough of that no good monkey. I get my big frying pan and..." He acted out a sideways swing. "I have it here. Good chop for us." Attah took them to the kitchen. In the refrigerator there was a bowl filled with meat in a marinade.

"Fucking hell!"

"Yes, I murder it." Attah began wringing his hands. "Miss Toffee, she cry. She not stop screaming. There are many children here, and make big noise also. She haymaker me. I do what I can. She has no money. Qwami give her one big drink, he give her two big drink. I feel infinite sorrow for her. She sit here very alone, very shaky, then that no good Mr Starry come for her."

"So where are they?"

Attah folded his arms and was silent.

"Dash him," whispered Drift. "Plenty."

Once more Chippo held out his change Attah took it all and was full of smiles. "Thank you, thank you. Miss Toffee, she beautiful woman. How could anyone not love poor Toffee. That Mr Starry he love her so much he escort her to Old Kofu funeral in village." Attah looked down at the coins still in his hand and put them away. "This now even better day for me."

Drift looked at him suspiciously. "Why?"

Attah's smile grew oilier. "Pastor Swingle give me many dollars to make telephone call. I thank the infinite powers above that my naughty machine was in good working order. He ring Mr and Mrs Shaler, poor Zach's parents in Nebraska, America to tell them that Zach has gone quite mental and tried this afternoon to drown himself. They must come immediately." Attah rubbed his hands together. "Oh, he dash me very nice indeed."

'We're gatecrashing that funeral," said Drift as they set off hotfoot for Tlula. Chippo walked close, cuddling into his newly beloved. "Mmmmmm. Chirrrrrrrrr!"

"Shut up." Once more Chippo Cherrynose's mouth got a smack.

"I said shut up!"

TWENTY: *It's All Good*

Oblivious to tensions in the air, Chippo licked out the very last of the grasscutter gravy and handed the bowl back to Lilibet Lanfal. The women's food stalls with their ravishing smells were being cleared away, the scratchy battery radios turned off. The sound of the drums grew loud in his ears. Just about everyone in the village was assembling next door to the Lanfal compound, a place where the street bulged and two lanes intersected. A place not far from Blossom Rokoku's petrol bowser, where the disabled trotro stood forlorn. With Sir Henry Kmango's new fluorescent bars all disconnected, light came in soft pools from palm oil lamps and kerosene lanterns. On verandahs, the moon flowers were blooming, their sweet jasmine smell impregnating the air. Swarms of pollinating moths had been attracted.

The drummers, led by Qaddo, were seated back to back on two benches in the middle of the red dirt street. In an oval around them, the village women had begun a slow shuffling dance. Spectators were soon pressed back into the laneways or against the houses, oh so intensely coloured to Chippo's newly-stoked eyes. Three frontages had been decorated with glyphs and calligraphic symbols that dealt with Old Kofu's life and passing. Torches illuminated the red that had worked its way up as though rooting the walls to the ground.

Dust, the smell of the fuel in which the firebrands were dipped, and the harsh chanting of the woman all hung in the air in eerie alliance. The stomp of bare and sandalled feet lent a power to even the gentlest of the drumming. Whistles held to the mouth blew shrilly with every other breath, and wails and ululations burst out from time to time. Those who had been laughing and chattering with their neighbours not long before, selling peanut and onion soup, roasted yams and hot sauce, sago puddings, chunks of boiled or smoked tuna, grilled palm worms and slow-cooked pork ribs, now mourned, their faces and forearms streaked with white, the colour associated with death. Clothes were threaded with twigs and creepers. Switches of fresh leaves hung from their hair. The charcoal seller, who had kept up an angry dialogue with herself while Chippo and Drift ate nearby, now danced, her eyes closed, hands thrashing the air.

These villagers were one vibrant community, linked by generational blood, isolation, and a timeless web of indefinable bonds. Chippo put two hands over his heart, lowered his head and mourned the absence of any such belonging in his life. He had followed Matilda when she left their small but friendly Federation home for the autocratic Melody Motherwell's roomier rectory. He soon discovered that sharing with Melody as father-in-law had echoes of the old adage, a house is not a home. Chipman's well-married sisters, mothers and housewives both, one in Toowoomba (to a chartered accountant), the other in Coonabarabran (to a local doctor), he had scarcely seen since Alfie's funeral. Wally Whitbread had never become 'family'. Bouts of lunchtime table tennis with him and schooners after work on Fridays did not really cut it. Chipman hardly knew his socialite wife, Janette. Their only child, Angela, was long grown up and away, now living with a tattooed mixed race 'muso' and their children in a fibro shack on the outskirts of Darwin, happily, Wally had told him, but still, at least in Janette's eyes, a disappointment. The extensive searches he had instituted for Tibor had come to nothing. It seemed the entire Radovan family had disappeared from the face of the earth. The note Tibor had sent, pressed like a precious flower in his Roget's Thesaurus, always made him cry. Yes, where was his village, where was a family for Chippo?

At that moment, out from the darkness, beyond the shuffling dancers, Starry and Cerisia made a grand entrance, and he knew indubitably where his home and family now were – with the Sanguinis and their magical gypsy bus.

Clinging to Cerisia's arm was Toffee, seemingly half-asleep. "Seconals," Drift hissed. Sensing his anger, Chippo placed a calming hand on the back of the Chicagoan's neck. Cerisia talked money with the enstooled Chief Akwa who was there with his wife and his blunderbuss. The Chief consulted briefly with the village elders and despite Blossom's objections, room was made for Starry on the central benches. He was looking dishevelled in a battered hat, an old black tail coat and not much else. He began to drum. A small curved dagger from the inner sanctum wall in the bus was hanging amid his chest hair. Cerisia, (who had been given a robe to cover her bikini), quivered and stomped in front of him, shedding avoirdupois and sending a million motes of red dust skywards. Other survivors of the Makeover, like the French triad, danced with her.

"Wake up!" Drift shouted, pulling Toffee roughly towards him.

"Leave me alone, I hate you." Toffee's words were slurred. She was scratched and bruised from the monkey's rampage, but Lotus had done a patching, attired her in a pretty playsuit, dabbed a fragrance or two on her wrists. "You shouldn't have been drying all that dope in there."

"Honeybunch, don't be like that. I'm really sorry about Lobelia. I gave Attah the third degree." Drift dared to cover her face with kisses, gave her wart a lick. "Why didn't you wait for me?" he asked plaintively.

"Quit giving me static."

"Massage her shoulders," he whispered to Chippo. "She won't let me."

For five minutes, Toffee went limp beneath the freshly sensitised fingers of Chippo Cherrynose. She brushed his nose with a kiss. "Thank you for your healing hands, Chipman, I feel calmer now. You loved my darling Lobelia too. She was my furrywurry lovebug baby." At Drift, she snarled, "And sex had nothing to do with it. That's what jealousy does to your headspace!"

"Honeypot, it's me who's paying for your phony therapies."

"Starry would never have let that happen to Lobelia." Toffee slapped his face and walked off, thud, into the symbol-chalked wall. Cerisia's dancing feet had her beating Drift to her side. She picked her up and warned Drift off.

"They've got her finally. Drugs, it's always drugs." Drift made no attempt to hide his misery. "The lesbo monkey might have been a better bet."

Old Kofu's widow went by, sobbing uncontrollably. When she pitched to the ground, no one went to her aid. Soon she was up and off again. Her face and body were covered with pale ash, her cheeks a delta of tears. There came the diversion of the carnivalesque Fangga; the raffia masklet, a necklace of bullet casings and parrot feathers, yet another pair of shiny custom-made boots. A basket of snakes was perched in his hair. His pointed tongue was going in and out, flickering like that of a serpent. Chippo smiled knowingly; even more than Drift, he thought, the Fetish Priest had no fear of snakes, had them dancing to his tune. Starry came bounding up to Fangga and made a deep obeisance. Fangga whacked him with his stave, stabbed at him with two fingers, shouted something that had to be a curse. Chippo gasped for Starry's welfare.

Fangga propelled himself around the circle, accompanied by a helper with a calabash of liquid. As each person stooped, the Priest frothed the liquid with a whisk of twigs and deposited drops on their foreheads.

"Protect from two-step," Qaddo explained.

Fangga halted when he came to Chippo, who stepped forward and kissed his forehead. "Thank you for what you did for me this afternoon." The words came out as a continuous chirring. Fangga, he knew, understood as a matter of course. The Fetisheur shook out a number of drops. Chippo thrilled as the bezoar stung his eyes, the pain a price to be paid for by the pleasure of initiation into an ancient spirit world.

Inflamed by rejection, Starry was weaving rapidly in and out of the women's circle, rubbing himself up against them as he did so. Being shoved away meant only a redoubling of efforts.

"His dopey Africanastics," said Drift. "If the elders don't stop him, I will."

"Mr Kmango he do many tings for de village," replied the massive, impassive Qaddo, the piece of work as Drift described him. "He pay for dis funeral. Chief Akwa he not interfere wid Mr Kmango's guests and de new order."

Starry pushed his way through the throng. "I tell you, Chippo Cherrynose, the Aortics of Abomey are mysteries to Starry Sanguini no longer. I will make them my gift to Tlula." Seizing an earthen bowl, he handed it to Toffee. "My bellissima, we will make beautiful music together tonight. Bring me water and we will begin."

Drift took a step towards Starry, fists clenched. "You're destroying her. Look what you've done to Chipman!" Starry put a hand on the dagger around his neck. Chippo stood himself between them, healing hands spread

"Twiddle off, you little upstart!" Cerisia shouted at Chippo, choofing forward to give Drift a mighty shove. "You'll be in like Flynn now the monkey's gone." He shoved back and made a grab for Toffee.

A change in the tempo of the drumming had Starry going up and down like a tramp on a trampoline, hitting the ground and shazamming four feet into the air. His hat went flying. Chippo found that numeracy was still his. Seven eight, nine, he mouthed silently, convinced that Starry was demonstrating the art of perpetual motion. As his count reached sixteen, Starry straight-armed Drift and plucked Toffee away. He bounced around the circle with her in his arms, up down, up down...

The women scattered; anything to get out of his way. Landing in front of Drift with a final, flat footed jolt, Starry flung Toffee high. Up she went, her arms and legs waggling, limp as a rag doll. Starry glared at Drift triumphantly, hands on his hips. It took Toffee an age to come down by which time it seemed that Starry had forgotten all about her, but at the last possible second, he reached out an arm, swung her upright and set her on her feet, miscalculating somewhat, like Qumqwat with her breakfast tray. "Ow!" went Toffee.

To Chippo's eyes the performance was such a phenomenon, it had him clapping. Oh, why not me next, Starry? Throw me way up and catch me, he wanted to say.

"Yes, Chippo Cherrynose!" cried Sanguini, reading his mind. "This exorcism tonight means that the widow will be free of her grief, in three months able to marry again. Such a ritual will also be my gift to you. Soon you will be applauding your own deliverance from grief." So saying, Starry seized the fuel bucket, flung the contents at one of the glyphed walls. A torch followed and a sheet of flame erupted. "The cleansing fire, Chippo."

The drumming stopped, the women screamed and shouted. Chief Akwa and his notables rose from their stools.

"Uh oh," cried Lotus, "Starry's in free fall."

Many rushed to join Qaddo and his wife – it was their house – as they beat at the flames with brooms. Drift darted forward to help his friend, but the antic Starry was up and away on the tin roof of the Lanfal home next door, making a great din with his dancing feet. Amid smoke and flames, he yelled. "Starry is the lizard up a palm tree. Starry is the lightning bolt..." From a box left on the roof, he began hurling handfuls of nails.

Gold-fanged, one time Olympic-standard shotputter, Blossom, got him with a considerable lump of conglomerate. It bounced off his head with, seemingly, no consequence at all. He hurled it back and a cry of pain went up in the crowd. Blossom snatched Chief Akwa's blunderbuss and fired a shot, a near miss, prompting an unprecedented reaction from Cerisia. "STARRY SANGUINI!!" Her voice was never louder, never more resonant. "TOOTS!!" It amounted to nothing less than a Divine Intervention. Starry stopped abruptly, looked in her direction.

Chief Akwa, who had copped a few nails, was angrily thumping with his staff. "All you hotel peoples, with your disrespect, begone! We have affairs to attend to, just like you."

"We're not playing games, old boy," shouted Starry, crashlanding in front of the Chief, bracelets and anklets clattering.

"Dr Sanguini, if you not depart, I will have Mr Qaddo here severely deal with you. You have aroused my ire."

"I'm the Fiend of the Dance, delivering this planet. You go!"

There was an outraged silence. Qaddo stepped forward, flexing his fists.

"TOOTS! It's TIME!"

Starry dodged Qaddo, seized Toffee and raced off into the night with her in his arms. Drift gave chase. Cerisia put her hand into the pocket of Chippo's shorts and gave the banknotes in it to Chief Akwa, doling them out one at a time. The process mesmerised Chippo but really, all he wanted to do was run after Drift and Starry. Impatience released him and as he ran, he heard the drums behind stuttering into life again, like an All Clear. The Tlula women once more began their songs and ululations. Ahead, by the fishing nets strung between the coconut palms, he saw Starry grappling on the sand with Drift. Milling around them, much enthused, were Qojo and the village boys who had been awakened from their slumber on a tarpaulin between the canoes.

Drift sent Starry sprawling but he bounced up in an instant. Cerisia, arriving at some speed, barged into Drift from behind. Unbalanced, he was an easy target and Starry got him with a jab to the side of the head and then a two handed combination that had the snake catcher reeling.

Chippo sang silently in a sweet delirium of concern. Torn between his new mentor (Starry), and his new sex and business partner and perhaps beloved (Drift), he decided the thing to do was fling himself down between them, like a Sabine woman. On the count of three. One, two… Long before Chippo got it together, Toffee was in there. Kiss, kiss, kiss. "Drift, honey, don't be angry, it's the next phase. My healing."

Her embraces were pushed away and Drift got his hands around Starry's throat. Starry fumbled for his dagger. At that moment, Qaddo came loping up. With an effortless, single handed movement, he plucked Drift out of danger. Starry found himself levered into the air by a mighty kick. Landing with a thud, he went rolling away over the sand. As the doctor rolled, he managed to yank the dagger out of its scabbard. Qaddo advanced and would have dealt with that also but Cerisia once more played her newfound role of Divine Intervener.

"TOOTS, that's enough! TOOTS! I'll have that. Ta!" She put the knife back in its sheath and it was over.

Imperturbable as ever, Starry led everyone off towards the sea. *Esther Williamsicals*! Drift stood stock still, paralysed by the sight of Toffee with her arm in Starry's. The night fleas, who lived in the dampish sand down there by the river mouth, began feeding on their ankles. Drift started to curse and scratch. Qaddo lifted him up beyond their reach, cradled him like a baby. The night fleas? Chippo Cherrynose welcomed them. He had only surging, ineffable love for everything in the universe, as came the bitter end – as the lovely Lotus would have put it – to the fabulous Full Moon Makeover.

PART TWO
Equatorial Manoeuvres

TWENTY ONE: *Is there anybody out there?*

The eastern sky was flamingo pink and the sea a sheet of silver in the first rays of the sun. The islet was partially obscured by a night mist which lingered close to the water. The palm tops and the promontory peak floated above.

From the roof of the bus, Starry took off his hip Siegfried shades and made a declamation. One of the fat hotel lizards was at his feet, blinking, furious, immobilised by Lotus with pretty coloured strings.

"Fellow Chakrans. Last night a name was bestowed upon me." He paused for effect. "A name with all the elements I have deservedly earned. This morning, I confirmed it by doing the impossible – catching one of these superbly adapted creatures for the very first time." He picked up the lizard and held it high. "From now on you are to call me – REPTILIO!" Cerisia nodded approvingly.

"Something like 'Lubricio' would be more fun, Starry," cried Lotus, clapping away, regretful that 'Starry', her own name for him had gone into history. Reptilio tossed the lizard to her for safekeeping. "Or Crocodilio," she called out recklessly. "Oops!" as she dropped the catch. Her giggles froze as Reptilio lanced her with an eye. The unblackened one.

"And Chippo, for you, I also foreswear my Siegfrieds." Reptilio flipped them to Lotus who arranged the shades on the lizard's head. "Let's call him Starry."

"I still respect Adolf, but he is Caucasio/Eurocentric. He would not understand the creative jump I am making here – the total transformation of his Reichian/Janovian therapies into Afro/Artaudian dance theatre."

Chippo Cherrynose was soon being treated to the Total Shaving, a ritual which symbolised liberation from the limitations of his past and perhaps also the hijacking of his future. "Not just you, Chippo.

All of us. Cerisia and I too, will make fresh vows. New new new. Now is new. In with the pink and out with the blue!" he chanted.

The cherubic curls of Chippo's head and the less cherubic of his chest were the first to go. Any associated vanity was already long gone. When deceptively youthful Stan soaped his groin, moving his genitals this way and that, the better to fulfil his task, Chippo's dick sprang to exuberant life. The ecstatic chirring in his throat accompanied its rise. "Hey, everybody, look here, it's good time, no hands Chippo." There was congratulatory clapping. Stan let out a wolf whistle. A sharp slap across his chirring mouth came from the lovely Lotus before she wiped him down with a wet towel. Reptilio raised Chippo's legs high and parted them. "Tidy up the fabulous anal orifice, Stan. Let's give breath to the winds of change that are already blowing down there. Reptiliozone is nothing if not an erogenous one."

Cerisia, or Mother Bub the Divine, as Reptilio suggested they might now like to call her, went into the bus and reappeared with a camera. His camera, Chippo noticed. She floated her bulk about, zooming in close on his posterior, circled back…

"More visuals for *Thug*," said Reptilio. "Get Danny psyched up about the lead article you and I are going to write, Chippo. Our ticket to fame, fortune regained. Wittering, who needs him!"

Lotus was polishing Chippo's best feature to a maximum shine, bringing out the true colours, the beetroot red of the ridge, the crimson of the nostrils, the rich aluminium tinge of the flanges.

"How about the Girard Perregaux." Cerisia closed an eye and coughed at the smoke from her Gitane which she kept in the corner of her mouth while she removed the watch from Chippo's wrist. Her lipstick was the colour of grenadine. Her newly exposed skull shone pearly white. "Toots, hand me that mirror."

The next hour passed in a dream of happy dissonance. Chippo was aware that Lotus, Stan and even Zach were also being shampooed and shaved. The Glasgow girls, Heather and Fiona, fled, as did the Parisian trio. "No clip go the shears for me, boy," sang Floralee, and Mad Oslo's rasta locks were untouchable of course, but Toffee's afro was soon no more. In compensation for the loss of one of her ethnic attributes, and in honour of her quest for her roots and Afro-authenticity, she was re-spelled Tophphi.

Chippo knew vaguely that wayward blasts of the harmattan were blowing hot dust through the usually sheltered grove, and that he was being carried into the bus. Bodily shaven, they were like a group of pre-pubescent children, pre-school even, in Chippo's case. All around was the smell of soap and sandalwood, of freshly sweaty skin. The former lawyer showed less than a languid interest in a child's soft toy that was Zach's dick, as the newly hairless groin of the Nebraskan passed by.

"Time for your tarot," came Lotus's voice. "Hey, I'll give you my really cheap deal." Chippo's shorts were back on and he had been settled in the boudoir at the back. "Yes, babykins," cried Cerisia, rummaging for money once more, this time in a side pocket. "Ooo, lotsa moolah! Thanksywanksy. Ta!"

There was nothing Chippo wanted to, or could, say.

"We'll start off with a three card spread." Lotus shuffled her cards. "Ignorance to Bondage. The wheel has turned but you're still stuck. Oh, shoot, I read the Full Catastrophe here." Lotus stopped. "These three card spreads suck, Cerisia. I'm going to give him my Everything's Coming Up Roses Special…" His head lolled against Cerisia's shoulder. His eyelids drooped. Stan was playing a kazoo.

He woke to find himself curled up in Mother Bub the Divine's arms, his head cradled between her breasts. He was sucking away at one of her nectarine dark nipples. There was an oceanic feeling, the taste of salt. Ensconced on her blubbery matriarchal life raft, he felt rescued, safe.

"Reptilio, toots, do your flowers for our day-old chick here."

Reptilio's shaven buttocks were thrust into Chippo's face. There was a chain of four or five not-so-delicate farts. "Smell," instructed Mother Bub in his ear. "Jonquils. Isn't that something?" Reptilio let out another rill. "Nasturtiums," she murmured. "Gorgeous, truly gorgeous."

There were many intimate odours, both foul and fair, but Chippo was beyond any real ability to make identifications or discriminate. He closed his eyes and drifted away again, accompanied by an undulant carpet of imagery drawn from Tlulan experience, child bright and as changing as Lotus's tarot deck. Mother Bub the Divine's rubbery nipple turned into the muzzle of the revolver in the drawer of the dining table in the bus, and he began a soft burbling.

TWENTY TWO: *In the depths of the temple*

It was still early that same morning that Chippo, fitted up with a pair of the Siegfried gangster shades, found himself crawling behind Reptilio, who was in babbling mode as he floated along the wide palm-fringed shore.

"Our zonked out zoologist still cannot accept that by pressuring Tophphi to give in to him night and day, he is part of the problem. I was not the least surprised she took to him with the cutlass. I'm moving her away from Drift into the bus. It will also be a tonic for Mother Bub the Divine. Her maternal instincts have been frustrated since her daughters were snatched away by the cruel forces of the law."

Chippo took the cool air deeply into his lungs. He found he could keep his eyes closed as he crawled and still see where he was going.

Came Reptilio's voice from above. "For a witchdoctor to be empowered like a living God he must also allow himself to be possessed like a living Dead. In the village last night, the music of the drums welcomed me into the Eighth Chakra Mode. I was imbued with the healing powers of a Farisha, the great benign Fiend who inhabits this land. On the roof, I accepted the jeers and stones of the multitude as part of my enlightenment, but there came Cerisia's magic voice and I realised in an instant I had been lured into the heart of Zombie Darkness. What does it mean, Chippo? It means that at last my bride and I have become one, indispensably welded to one another." He waited for Chippo to catch up. "To live at the limits of what is possible, the artist must be free to explore both the Farisha and the Zombie within. If the artist has to worry about which is which, his energies are squandered, nothing of value will be achieved. Now that Cerisia is the guardian of the cosmic gates, I can release myself with unfettered confidence into the creative universe. How serendipitous that she too has been divinely transformed. I trust her judgment unreservedly. How could I not? The Twitchleys have been leading English scions since the time of the great Elizabeth. The family successfully rode the industrial changes of the 19th Century. Cerisia's great grandfather invented a bleaching process that quadrupled their chocolate and slavery fortune. The accumulated wisdom of centuries of privilege is now at my disposal."

"My scar." With his fingers, the former Starry Sanguini traced the freshly revealed angry disfigurement in the middle of his depilated chest. "The Manhattan mugging. Now that I am forever bonded with Cerisia, this sort of thing will never happen again."

A breaking wave knocked blind crawling Chippo Cherrynose sideways. Somewhat shocked and spluttering, he got himself to his feet. "In life, you must watch where you are going," came a sententious voice as Reptilio put an ear to Chippo's skull and did a quick auscultation. "I don't think my new born cicadababy has any idea of what I have been talking about."

He was spot on. Chippo did not have a clue. Unquestioning acceptance of Reptilio, this exalted exemplar, this eminence, was now his vaunted lot.

"What a giant leap you made yesterday. It is not often that one of my patients can so excite and amaze me. Thank you, I am most flattered. I do believe that soon I will be able to rely on you, as well as Mother Bub the Divine, at crucial creative junctures." He pulled Chippo close. They gazed intently into each other's eyes and both felt a cosmic fusion of their souls.

"Ray Grable?" the balded Reptilio asked, passing a hand slowly back and forth in front of Chippo's eyes. "Captured after I eloped with Jane Coolidge from the West Wahroonga Psychiatric Centre? Oh, Chipman Smith, observer of my leap from the courtroom dock these ten years ago now, almost to the day? Do you not recognize Raymond Vincent Grable, standing in front of you?" Chippo returned his look blankly. After a pause, Reptilio took his arm and resumed their walk. "As I thought, you never have, and now you never will." He gave Chippo's arm a squeeze. For once it was not

Reptilio's intention to boast, but he could not prevent a triumphant "Gotcha!" passing his lips.

They had reached a section of the beach where a spur of the palm grove thrust out into the sand. "Dig me a hole, would you?" Reptilio gazed towards the sea where Floralee and Mad Oslo were playing water frisbee, then removed his sarong and squatted. Stan had been instructed not to shave Reptilio's eyebrows. They were like two furry black caterpillars dozing on his forehead..

Post-primal pigs waited in the near distance. "The miraculous evacuation, my insect friend, is not yet to be." Reptilio stood up. "As usual, the opium has gummed up my works. Those bloody Frogs."

Chippo had no such difficulty.

"Good boy, let it out," Reptilio said automatically. "You know, my effusive young cicada," he continued in a dreamier tone, as he savoured the dense faecal smell, "Why not organised group defecations? How can we all love each other, attain Nirvana together, if we can't all shit as one? After all, there is no difference between the sacramental and the excremental." There came a wide grin and Chippo marvelled at the quantity and perfection of his teeth, snaggle notwithstanding. "I'm a wordsmith and don't I know it."

The lizardian Reptilio closed his eyes, let the early morning caress him in all his newly shaven glory. Chippo stared up, still squatting. Reptilio's penis was there in the sunshine, the exuberant dark forest it once hung from, stripped away. It was now clearly seen to be remarkable for its length as well as for the empurpled mushroom of its cap. Chippo reached up and held the heavy testicles. He was appreciating the smoothness of Stan's barbering when from the central eye came flowing a golden stream. It splashed down hot on his face, spread over his body. "A gift for you, my friend. My sacred water. Drink!"

Reptilio sluiced him in the turquoise sea, gave a ritual baptising by holding his head under water for (some might say) an inordinate length of time. "Ah, Chippo Cherrynose, my son, Cerisia might prefer to have you in a vain struggle for air, but to me, this morning, you are an advertisement for tropical travel, a satiated tourist lounging on a tranquil shore beside a warm glittering ocean, decorative beverage in hand, a handsome Qwami hovering nearby. La Dolce Vita. I congratulate myself. Finally, I have you experiencing the real meaning of Leisure Beach."

Self-congratulatory tears came from Reptilio's eyes. In a sudden cascade, empathetic ones coursed down Chippo's cheeks as Reptilio helped him put on his shorts and danced him in the direction of the hotel, where flush with cash from the Makeover fees, and other sources, Cerisia had permitted Reptilio to order a late Full Breakfast for the Chakrans.

It seemed only fitting to be granted the sight of a gleaming pod of dolphins surfing in front of the hotel. Billy Carpenter's workmen, grouting the cinder block walls for the Liberator's luxury chalet, were full of friendly jests as the duo capered by. Bonnie & Clyde in their greeting were no longer fierce, but flirtatious and fun, their head splitting yonks and yells experienced as the sweet nothings that they truly were. The vultures were no more rapacious than a flock of Thanksgiving turkeys, Old Idi in the exercise of his authority, a lovably pompous gobbler.

An unstoppable chak-a-chak chak came from Chippo's larynx at the sight of his breakfast eggs, two full moons, newly risen and smiling up with such a shimmer that he shielded his eyes with a hand. Qumqwat, undulating before him in her kindergarten mini-dress said, "Oh, Mr Chipman, you good man," and fished herself a dash from the coins Cerisia had left in the helpless Chippo's shorts, kissing him on the cheek as she did so. Qwami, seeing her get away with it, kissed and self-dashed also.

"Hey, baldy, let's do business." It was Floralee calling from the next table. "I got passports, I got yohimbine, I got crystal meth. I got...."

"Call me Reptilio."

"Well, excuse me, oh Great One."

It did not disturb Chippo at all, the sight of Chief Akwa's delegates running ignominiously away through the palm grove with Ntank lumbering in pursuit, cracking his whip around their ankles. Their complaints about Reptilio's behaviour at the funeral had received short shrift.

It seemed only inevitable that Sir Henry Kmango make a pretty arabesque with his fly whisk and summon Reptilio and Chippo to his table. "So gratifying to see you enjoying Chef Lalwani's excellent cuisine. He can do a Full Breakfast like no other," he said by way of introduction. He smiled. "Dr Sanguini, I spoke by telephone this morning with dear President Mguavas. I have both good news and bad news for you." After his exertions, Ntank was sucking his lips in and out, delicately applying a layer or two of a coloured salve. "First the good news. I mentioned to the President your concept of an 'African Homage' for Ulysses, and I am pleased to tell you that he looks upon it favourably. I myself would prefer that you could come up with some light Shakespeare, *All's Well That Ends Well* for example. Gilbert and Sulllivan's *Pirates of Penzance* would be too much to ask, but that is neither here nor there. Much is at stake. I am sure that together we can devise something appropriate to the changed conditions under which the People's Democratic Republic of Bomzawe finds itself. In short, Dr Sanguini, you and your extremely talented players are hired."

The plangent chirring erupted spontaneously from Chippo's throat. In elated accompaniment, he began executing dervish spins of (to his mind) undeniable perfection.

"You have obviously enjoyed Attah's fried eggs, Mr Chipman Smith. Wobble on!"

"Mr Cherrynose from now on," said Reptilio, terminating Chippo's unique vocals with a slap. "I do believe he has become a cicada."

"Ah. A very apt appellation if I might say so. But do let him sing! Mmm. I enjoyed those eggs myself. From my white-breasted guinea fowl flock."

"Sir Henry, I too have been given a new name. In honour of the inspirational orange-tailed lizards that adorn your beach-front pavilions, I now present myself as" – his arms flapped upwards in a grandiose theatrical gesture, his shaven head was thrown back. "Reptilio! At your service!"

"Very well, if you insist. Your appearance would seem to be much changed, Dr Reptilio."

"For performance purposes only, my excellent Sir Henry," Reptilio replied, making a deep obeisance. "And the bad news, my Liege ?"

"Ah well, not so bad. President Mguavas no longer believes that Ulysses took the Bronzes to Haiti. The President's not necessarily reliable intelligence sources have given him reason to think that the Bronzes are still in Bomzawe. Almost certainly here at Tlula itself. As you know, Ulysses was my dearest friend and confidant. He would not have lied to me, so I have my doubts but if they are, we will find them. My journey to Okidoki this noon time is to ensure that whatever the truth of this rumour, the decree for Ulysses' Return will be signed by the President as promised.

Sir Henry Kmango smiled graciously and dismissed them with a flick of his fly whisk. Ntank showed Chippo his serrated teeth.

TWENTY THREE *Where is the life once led, where is it now, totally dead*

Whatever changes the neuro-chemically induced ischemic attack on Chippo Cherrynose's brain had induced, the days that followed would have to be described as blessed; a time without any suggestion of care, responsibility, or (for the most part) pain. He may have had the emotional range of an insect and a total inability to distinguish friend from foe, but what price bliss? What price freedom? Is infantilism not eternal delight?

Like a proud father, Reptilio decided that prolongation of the Cherrynose prelapsarian Baby State for as long as possible was essential as a preliminary stage in an ultimate and curative Coming Out. To protect the shaven Cherrynose skull from the sun, Cerisia provided him with her second-best flower-bedecked straw hat, one she had purchased some years before from the Chelsea Antique Market in Kings Road, and Reptilio sent him off every morning to frolic by himself, free to chirrup and wank, splatter his seed, all to his heart's content. According to Reptilio he was re-living that first cicada summer of his Tibor Radovan boyhood, organically at one with the plant and animal kingdom around him, making up for wasted years, doing all the things he would have done the first time around, if only he had not become derailed by such calamities as the departure of Tibor, and his father's sudden death. Not to mention societal and legal prohibitions and Old Testamental homophobic savagery directed at him on a daily basis by the manipulative and single-minded Reverend Melody Motherwell who agreed with Matilda that Alfie had corrupted him into an unnatural gayness.

The triumphs of Chippo's euphoric and unexamined Tlula days were exceptional – the ability to dine with Old Idi and his flock, for example. He was delighted to squabble with them over the attractively odoriferous kitchen scraps. One time it was he who caught the monkey head. He also scrounged with them in the hotel's garbage dump behind the cheapest row of bungalows, sniffing away at the acrid incinerator smells.

Although he may have been traumatised by a pair of black swans as a boy, he also became a constant companion to the heavy-casqued, knockabout hornbills. His especial friends were Bonnie & Clyde (so named by the former Starry) whom he had met his very first day at Tlula. They showed him how to rip berries off the bushes, how to crunch down on the unwary cicadas. If he tickled Bonnie & Clyde's long necks they would generously regurgitate their repasts into his waiting mouth. The avian couple, roguish and loving, seemed forever on the point of falling over, but never fell, and the simpering, giggling Chippo was able, day after serotonined day, to accomplish the same. He was led to the cavity in a tree trunk where their latest brood had been hatched. With them, he honked and crooned songs to their half-grown nestlings and they danced around him with much clattering of beaks, their wings flapping with an oilskin raincoat sound. Some nights, he slept close by them, his roost a comfortable nook in the spreading roots of a strangler fig.

Other nights he dossed down with Billy Carpenter and Sir Henry's other city workmen who all slept together on floor mats in a single back bungalow. Practising the pronunciation of their English, they asked questions about Australia he could not answer. They laughed and chirruped along, ruffled what was left of his hair, spoon-fed him and played jolly games with him as though he was an exotic doll. Passed him joints. Shut him up (as Reptilio instructed) when that excited childlike trill got too much for them.

The mambas checked Chippo out but always slithered by, protected as he was by the foul fetishes that the ambiguous Fangga, seeking him out, took to hanging around his neck. Yes, Fangga, exiled but still in the vicinity, biding his time.

Chippo did not confine himself to the hotel grounds. One afternoon he wandered up the only road out, became lost and was rescued by Josiah Lanfal in his repaired trotro near the edge of the Tlula escarpment, high above the village. Other times he wafted to areas so wild that Lilibet Lanfal and the village ladies would never be forced to tame them; tangled paradises where the ripe fruit dropped, the yellow billed turacos flew and the bats flapped, the monkeys marauded and the duikers darted, where stalked the solitary ocelot once a beloved pet of Ulysses Oratorio and where Drift and his assistants engaged in many herpetological forays; the noose and bag or the fatal shots.

At dead of night, Drift (even more paranoid after Sir Henry's 'not so bad' news about the Bronzes), transferred the precious, purloined artefacts to the wardrobe in Chippo's unslept-in room to which Drift had commandeered the key. Not even Tophphi, tightly sequestered in the bus, knew that the Bronzes were no longer in Qaddo's shed. "I trust her with my life, but I particularly don't want you to tell her," the ever optimistic Drift impressed upon Chippo more than once, waiting patiently as he was for his dysfunctional buddy to become functional enough to begin work on his cages. In the meantime he made 'curative' use of Chippo's oral skills but the former public servant's flashing of naked buttocks at him, like a mandrill in oestrus, had Drift good naturedly smacking those buttocks and moving well away.

The complaints about his "schizoid" or "disgraceful" behaviour were of no concern to Chippo himself. The mining company officials and USAID workers who still rented the beachside bungalows for weekends suggested he should be taken to Doggone and hospitalised. "He's probably had a stroke or something."

As far as Qojo and the village children were concerned, "Witchdoctor Starry" had put a "sweet swear" on him. They would hold Chippo's hands and treat him like a friendly bush imp, or good luck charm. He would be taken to Tlula to do his song for their families. He sang as he watched Lilibet Lanfal pound fufu in the compound of her 'small small' house. He sang as he lay with mothers suckling their babies, all somnolent in the noon shade of the orange flowered tulip trees. He sang as he sat under the gay umbrellas of the market ladies, sampling their aspirin and cigarettes, their grilled fish, toasted yams and the delicious sour kenke mash which they wrapped in banana leaves for him. He loved the magic stall which had bat wings and baby monkey skulls with which to play, seeds and pods and mysterious roots to chew on. One day the murderously inclined Blossom came out with her bucket of slops as he crawled by in his "happy nappy". Chirr, chirr, chirr! Slosh, not just his feet this time, but all over. And she made use of her horselike kick.

Some of Chippo's most enchanted hours were spent at the top of a particular mangrove tree in a brackish lagoon behind the far beach, where he could be seen squatting on branches almost too attenuated for a man's support, surrounded by his brother and sister cicadas; each one as big as his thumb, so very similar to the cherished Cherrynoses of his childhood; the same blood-red postclypeus; darker in the head but the same white pubescence coating their tymbal covers, the same opaque orange cachous for eyes, the strength of the brown thoracic markings the only difference.

Yes, it was aural heaven up there in that grandaddy mangrove tree. Touching the sky, Chippo sucked juices and striduated with the cicadas, let his sound blend with that of the homopterous insect rattlers, let it rive deep into his skull. He would slowly turn his head from side to side, the cacophonies filling one ear, then the other. Bonnie & Clyde came by more than once to check up on him.

One day, a stranger to his eyes lay down on the beach not so far away from the mangrove tree. Chippo watched him read a book and continued to watch when he put it aside, sit up and slash the top off a coconut with a machete, drink the milk. The man smoked a cigarette, his eyes scanning the sea. Someone Chippo did recognize came by, Fangga, who gestured for a cigarette. The two men talked and smoked together until the fetish priest moved on. Chippo continued to watch. He didn't have an idea in his head as to why he found the first man's presence so absorbing. There was nothing in his gazing that could be interpreted as sexual desire.

After some time the man stood up, turned and began walking towards him. Closer and closer he came until he was standing below looking up.

"Come on down, Chippo. You idjit. You been there long enough for today."

Oh, it was Zach. Chippo could only stare at him.

"If you're not back before sunset we're coming to shake you down."

Chippo's preternaturally bright Henri Rousseauan world did not last, and rents in that steady-state mantle began to appear. There came fits of frenzy, fits of crying, bouts of stuporous despair. There were stark moments of awareness, of naked terror when reality manifested itself; regret for what was surely forever lost – the working life he had enjoyed under the patronage of Wally Whitbread, the ordered, monkish years he had endured in the rectory. Once he was on his knees screaming for help to Reverend Motherwell's God the Father, but the heavenly skyman deigned not to answer, bringing to Chippo's tortured mind, the certainty that at Tlula Leisure Beach, he was trapped in squalid depravity, in a realm populated by saboteurs and slavers, bandits and buccaneers. Monsters all.

Reptilio was carefree, confident that matters were merely going according to plan. "There is a natural plasticity in here," he said, tapping Chippo's skull. "The right hand brain requires time to get into the acculturating, tap dancing mode."

Zach was not so sure about this and offered assistance which Reptilio unexpectedly accepted. It was a turning point for the possessed cicadan to find himself invited into the hotel room of the Nebraskan who had a laugh when Chippo smelled the man's sheets and cradled his pillow to his face. Chippo became a mindless puppy, surrendering to the tenderness with which his ears were played, with the massaging of his scalp and shoulders. He sat on the floor gazing blankly up, while unshaven Zach sat bare-legged on his chair, trying to bring back common sense to Chippo by playing songs like *Mr Tambourine Man*, and reading from the collected Dylan lyrics. Then there was *Ode to Tamalpais*, a poem by Lew Welch, one of the West Coast beat writers whose work he had been introduced to some years before. *'Not the bronze casket, but the brazen wing...,"* Zach recited. Welch, he explained, was a man who had gone off into the Sierra Nevada one day with a rifle, intending to end his life, and have his body devoured by buzzards...*'the very opposite of death...bird of rebirth...the bronze winged silent ones...praises Tamalpais/perfect in Wisdom and Beauty/she of the wheeling birds...'*

Chippo chirred (ecstatic but uncomprehending) through such lines until a sharp flick of Zach's hand would silence him. Another day, the Nebraskan read from *Keep the River on Your Right* by Tobias Schneebaum. A book about a Roman Catholic priest whose desires could be fulfilled only by being ritually killed and eaten by cannibals in the Peruvian jungle. The priest got his wish. "A true story," Zach said as he led Chippo back to his room next door and locked him in for the night. "It's all about pursuing one's destiny, accepting with a stoic resignation, even a happiness, whatever you want to happen, whether it is life or death."

Reptilio decided that Zach's ministrations had unsettled Chippo more than saved him, and therefore anointed Lotus as Official Nurse. "Starry calls me Flotus Nightingale," she giggled. "That also stands for First Lady Of The United States," she added, giggling some more. "Ommmm" she went in accompaniment with the ecstatic utterings of the former protégé of Wally Whitbread. She kept Chippo clean enough, fed enough, and after fitting him with a collar and a leash, controlled enough. It was Flotus who trained him not to eat any more of the poisonous flowers of the trumpet shaped Brugmansias.

Ultimately, more than anyone else, it was Lotus who slapped Chippo back into shape. By the tenth day, following Zach's example, she had him locked in his own room and sleeping soundly. Recognizing the restorative value of hard labour, she hired a canoe and had Chippo row her and Stan Francisco two hundred yards up the Wawa River to where the three of them hacked a load of clay from the bank below the Tlula Escarpment. Soon he was also helping her and Stan Francisco in the Easter Carnival workshop. Chippo was even taken on a trip to the Kassini Junction market where she bought what she needed for the Chakra Dancers multifarious performance plans. Stan drove the bus there and back with no mishaps, and chose parts to fix the handbrake. On return, Stan and Chippo duluxed the bus a limousinish black. A single red Africanesque motif was added – a Reptilio Rampant as the Farisha Zombie Lizard. *The Beautiful Afreakans* lettering was no more, replaced by the 'more philosophical, more forgiving if not fatalistical' *WHATEVER FOREVER* in a marginally more legible script. "Perfect," Reptilio appraised. "Now Reptilio is – we all are – ready for anything."

It was a major rehabilitatory experience being with Stan. Chippo Cherrynose, former Attorney General departmental crime researcher, Chipman Smith, and Stan Francisco, former teenage truck driver, Stanford Gutnick, often found themselves contemplating each other with open admiration. Encouragement from Lotus had Chippo attempting baby talk with Stan. They sat beneath a striped awning in tie-dyed jock straps, working together on masks and costumes, both with total concentration, tips of tongues showing. Reptilio and Mother Bub came by and expressed deep satisfaction at their display of creative skill. "Take pictures of me and the boys with Chippo's camera," Reptilio said to Lotus. "For Danny and Professor Adolf."

A few days later, after the negatives were developed in Kassini Junction, Lotus showed her favourite one to Stan and Chippo. Stan had a grin on his face as he gave the finger to the camera. Chippo was looking adoringly at his master, the light catching a thread of goo arrested in descent from his lips. Reptilio had positioned himself between the two of them; a hairless, sunglassless, sky clad persona. There was no suggestion that Chippo knew or desired to know, the man with a past behind Reptilio's vaingloriously present self-creation.

TWENTY FOUR: *Shine on crazy diamante*

Except for one or two monosyllabic utterances, in a voice certainly not his own, Chippo remained unable or unwilling to talk. But Reptilio was delighted to find at the end of that second week he had begun to 'fire on more cylinders than one' and was ready to re-join the adult world of Tlula. He became well capable of wielding any pen given him, even if his writing turned out to be micrographic. Together with a biro and a magnifying glass, Reptilio hung a note book around his neck so that he could record for him any thoughts he might have on the 'insect spirit forces' that were guiding him. And more significantly, any revelations he might have about Reptilio himself – or Raymond Vincent Grable.

"Time for an assessment of your progress," The Exemplar said one night, piggy backing him to the bar. Set down on a stool. Chippo gazed about as though for the first time.

Sir Henry's workmen had washed a five year accumulation of mould and grime from the mural of the tuxedoed Great Liberator and he beamed down on the two of them with the benevolence originally intended. Qwami, going for a more romance-infused atmosphere, had his counter lit by the glow of a couple of hurricane lamps.

"Mr Kmango is go Okidoki two day again now. Big trouble there for him." Qwami was taking advantage of his absence to play the latest turbo rhythms from Brazzaville and Accra on the Dansette, instead of things like Freddy and the Dreamers' Greatest Hits.

"Get that thumb out of your mouth," said Reptilio, looking through the Savoy Hotel cocktail recipe book (always on the counter), "and order one of these horrible drinks for yourself. And my usual."

"Hopgrasser, and Trepioli for a skiwhisk. Led Rabel' Chippo's request came out in his new, crackly little voice and everything was backwards.

Qwami handed Chippo his bar pad.

"A Grasshopper for me, and a Scotch whisky for Reptilio." he wrote for him. "Red Label."

"What is dis? De light so bad." Qwami's reading skills were not high, light or no light and magnifying glass notwithstanding.

As the crème de menthe and Nestles condensed milk were being added to the vodka, Reptilio said, "Don't forget to mix in extra palm sugar for him, Qwami. Little Chippo, we want you to forever stay as sweet as you are."

Chipman Smith's formerly repressed taste for the Pink Lady category of cocktail had surfaced. Chippo Cherrynose freely exercised his attraction to the highly coloured ones, the more syrupy the better, preferably with maraschino cherries.

"Chippodeo of the Rodeo, you are my finest creation! Now, nothing can obstruct my grand Coming Out for you at the Carnival. Every Jewish boy has his Bar Mitzvah, every gay man must have his Coming Out."

"Vahbah Mitz?"

"I envision your Coming Out as a maiden voyage, told as one of those folkloric morality stories that Bomzaweans love. We have our team destroying your old puritanical Aussie-Celtic Motherwell karma. You're releasing! You're kicking on your back. Lots of percussion. I hear didgeridoos droning somewhere, the band playing *Advance Australia Fair* if you insist. We take off the ceremonial nappy, do a ritual douche. Gaga, gurgle, gurgle, goo you go, you little chirrerboy. Cerisia greases you up. Then I perform what they call the *Jewel in the Crown*. You don't have a clitoris, Chippo, but we men do have a prostate. The anal orgasm will be yours."

It sounded ideal. What more could Chippo possibly ask for in a Coming Out? If only Matilda and her Reverend might be here to witness it. Reptilio must invite them. And it would be followed of course by Reptilio's presentation to Chippo of his Ideal Friend. His new longings, with their not so subtle excruciations, way beyond impatience, would be over.

"Toots!" Mother Bub the Divine's call came from the near distance.

Left alone, Chippo lit a Pioneer. No more Camels to buy, but he liked the local cigarette which had a touch of Cerisia's Gitanes about it, but sweeter and milder. He sipped away at his delicious, eroticising Grasshopper. Qwami changed the sounds; off went Leopoldville's Mbilia Bel and into the hot night air went mood music just for Chippo. "All you need is love, love love, Love is all you need," John Lennon sang. His eyes soon fell on the caviar glisten of the sweat in the hollows of Qwami's torso. Reptilio had raised sky-high his expectations for a long term partner, but he had also been spreadeagled to short term lust.

"...yes," came Qwami's seductive tones, "I hab ambition for better tings dan barman."

Qwami had been gone for ten days and had only recently returned. Chippo wiggled his backside into a position of maximum comfort if not anticipation on his stool and listened to the story of Qwami's attempt to become a sailor. He had hung around the Doggone docks all day and in the evenings squandered his savings on records, booze, cards and "bad bad" women.

"I fight rascal who rob my money. Like dis." Qwami threw a playful punch past Chippo's nose, the nose that he now found so acceptable that it was rubbed over the faces of all whom he greeted. "Rainbow hued and sexually alluring," Reptilio had confirmed for him. "You handsome little cicada you."

"After Easter I want go again, but I skint. Mr Kmango pay me small small. Money to save, it hard hard." Qwami leaned forward until he was no more than a few raised hair follicles away. He scratched with crossed arms at both his armpits. He had very lovely breath, his skin so satiny, his teeth so white; there seemed to be pretty creatures crawling in his eyelashes.

"Little animals," Chippo tried to say, moving delicate fingers, pincer-like, towards Qwami's eyelashes, hoping to capture one and pop it into his mouth.

Qwami's lips closed firmly on Chippo's. His firm, fragrant tongue went into his mouth. The sounds of a quarrel came from the palanquin, parked out in the velvety dark by the pavilions.

"That was good kiss, Mr Chippo. We go for quick one in de front office. Attah he never wake." Chippo gave a preliminary caress to the erection that had leapt to attention out of the shorts he had forgotten to button up, but he wasn't sure about the office, even with Attah snoring away in the back. "Or for extra dash, I fuck very good with plenty dick in yo room."

Chippo went behind the bar. Qwami already had his 'plenty dick' well out. Chippo wanted to savour the look of it, fondle it for a while and grasped it, but Qwami whipped him round, massaged his buttocks, pressed into him through the cotton. "Dis bar look after itself for five minute." Chippo was happy to be pushed towards his room at the back of the hotel until he suddenly remembered the bat shit stink seeping from the wardrobe which contained the Bronzes. There was even one that Drift had taken out earlier that evening to adorn the room's table. He began shaking his head vehemently, but by this time Qwami wasn't taking no for an answer.

Reptilio's voice, coming in from the darkness, interrupted. "Ah, Qwami, Cerisia has her back problem again. I want you to give her one of your special massages. Now! She needs to be pain free for tonight."

"Lady Cerisia back problem?" Qwami's eyes lit up. Reptilio counted out some coins for him and the bartender dashed off.

"It's her Dance of the Duika, choreographed by me and guaranteed to take off lots of avoirdupois," Reptilio explained, as he led Chippo away, glancing down as he did so, at Chippo's shorts. He pushed his penis back in, buttoned him. "Yes, my boy, what a ripe blackberry Qwami is, always so ready to shove it up, you lucky little cicada. But what do you think? Perhaps such priapic excitements might be better left until after the Carnival. As I said, nothing must lessen the impact of my sensational Love Ritual, my Final Solution for you." Fingers and thumb dug deep into the sides of Chippo's neck and he found himself being propelled in the direction of the beach. "We're heading for the healing waters."

The quarter moon shone down, the ocean ahead reflecting the clear night sky like a star-filled mirror. As they passed through the domain of the red hot poker tailed lizards (asleep and safe in the thatch of the pavilions), Reptilio let go Chippo's neck, raised his arms and gave them a double salute.

They played Follow the Leader along the sea wall with Reptilio presenting him with an idealistic picture of himself in his new incarnation – he was a tabula rasa, but also an artist savant, divinely inspired, latent skills now activated, thanks to Professor Siegfried. With the Office of the Clerk of the Peace now the deadest of dead ends, the Public Service a wrong-headed career move, associated with years of perverse and unrequited lusts, Reptilio unfurled a new path for Chippo; now he would be a counsellor for the coming new age; informing the world of his interspecies communication experiences, about Darwinian interconnectivities and mathematical, mystical symmetries, showing people how to make love not war, how to sing and dance, how to be happy with a biophilically-sensitive, less-is-more life; and most important of all, preaching the evils of sexual repression. "And wasn't it Gore Vidal who said that homosex was as natural as hetero?" Chippo's shining red-on-red nose would be a beacon of light for the rest of humanity, all that. "Yes, yes, yes," his cicadan heart thumped in agreement.

"Once, my dizzy little cicadawada," Reptilio went on as they discarded their shorts, "I lived to shock the shit out of the old Anzac farts. In Europe I was fuelled by barely controllable Baader-Meinhoffian rage at the decadent bourgeois Establishment, the corporate elite, Mr Nixon and the war in Viet Nam, but now I am Reptilio, the passionate artist and star, bringing universal joy through entertainment. That is the way to happify the happiless, smilify the smileless."

He made a lizardish slither, a newly-added move, over the wet sand by the water's edge. "Mot for ne," Chippo suddenly shrilled, the sea an element he had avoided while up in the trees. Reptilio slithered back, held out an encouraging hand and inevitably the two were soon swimming in commune. In that phosphorescent pool beyond Tlula Leisure Beach's family friendly breakers, Chippo was enraptured when naked Reptilio entwined his wrestler's legs around his waist.

"Mmm. I can sense your song coming on, Cicadaboy. For the first time, you are about to sing for me. For me alone."

As they pressed together, there came easy tumescence and with it that ecstatic rush, the magical fibrillation. Mmmmmm… A vivid remembrance erupted of that childhood time when a naked Tibor, the wicked outlaw, had hugged him, nuzzled his neck, knowing he would be forgiven for having done the 'beyond the pale' thing; when Chippo's Dad had come in and kissed them both on the lips, wishing them good night, switching off the light as he left. It was the last time Tibor ever slept over until morning. Now Reptilio was Tibor, now Chippo would relive the kisses and more of that night. He wanted to share Reptilio's mouth, his lizardy, sea-salty tongue, his life. Reptilio loved him. He leaned forward, their lips were as one. "We are in love, Reptilio dear," sang his 'cicadaboy' from deep within.

There came a yell. It seemed to boom from a vast distance. "Repti!" A siren call. "Repti, Repti!!!" He turned towards it. The passionate kiss managed no more than a brief mingling of marine-cooled breath. "TOOTS!"

The yell from hell. Mother Bub the Divine's cattle prod to Reptilio's chromosomal core. "You don't have to leave me because of her, do you, oh master and guide?" Chippo's fading fibrillations queried.

Reptilio caught a wave to the shore, paused to put on his shorts and did not look back. Mother Bub, revived after her session with Qwami, unfolded her arms in a gesture of welcome. They performed an all-enveloping loving embrace. Flanked by torch bearers and djembe drummers who created a wall of sound around them, Dr and Mrs Reptilio sashayed off the beach, cavalcaded across the cleared field beside the hotel, rock and rolled over the rickety wooden bridge above the tidal swamp, and then were gone.

Chippo felt the melancholy of abandonment. Treading water, he let the waves wash away any idea that he could be so mean-spirited as to be jealous of – The Honourable Cerisia Twitchley!

In the teensy, childlike hand that was the calligraphy of Chippo Cherrynose, he dashed off a card to Matilda and Melody, together with a letter, a thing of beauty in its size and spontaneity, to Wally Whitbread still at home at Waverton in Sydney, yet to board his flight to Nigeria.

...so sorry, my sweet, so adored Wally, that I have not yet looked up your very good mate, whose name escapes me for the moment, but I will do so on my way to Lagos after the big Easter Carnival here. Heaven knows where my new life will lead me beyond that. Maybe an existence devoted to the realm of the senses. Certainly I will be travelling with my new Tibor Radovan, the LOVE OF MY LIFE – who he is, still a secret being kept from me but I have some heavenly suspicions – it can't be Zach unfortunately but it may be Drift, my snake catcher buddy, although he is promised to Tophphi, or it may still be my dear cosmic guru himself, Reptilio, who lives in WHATEVER FOREVER the wonderful, wonderful magic bus. I am sure you will welcome him and his wife, the aristocratic and free loving Cerisia Twitchley, Mother Bub the Divine, into your ever accepting heart. I send you big hugs and kisses. Maybe you also can be a new Tibor Radovan for me. The more the merrier.

Chippo Cherrynose. This day in March

"No word of the long lost Ray Grable? Too bad for Wally, of course," said Reptilio, vetting both the card and the letter. Chippo had no idea who he was talking about or why he was grinning so very broadly. "It's what's left out that says it all, Chippo. How can you do anything but agree?"

TWENTY FIVE: *A robin redbreast in a cage puts all heaven in a rage*

"Vamos buddy, vamos! We need them finished NOW!"

Oh yes, the cages. Construction was taking place in a disused outbuilding in a remote corner of the Hornbill Palace grounds. Once Chippo had moved on from Stan's masks and musical notation, he found his years of apprenticeship with his Dad coming back and in good stead. With some pencil sucking and brow furrowing, his rearranged mind did not find it difficult to prepare a template for the sixteen cages. Pickled light-weight coconut wood planks provided by Sir Henry, had been sawn to his specifications in the village by Qaddo who knew well the real reason for their somewhat unusual shapings. The sights and sounds of the planing and the smells of sawdust took Chippo back to the charmed days of paint, pinewood and turpentine in the backyard shed. Sir Henry Kmango, anxious to have all the snakes either confined or killed, had the lithe Jimmy Carpenter make available any tools required.

Yes, Drift's cages kept Chippo busy; his earlier sometime thoughts that he had 'fallen among thieves', no longer crossed the Cherrynose mind and he completed, dovetail joints and all, twelve of the sixteen in quickish time. Each cage was 4' x 2' x 2', the front covered with a fine wire mesh. Feeding could be done through a top frontal entrance, but in the solid odoom wood backing of the cages, there was a hatch door which enabled Drift to release a captured snake into the dark of its sleeping box, an area which stretched the length of the top third of the cage. From there the snake could descend through an aperture onto a slope which dropped to the floor of its home. Beneath the sleeping box was the secret compartment for the Bronzes which made use of the extra space under the snake's slope and was accessible only through a wide, lower door, also at the back and which had to be 'invisibo'.

A shard from Chippo's past unexpectedly came piercing; a rare chiding from Alfie for a mistake he had made. He had begun to cry. Any such chidings were gentle but Chippo had never liked his father having a low opinion of his abilities as a cabinetmaker. He determined, with a rush of unconcealed joy, that this project would prove him wrong.

Qaddo's sensimilla, tightly packed in double plastic around the Bronzes was to be the padding to keep everything secure. Qaddo was already holding Drift's order for him in the village. A gradual transfer of the Bronzes from Chippo's room as each compartment became ready, might have been the better option, but Drift decreed that with a late night, last minute, one time operation, the chance of detection was much lower. Chippo was as powerless to disagree with Drift as he was with Reptilio.

The unhappy mambas created an extremely menacing atmosphere. Freedom loving creatures as they were, accustomed to getting their own way, they discouraged any unwanted inspection of the cages, by lunging at all who approached. Chippo, free now of anything so unfortunate as paranoia, soon came to feel that Drift's suspicions of everyone, even his own Family, even Zach, who was showing interest in the snakes, were completely unnecessary.

The Nebraskan's visage, increasingly handsome to Chippo's eyes as the days went by, was an object of rapt interest for him as Zach described how he had a couple of narrow escapes from those rattlesnakes on the Idaho valley ranch. "I do enjoy listening to Zach's voice, the way he tells his stories," he wrote. Chippo liked to think it was for his company that Zach was hanging around, not the snakes at all, but Drift thought otherwise. "Muchas gracias for your interest, Zacho hombre, but I want you outta here. Hasta la vista. I mean, fuck off. Now!!"

"We're all one happy family here, Drift. Whatever small disagreements we have, we are all in the same boat, surely?" Chippo wrote on his pad for him. "Zach is no thief and has too many problems of his own to even think about what we are up to.

Don't you know he found a ripped piece of Zoe's broadshorts in the mud up by the crocodile ponds?"

"Okay, amigo, whatever." Drift let Chippo's magnifying glass drop to the end of its string. "I sure don't want any Mr Negativos like him skulking around, that's all. I've seen him and Fangga heads together out on the far beach." Drift tore the page from Chippo's pad into little pieces. He gave him a friendly shove. "Go fix that latch you fucked up."

From his ocean of bottomless bliss, Chippo found that his cousin-once-removed kind of love for Zach was sustained by a peripheral chunk of pity. Poor Zach. He had been carrying that old weatherworn piece of blue cotton around with him for days. He slept with it, stroked his face with it, refused to wash the smell of swamp off it. Everyone but Zach knew it could not possibly have come from Zoe's shorts. There was all sorts of detritus up there at the ponds, observed the adventurous Drift, a sometime visitor, scraps of cloth from all manner of bodies, but fifteen wet seasons before?

As for Reptilio, he was impatient with the 'uncooperative obsession' with a piece of denim that the Nebraskan had developed. "Zach has ripened and is ready for the plucking. But I needs me a clue. A sign! Time is running out."

Cerisia, wearing a toque to shield her skull from the sun, had herself carried by. Drift had captured a diamond python and she wanted to train it for her belly dance at the Carnival. Accompanying her in the palanquin was her latest conquest, Yukio, a shock-haired young Japanese poet and daredevil who was travelling around Bomzawe on a unicycle. Yukio had managed to interest Reptilio in the seventeen syllable form of the haiku. *The Okidoki Post* had already published several of the poet's verses in an article about his penchant for large African market women.

"Couplets are more my speed," Reptilio had said to Yukio, "but the haiku is something to aspire to, like limericks. I have recently honoured Cerisia with one of those. Would you like to hear it?" But unexpectedly, Cerisia had put her foot down and was insisting on changes.

Negotiations over the use of the python were in progress. "Will this mean I've discharged my old dinner debt?" Drift asked.

"Yankee tightwad. I'm enjoying torturing you about it. While I'm here could I say twit and twoo to the mamba you named after me?"

"It was the one that got away."

"Well, zippedy do dah."

Drift and Cerisia smiled grimly at each other. Drift bent his head and gave the two handed flick-back of his hair. Implacable enemies they might be, but now a truce was in place. Drift had been scarified when he first saw a balded Tophphi, her apricot highlighted megafro entirely shaved off. Close to tears, yes, but realistic. He was in two minds about the Africanistic spelling of her name but conceded that for her future well-being, it was best that he absent himself from her company. "Ten days, tops. I've got my health needs too."

It was also okay by the enslaved Chippo. It kept his snakecatcher very 'horny', the condition Drift used to justify his infidelities – and their frequency. One drunken intercrural night, a desperate Drift had even shoved him up against a tree trunk and orgasmed between his thighs.

TWENTY SIX: *Taking it to the limit*

"Oh, Reptilio," Chippo trilled on his pad, "I have become bereft with impatience. What about me living the full fairytale with my new Tibor as you have promised? Someone fabulous and simply loving of me with true reciprocity. I am not criticising Drift, but reciprocity is not his strong suit. I know my secret love could be you, Reptilio, but when my mind and feelings trespass deeper into the chambers of my heart, it is Zach I picture, with doves cooing, blue birds of happiness warbling all around our heads. Why do you always say it can't be Zach? Does straight always mean straight? Isn't there room for flexibility here?"

"Now you're turning into Wordsworth," said Cerisia, fanning her crotch as she read "or even Doris Day. I preferred your days as the Tlula twit." She lay back, hand behind her head, a perspiring odalisque. That morning, Lotus had given Cerisia's skull such a shave and wax job, it presented a surface resembling a celluloid of rare quality. With her eyes concealed by triangular dark glasses (they were polaroids, from the Sunday market in Kassini Junction), she reclined, a bare-bosomed Jane Mansfieldish glamourpuss, in a sumptuous skirt, with no sparing of the dried elephant grass from which it was confected. It was a gift from Lilibet Lanfal. To round out the Hollywood via Tonga illusion, a fumy garland of flowers from a tree outside Bungalow Thirty was draped around her neck.

They were all sharing a farewell lunch with Yukio of the lustrous black hair who was on his way back to Okidoki. One platter of deep-fried bush meat in batter had been consumed, and they were starting on a second.

"Mmmm! Scrumptious," said Cerisia, her mouth full. She had announced a final indulgence before getting into shape for the Carnival. "My farewell to fat. Not to mention that Sir Henry has forbidden Attah to serve bush meat. He told him it was not pukka!" She let out a little cackle.

Yukio was tossing the bones out the window, where Old Idi and his flock were doing what they did best.

Floralee, Reptilio, Yukio, Cerisia ('Mother Bub the Divine' had not really flourished as an appellation in the way that 'Reptilio' had) and Chippo, were sweating it out in the sanctum at the back of *Whatever Forever*. Cerisia was about to conduct one of her pleasure shops. As usual, no one new had signed up. The gipsy grannie's contribution was a card she was writing to her mother back in Bendigo.

Dear Mum,

You'll be pleased to hear I'm taking it easier lately. I slept with every available man in Tlula more than once and was half way through the unavailable before I realised. I've taken myself off the 'bine before they run me out of town."

"The old chook is 85 going on 25," Floralee chortled. "Give or take a few years. She's not on the way out yet. Gets stuck into the Amontillado every night. At her age there's no point in anything except going for broke. She's still smoking and dancing, getting fucked by potbellied studs younger than me."

"Yes, beautiful things come with age," Reptilio waffled, as he blew a kiss to Cerisia as dowager and twanged Chippo's notebook back at him. "My boy, the Carnival will reveal all. Until then, not even the great Reptilio knows the answers to your queries."

A plaintive tear or two escaped, then unstoppably, another and another. With Chippo continuing to weep uncontrollably, Reptilio went priestly if not professional on him. First of all he smoothed his hands up and down his disciple's bare back. Then he snatched a monkey bone at which Cerisia had been sucking and gave Chippo's one time public servant perineum some preliminary prodding.

"Perhaps, after all, something can be done to calm your emotional and sexual turbulence. My learning at the Convents in Abomey will come in useful here. The priests selected certain prime specimens for preliminary manhood rites. We can adjudge it is time for Reptilio to initiate you in similar fashion. We don't want to fail our audience at the Carnival, do we, for lack of rehearsal?"

"Toots, my darling toots, I won't see you sacrificing yourself like this."

"My mummie bubbie, my seafood grotto. Your jealousies have no place in our new world order, least of all in our sacred and profane rituals. Play the role of Priestess, and it will make us all feel that much better. Floralee will act as Hand Maiden."

Cerisia threw out the remains of the monkey. Yukio threw out the platters. The vultures made their noises. Cerisia rolled close, burping the smell of fat and Attah's hot sauce in Chippo's face. She applied a generous amount of oil to both of them and showed how Reptilio liked to be readied for ritual. Yukio was looking at his watch.

"There! Once he's up he stays up. Instant Shangri-La for you."

Chippo had stopped crying. He did not detect the unfriendly tone. "Yes indeed," he scribbled. "For both of us."

"We will commence in the context of one of my tantricks. In minutes, a Spinalini Surge will shoot up from the root chakra and explode in our brains. Divine flowering loti will illuminate us."

Floralee picked up her dilly bag, let her glasses dangle. "You kids call me a leftover piece of Victoriana, but this old slag is on her way to the post office. You want that lift to the Junction, Yukio pet?" The unicyclist gave Cerisia a quick kiss, scrambled to his feet.

"Ah, Yukio, before you depart," said Reptilio, momentarily distracted, reaching for a sheet of paper. "Let me recite for you my very first limerick." As Cerisia tried to grab it, he added. "With that change you wanted, darling one."

One Wagnerian night in Korea
My bubby was douched with sangria
While the lady was burping,
Sanguini was slurp…

"No," screamed Cerisia and hit him with the gold silk cushion.

"Take no notice of her, Yukio. I've signed it for you. Not yet perfect, but one in the eye for Zach's no rhyme Rimbaud, the tadpole. You're looking mystified. Never mind, you've got Dr

Reptilio working on a haiku. He intends to conquer all the forms. The Byronic epic is not beyond him."

"Bye Floralee. Bye Yukio."

Chippo had no interest in what Reptilio called it, priestly initiation or psychotherapeutic whatever, he did not want to remain an arsehole virgin a second longer. How he thrilled at the thought of his maiden voyage. No longer would his impatience have him dying a thousand deaths awaiting the Carnival, which was still several long, not-so-leisurely days away.

Reptilio liked a bit of reddening and primed Chippo's prized bottom with some well-aimed slapping. The euphoric shrilling erupted from Chippo's throat. Thank you, thank you, Reptilio.

"Oh, for heaven's sake." Smack! came Cerisia's beringed hand.

"Mmm, this fine contouring, I appreciate an unexplored male arse. So tight, so muscular." Reptilio's voice was syrup in Chippo's ear. "I don't know sometimes whether it's the male or the female that I prefer. You have the perfect rose of a pucker. What colourations – the mauve, the dusky pink. And mmm, what aromas." His nose was at him. "Tangy fruits, the fading hyacinth, a touch of fresh sawdust." His tongue was in there. Chippo gave a gasp and almost ejaculated on the spot. "I'm searching for a better name for your Coming Out, Chippo. Flower Dance, Deflower Dance? Something pretty that our audience can relate to. Maybe something Englishy, kiss of the lashy. Cerisiewiesie, help me here."

From the corner of his eye Chippo noticed that Cerisia was not enjoying Reptilio's musings and explorations. It was a banging on the side of the bus that cut short her descent into distemper. Someone at the front entrance. Up the steps. "Hello, Doctor, I am not intruding I trust? Lady Cerisia?" came a familiar voice. Toe-peeper shoe steps approaching through the dining area. Sir Henry Kmango.

"Bugger!" Reptilio had not even begun. "Don't despair, Chippo." He gestured towards Cerisia. "The rehearsal will continue in hands even more experienced than mine." He wiped oil off with a towel, threw on a tunic, made a pointless attempt to tuck himself away. "Le bon hotelier and I have much to discuss. He

wants the presentation of my Tophphi, my Chippo and my Zach –
if I ever get that recalcitrant country bumpkin conquered – to thrill
his guests like a first night at the Proms. Little does he know that
we will also be subtly re-educating those guests in some of the
admonitory African virtues. That the wooden horse is within his
gates."

The footsteps passed Lotus and Stan's quarters, stopped in the
'bunkhouse' – two tiered beds on each side of the central
passageway. "Are you back there, Dr Reptilio?"

"One moment, Sir Henry." Reptilio's eyes flicked to the ebony
phallus in its nest of raffia. "No rough stuff, darling." His lowered
voice was accompanied by a carefree gurgle of amusement. "No
blood sports." She rolled her eyes.

"Ah, my good chum," Sir Henry said as Reptilio eased into the
passageway, pulling the portiere closed behind him. "I am here to
request your presence at a momentous occasion. Less than one
hour ago, I spoke long-distance with naughty Ulysses. He outlined
in fine detail the location of the Bronzes. They are, after all, here in
Tlula, right under our noses. My joy at this serendipitous moment,
has been impossible to contain."

"Here, Sir Henry?"

"I understand your amazement at this absolutely incredibly
sensational news! It hurts me deeply to think that our Great
Liberator did not long ago share with me this information. I am sad
that Ulysses had no-one in all Bomzawe that he trusted to restore
them to the National Museum where they so rightfully belong. He
swears he always believed, from his first day of exile, that his
return was nothing less than imminent. I weep to think that it took
five years and a terminal illness. Oh, the Shakespeareanity of it all.
It is a tragedy on the scale of King Lear that may well sweep us all
away."

"And where were the Bronzes secreted, may I ask, Sir Henry?"

The hotelier seemed in no hurry to either impart information or
move away down the passageway. Cerisia lit a Gitane.
Detumesced, Chippo looked around for his shorts.

"The interior of your bus is an unexpected delight, Dr Reptilio. Traditional English furnishings and fittings."

"Lord Wittering's daughter has the taste that comes with her impeccable bloodstock lines."

"Lady Cerisia will honour us with her company, I hope?"

"Taking her afternoon nap, Sir Henry."

"Ah. The corridor ceiling is a masterpiece. Very Gainsborough with the copper beeches, but without clothes. Did she pose for that herself by any chance? Well, I suppose we will move along. It is impossible to persuade the locals to go down into the haunted dungeons of Castle Vinkenoog, but I have Billy Carpenter and my city team already there. They welcomed a diversion from their proud chalet toil. Even now the Bronzes are on their way to the village. Chief Akwa and his drummers and dancers will welcome us in the square by my latrine. Freshly scrubbed, I might say, by your excellent Zach Shaler We have the Dettol now! I have arranged for champagne to be opened. We will discuss your Carnival performances en route. I want to make sure we get the balance right. Colourful, yet discreet. Exotic, yet indigenous."

"Exactly."

"I am thinking a name change for your company would be wise. Do we really need, 'Evolutionary'? I would prefer something more essentially English. Let us think Noel Coward rather than *Hair*. And what exactly is a chakra? Attah, my devout Punjabi, may be the one to ask, but I don't think that..."

"Just a moment, Sir Henry. For this momentous occasion I will attach my best sandals."

"Dr Reptilio, you may not be aware that the Hornbill Palace was built specifically so that the Liberator could relax from the cares of state. To be at leisure, so to speak. I am sure all governments have such places." Sir Henry gave a soft cough. "It is time to fill you in on The Rites, or Customs as Ulysses called them, that we have always celebrated in conjunction with the Carnival."

The voices receded.

"Sir Henry sounds somewhat prematurely excited," Chippo commented, attempting to keep any knowing tone out of his voice.

"There he goes, my wild colonial boy." She let out her cackle. "I suppose he's told you I've buried two husbands. He adored that Tattler trash they used to write about me. I've grown even trashier, all this new-age improvement twaddle Reptilio is throwing around like confetti, but I have no intention of burying him." She picked some tobacco off her tongue. "He's a worry though. Do you know, he…"

Chippo had not encountered Cerisia in a ruminative mood before. It was the moment to make his excuses, alert Drift as to what was about to happen. The Bronzes were, after all, stacked in Chippo's room. The words 'complicit' and 'accomplice' came drifting in from somewhere in a past life, activating another phrase in Chippo's Siegfriedianed brain. "Firing squad!"

He wondered how the Liberator knew where the Bronzes were. There had to be more to the Qaddo story? He reached for his shorts. Cerisia whisked them away. "I can see my sweet spouse has you all of a twitter. Let's rooty toot toot!"

Cerisia stubbed out her cigarette and manoeuvred herself between him and the portiere. She let out a tee-hee of anticipation. "I don't mind telling you, Mr Cherrynose, Reptilio's always getting diverted by weasely nosebleeds like you. If I had known about my toot's omnisexual pretensions back in Switzerland, I would not have married him." Kneeling, she chucked him cheerfully under the chin. "Nor do I mind telling you that your certified virginity has been arousing my sodomitic impulses ever since Stan has been shaving the baby fuzz off that posterior of yours."

Cerisia whipped off her grass skirt and flashed the scarlet pubic heart Lotus had fashioned and dyed for her during the previous day's Eroto-rituals. Cerisia had proved herself touchingly vain at the result. "My topiary!" she had announced.

She grabbed the phallus. Lotus had recently revealed that the close to rolling pin sized object with its strappings had come from a sex shop in Amsterdam, not from an animist village in backwoods Mali. It was made not of ebony, but vulcanite, a tough and shiny rubber. "Tweet, tweet, tweetheart!" Cerisia was singing to the tune of Conway Twitty's *It's Only Make Believe,* as she slapped grease onto the shaft.

Chippo should have welcomed the unique opportunity and he did find Cerisia's enthusiasm endearing, but found himself struck more with an abject terror, a terror that had him scrabbling backwards, his mouth and jaw, his throat muscles working in strangled, febrile fashion. Something anatomical and vital was happening to his vocal chords. "Aahhh." He clutched his neck and suddenly, after hesitation and then some gargling to reassure, there materialised an understanding that he would be not only be able to speak but able to do so in a proper and harmonious voice and not necessarily backwards.

Yes, the glorious human ability to communicate verbally was once more available to him. The unique gift took the form of a gabble of flattery and sweet talk intended to get him out of a predicament. "Reptilio says that with the help of Floralee's crystal meth you have taken off forty pounds, Cerisia. He tells me that lovely Lotus has been staying up late, taking in the waist of all your harem pants. That you are buoyant again. Dancing divinely for someone your age. More divinely than ever before. I mean…"

The tone and tempo of his recovered voice were different. Not unpleasant by any means, but harsher and higher, with a dry leaf, coastal banksia-man catch in it.

"Well, well, well, grammatically correct sentences, Mr Smith! I always knew you were faking it." Cerisia was exhilarated, buckling up, positioning the awesome artefact with fearsome expertise.

Standing up on the mattress, Chippo managed a set of post-insectoid undulations for Priestess Bub, in sincere homage certainly, but which also brought him closer to escape. It would not be the first time he had run naked through the hotel grounds.

"Spread 'em, Chippo. Your hour has come."

"Please, Cerisia, there is no need to go to all this trouble."

"No trouble sweetie, I assure you. Like Reptilio said, time for rehearsal is running out."

"It seems so loveless, so impersonal. As you know, I'm seriously all gay abandon now. But for a virginal first time, something so precious, I insist that only a real male person and a real male body part will…"

Cerisia was in total command of the exit.

"I fully appreciate that you are carrying on the assertive traditions of Mary Kingsley, the proto-feminist, your distant relative who was awakened to lust and sexual freedom in Africa, not far from here but…"

"I think we're ready Mr Sydneypants. Gently does it."

"I could do your feet." Cerisia's feet were her daintiest feature. Starry was prone to eulogising them. Parked in the palanquin she always pointed them most appealingly. Lotus kept the nails buffed and lacquered.

"Let me do your toes. I'm the sucker to end all suckers. Ask Drift"

"What could you do that Lotus and Stan don't do for me already?" She dragged him down, forced his knees apart. "Come on, legs up! Let me at it."

"No no no…"

"Keep an eye on yourself in the ceiling mirror."

"Good Mother Bub the Divine, perhaps I could fuck you instead. Celebrate your new topiary." Yes, make an effort, be generous. It was now clearer than ever that he had been born without any attraction to female genitalia, but heterosexual doings (as he had come to know, with so many secretly gay men dutifully marrying, fathering children) could not be entirely impossible! "With a real one. Look, it has risen to the occasion!"

Nothing seemed to deflect her. Utterly desperate, close to tears, he made a further offer. "Darling Cerisia, let me explore your ocean cave, drink in your warm moist succulence, sip your aromatic vaginal juices."

"Chippo? You there? Mamba Emergency." The cavalry, his partner in crime, his handsome smuggler, his secret dick mate had pulled back the portiere. He was going to kiss him, he knew, for rescuing him yet again.

"You did a twiddly, Drift. Party of sixteen. Nobody did that in my restaurant, nobody. Bugger off!"

"Yesterday we had a deal. I'm already easing your python in for you."

"Fuck the deal. We've got unexpected expenses."

Drift's eyes went to a hypodermic resting in an open camphor wood box. Floralee's crystal meth sachets were visible beside it. "Yeah, right!"

"That debt is still rankly wankly, ain't it, Drift."

"You're the one who has got something rankling. Wittering dumped you and hired me. You've still got my honeypot kidnapped. It's time you gave me a break. What are you up to with Cherrynose?"

"She hasn't suffered her tormies since she moved in. She had her period finally. We have her dancing again. You're getting more than your money's worth." Cerisia had one of Chippo's arms twisted behind his back. "Stop giving me the tomtits, twinkle off and let Cherrynose and me get on with our workshop."

"Where is she?"

"I've got my Boys gangbanging her in the palm hut. Get out!"

"Formation swimming with Lotus and Stan and the others at the river mouth," Chippo put in quickly, seeing that Drift was unable to appreciate Cerisia's remark as jest. *The Afro-Esthers.*" It was the new, new name for the *Esther Williamsicals.*

Drift stared. "You're talking again. Congratulations!" He took hold of Chippo's other arm. For some moments both of them were tugging. Then Cerisia let go. She unbuckled the dildo, reached for her Gitanes. Chippo grabbed his shorts and leaped for the portiere.

"Twanks!" Lord Wittering's disinherited daughter let out a laugh that had the sound of defiance about it, rather than defeat. The dildo hit Drift's back with a dull vulcanite thwack as he pushed Chippo into the passageway.

TWENTY SEVEN: *Everything is broken*

"Two?" Sir Henry Kmango clutched the low-relief plaques, blackened and odorous. His voice rose to a high pitched scream. "Only two?"

Feeling foolish for having counted his chickens before they hatched, he had Ntank organize a search team.

"Recently removed," was the opinion of the chauffeur who had made his own inspection of the hiding place. He appointed a Chief Enforcer who set out to inflict maximum terror upon the village. Fangga, a known frequenter of the castle dungeons in his quests for bats' droppings, was put in leg irons. As chief suspect he would be held until he confessed. Those frequent trips to the capital. What was he hiding under his smock each time? How did he pay for those shiny custom-made boots? Everyone was aware of Blossom's track record with the Liberator and her bar was nailed up until further notice; the redoubtable proprietor herself put under house arrest. The single road out was blockaded and departing vehicles were searched. Up the Wawa River, The Great Liberator's humble cottage of his birthplace (now opulent mansion), was turned upside down and his centenarian mother and staff interrogated. Qojo reported that his parents' backyard had been dug up. Next door, massive Qaddo and Afreya, his petite wife, had been subjected to a brutal cross-examination. He had held fast and not given Drift's game away.

Drift had an evening of paranoia but had not panicked. He was more pissed off that he and Tophphi had managed to overlook a couple of the Bronzes.

Qaddo, still recovering from his battering, came knocking. "Excuse me, Mr. Drift. I apologise not telling you full story. I go next day to see Liberator. He sick but has doctor with him. I tell him we not want evil Bronzes. Not good for our village. I tell him where they were in the dungeons and he must take them when he go to Haiti. But they come after him and he has to go quick. I think I was happy then that the Bronzes were there in their grave with nobody know. Now I fear for you and for Tlula."

Drift accepted Qaddo's apology, "My loyal Qaddo," and sent him away. After smoking a chillum, he came up with a decision. At midnight, with the generator off, and everyone in bed, he and Chippo buried the Bronzes deep in the hotel's garbage dump, well away from its smouldering centre.

Before dawn, the very next morning, they were all rousted from their beds by the Enforcer and his team who made a thorough search of bungalows and rooms. Chippo's carefully constructed cages, out in the far hotel grounds, were also given a once, even a twice, over. He was pleased that his soon-to-be finished workmanship passed this preliminary test. The Hornbill in fact, was not under suspicion. Grand Larceny of a National Treasure (a treasonable, executable offence), was assumed to be something to which those few foreigners still remaining would never stoop.

News of the Bronzes' disappearance travelled quickly. Working the capricious hotel phone, Sir Henry had dictated a positive spin and it was the front page story in his *Okidoki Post*, editions of which were now making their way to the Hornbill more frequently.

BRONZES BEING SPIT & POLISHED UP
OFFICIAL VIEWING DELAYED 24 HOURS
NATIONAL REHABILITATION COMMITTEE
OUTRAGED AT OPPOSITION ATTACK ON
BELOVED ORATORIO'S RETURN

There were flattering images of Sir Henry and Ulysses Oratorio, an unflattering one of General Kporpor, and ironically, Chippo's photographs of the two cleaned-up Bronzes. From his northern stronghold in Larrakini, Kporpor, aligned with the Opposition, stated defiantly that a Public Expression of Remorse was no longer enough.

"Remorse for what?" Chippo Cherrynose asked as they watched Sir Henry's Silver Cloud leave for Okidoki. "Wasn't it just unfortunate internecine political squabbling?"

The Rolls Royce convertible reappeared in the palm grove late the following afternoon. The tycoon had spent his time in Okidoki in urgent consultation with President Mguavas.

Easter was very close. The Chakra Dancers were rehearsing final adaptations to the stage of their various entertainments. With Reptilio indicating that Tophphi would be one of the performers, Sir Henry was prevailed upon to watch.

"Very well. A few Sadler's Wells moments will soothe my jangled nerves. But I warn you, I have some good news and some bad, but the bad is very bad indeed." He sent Qojo running for the Chief Enforcer and sat down wearily. Ntank wiped sweat and dust from Sir Henry's forehead, massaged his shoulders.

"Tophphi, Tophphi, Tophphi..." they chorused, softer and softer. The gentle rhythmic thrumming over her body with tips of fingers sent the former Miss Georgia Peach runner-up and the participants into a dream world of pattering mudras. Their 'angel baby' was rotated and flown into the empyrean without permanent mishap.

Drift, watching from a canvas chair on the roof of *Whatever Forever*, was pleased that Reptilio and Cerisia were allowing Tophphi to regrow her hair. One morning after breakfast, Qumqwat had taken her to the Amazing Grace Fast Hair Salon and she had come back with a coiffure of baby corn rows and hundreds of tiny red and white beads. "Now you is real African girl, like us," cried Qumqwat giving her a high five. "Tophphi, you is black and beautiful!"

Sir Henry sipped Chivas, soda on the side, popped a pill. He applauded but his smile was absent.

While Cerisia, Lotus and Tophphi prepared for their triple baladi, Reptilio presented a truncated version of Chippo's Coming Out. Sir Henry listened abstractedly to the former lawyer's robust screaming, watched his frenzied bodily contortions as the Reichian massagers dug deep for primal information and prepared him for absolution. As he cleaned himself up afterwards, and polished his nose until the adamantine lustre of its carmines and vermilions was brought fully to the surface, Sir Henry complimented him on the technicolour chunder he had managed, and raised his glass. "Thank you Mr Cherrynose, most spectacular."

Chippo delivered a deep bow, much pleased. "I am glad, Sir Henry, that you understand that our eroto-psychotherapy makes for excellent theatre."

"I'm touched that you so see it, Mr Cherrynose."

The Chief Enforcer came bicycling up and spoke solemnly into the hotelier's ear. His gestures indicated a final frustration. Sir Henry drained his glass, stood up.

Floralee Bush, in her designated role as group cheerleader, was taking the chance to brush up her Byron Bay pompon routine. "Old woman, I must ask you to desist," cried Sir Henry. Ntank gave a crack of the whip in her direction. Qaddo stopped his drumming.

"My good Doctor Reptilio, I have a grave announcement to make. Two Bronzes are not enough. Under intense political pressure, President Mguavas has now decreed that the primary condition of Ulysses' return is that all Bronzes be located. If he enters the country otherwise, there will be no official recognition and his personal safety will not be guaranteed."

He held up a folder. "Mr Samuel Ichoko, the director of the National Museum has prepared an itemised listing of each piece that disappeared those five years ago. So there it is." He slapped the folder down on the card table Ntank had set up for him. "Crisis upon crisis is raining down on us. Ulysses Oratorio, our Great Liberator, has quarrelled with Baby Doc Duvalier and has been forced to leave Haiti. The good news is that President Houphet-Boigny of the Ivory Coast has granted him temporary asylum and even now Ulysses is winging his way to Abidjan. My Carnival is less than a week away. I am now tripling my reward for the Bronzes' return. Exhaustive searches are continuing. Ulysses' banshee of a mother is still proving intractable. We will keep putting the screws – is that how you say it – on her and on Mr Fangga and his nefarious connections. It is inconceivable that the bestial Blossom is as innocent as she claims. I am entirely confident, but if my confidence is misplaced, then of course, Ulysses will not be welcomed back to Bomzawe. There will be no Carnival. No Carnival at all. Now if you will excuse me, my heart is breaking."

Tophphi and Drift's eyes met for the first time in many days. "You gotta get them outta that shed and put them back," she said. "Over my dead body, Missy Minerva," Drift re-joined.

TWENTY EIGHT: *What is stress without the strut?*

Later that same afternoon, when the trotro delivered a package for Reptilio from Danny Dudgeon, it seemed to ensure in his mind that the Carnival could not possibly be abandoned.

"Wanda wandered out of Wooky Hole in the West Country. She's bedraggled, she's battered, she's suing, she's headlines in *News of the World*, but all criminal charges against Danny have been dropped." Reptilio hurled the latest *Thug* at Chippo. "Danny's published that picture I set up for you. One in the eye for Leni Riefenstal and her Nuba nudes even if I say so myself."

Thug's centrespread was a full colour reproduction of Chippo's photo of Tophphi and the Lanfal brothers, Qwami and Qojo, all cavorting naked on the beach by the hotel. A bare-breasted Cerisia waved from the palanquin. Her four 'Boys', their shorts around their ankles, mooned for the camera in the background. It pleased Chippo to see that the photo had been credited to *The Reptilio Love and Leisure Family*. Below it was an announcement 'for all thuggers and thuggees':

Coming up in our supercharged ORGASMATRONICAL summer THUGGERY, super skulduggery SPECIAL, the continuing TRASH and PULP sexploits of Starry Sanguini, our third world, third eye dingaling-danceman, now rebirthed as the rootin' tootin' REPTILIO. The shamaniacal MAGIC of his COCK and CUNT bus will guide us to a first time ever HAVOC and HEARTBREAK high. His FIST FUCK and PISS PIGS safari will take us past the JUNGLES of JEALOUSY to the QUICKSANDS of SEXTASY. We will JERK OFF to the sensational BUTTHOLE antics of anti-establishment FAGGOT, the singing INSECT, Chippo CHERRYNOSE. We will EJACULATE to the BALLET to BELLY dances of legendary Swinging London hostess, LADY LUST of LEISURE BEACH, Lord Wittering's degenerate daughter, CERISIA O CERISIA, now the maddeningly FAT muse and titivator of the regurgitating, ever rutting, aforesaid REPTILIOSO. It's

"Danny Dudgeon certainly seems to have captured the essence of carnivalesque exuberance," Chippo observed. "What exactly is clutterfuck?"

"Too bad it's off," said Drift drily. He had not been amused by the sight of Tophphi in *Thug*, but the more anxious Sir Henry and Reptilio grew, the more blithe he became.

"Dudgeon lays out the sexual possibilities like a blitzkrieg," cried Reptilio, all charged up by Danny's hunky-dory way with a phrase. "Our edition of *Thug* will be the last dress rehearsal for the next apocalypse but one, an aberrant danse macabre with Scotland Yard's Porn Squad. It will be playful, perverse, pederastic, pyroclastic and of course, primal. It will be our finest hour."

He palmed Chippo's eyes, cracked his spine, did his usual straightening of his posture at all possible speed.

"Thanks but no thanks Reptilio. One more twist and my head would have been off."

"A rat, you're becoming a rat in the ranks?" Chippo received a scarcely controlled backhander above his ear. "Danny and I bathed on the Left Bank with Angelo Quattrocchi's Situationists. We organised the Water Bed Screw-In at the Institute of Contemporary Art. Danny and I were guerrilla cupids, freedom fighting for bourgeois society's mangled soul." He spun himself from the fast into the frantic. "Danny's sexuality is as warped as the next budding tycoon's. As warped as yours, Chippo, before you landed in my lap. I'll get him down here for the Carnival, prise open his tin heart with our artistry! Adolf too! What has happened to Seamus Shamrock? He must know our supplies are long gone. It seems to me, Mr Chippo, you might be in need of a top-up. I'll dictate letters, make calls! How can those Bronzes still be missing?"

Reptilio and Cerisia had been skidding along on the crystal meth for days, talking up a tempest, changing outfits every hour or so, not eating. At that moment they were both wearing matching purple skull caps with upturned red trimmed brims. There was a monkish, Tibetan effect.

"They're losing it," said Drift. "Floralee, you should be shot. Selling them that poison."

"So shoot me, mate. She drove one mean fuck of a deal."

There was no time to lose. A serious talk with Drift was in order.

The talk did not amount to much.

"Reptilio has promised that my new Tibor Radovan will appear at the carnival. I know you are paying me well, Drift, or will, but I have to value love more than money!"

"Chippo, we're not putting the Bronzes back. I'm working Tophphi over and she'll come round. Reptilio's got her brainwashed but she's not mindblown. I trust her absolutely." Drift locked eyes. "Like I trust you. And Qaddo."

Again the erotic hand clasp, a finger tickle of Chippo's palm. "My buddy. I want you to take some more shots. With that el cheapo camera of yours. Decent ones this time, with clothes on. Some shots that will make both of you famous." He ruffled Chippo's regrowth. "How do you know your Tibor is not here in front of you?" The body came rubbing roughly, and the raggedy revealing Bermudas were presented.

When it had become apparent that there was not going to be any more searches of the hotel, Drift had dug up a couple of the Bronzes and stashed them in Chippo's wardrobe. The Chicagoan had taken them out, removed the plastic and placed them on the floor so they could admire them together. The artefacts stank, but yes, the cicada totem head was sitting there, with Drift promising once more it would soon be Chippo's.

Lying on his back on the floor for once, rather than standing up, a pillow from the bed supporting his head, Drift began fondling his Bronze, even giving the foul surface a kiss. It was no small sorrow that he always found something other than Chippo to excite him while he was being serviced. It could be a copy of *Thug* or more likely, the remains of an old *Penthouse* or *Screw* that the late Lobelia had ripped apart. Chippo's photos of Qumqwat in her puff-sleeved mini-dresses could also come in useful.

Drift put down his Bronze, placed his hands behind his head and watched Chippo. "I hold the trump card. Carnival's off. You saw my Georgia Peach dancing up a storm this afternoon. She's back to her supercharged best and it's time for her to choose between Reptilio and me. He lusts after her, but he doesn't love her. It's all a power trip. She'll choose me. If Starry's capable of loving anyone except himself, he loves Cerisia. Or even you maybe. Have you noticed that?" Drift looked at Chippo between his raised knees with sudden suspicion. "You're not giving him head too are you?"

"Sir Henry has two Bronzes already. You could put a few more back in the dungeons somewhere and claim the reward. A compromise would enable Kmango to do a deal with President Mguavas and keep the carnival on track. Stop him giving Tlula a hard time. Get the best of all possible worlds. And Tophphie would be..."

"Still can't believe we missed those two. Hey, I'm sorry about the village, but hear this, buddy, and hear it good." Drift sat up, and grabbed him around the neck. "Listen here, my Tophphi Project needs every dime I make on this venture. It's a once in a lifetime opportunity. And secondly, I'm glad you're queer, but if you were capable of loving Tophphi like I do, you would never never never permit her to perform naked in front of a bunch of strangers at a sleazy carnival on the fringes of the civilised world. I've got standards. Even if she doesn't. Now get back to work." Drift lay back and closed his eyes. A light snore indicated that he had fallen into an instant sleep.

Chippo could have turned his interrupted toil into a labour of love, but he was tired of being impaled on the horns of a dilemma. The answer was to escalate, test Drift's sincerity. A lie down with him, a horizontal embrace, something Drift had never permitted.

Chippo took off his shorts, kicked them aside. Once stretched out beside Drift, deliriously close but not touching, he felt the heat of the snakecatcher's skin, savoured his jungle hunter not-washed-for-a-few-hours smell. Drift is really gay, Chippo breathed to himself. As Reptilio himself preached, no matter how deep one is in the closet, there is always someone else even deeper. It was enough. Electric with anticipation, he gently lowered himself on top of Drift. As hoped for, Drift's hands went to his bare buttocks and began a caress. Visions of a more pleasurable impalement than being dildoed by Cerisia erupted. Yes, a profound penetration in the masculine manner that he craved; the manner that Reptilio had promised would finally make a whole man of him. He sought Drift's mouth. The snakecatcher's his eyes opened. "Hey!" Drift fractionally jerked his head and Chippo's tongue tasted only the droopy Colonel Custer.

"Back off, my little buddy, back off." The now wide-awake Drift pushed him roughly away. "No lip action. We're going to do the sleep together thing real soon, a triad, you, Tophphi and me. No monkey business." Drift inflated his lips like a frog, gave a double thumbs up.

It was not enough. Chippo's mouth turned down, tears welled up. Drift's commitment to Tophphi was unconditional, and despite the current impasse, she would forever be his baby. Stubborn as the former lawyer could be, he finally accepted that Drift could never be his new Tibor Radovan.

Drift pulled up his ragged Bermudas. "It's late. I'm still horny but to-morrow will do. You get better at it every day, Chippo. You'll get the Pulitzer. And the Oscar! Sure thing, buddy, it's the number two slot for you on the ranch in the rainbows." On his way out, he gave Chippo a peck on the nose. "Love that schnozzle."

At that moment the generator was switched off and the lights went out.

TWENTY NINE: *Yes, the lonely hunting heart*

With Drift gone, Chippo lit candles and began to clean the cicada head with a wet cloth. Then he rubbed it like an Aladdin's lamp, and politely requested a confirmation of his changed feelings about the duplicitous Drift. "Rainbows and showers on a ranch in Hawaii?" he whispered. "I don't think so." After five minutes, the cicada head's magic began manifesting in the form of a brassy, unearthly glow, the emerald eye had turned to neon, thirty seconds later, came vibrations…

There came a soft knock.

Chippo knew it would not be Drift. He peered through a gap in the louvres. It was Tophphi. She was looking frumpish – fetching nevertheless – in a nightgown, flimsy and a pale pink, more of a negligee really, much too large, one of Cerisia's; it even had food stains. He was in an immediate panic. "Just a moment."

The wardrobe was locked, the key gone. It was unfortunate that Drift, having done the locking, had absently put the key in his pocket. Hurriedly he moved the two Bronzes from the floor to the bathroom alcove. Ever accommodating, he slid the little bolt back and let Tophphi in. Equatorial night notwithstanding, she had brought him a mug of steaming cocoa from the bus. "I figured you'd dig a nightcap." Her eyes were stricken, flashing warning lights. She had been biting her luscious berry lips. She was still at her nails. "How do I tell Drifty I'm going to reveal the hiding place of the Bronzes?"

Chippo gasped. "You can't. Everything Drift does is for you. He has wonderful plans. Hawaii, Waimea, above the Kona coast..."

"Everything is for him, the jerk. I'm a specimen, like one of his mambas. A trophy that he gets off on, part of his stupid vanity. A vessel for the brood he has in mind. Having babies with him is just not on. He's so white Wonderbread. He'll dilute my ancestral blood even more." Tophphi clutched his arm. "But don't you go telling him that. Promise?"

"I promise."

"I feel more in control of my life when I'm with Reptilio than with Drift. I want to share my nakedness at the Carnival. Reptilio has created everything from the true spirit of Africa. He's even going to help me find my tribal name and an African father for my children. I'm so proud to be part of his love rituals."

"Me too. My gay origins. I'll be a sexual refugee no longer."

Drift's snores had started to come through the wall from the room next door. As instructed by Sir Henry, Attah had moved him out of his bungalow, which, like all the bungalows, was being refurbished for the Easter guests.

"There's no need to whisper," she said. "He goes to sleep on the ganja, nothing ever wakes him." Tophphi gave a laugh. Loud and crazed. Yes, as Chippo suspected, her torments were a-teetering inside that laughter. His eyes went to Drift's chillum, unsmoked, on a chair. He had forgotten his Zippo lighter as well. He put a finger to his lips. "Shhh." Despite the heat, an involuntary shiver ran down his spine.

Tophphi jiggled the poultice under which her wart was struggling for survival. Drift had been pestering Floralee and she had found a herbal remedy in Kassini Junction. "It's stinging like a wasp. Gotta get a good look at it." She picked up a candle and moved with its glimmering light towards the bathroom but Chippo managed to get in her way, handing her his Savlon instead. "Use this." He remembered his solemn promise to Drift, not to tell Tophphi that Bronzes were anywhere else but in Qaddo's shed. No longer his suck buddy but ...

"Oh, okay," She poked aside the poultice, began dabbing with a finger. "Ah, that's better."

"It's a beauty patch. Like Madame de Pompadour. Sexy."

"Why thank youuu! Try telling stupid Drift that."

Tophphi's temperature was rocketing up and she wanted to stick her head under the shower. He took her by the arm and fanned vigorously. She was dehydrated and wanted to get herself a drink of water. He handed her his half-finished bottle of warm orange Fanta. She still wanted water.

"Outta my way, handsome." She grabbed a candle again. "There's something you don't want me to see. Is Qojo hiding back there?"

"No, no. Ah, Attah's cut off my water. I'm late with the tariff."

Chippo fanned her anew. Tophphi subsided. "Drift get's so horny when I'm not there for him. When I was in love with Lobelia, he was having these horrible fantasies about kidnapping Qumqwat and fucking her in that hole below the sea wall. Sometimes I'm just not black enough for him! Are you doing it with him yet?"

The dim lighting concealed Chippo's rushing blush. "I've had my fantasies about him. Did he really get it on with Stan one time?"

"With Lotus. Poor Stan went ballistic. I was pissed off too. The creep!" Tophphi put her lips close to the former alcoholic's ear, drew her fingers teasingly down his cheek. "I dig you, Chippo Cherrynose. He'll always take a blowjob. I told you. Or bend over for him. That'll really take the heat off me. Better you than Qumqwat."

Despite her frazzled manner, Chippo was delighted by the forthrightness, the fondness in the two handed finger stroking, and indeed, that encouragement to bend over for Drift, even though it had come too late. Her warty nose came nuzzling into his. "I really dig your nose. I'm glad you've stopped making that weird noise." Next second she said, "I agree with Cerisia. I'm beginning to hate men who put animals in cages. I prefer Reptilio's dream for the future. His Ninth Chakra Plan. I want to go with them in the magic bus when they continue their African safari. They're like the parents I've left behind. They smell so nice when I curl up in the big bed with them. The flower farts are so delicate and funny. And Mother Bub really is Divine. Oh Chippo, I need that Final Healing at the Carnival so bad. Then I can fully embrace my African self. I have to choose happiness over the illusion of material things like the Bronzes."

Tophphi had been breathtakingly close. Now she came even closer, preparing herself for the real reason she had arrived so late in Chippo's room. Her breasts quivered under the negligee, she gave her hips a shimmy. "Did I put enough sugar in your cocoa? I know you like lots," she purred. "Chippo, I've figured it out. Drift won't put the Bronzes back so I'm writing an anonymous note for both of us about them being in Qaddo's shed. If it's okay with you, I'm gonna slip it under Sir Henry's door tonight. I know you'll agree. It will break Drift's stupid heart, but I've broken his heart before. It always mends." She picked lint out of Chippo's belly button, ripped a hair from his left nipple. "He has no business stopping our Healing and that's that!" She pushed. "Outta my way, water or no water, I gotta pee."

There was a loud snort from next door and the snoring ceased. A cough, a footfall. Tophphi was flying down the wooden steps so fast it was almost as though Chippo had imagined she had been in the room at all. Drift came in yawning, flicking back his hair. "I heard voices." He sniffed the air. "Was Cerisia here? Can't believe I'm awake."

Drift gave another huge yawn. "There's no reason now not to get my Bronzes outta Bomzawe pronto. Qaddo will be pleased the curse has gone elsewhere. Kassini Junction manana what's wrong with that, book a truck. How much more work can there be – another hour or two in the morning?"

"Drift, I'm pretty sure Tophphi won't be wanting to miss the Carnival. You know I am eager to be here for it too. We both have made commitments to Reptilio and Cerisia."

"Oh give me a break, Chippo. You know Reptilio's Coming Out Tibor Radovan thing is all a bunch of bullshit." Drift was glancing around. "Hey, there's what I came back for. My fucking chillum. What kind of best buddy lets an all-American guy forget his chillum?"

"How about you give me back my wardrobe key."

THIRTY: *Somewhere over the rainbow*

The chillum sent Drift back into dreams sweeter than those from which he had woken, but Tophphi was not so fortunate. By the time the Georgia Peach runner-up got back to *Whatever Forever* that night, her tormies had spiralled in and struck without mercy. Reptilio and Cerisia seized their opportunity and pounded her for more memories of her father's doings in the turkey sheds. There was a fragile period of calm, but by dawn, she was in a stratospherically high state of anxiety, with her screams reaching such a pitch that her lapse into a coma was a welcome diversion. "Her neurones have had enough for the moment," said Reptilio. "She's escaped into cataplexy." They gathered as if to a dying. Old Idi and his gaggle, passing by the bus on their way to the dump, paused.

"Oh, cupcake, what have those two monsters done? If you could only see what you look like," murmured Drift, who had been permitted entry. He entwined his fingers in Tophphi's beads and cornrows. There had been a sudden eruption of pimples around her chin. Her eyes, when they were open, were dulled, inward-looking. Drift picked off the nose poultice, threw it to the floor. When he gave her a kiss on the lips as if to awaken her from her comatic state, she did in fact, like Snow White, suddenly rouse herself.

"The Bronzes," she screamed. "Reptilio! Cerisia! Drift stole the Bronzes!"

Drift still had a hand clamped over Tophphi's mouth when they came rushing back from the dining area, even though she had relapsed into unconsciousness.

"What was that?" Reptilio demanded. "Her father?"

"You'll be the death of her," Cerisia shouted, giving Drift a push. "Twiddle off!"

"I insist on being here when she fully wakes."

"She's not waking up any time soon," said Reptilio. "She was her father's little mistress for years. When she began to object, he raped her in the turkey sheds and she tried to kill him with a sabre. A Civil War sabre. That's why she ran away from home. That's why the brute's in jail."

"This is total garbage," Drift shouted. "He was incarcerated for turkey rustling. He had to destroy his own birds because they got a virus. Theft, that's all and so what! I visited him with Tophphi more than once. They hugged and kissed. He's a cool guy. A southern gentleman. Once a month she sends him a postcard. She loves her father."

"Drift, the truth has been emerging consistently in the sessions, day by day."

"Torture people enough they'll say anything. Her father and mother both came to see her one night in the Candy Bar. When Rosarita had the Petting Zoo going. They saw what a star she was and stopped worrying. I was there."

Reptilio shrugged and Drift went off to his Menagerie, where he had scheduled an "Open House". He was expecting Sir Henry and Ntank to be there shortly.

With the Carnival so close, Reptilio took a chance and decided on an all-or-nothing emergency exorcism, a treatment he said he had seen employed successfully in a fetish house at Lubarra, a remote desert town in the far north-west of Bomzawe, but had never before dared to employ. Cerisia nodded sagely.

Chippo could not help but blanch when Reptilio went into the details.

"You tell Drift and I'll tie you down and fuck you," said Cerisia, letting out a cackle. She reached out and gave Chippo's ear a twist.

"Darling, please."

The Menagerie was located in the Polynesian Long House. The hotelier had abandoned its restoration for lack of time, but had agreed in the days when the Carnival was still on track that it was just the place for Drift's snake collection and the other animals and birds he had collected for display at the Easter Carnival. As each cage was finished, it was transferred there.

Drift's labelling was in place, printed on a press owned by Sir Henry in Kassini Junction. *DEADLY – KEEP AT LEAST THREE FEET FROM WIRE MESH,* each well-designed sign read. Beneath, was the title of a cage's occupant. *BLACK MAMBA – Dendroapsis polylepis.*

The snakes hissed restlessly. They were not fond of the old monkey hunter and his adept grandson who comprised Drift's collecting team. Zach, flagon of palm gin in hand, took a lurch around. Over the past few days he had been withdrawn, melancholic and drinking hard. He knew that his parents, having been told of his 'suicide attempt', were already on their way to Bomzawe, and Chippo, with Drift excised from his radar of love, was well aware that this was affecting Zach in ways the Nebraskan was not emotionally prepared for.

Reptilio and Cerisia, much to Drift's surprise, also turned up. Cerisia was snacking as usual, but now on a tropical fruits diet, which, along with Floralee's crystal meth, had her getting ever slimmer and worse tempered. Tophphi had been left behind, with Lotus and Stan in attendance in case she came out of her coma.

The Menagerie was, as always every morning, a feeding scene. Qojo and Aqosua, along with several other children, had delivered their piles of small birds, rats, rotting fruit, clover and spinach, bamboo shoots, and nettles. Flies and ants were laying siege. Chippo had negotiated a price with the children and, as usual, helped with the feeding. Bonnie & Clyde, always curious, always around, were kept at bay.

Nothing was said by Reptilio and Cerisia about the exorcism planned for Tophphi. Nor by Chippo. Drift in fact had his own news to impart.

"I'm taking Tophphi to Doggone General later today. I've fixed up a bed in the back of the Rover."

"She's not fit to travel," said Reptilio;

"That hospital's only good for cattle," said Cerisia.

"Private room. She will be staying over Easter. Out of harm's way. Out of your fucking way! I've got a truck coming from the Junction for the snakes."

"Not before you pay your rotten restaurant bill."

"What's happened to your sweet and slovenly side these days, Cerisia? I preferred you fat and depressed."

"Fuck you too. I hear it's the bilge for poor Tophphi on a fishing trawler."

"First class. The *Star of Casablanca's* a Norwegian boat. Squeaky clean. Chippo's coming with us. Aren't you, old buddy?"

"Chippo's here for the Carnival. He's not throwing away the chance of a lifetime."

"There's no Carnival. Forget it, fuck off, es terminado!!"

Reptilio and Cerisia stood their ground.

"Sweet papaya, tweetikins?" Chippo was offered her fruit bucket.

"I have to admit you handle these creatures with great skill," said Reptilio as Drift began the transfer of an eight footer. He and the monkey hunter's grandson had trapped it – a bush rat in its mouth – slithering out of one of the bungalows still awaiting repair. Drift never wore gloves and always made it look easy. The snake stared straight ahead. Its eyes glittered, long black tongue flickering in and out. The tail was vibrating, not with the noise of a rattlesnake, but the rapidity equally a warning to move back.

Zach bent down to observe and in Chippo came a foreboding. There was a feverishness in those dark green, gold flecked eyes of his. "Not too close, Zach." Drift released the snake into a cage's hiding box. Before anyone realised what Zach was up to, he had come up behind Drift and thrust his arm in, open palmed, as though he was offering himself. Many things happened quickly. The mamba struck his wrist with three, maybe four strikes, before exiting the cage. With extraordinary speed it slid out into the grove, disappeared into a pile of dead brush.

Chippo caught Zach as he fell back. Blood oozed from the hits. Everyone panicked except Drift. He had the fang marks incised and Zach's upper arm tourniqued within seconds. Before long he was spitting out blood and venom. "Stay quiet, you stupid fuck. Don't touch him. I'll be back in a flash."

By the time he came running back with the venin, and found a vein, Zach was blue in the face, suffering cramps and in agony with chest pains. "Heart attack," said Drift. "It happens."

Cerisia lit a Gitane. Close to the last of her supply. "There's no obligation to hang on forever." Coolly, she blew smoke down in Zach's direction, spat a shred of tobacco off her tongue. "Let Zach zippity doodah out if that's his wish. He's clearly reached that point. Again. I'd say he's happy to put an end to fifteen years of fuck all. Suffering, if you want to call it that."

"Oh, Cerisia, please, he…"

"We all die sometime, sweetipie. I admire people who are brave enough to take matters into their own hands. Zach's one of the lucky ones. Mango?"

"You're wrong. He doesn't really want to." Chippo was close to anger (an emotion hitherto unknown to Chippo Cherrynose), his body constricting with many feelings, both vague and precise. A memory of his Dad telling him there was "nothing else but this life, so hang on to it," came into his head, "respect your future" and there was a welling of tears. "It's a cry for help. He knows there are people around to rescue him."

"Suicide can be fond of an audience. Believe me, I know. Death as performance."

Cerisia may have leagued herself with the Grim Reaper, again, but Reptilio had had some kind of a light bulb moment and was in full *furor sanandi*. Launching into a major Africanastics, he danced, he mimed, he made sucking noises.

"Toots, you're wasting your time. Let him go."

"Quit the Swan Lake crap, asshole." Drift snarled, shoving Reptilio aside. Just as violently, Reptilio shoved back.

"Like stags," whispered Lotus. "Don't you just love it?"

Attah, Qumqwat and the shocked hotel staff clustered around as they laid Zach on his bed. Lotus applied a cold compress. As the day wore on, Zach's larynx became paralysed, his whole body less motile by the minute, his sight partially lost. Drift injected him with more venin. Reptilio applied the full extent of his hyperactive energy to the nursing. He arranged for Lilibet Lanfal to give Zach solutions of saline and glucose every hour and even drew up a roster for his care. "I'm not going to lose my greatest challenge. I've been putting a lot of my best work into this one."

Deep into the night, just when it seemed the angels were about to hoist him up to heaven, as Melody might have intoned, Zach's eyes fluttered open.

"Home is where the heart is," he murmured weakly. "Dorothy said that."

"Who's Dorothy?" Chippo asked.

"His younger sister," said Reptilio. He waved Chippo out of the room and moved in close.

It was the beginning of a recovery, some kind of miracle, but it seemed only a matter of time before he would try his luck again.

Next morning, Reptilio instructed Chippo to shave Zach's beard and moustache, his chest, brush-cut his fast growing hair, so that he would once more achieve 'visual unity' with the Family. "And behave yourself. No point losing your mind to yet another loser."

As Chippo scraped the razor across his chin, Zach did little but stare unblinkingly at a picture of a crucified Christ on the wall in front of the bed. Reptilio had hung it there. Beneath, on his small cane table, was the ripped piece of faded blue cotton that Zach believed came, fifteen years earlier, from a leg of Zoe's broadshorts.

"Zach, the island and now this, you have to start taking your medication again. I'm sure Starry would agree with me that…"

"Our spirit forces are in me. They come and go as they please. I have to follow. Were they beckoning from the cage, Chippo? I reached out…"

Chippo shut his ears. Having escaped his own delusions (as he thought), he wanted no part of these ones. He turned shaving Zach into a making of love to him. Particularly in light of the fact there could be no loving beyond loving care.

Chippo sensed a gradual withdrawal as Zach became aware of an intimacy beyond his ability to relate to. His hand was given a single pat. "Thank you, Chippo." The tone was heartfelt but also dismissive, his eyes not on the man who had been shaving him, but on the Christ. He caressed his cheek with the faded piece of blue cotton as he gazed at the Saviour. That gaze did eventually come back to Chippo, who looked earnestly for something of bad boy Tibor's loving glances in there, but Zach eyes registered only opacity. A fervent wish came that now Mr and Mrs Shaler were on their way, they arrive soon and rescue their son from a fate that no one else, not even Reptilio, seemed able to deflect him.

In that very moment, as though he had read Chippo's thoughts, Zach said, "Reptilio has come up with a great idea. A burial behind St Bedes. When my parents front up, Reptilio will show them the fake headstone. Hand them all my papers. Cerisia will use my money to buy a new passport from Floralee. Reptilio and I have worked it all out. I will be born again. We dash Attah and everyone not to tell."

THIRTY ONE: *Oh my beloved father*

It was the Wednesday before Good Friday. The Great Liberator, existing now in homeless limbo, had arrived safely in Abidjan, less than 80 miles to the west.

Poised in a crouch like a stone age hunter, Reptilio stalked the vultures. Scraps of offal lay on the ground. As the flock approached, he uncoiled an explosive burst of that same kundalini energy he had discovered how to access on the night of Kofu's funeral in Tlula. He soared in the direction of one of Old Idi's subordinates, grabbed it in mid-air. Click! Reptilio had reminded Chippo to bring the camera.

"You crazy man, Dr Reptilio." Attah (who for another dash had sharpened a cutlass for Reptilio), scratched his head as the flapping, croaking bird was stowed in a sugar bag. "That fellow, he bad bad chop."

"I'm going to walk," Cerisia announced. She had volunteered the palanquin for the occasion. Her Svelteness, as Reptilio had dubbed her, was continuing to shed freight at an alarming rate. A sedated Tophphi was gently laid on the cushions, the curtains pulled. Reptilio sent her on ahead with the Boys. Cerisia, in a dancing mood, went tripping along beside her. At the early time set for the exorcism, Drift was still fast asleep, as Reptilio well knew he would be.

"I really think he should know," said Chippo. "I'll go wake him."

"In your heart you know it's better for Tophphi if you don't."

"Reptilio, you're breaking your promise."

"I forbid you!" Reptilio hooked him around the neck with a proprietorial arm and gave him a kiss.

By the time they were halfway to the palm shelter – for a verisimilitudinous atmosphere, Lotus had decorated it in a manner she imagined a Deep South turkey shed might look like – Chippo was having enormous qualms. He lingered, slowly fell behind the procession, managed another small revolt and ran back.

Drift had carried Tophphi from her bed in *Whatever Forever* with such determination, there was no stopping him. He had parked his Range Rover right outside the bus, but she came out of her coma, took in what he intended and had another attack of her torments. The screaming began. At one point her eyes had rested on Chippo. "The note, put the note under Sir Henry's door," they seemed to insist before they lost focus and rolled up, revealing the whites. The screams did not subside until Drift had removed himself from her presence. She sank back into insensibility. Distraught, the snakecatcher had given way. But not before Drift had exacted a promise. "On one condition, Reptilio. If you start any new-fangled treatments, I want to be there to supervise."

"Absolutely, Drift. I give you my word."

A chillum, fully smoked, lay beside Drift's head. Chippo began the difficult task of arousing him. As ever, the herpetologist was slow to get going, and that morning he did not seem to understand the need for haste. There had to be the meticulous packing of the chillum he required to set him up for the day, the ingestion, the recovery. There were several minutes before he could talk, a few more before he could walk. A lengthy shower. There was the extended brushing to bring up the shine of his hair. By the time he stopped by the kitchen for the Full Breakfast with the Poached Guinea Fowl Eggs Special, Chippo had given up, realising that the Chicagoan hadn't wanted to supervise the exorcism after all. Drift was still there exchanging barbs with Qumqwat and flirting with another of Attah's favourite girls when they saw the palanquin and the Boys coming back. Drift left his eggs and rushed to Tophphi's side. She was out of her coma, sleeping peacefully.

"We were turkeys," cried Lotus. "It was fun. Gobble, gobble!"

Reptilio was triumphant. "She killed her father." He reached into the sugar bag and held the vulture's severed head high like a trophy. "Behold, the evil Daddy Fuck. Tophphi woke up and did the chop herself! Perfect!" He threw the grisly object to Old Idi and his flock, already milling around. The rest of the corpse followed. There was fierce squabbling.

"You twiddled out, Cherrynose. You were supposed to take pictures." With a stick, Cerisia starting whacking him on the backside. "Scared of a little blood? Think we can destroy the patriarchy without it?" One final whack and she stormed off.

"Darling one..." Reptilio cried after her.

"What's the patriarchy?" Chippo asked, rubbing his bottom.

"Momma whack, but she doesn't mean it. She's temperamental, papayas and bananas will do that." To Drift, Reptilio said "An incredible success. You'll find that Tophphi's torments have gone for good. We will confirm it in a more ritualised fashion at the Carnival. Stan is already thinking of music. The lovely Lotus is whipping up masks and costumes." Reptilio's nostrils were flaring arrogantly at the thought of aggressions and triumphs to come. He pulled out the hand mirror he had appropriated from Chippo, checked the strength of his gaze, eyed his profile. "Reptilio. No witchdoctor but a Dancedoctor. C'est moi! I'm moving on again."

"If anyone's evil Daddy Fuck, it's you," shouted Drift. "How about Tophphi chopping your head off. What do we know about your past? The past that has turned you into a monster?"

"It's beyond your comprehension, Drift," Reptilio snapped. "Let it go!" He commanded a departure, and accompanied by the slumbering Tophphi and Cerisia's Boys, he slithered off.

"It was nothing, Drift. Easy as falling off a log," said Lotus soothingly. "You'll see. Cerisia got it all documented on video."

"He was Daddy Fuck all right," said Floralee. "Out of control again. Cerisia had to do her tootsie wootsie devil yell. But Drift, the vulture's the turkey and in Reptilio's mind, Tophphi's father and the turkeys are one and the same. By association. Reptilio's mind is warped, but don't you see?"

Drift would not be mollified and kicked at the cannibalistic vultures. Chippo too was troubled, but more by the fact that it was only Mother Bub the Divine who had the power to call Reptilio back from that perilous world that he insisted – for the sake of the artist's unfettered imagination and for the sake of access to ecstatic healing – on letting himself spiral into.

"It was disgusting," Floralee conceded, "but I've run into this stuff before. In the Philippines, chickens and things. Dogs. It's all the go these days. Rock stars are into it. Ever heard of Alice Cooper? After a while you wind up inured and let it go."

"Cerisia is making it extremely hard to appreciate her many qualities." Chippo's backside was still burning.

"Oh, Chippo, she told me you were rude the other day about her topiary." Giggling, Lotus pulled down his shorts, knelt and began kissing his bottom better. "How could you? You of all people? Stanford, darling, hand me my Calamine."

THIRTY TWO: *Love or what you will*

Reptilio arranged an urgent meeting that night with Sir Henry Kmango in the bar. The old Dansette had been replaced by a new turntable and a powerful set of speakers. Cliff Richard's *Living Doll*, one of Sir Henry's favourite songs was playing but he was in a low mood. When Tophphi was presented, the hotelier managed only a faint smile. "Poor Miss Afro-America, our broken beauty. On the brink, like me this darkest of Churchillian hours."

"On the contrary, my dear Sir Henry, not broken, mended..." Reptilio began.

Tophphi had slept soundly throughout the day. Now she was radiant. Her eyes sparkled, once again her skin was unparalleled in its silkiness, and graced with a baby-dollish flush. Her shoulders were bare above a pale halter-top and pleated skirt. Despite the milk chocolate skin, the cornrows and beads, she seemed a figure straight out of the all-white Tinseltown fifties.

Reptilio was eager to explain the *Sacred Vulture Daddy Dance*. "...in short, my new healing ritual is what I have to call a Supreme Triumph, a breakthrough, greater than anything I achieved in London, Vienna or Amsterdam, even New York. After what you said about The Customs of Ulysses' days, Sir Henry, the ritual may remind you of the spiritual practices and mysteries of animist forebears. Arouse in you ancestral memories from the days when..."

Sir Henry had been distracted throughout this peroration, had scarcely heard a word. "My dear Dr Reptilio, it all sounds wonderful, but I am unable to share your joy. Time has run out. My searches have turned up nothing. The Bronzes are gone. Ulysses is doomed. He is now a man without refuge, a man without a country or a home."

Reptilio slithered low into some lizardlike press-ups. Yet another added move. Even before he came to a stop, Chippo realised that the former Dr Sanguini had been withholding information.

Reptilio sprang into an upright position and cried in great glee, "Sir Henry, the nothing less than absolutely gorgeous Tophphi here, will tell you where the Bronzes are."

Drift stifled a gasp, made an involuntary movement forward. Sir Henry's hands came together with a soft clap and in his genuine shock he could not help rising. "And where might that be, my dear girl?"

"I can take you there."

Reptilio gave the tiniest flicker of indication to Tophphi who went to Drift. She wrapped the full bloom of the Georgia belle around him. "Honey, it had to be."

"Tophphi, peach, what's to be?" he asked, in bewildered tones. "You are so innocent. Your illness, your roots, you are being misled to no good end." He blew gently on her blemished nose as if to soothe the sting of yet another corroding poultice.

"Sweetheart, you've got it all back to front." She twirled strands of his hair through her fingers, flicked it back for him. She traced his lips beneath the General Custer, circled his nipples with the tip of her tongue. "The moral thing. The age-old raptor exorcism is the best thing that's ever happened. It has set me free. Bomzawe has become my heart and home. I have to share everything with the African world at the Carnival. Be a part of it with me."

"Tophphi, kitten, you don't know where those Bronzes are. No one does."

"Quit it, Drift," Reptilio advised. "Game's up."

"Reptilio sexually violates women in the name of therapy!" Drift shouted, pushing Tophphi aside. "There has been an animalistic rape! There's a video to prove it." He towered above Sir Henry and Ntank, his fists clenching and unclenching. "Tophphi is my responsibility, the mother-to-be of my children. I'm taking her away from all you slimy fuckers forever. I love her."

Ntank's teeth began to gnash and snap in a terrifying periodontal display. He surged towards Drift in a sharklike attack. Attah, hovered nearby with his cast-iron frying pan.

"Not before she takes us to the Bronzes, Mr Drift. I am warning you. Ntank, a moment please!"

"She's a mad woman. Look at her."

"They're in Qaddo's shed in the hills," cried Tophphi.

"Ha ha ha! I told you she was off her rocker." Before Ntank could stop him, Drift scooped Tophphi up in his arms and ran off with her. She screamed and beat at him with her fists as they vanished into the night.

"Qaddo's shed was searched." Sir Henry and Ntank were more than disappointed, enraged! "Every shed in the hills, we burned."

Chippo hesitated no more than a second or so. "There are two Bronzes in my room. The others are buried in the hotel dump."

Twenty minutes later, a jubilant Sir Henry was on the phone to President Mguavas. When he returned to the bar, he was mopping his brow, breathing heavily. He had Qwami pour Nwalabi Hills champagne for everyone. Over ice. "Dear President Mguavas. Now he has the ammunition he needs to deal with the appalling Kporpor plotting away up there in Larrikini. Puking for partition!" A call had also been made to Abidjan.

The Bronzes, checked off on the Museum's list as all accounted for, were under lock and key. For a few moments Sir Henry watched the etiolated Qojo at play with one of Cerisia's Boys at the ping pong table. "Such is the President's enthusiasm, he is sending monitors from the National Crime Authority, the "Morals Squad" as they are known. My carnival will be flattered. Please talk freely with them. Emphasise particularly any Shakespearean and other English aspects. The precision of your techniques. The healthy western therapeutic values. Make sure they see your resume, Dr Reptilio, your quality credentials. Some representatives from Amnesty International who happen to be in the capital will honour The Great Liberator with their presence as well. I will have my excellent Ntank ensure that they are shown every courtesy."

A retrograde revved-up mmmm squeezed out of Chippo.

"Ah, the always chirpy Mr Cherrynose. Jolly to a fault. Our saviour! How blessed I am. You reveal Mr Drift's naughty prank, Dr Reptilio in all his cleverness shows me how to give the Carnival a necessary nip and tuck. At the very last moment, we are on track for a good time to be had by all." Sir Henry tossed a digestive the size of an all-day-sucker into his mouth, patting his oesophagus as a flood of champagne washed it down. "Enough for the moment of my tribulations. How is our sad friend Mr Zach, our non-existent guest." He laughed softly.

Chippo was somewhat amazed that Sir Henry was privy to Reptilio's headstone lark.

"I wish there was something I could do to speed his recovery. Bubble and Squeak? Which is, as you know, or should, one of Chef Lalwani's signature dishes. What about a delicious dessert? Your world famous Australian delight, Mr Cherrynose? Aeroplane Jelly. We have the packets." He looked at Chippo knowingly, unleashed his very best smile. "We do need Mr Zach back on his feet."

Glasses were raised and everyone toasted to the full recovery of Zach.

To confirm there were going to be no recriminations or hard feelings of any kind (and no reward to be paid), Sir Henry sauntered over to Drift who had returned and was sitting with Tophphi on his knee at a distant table.

"My gratitude to you, with your serum, sir, is unbounded. It can be difficult if one of your citizens meets an untimely death in our poor country. US funding is withdrawn, and as we say, the ton of bricks comes down."

Drift's sugar baby was giving him every possible attention but he was inconsolable.

"Mr Drift, might I ask how you were you proposing to get the Bronzes out of the country? These matters are not as simple as you might think."

"My connection in Okidoki was coming here to appraise them, take them off my hands."

"Your connection. I see."

Drift began kissing Tophphi passionately on the mouth. In case she blurted out anything different.

THIRTY THREE: *The eyes have it*

Love Love Me Do's beat chugged into the hot night, never louder, never more familiar. Chippo watched Tophphi and Drift dancing in the centre of the floor, the almost Miss Georgia Peach singing along and moving with a winning abandon beyond anything they had seen from her in the previous weeks, except perhaps that one-off day of her cartwheels with Qojo and Qwami, the Lanfal brothers.

After a short celebratory shuffle with his chauffeur, Sir Henry retired to a pavilion with Mr and Mrs Reptilio. Attah himself carried out to them a platter on which was an example of his new 'lean cuisine', a whole roast duiker (a forest deer the size of a doberman) with absolutely no fat, as Cerisia was now demanding.

"Lotus, dear, what they talking about?"

"Cerisia's not selling the *Vulture Daddy Dance* any cheaper than your *Deflowering*."

"You mean they're discussing our performance fees."

"You bet. A real big fat one for Zach's *Supreme Triumph*."

"I beg your pardon?"

"Whoops!" Lotus zipped her lips closed. "Let them handle these things, Chippo." She tossed her braided head, sent her favourite earrings, those dinky ceramic teapots, a-jiggling and danced herself over to Stan.

Chippo was feeling very alone under the central fan as he watched the entwined Drift and Tophphi. In return for a solemn promise from Drift that he would not in any way interfere with her performance of the *Daddy Dance* at the Carnival, Tophphi had agreed: (a) never never never to reveal that the cages with their ingeniously Cherrynose-engineered secret compartments, were for anything but the snakes, and (b) out of the 'goodness of my heart', she would move out of the bus and back in with him.

A desperately dark mood was advancing upon Chippo. It was okay that Drift would no longer honour him with his male endearment, 'buddy': or when stoned, present his most beautiful body part for service. Yes, even sex, after betrayal, was sadly, too much to hope for. But then again, he had already tested Drift in the more important matter of love and found him, as far as Chippo was concerned, wanting. He should just wish them both all possible joy. True togetherness in life was so very rare. How glorious to see it in the symbiotically partnered Drift and Tophphi.

He regretted having to say farewell to the totemic cicada head. But it was, after all, a National Treasure, and about to be returned to a Grateful Nation. Yes, it had to be. Now they would all be able to enjoy the immeasurably greater pleasures of the Easter Carnival, celebrate the Essence of Family and the Priceless Fulfilment that it would bring them all.

Chippo raised his cocktail glass in a lonely salute to an emotionally rich and civically responsible future and all at once was bucketing tears. He signalled urgently to Qwami. By the time the slothful bartender had completed the admittedly complex task of mixing a fresh Pink Squirrel, with triple Amoretto and extra palm sugar, he was recovering. He managed to give Qwami a look he hoped would be received as amorous. It was. Qwami, butterfly of the night, batted his crowded eyelashes, dried Chippo's cheeks with his bar towel, once more presented his lips. Was the handsome, well-hung Qwami merely representing the satisfaction of lust, that all too temporary release from loneliness and despair? Or was he the one to make a commitment to, the elusive love of Chippo's life? They fabricated a kiss which was more than perfunctory but the answer was NO! A blade of pain poleaxed Chippo's head. He slumped forward, left cheek on the counter in a puddle of beer. More tears gushed down. Stan in his jerkin and jock strap, blissfully banging away with a couple of tumblers on a nearby table, the ever loving Lotus fondly helping him keep time, had it all over poor Chippo Cherrynose.

He felt an onset of his spasms, those unfortunate side effects of his otherwise extremely successful therapy. He remembered a Reptilio dictum – the spasms would stop for good only when loving concord with another human being had been achieved. Yes, the Carnival, but what about NOW! And who was it going to be anyway? Like Drift, Qwami was out of the question. Stan? With the rapid escalation of civil unrest in the rest of Bomzawe, there had been repeated consular travel warnings and the supply of 'hippie dreck' (more than once recommended by Cerisia as a satisfying substitute for Drift) had ceased to pass through Tlula. Reptilio himself? He did not like to think that ultimately, that was what Reptilio was up to; Chippo's sacred Coming Out only a snaring for him of an additional bride He rubbed his still raw backside and could not help giving a shudder as he pictured the probable nature of a Cerisia reprisal if that was the case. The word 'harem' came to mind.

He realised, for the first time since his 're-birthing', that he was having a truly retrogressive moment. He was no longer Chippo Cherrynose, but the former Chipman Smith. He saw Reptilio once more as a stranger with a past and was there not another life in that past of which he once knew but now was lost to him? The moment drifted away. "Wally," he cried silently, "where are you when I need you?"

Chippo went out into the night and up the wooden stairs. Zach was awake, bare torsoed, propped up on pillows and staring at the bubble-gum pink wall, blank but for the picture of the Easter Christ. His hands were clasped in front of him. Chippo had a tray with drinks for both of them. "Kool-Aid?" Zach had told him, some weeks earlier, that it was the official state drink of Nebraska.

He got the invalid to swallow a mouthful. No alcohol, Drift had said, but Chippo had Qwami pour in a touch of Wild Turkey – in the absence of any Jack Daniels. He put Zach's glass on the bedside table and settled down in a chair with two more sugared-up Pink Squirrels. With straws. He lit a Pioneer, his first for some days.

Several minutes of silence followed. Zach's sweet melancholy began to have a most calming effect. His wasted state gave Chippo the confidence to openly feast his eyes on his face and body, commune with his very being. He had shaved Zach's chest, but he had certainly left the neat dark hairline that began at his navel and spread as it disappeared into his nakedness under the sheet. It was a while before Chippo even noticed a sheet of paper on the bedside table. In red laundry marker was written, *"THE SIAMESE REJOINING. Think about it!"*

"This is Reptilio's writing."

Zach's lack of response induced a fierce desire to lie with him on the bed, cover him with kisses, fold him in his arms; yes, loving him would fast track Zach back to health, save him from himself. Chippo cocked an ear for the possible approach of the overly attentive Reptilio, but it was time for tenderness, but not so tender as to be disrespectful of a straight man's space. In the end, he did no more than once again put the Kool-Aid cocktail to Zach's lips. When he swallowed, their eyes met and momentarily stayed. When he indicated with a sideways flick of those eyes, Chippo gave him a drag of his cigarette.

To continue the drowning and the disowning of the spectre of former public servant Chipman Smith that had so rudely and unexpectedly inhabited him that momentous evening, he sucked up the rest of his first Squirrel and began on his second.

"Zach, I am beginning to realise that I don't remember much since the Makeover, but things are now coming back. Floralee said that Reptilio in his earlier days created a lot of mischief, peccadillos, student fun, for which he had to leave Australia. His passport is illegal, but he devotes his life to us, to Tophphi, to you and me. Our performances at the Carnival will be our final restructuring. Whatever he did back then, he's now in full redemptive mode. Should not full redemption be fully rewarded?"

Zach's green, gold flecked eyes engaged Chippo's grey, unflected ones in a way he had perhaps never allowed before. He smiled the friendliest and most resolute of smiles. He even reached out and long held Chippo's hand in both of his. "Yeah, Chippo, I'll go with all that. Dr Reptilio, the guru, the great redeemer. The architect of my *Supreme Triumph.*"

THIRTY FOUR: *Coming ready or not*

"It's Good Friday," Reptilio announced, shortly after dawn, "You're designated to take poor Zach to church."

"St Bede's? Are you sure?"

"In the final throes of training for your performance tomorrow night, Chippo Cherrynose, you will do as you are told." Reptilio unleashed his snaggle-toothed grin. "And, I need once more to remind you, Zach is no more your new Tibor than is Drift."

"I have to sit up close," said the Nebraskan, "so I can meditate on Reverend Adomako."

"...do thou oh Prince of the Heavenly Host, by your Divine Power, thrust into Hell, Satan and all the other evil spirits who roam through the world seeking the ruin of souls. Most sacred heart of Jesus, most sacred heart of Jesus, have your everlasting mercy upon us. In the name of the Father, the Son and the Holy Ghost. Amen."

After the service they visited, at Zach's request, his brand new grave and headstone. He bowed his head, as though someone really was buried there. The foliage drooped in the liquid air of the morning. Twice in the past week there had been showers of startling warm wetness, and it felt like another was about to descend. With the harmattan long gone, slow moving kamikaze mosquitoes were attacking. Chippo slapped away for both of them, (delicately when it came to Zach) and got them all. Of the human bone pile on the collapsed creek bank, there was no trace. Sir Henry had orchestrated a meticulous clean-up.

They moved – Zach shuffling in his weakness, Chippo emulating in empathy – back towards the Hornbill. It seemed that finally, with Reptilio's help, he had put behind him all thoughts of doing away with himself. There was method in the Dancedoctor's mad headstone manoeuvre after all.

"The sermon seemed to carry you off to somewhere peaceful, Zach. And the choir too." His mood had in fact, been close to rapturous.

"It was cool. Spiritual vacuuming."

"Vacuuming?"

"Yeah. Sucking out the parental, generational crap, stripping me down for The…" Zach glanced at *Whatever Forever*, just ahead and stopped. He looked at Chippo uncertainly. "I may have already mentioned something. Reptilio has had this wonderful idea. It first seemed too over the top, but while I was listening to the choir, everything began to make sense, to be so absolutely right on. He made me promise on my oath to keep quiet about it but I feel I can trust you." He paused and took Chippo's hand. "I've been following what Reptilio has devised for you. Your *Grand Efflorescence*, your coming out ritual…" His voice faded. "Are you really happy with Reptilio's plans? Sure that they work?" There was no mistaking the terrible doubt lurking in Zach's voice and Chippo reassured him. "Well yes, I'm really happy. I have every confidence that the ritual will succeed for me in the way he envisages."

"Specially tailored for you." Zach withdrew his hand. "Well, here we are, we've both been blessed this morning. As Reverend Adomako said, we're on God's golden shore, about to embark on the greatest adventure of all."

"He said that? Zach, you are sounding strange to my ears. And not in a good way. Is it your *Siamese Re-joining* thing?"

Before he could respond, they were interrupted.

"Mr Shaler, Mr Chippo, double the pleasure, double the fun!" Sir Henry, linen-suited, panama-hatted and also returning from St Bede's, caught up with them at that moment. A tank-topped Ntank, seductive in mirrored wraparound shades and tight red leather short-shorts, stacked-heel combat boots and knee-length white socks, was a step behind. In the church the two of them had sat in isolation in the front row, with no one in the pew behind them either. Every other pew had been full, with many of the Tlulan villagers standing. It had been either the lonely grandeur of power, or a deliberate ostracism.

Sir Henry gave a smile, one of maniacal intensity. Similar in fact to Reptilio's. Both were feeling the strain of production, both overly concerned with minutiae. Reptilio was certainly giving Lotus a hard time in her Carnival Studio, employing as she was, half a dozen women from the village to help with the cutting and stitching of costumes.

"Qumqwat's mother refused to shake my hand this morning. Lilibet Lanfal too. Foolish creatures. Qumqwat and the adorable Aqosua, developing so nicely, will be the prima ballerinas on Easter Sunday and will bring joy to the heart of brave Ulysses. The Maypole! A revered symbol of Ye Olde England herself. The mother country!" An aggrieved tone had come into his voice. "The regatta is turning into a shambles! Tlula wants triple what I paid them last time. They should be paying me. For the sublime honour." He wiped his brow with a handkerchief. "My difficulties have usually been with the farmers and the overly ballsy Blossom. Now even the fishermen are turning against me."

Sir Henry looked Zach up and down, at his tentative gait, the stave he was employing. His cowboy hat had gone askew and Chippo straightened it. "How moved I am that you managed Reverend Adomako's sermon, Mr Shaler. On this special day. The day we renew our faith in a crucified man. What a noble thing, Christ laying down his life for our sins like that. What was that wonderful text? The Gospel of John Chapter 3 Verse 16 is it? 'For God so loved the world He gave his only begotten Son...'" his voice trailed off.

"... that whosoever believeth in Him should not perish but have everlasting life." Chippo finished for him. Something from the St James Version that Matilda and Melody had managed to cement in his head. "Sort of like the ends justifying the means, I suppose."

"If the ends don't justify the means, what does?" Sir Henry queried tartly. "But thank you, Mr Cherrynose, for that." He turned to Zach. "Your recovery continues, I trust?"

"I'm up and at 'em." Zach raised a friendly if limp fist. His lips moved in an affirmative moue. He was looking sideways at the plump hotelier and on his face there was once more the beatific expression Chippo had become aware of during the church service.

"Excellent," came Sir Henry's voice which had a contradictory edge to it. "How nice to find you are taking an interest in life once more."

A flat-bed truck went by, gushing foul exhaust fumes. It bore several mature poinsettias and two Canary Island palms and pulled up by the chalet de luxe. Holes for them had been dug. Billy Carpenter and the workmen were applying a second coat of paint, hornbilling the chalet yellow, black and white, the ubiquitous national colours with the red star in the black already added. The toilet flushed and the electricity had been connected. Window panes were in. Security bars were to be added if they arrived from Doggone in time.

"Excuse me, gentlemen." Sir Henry broke into a lope. "A poor man's work is never done." He called back, "I am still unhappy with the guest menu Attah is preparing, but I recommend his all-weekend Breakfast Special – defrosted English muffin with Tesco corned beef and shirred egg. Heinz baked beans on toast. Fresh hot cross buns. Dundee marmalade. Chow down!"

"Mmm. Defrosted!" They said it at the same time and erupted into giggles, catching each other's eyes like complicit schoolboys.

Zach gave Chippo another look at his new passport. A photograph taken with Lotus's Polaroid camera had been skilfully patched in by Floralee. The forgery was virtually undetectable. His name was now Wilbur John Fedoroff, U.S. citizen, born in Atlantic City, New Jersey. Cerisia declined to turn over any of Zach's money and it was Chippo who had bargained with Floralee and paid for it.

Apart from the new structure for the Liberator, everything was ready. The jungle had been hacked back, the hotel gardens pruned up to a point. The bungalows had been scraped clean of bat and bird shit, the interiors of mould, fungus and long-established arachnids. Every dwelling had been repaired and painted in the best and brightest of tropical shades. Any mambas who had not been either captured or terminated by Drift, had departed the hotel grounds in dismay. Sir Henry had expressed much satisfaction and paid Drift the contracted sum and more. The only First Worlders left at the Hornbill were the members of the *Westminster Dance Theatre*, a name chosen for them by Sir Henry, who had more than once let it be known that the *Eighth Chakra Evolutionary Dancers* was at odds with his scheme of things.

The sounds of Led Zeppelin's *Stairway to Heaven* and usurious linkage came through the wall of Drift's room. Tophphi was content making good on her decision, but Drift was not. He was still obsessed with preventing the "totally unnecessary, totally deranged, totally demeaning" *Daddy Dance* from taking place. "What if I shoot all the fucking turkeys? The vultures, I mean. Who's going to miss Old Idi and his brood?"

Sir Henry had refused point blank the demand from the powers in Okidoki that the Bronzes be returned at once to the capital. In frustration, President Mguavas had instructed Mr Samuel Ichoko, Director of the Bomzawe National Museum, to make a special trip to Tlula to verify their presence and authenticity. Mguavas had issued a dire warning. "Kmango, if anything goes wrong, it will be on your head. And I mean your head."

Sir Henry assigned heavily armed guards to a full-time watch. The Director, who arrived in a white Cadillac, chrome encrusted and with fins, began the task of readying the Bronzes for display at the Carnival, where, with appropriately grand ceremonial, they would be handed back to the people of Bomzawe.

An olive green Humber Super Snipe stole into the grove. The car, long and low, with its lustrous paint job and black windows gleaming through a fine coating of reddish dust, stopped in front of Bungalow One. The piteous bleating of goats, and the sound of a tenor saxophone came from inside. The driver's door was flung open and out stepped a tall woman, negroid with a muscatel bloom to her skin. She was dressed in a Norman Hartnell travelling outfit, her hair coiffured into an African beehive. This was Lady Chompia, Sir Henry Kmango's wife.

Other occupants soon debarked; Qofia, a former local, who had for over two years been Lady Kmango's hairdresser and personal beautician, and Chunkia, Lady Kmango's succulently-figured older sister, also fashionably if garishly dressed (Zandra Rhodes) but nibbled at by the goats, and much in need of a touch-up by Qofia. The saxophone ceased. A man with a potato dumpling of a face appeared. Fortyish, with mutton chop whiskers, his greyish receding hair was pulled back into a pony tail. He was dressed in papal black, perhaps to hide a considerable girth. Siegfried gangster shades.

"Shameless Seamus!" cried Reptilio, prancing up. It was the tardy Seamus Shamrock. "Not a moment too soon! We've been reduced to Floralee's hideous crystal."

"Starryo!" Seamus and Reptilio hugged mightily. "Back off, Twitch," he said to Cerisia. "I remembered." Seamus rummaged in an overnight bag and produced six cartons of Gitanes. "Smoke up. Have a ball."

Lady Chompia Kmango had come upon Seamus hitchhiking and given him a lift on the understanding he would help control her cargo of sacrificial goats which had inexplicably begun to rampage. An old hand at this sort of thing, Seamus had kept the sensitive beasts soothed with sounds. "Me auld Ireland Bing Crosby selection, heh, heh, works every time."

Sir Henry emerged from his bungalow. Not as dark, and shorter than his wife, he stood on tiptoe to kiss her lowered cheek and they conferred. She slapped with the back of a beringed hand at the newspaper she had brought. Sir Henry's brow began to crease.

Qofia, the beautician, straightened hair, bobbed and shiny with gel, wearing a short Japanese style kimono over blue sateen shorts the better to display long slender legs, disappeared with her equipment and Chunkia into their bungalow. Chippo noticed that Qofia had already established an intimacy with Seamus.

The Snipe was loaded with foods and fireworks. Attah and two of the village girls who had rushed up, began carrying delicacies into the Kmango quarters. Several hams, braces of trussed guinea fowl and much else went towards the hotel's kitchen area, as did the goats. The boxes of Chinese fireworks, mostly bangers, flares and coloured smoke bombs, some of which Sir Henry wanted incorporated into their performances, had Stan chortling with glee. Lady Kmango had also brought the Carnival Programme which looked very sleek in black and pink on gold card.

"Sweet Jesus, I'll have their necks!" cried Lady Kmango as one of the Canary Island palms missed its hole and crashed on its side. "Where's that sleazy Ntank? Never here when he's needed!" She turned to Reptilio. "So! You find Henry's Easter nonsense to your liking?"

"Chompi, my dear..." said Sir Henry reproachfully.

"The Great Liberator," said Reptilio. "It does him honour."

"He won't even notice. Henry's Rehabilitation Committee has restored the name of a man as good as dead. What was there to restore, I have always said."

"It is a Christian gesture," pleaded Sir Henry. "President Mguavas..."

"Bnana Mguavas is an imbecile." She threw Chippo a tempestuous look. "Do you know what happened yesterday?"

The *Okidoki Post* that Lady Chompia had brought, carried the worst possible news. For fear that the rebellious General Kporpor might move on the capital with his two tanks, the government had blown up the bridges on the only highway to the north. Tear gas and rubber bullets were being used to quell strikers. Hundreds had been arrested. The day before, the entire National Rehabilitation Committee had resigned.

"Henry, the telephone is down again. Why don't you get the newspaper delivered? You stay here in your fool's paradise. You should be in Okidoki making sure that everything goes well with Ulysses' itinerary. Events are conspiring against us."

In the Esteemed Presence of His Most High Excellency
ULYSSES Q.ORATORIO, THE GREAT LIBERATOR
SIR HENRY Q. KMANGO
presents

TLULA LEISURE BEACH

EASTER CARNIVAL

In the beautifully scrubbed up grounds of the HORNBILL PALACE HOTEL

We welcome the Friends of Ulysses to Honour the Safe Return to the Place of Birth

DELIGHTFUL PROGRAMME

EASTER SATURDAY

Afternoon: Volley Ball, Ping Pong Tournament, Darts Competition, Soccer Match
followed by
OFFICIAL UNVEILING of the world famous
ORATORIO BRONZES

Evening: Direct from their acclaimed LONDON season, the all white
WESTMINSTER THEATRE DANCE COMPANY
Multi-ethnic Educational Song & Dance Routines in an officially approved style
Blessed and Funded by British Medical Association followed by the fabulous
HIGH SOCIETY BALL
featuring the very remarkable
UHURU CONTEMPORARY DANCE ORCHESTRA

EASTER SUNDAY

Dawn: Service at St Bede's Anglican
Morning: Traditional Wawa River Pleasure Cruise
Afternoon: Sports Jamboree: Athletics, Thread the Needle, Egg & Spoon, Sack Race, Coconut Eating, Traditional MAYPOLE, Tug of War climaxing with our unique REGATTA featuring Canoe Race around Oratorio Island and back
Evening: SUPER COCKTAIL PARTY and SUAVE DANCING

EASTER MONDAY

The Great Liberator's time honoured
CRICKET MATCH
Al fresco Breakfast Lunch and Dinner, courtesy of our WORLD CLASS Chef,
Attah G. Lalwani formerly of prime Mayfair eateries

SPECIAL ADDITIONAL EASTER WEEKEND ATTRACTION
Mr. Drift's Polynesian Snake House and Zoo

"Chompi, Chompi! Regulator Ronson and his crack team are there. Please do not discuss these things in front of my performers."

Attah appeared, sweating, having run from his office. "Sir! Telephone!"

"It's working." Sir Henry galloped off. "It will be the Regulator. Qweku Ronson always keeps me in touch."

Reptilio and Cerisia were invited to high tea with the Kmangos. Zach and Chippo spied on them knocking back tinned pheasant on toast while they quaffed pink champagne from the Nwalabi Hills vineyard. The Director of the National Museum was pointing out some of the finer details of the table's centrepiece – one of the legendary Bomzawe Bronzes. The cicada-embellished head that so nearly was Chippo's.

THIRTY FIVE: *A walk on the wild side*

Reptilio's plan was to celebrate the arrival of Seamus Shamrock by breaking out one of the many treats he had brought, a truly new and mind-blowing killer called DMT. It came on dried, super-saturated parsley flakes. But Seamus put the kybosh on that.

"Real people don't do psychedelics any more. It's over." Reptilio was whacked consolingly on the back. "Let's soak up some of that authentic village atmosphere you've been raving to Adolf about."

Blossom's Leisurely Chophouse had been permitted to re-open and there was exultation in the air. Unlocked from the Chief Enforcer's chains, Fangga squatted in a position of honour on a high stool. Hung with amulets and freshly gnawed bones, the ever popular feticheur was showing his chafed ankles and wrists to Blossom. In whale boned brassiere, battle boots and cargo pants, she was brazenly sporting a WE LOVE GENERAL KPORPOR baseball cap.

Blossom banged down a couple of fizzing buckets in front of Reptilio. Palm gin, the establishment's preferred and sometimes only drink. There was haggling over the price. Seamus was soon gagging on the stuff.

Congolese singles on the antique juke box played at high volume. Sir Henry's donated spittoons were a successful addition to the amenities.

Seamus had invited Qofia, who had dressed, perhaps over-dressed, for the occasion; a ginger fright wig, scarlet lipstick not only on her mouth, but also smeared over the triple tribal cicatrices slashed diagonally across both cheeks. A low-cut tangerine bubble nylon blouse tight over her brassiere, similar slit skirt in turquoise, and platform mules, completed her ensemble. She exchanged incomprehensible Qahatan insults with a table of copra workers, lolling with their cutlasses amidst a fug of ganja smoke. When they withdrew, blushing somewhat, she blew a kiss in their direction, tilted a muled foot. "Dey jealous ob me. I hab fine English gentleman in Okidoki, he dash me dese fashion items," Qofia said, making eyes at Seamus. Her voice was low and breathy, hard to hear over the racket.

"Cool," said Seamus. "Super cool."

"I not cool." Qofia pouted. "I hot. Hot fox." She found her drink unsatisfactory and had Qojo threading his way back to Blossom's counter. When he returned, a big chunk of pineapple, a maraschino cherry and a plastic stirrer graced her glass which was the size of a schooner. Qojo had been lured into Blossom's by his admiration for Qofia's high style and city ways, her talk of the "Purple Heart pill scene" in the discotheques of the capital. Qofia, it turned out, was his cousin.

After half an hour of the fecund Chophouse, the faux-English world of the Hornbill seemed far away indeed. In the courtyard, where celebration of the re-opening was at its height, pots of stew were bubbling and staggering quantities of meat were being barbecued; mostly pork or bush meat, which meant monkey, grasscutter or duiker. Fish and seafood were less preferred in Blossom's. Pigs, Pharaoh's chickens, rats, gigantic centipedes and winged cockroaches wandered about, competing savagely for scraps. Inside, chooks and guinea fowl were roosting in the rafters. In the side booths, pipe smoking old men played warri by the light of storm lanterns. In the centre of the floor, Scarlet the Harlot, who was in fact the village madam and four of her micro-skirted fancy ladies held sway, surrounded by a dozen male dancers, their sweating club chocolate torsoes swallowing up what little light there was coming from the dim 25 watt bulb hanging above them. White eyeballs kept popping into Chippo's view, glaring briefly before sliding back into the gloom.

"So Starryo, which bourgeoisie are you shocking the shit out of this time?" Seamus yelled. "The Kmangos look your unlikeliest prospect yet."

"I will never deny the value of shock, Seamus," Reptilio yelled back, as he danced about with Cerisia, "but I have raised both the stakes and my standards. Kmango's Carnival guests are more of a challenge than the scruffy radicals we were performing for in Europe. High rollers from Okidoki, more English than the establishment English, just as ruthless and just as rich. To target them I have moved from Reich to Ritual, from *sturm und drang* to sweetness and light. I bring only joy."

"Trapdoor man Chippo here," Cerisia put in, derision evident in her cackle, "has been a most positive and delightful influence."

"Backdoor," Reptilio corrected.

"The joy of that tinned pheasant?" queried Seamus. "I smell the stink of corrupted values here."

"What other values are there?" snorted Cerisia as Reptilio made good use of her to forge their way through the unfriendly male backs.

"Enough, Seamus!" shouted Reptilio, "I have travelled far since our angry sparagmatic dismemberment days."

"Sparrow... what was that word?" Chippo asked Seamus politely.

"You know, all that libertarian sixties weirdness. The orgy mystery theatre. Community cauterisation in order to restore a more chthonian sensibility, more earth based, more Dionysian, less Apollonian. Cathartic dramatisations of man's sin and guilt, acting out the bloodlust, the rite of the scapegoat as the fountainhead for world purification."

"Oh."

"Sanguini jumped into the goose neck fuck thing on stage with Otto Meuhl. *The Amsterdam Wet Dream* folderol."

"Goose neck?"

"You know. Chopping off the head and fucking his woman with the neck. Heavy shit. Even people like Heathcote Williams and Germaine couldn't handle it. 'Fascists,' they hollered. All over Europe we got shut down. No venues, no funding. Otto let on that his priority performance objective was to explode a live cow and have a cluster fuck in the guts. After that, no-one wanted to know about us going into the darkness to find the divine. They just saw the entrails and blood on the stage and the stinky mess it was for their staff. Otto didn't clean up. Neither did Sanguini although that was his job. He was low man on the Otto totem pole."

"That doesn't sound like Reptilio at all," Chippo ventured. "He is into the transformation of others through public pleasure rituals based on sacred African traditions. The therapeutic value of the ecstatic and the erogenous. Anality." A lump of emotion developed in his throat. He found himself on the verge of tears of triumph and happiness." The right to sexual freedoms. The achievement of true love. The love that never dies..."

"Same old bollocks if you ask me. I'm not saying there's anything wrong with that, but..."

The thick smoke had Chippo coughing. He made more or less accurate use of the ceramic trough that was their table's popular and pretty spittoon. Someone had decorated it with a caricature of Sir Henry's face. "Perhaps you can tell me something I've always been curious about. How did Reptilio get that terrible scar on his chest. Where the hair has not grown. He says he was mugged in New York's Central Park, but..."

"Well, he would, wouldn't he, make up a piece of poetry like that." Seamus pulled a face. "No way, bro. Heh heh! Nothing so honourable. Sanguini got that beauty when..."

A shoving match had erupted on the earthen dance floor. Reptilio, feeling that with the creation of the *Vulture Daddy Dance* he was finally entitled to become a Companion of the Order of Fangga or some such, had endeavoured to shake the feticheur's hand and had once more been roundly rejected. A bone had been pointed, an overflowing spittoon had been thrown. Soon it was a melee, Reptilio and Cerisia were threatened with a broken pool cue. Kmango's name was being cursed on all sides. Blossom bore down hard with her truncheon.

"You hit an Englishman," Cerisia yelled. "If I was Sir Henry, I'd have your shit-hole bulldozed."

"Adore your cap," said Reptilio, holding his head. "And get rooted, you crazy dyke!"

Blossom pumped up her biceps, showed her gold fangs. Fuck off you sonofabitch or she and her boys would beat all the hotel trash in her bar to pulp.

Zach had not come to Blossom's but it seemed he was on the way to full recovery. Chippo leaned over the rail in the dark outside their rooms, sharing with his friend what was left of a joint of Qaddo's finest. There was a sexual frisson for him in the dampness left from Zach's lips on the unfiltered paper. Their forearms were touching, warm skin on skin. He melted as came the sensation of two souls merging, but he could not help but remind himself that this intimacy was to be experienced as the beauty of mateship. It was never going to lead to anything beyond or different, even as he was loving the moments as lasting forever. He dared to rest his head on Zach's shoulder. Zach put an arm around him. The unrequited too, had its ecstasies. One could never tell a libertine like Reptilio that. A footfall sounded on the wooden stairs. It was Qojo with an exercise book. "I learn de type." He was scowling.

"It's way past your bedtime, Qojo. How much of that gin did you drink?"

Zach flicked the finished butt onto the beaten earth below, gave Chippo's spine a farewell rub and moved to his door. "Wait, Zach. I have to ask. Lotus mentioned a big fat fee. Why…" but Zach was gone. Never was there a bloke more impossible to have a real talk with.

Qojo stalked inside. Chippo stared at Zach's closed door, listened to him clearing his throat. Lovelorn, he walked with reluctance into his room where the late bloomer was sitting with his fingers on the keys of Reptilio's Olivetti. "Qojo, it will be difficult. We should focus on your English first."

"Show me dis, please."

It soon became clear that Qojo had something else on his mind. He began to cry. "I hab no juice. I sixteen now wid no juice. What is matter wid me? De boys dey all laugh. Qofia make big fun ob me just now."

"I'm sure you will have some soon, Qojo." Chippo drew the weeping boy close, kissed him on the forehead.

Qojo looked up through his long wet lashes, put his hands on Chippo's backside. "I dat amorous ob you. We practice foh me."

Chippo's ears were acutely attuned to Zach pacing his floor, arguing with himself now, probably about the mysterious *Siamese Re-joining*.

"I think you should go see Cerisia. She's very good at these things. Or Scarlet the Harlot."

Qojo was trying to take down Chippo's shorts. It was time to kick the boy out, but through the ether there came a far off, falsetto version of Reptilio's voice from the Full Moon Makeover, "You're peaking, Chipman. We're taking you out of the frying pan and dropping you into the fire." Suddenly his stoned state had him drowning in a flood of neurological dislocation, another Chipman Smith flashback, not 'beyond the pale' as far as Tibor was concerned, but of phantasmagorical intensity. There came Qojo's soprano voice. "I know you want help me make juice. I nice and small fo' you..."

The last thing he remembered was Qojo's hand inside his shorts, priming his buttocks with a slap and his anus with some spittle. Undeniably pleasurable it would be, but...

The plates, six of them all juggled in the air at the same time, plates flashing in the spotlights, and he and Tibor and everyone were clapping and then more plates being twirled on top of Uncle Radek's sticks as the Shetland ponies dashed around the sawdust ring, their riders jumping off and on their backs, chased by cartwheeling clowns and then they were running and trying to cartwheel with the clowns and the applause until they were out under the stars in the cold and then he and Tibor were warm again in a big bed with Uncle Radek in the stables, with the smell of old sheets, Radek's hair grease, of ponies and chaff, deeply dozing, floating away on clouds and kissing and floating again in heaven and dancing cheek to cheek. He could hear the music and then he and Tibor were falling hand in hand, falling and falling – beyond the pale, or at least beyond the blue horizon.

Chippo found himself still standing as he had been before, palms resting on his table. His shorts were not round his ankles, his virginity, fortunately, was intact. He felt down there, just to make sure. It would have been awful not to have been present at its passing. Reptilio would have been most upset.

Yes, in the school holidays, he and Tibor had secretly run away to Canowindra where Tibor's disowned Uncle Radek was performing with a circus. They had taken the train and lasted three days before Radek brought them back in his truck in the early hours of the morning over the Blue Mountains. He had Brylcreemed black hair with a ducktail and an Elvis Presley profile Chipman could not take his eyes off. There was something of the irresponsible sexual vagabond about Radek, but in fact, the runaways were not being as wicked as they wanted to be, as unknown to them he had alerted their parents soon after they had arrived. Alfie gave them both a rare cuffing about the ears when they turned up again.

Qojo was seated in one of the room's canvas chairs, fiddling with Chippo's long defective Toshiba transistor radio. "You smoked proper," he piccoloed, picking up a pencil. He stuck it in the hole where the aerial had once been. A burst of music and static startled them. "Doggone. Bob Marley Reggae Jump-Up." A grin split his face.

"That's the first time it has worked for days. Take it."

"Sir, we dance." Qojo turned the sound up loud, put both arms around Chippo's waist, bent low and moved about with his cheek to Chippo's stomach, his thin torso stretched out horizontally. Chippo turned round and became the front legs of a two-man circus horse as though they were back in Canowindra those many years before. It was the funniest of dances. They were both laughing. Is someone like Qojo to be my life companion, he pondered, or a son for me? It was probably more that he was a bit of a spindly kid himself, stuck forever with Tibor Radovan in his cicada summer. Qojo changed position and swung him around. They pressed foreheads together. "You my white fader." He smelled the sweetness of the boy's breath together with the gin he had drunk. His leg knocked a chair sideways, Zach banged on the wall for them to shut up. Qojo's lips kissed Chippo's. "I dat amorous ob you."

"You'd better go now," he said, gently putting Qojo away from him. "Watch out for Hamid." Qojo turned down the radio. Boys from the village in the Hornbill grounds late at night, visiting foreigners in their rooms, just before the Carnival when security was tight on account of the imminent arrival of not only many distinguished guests, but Ulysses Oratorio, The Great Liberator himself, well, they were worth quite a substantial dash.

"Ah, is Hamou, I too quick for him." Qojo went to the door. "I's coming," he added, and disappeared into the night.

Bathed in a light that seemed to come glowing through the wall from Zach's room, Chippo was soon overcome by a lovely drowsiness. He slept long, a sleep of untrammelled kid simplicity, the sleep of a metamorphosing Chippo Cherrynose.

He was awoken by the clatter of vehicles, the bang of doors, unfamiliar voices calling. The air was hot, the sun well up and making its inexorable ascent towards zenith. He looked through the louvres. It was as though he had woken in an entirely new location.

PART THREE
Carnival

THIRTY SIX: *Take the best and leave the rest for somebody else*

Chippo was joined at the side railing by Drift and Tophphi. The Bomzawean hi-life music which had roused them came from a boombox radio on the verandah of a bungalow close below. A striking young woman with a bare midriff and café latte skin, even paler than Tophphi's toasted caramello, was dancing desultorily and licking her fingers of something sticky. She wore befitting black hipster jeans and a lavender silk shirt tied in a loose knot below her breasts. Her cropped hair had been blonded then Reckitts blued. Her stiletto heels must have given her considerable difficulty traversing the treacherous sandy terrain around the bungalows. Excited female chatter came from inside.

Samuel Ichoko came puffing over from the adjacent bungalow, behind which was parked his white Cadillac. The Director of the Bomzawe National Museum was a porcine, balding gentleman in tartan shorts, red and white tennis shoes. A gold medallion (it was the size of a beef pattie) bounced about uneasily on the wiry whorls of his chest hair. The café latte girl gave a merry poke to the upturned cup that was an umbilical hernia, distending from his navel. It was soft and her finger disappeared into it. She drew him, beaming, inside. A twittery chorus of greeting went up.

Nearby, Sir Henry was giving instructions to the round-the-clock contingent of guards he had hired to keep Fangga away from both the menagerie and the Bronzes. "My deepest fear," he had said, "is that at the height of the festivities he will release Mr Drift's specimens among my guests. He has done similar things in the past."

A sleek shuttle bus with tinted windows let out partygoers, turned round and headed back towards the road, almost colliding with a semi-trailer loaded with Red Star beer. Two Bentleys and an

Austin Princess purred through the flagged entrance poles, followed by a noisy pair of duelling Porsches.

Chippo turned his eyes to the Tlula Escarpment, that precipitous drop where the road made the sharp corner before the long descent into the village. There were vehicles stopped by the edge.

"Checkpoint," said Drift. "Ntank's team asking for everybody's credentials. These are the aficionados and supporters of old Ulysses. Reunion time. I don't know what sort of ship Ulysses ran. It may have started off as a socialist utopia, but you can bet it was something else by the time he was kicked out. They're probably like rich Republicans roughing it in the California redwoods for the weekend. Expect a few corporate gangsters."

"Well," Chippo said bravely, "that's grist to our mill, isn't it?" Determined he wasn't going to chicken out now, he closed his ears to Drift's current disenchantment. Thanks to Reptilio, he had never felt so focussed, so strong, almost messianic, in his belief.

The Great Liberator was scheduled to arrive in the early afternoon. Revellers continued to roll in. Freshly painted mammy wagons and trotros with candy striped canopies drew up, each with its aphoristic, sometimes cynical slogan – *SKIN DEEP FLESH WEAK. BE BUSY LIKE BEES FOR TOMORROW WE DIE. MONEY HAPPINESS FOR YOU, WHAT ABOUT ME?* Passengers in voluminous, vision-impairing clothes debarked, a dozen at a time, and spread out through the sunlight and shadow, animating the palmery with rivulets of riotous colour. Motor scooters buzzed around the ornamental shrubbery. A trio of 600cc Kawasakis went roaring off towards the distant wreck of the *Accra Queen*, making use of the firm sand at the water's edge.

Many of the sophisticated cosmopoles from the capital took to promenading along the broad white beach. Many dark heads were in the water. An unusual sight. The strains of Mantovani's *Beatles for Strings* soared from the new sound system. Forty people, ten a side, were playing at the two volleyball nets. Qofia, given time off after a gruelling morning in the Kmango bungalows, kicked off her mules and joined in. She proved to be a tough, aggressive player.

Seamus, avid eyed, followed her every move. She had spent the night with him in the luxurious enough back seat of Lady Kmango's Humber Super Snipe.

Elaborately dressed and coiffed Tlula women had arrived, loaded enamel bowls or aluminium trays on their heads, charcoal braziers dangling purposefully from their hands. Enraptured, freshly scrubbed children played at their heels. Under the palms, the women began setting up stalls for sale of afternoon snacks. The women's friendly presence was a welcome relief from the snooty city chic.

By lunchtime, the Hornbill Palace dining room was crowded for almost the first time since Chippo had been at the hotel. Qumqwat and a dozen post and pre-pubescent waitresses ran to and fro between the pavilions, the new cement tables along the promenade and the old Formica-topped ones in the bar. The hornbills went thrashing up into the treetops, vociferous in complaint at their loss of control of the terrain. Old Idi and his gang circled slowly in the haze above the palm tops, watching for frailty and other openings. Two small boys, deputed to keep the vultures away from the dining room, roamed up and down waving sticks.

Beneath an opalescent sky, the arrival of The Great Liberator's motorcade was imminent. With the absence of the harmattan, or even a breeze, the heat and humidity had an ominous intensity. A large sea-going pirogue, motorised and with a gold-trimmed burgundy baldachin, was drawn up on the sand, available for The Great Liberator should he choose to take a post-prandial trip out to the palm-clad island, which had been, along with the wreck of the *Accra Queen* and the picturesque ruins of Castle Vinkenoog, one of his favoured childhood haunts.

The tide was out, the surf slight, the sea so smooth its surface had an almost oily sheen. Those who had been swimming or playing in the froth of the waves came back to change. Mingling with the throng under the palms and poincianas was like being in the midst of a chattering cloud of brilliantly pinioned birds. For once, Bonnie & Clyde and the other hornbills were out-plumaged, if not out-beaked.

A battered lorry arrived, belching poisonous fumes and adding to the mounting excitement. It was crammed with over fifty fans of the soccer match for which the players were already warming up on the field. They crouched on the mudguards, they sat on top of the cabin, they clung inside and outside to the wooden cattle rails enclosing the back. It was like Chinese acrobats twenty to a bicycle. As it ground its way through the bungalows, Chippo took out his camera.

"You take picture to laugh at us in Australia," complained Qojo. "Our transport system runnin' down. Our government very bad. Dis is trotro pretendin' to be bus."

It was just a few minutes later that the Ulysses Q. Oratorio motorcade – three silver-grey, smoky-windowed Mercedes Benz limousines – entered the grove. The squad of elite motorcyclists provided as escort by President Mguavas from his own Palace Guard had unaccountably peeled away as the motorcade had swept past the Doggone Barracks, leaving the Liberator to travel on unguarded if he dared.

The antipathies towards the return of Ulysses, present elsewhere in the Democratic People's Republic of Bomzawe, were absent. A solemnity swept the assemblage and there was contrivance on all sides to look dignified. The volley ball games were gladly halted. Only the ever-ecstatic song of the cicadas and the excited honkings of the 'bills' (as Floralee called them), disturbed the reverent hush. The sounds of Mantovani were turned down and *The Uruhu Contemporary Dance Orchestra* struck up the National Anthem.

Chippo stood with Zach and Qojo on the seawall, and watched as a figure, Orson Wellesian large, in a beige polyester suit and a broad-brimmed overseer's plantation hat, was lifted from the back of the first limousine and decanted into a customised wheelchair. Ntank and his bevy of bodyguards kept the crowd pressed back as the Kmangos greeted him. He was propelled a short distance along the promenade and straight into his new quarters. High security it might be, but the maxi-chalet was still toxic enough with its fresh paint fumes to convulse any insects that might venture inside. The other two limousines seemed filled entirely with luggage.

"He lose much weight," said Qojo, "since I see him."

The Liberator had had a difficult time since his Air Afrique jet had landed him in Abidjan. His current wife and the two (out of his total of ten) children accompanying him had unexpectedly sought and received asylum from President Houphet-Boigny. In an attempt to calm the populace protesting in the streets of Okidoki against his return, he had not been given the regal welcome by President Bnana Mguavas that had been promised by the National Rehabilitation Committee; his desecrated statues remained overturned and unrestored. The President had received him privately, but bowing to pressure, had sent his Vice to attend the all-important Public Declaration of Remorse in Red Star Square. Riot police quelled the anger and arrested the rock and flame throwers. There was an indiscriminate use of tear gas. A fresh disagreement erupted about how much money he was restoring to the government coffers, yet another of the conditions of his return. He had in fact, been extremely lucky to receive clearance to proceed to his place of birth. Nobody seemed to know what General Kporpor was up to. Telephonic communication with Larrikini, his northern base, had been cut.

It did not augur well.

Ten minutes later, The Great Liberator appeared without the wheelchair – the toxic fumes seemed to have given him a boost – and shuffled unaided to a seat which was a freshly gilded throne under a makeshift arch of bones, beaks and claws. An expectant buzz developed as he began an audience. Reptilio and Cerisia were two of the very first. Sir Henry had a copy of the *REPTILIOZONE* flyer in his hand as the introductions were made.

Chunkia, formerly his Mistress of the Bodily Comforts, briskly wielded a tea towel, and swatted away the myriad of insects eager to get at him. His sizeable physician, a Dr Ali Imensah, directed squirts from an aerosol can at his face and hands. Scattered through the crowd were bulky gentlemen perspiring in dark suits. "The National Crime Authority's Morals Squad," said Drift.

"Is this the bloke we're performing for tonight?" asked Floralee, fresh from a foray in the surf. She offered around her jug of palm wine and a joint. "I was out by the palisade. He gave me such a dirty look as he went by. Doesn't he have an eye for a good looking Aussie sheila?"

"He's ill, Floralee," Chippo admonished. "He has come home to die with dignity, not to flirt."

"Seen photos somewhere. He's not the old geezer who ate the schoolgirls, is he? The one with the heads in the freezer?"

"Please, Floralee. We are out to raise his consciousness, not to malign him."

Sir Henry noticed Chippo on the seawall with his camera and beckoned him forward to be with the photographer from the *Okidoki Post*. On closer inspection, Chippo found Ulysses Oratorio to be more than merely obese. His bald skull was as lumpy as a custard apple. His rubbly facial skin hung in heavy skeins around the lower part of his face, making it seem to have sunk into his neck, which flowed out over the collar of his suit like a zebu's dewlap. Set with carnelians and other semi-precious stones, the many gold rings which adorned his short fingered hands were almost lost to view under folds of flab. He did not look like a cricketer. Or even a croquet player, his other favoured game.

His lips were cobalt blue. He frequently passed a whitish looking tongue over them as, in a weak and wheezy voice, he greeted local potentates and one loyal supporter after another. His troubles temporarily behind him, he tittered frequently and seemed in an excellent mood. As Chippo took photographs, the Liberator's red-rimmed, rheumy eyes occasionally swerved in his general direction. Eyes which still retained some of the acumen they had radiated when he had been one of the great architects of African liberation from colonial rule. Several times, Dr Imensah wiped away the copious accumulations of sweat on his forehead, the green froth fizzing from the corners of his mouth. The squirts from the aerosol can smelled like Pine-Fresh.

There was not a moment when the Liberator was not surrounded by a crush of well-wishers. After twenty minutes, he was clearly exhausted and the remainder of the queue was waved away. He rose and was helped to the crimson canopied Presidential Litter where beefy bearers were ready to transfer him to the far side of the soccer field. There he was scheduled to make a speech and, after the match, present pennants and cash. Crates of free beer were already being drunk.

The Liberator sank into the Litter's soft pillows with relief. A flunkey positioned a pair of dark wraparound shades for him, another handed him an immature hornbill to fondle. Dr Imensah popped an ice cube into his mouth. Applause broke out. The returned exile sucked, smiled, waved and fondled. Flanked by percussionists and the exuberantly chorusing back-up singers for the *Uhuru Contemporary Dance Orchestra*, his conveyance swayed out of the shade into the furnace of the afternoon sun.

THIRTY SEVEN: *A tea ritual and other diversions*

Ulysses Q. Oratorio was not the only one who arrived that afternoon. Jeb and Corrine Shaler, Zach's parents from Omaha, Nebraska, made it through the check-point and drove up in a rental car. Attah came puffing out to *Whatever Forever* with the news.

"Bring them to the bus, Attah. And make sure that Zach knows they are here."

Cerisia gestured for money. Chippo dashed Attah.

"Cheapskate!" Cerisia snapped her fingers impatiently. "More. Much more. Any slip-ups at this stage and I'll have you strung up."

Jeb and Corrine wanted to see the headstone first thing, and were taken to the cemetery behind St Bede's. Roughly carved letters read:

ZACCHAEUS GABRIEL SHALER
Born Omaha, Nebraska, August 12 1941.
Died, Tlula Leisure Beach, Bomzawe, March 20th 1972.
Unfortunate victim of a venomous snake.
REST IN PEACE

Corrine sank to her knees and mouthed a silent prayer. "If only we had managed to get here a little earlier we might have saved him." Jeb bared his teeth and gave a sharp intake of breath that sounded much like a hiss. "He was an Unbeliever. The Lord's will has been done."

"Place is twiddly widdly with snakes," said Cerisia. "Could have happened to anyone."

"So ironic it should occur this way," said Corrine who had frowned at Jeb's response. "Having lived so long in fear of him doing away with himself. Well, you must know what I mean. May the heavenly host look after him well, poor boy. Free at last, free at last, God Almighty free at last, as someone said."

"We brought along a fresh supply of his medication," said Jeb. "I always knew it would be a waste of money. You're not going to tell me it was an accident."

"It happened so unexpectedly, we are still in shock," said Reptilio. "I was intending to forward his passport and papers to the Embassy in Okidoki, but now that you are here..."

"Of course, we will take care of everything," said Corrine. "And thank you so much for putting up this most serviceable headstone."

Back at *Whatever Forever*, Jeb and Corrine seated themselves around a table cloth spread under the palms. Festive sounds came from the hotel and the soccer field beyond. Lotus began preparations for a 'tea ritual' in celebration of Zach's life. Corrine wanted something stronger than tea, and Stan was sent to the bar.

Jeb Shaler, former missionary, construction engineer, now a city planner for Omaha, tall and strong-featured, took off his straw hat and blue-striped seersucker jacket. Corrine, not at all petite and looking smart in a pink polyester pantsuit, sat down, unpinning as she did so, her panama with its gauzy spray of pansies. Jeb and Corinne were a good-looking, if overly large, fundamentalist Christian couple. Chippo felt he could detect in Jeb's face, traces of Zach's Coptic ancestors.

"We have memories of this place," Corrine murmured. "Sad memories."

"We understand," said Reptilio.

"There were difficulties with our son, Dr Reptilio. I hope he was not a trial for everyone here. If he was, I'm sorry."

"Not at all, a typical American, I would say."

"Well, thank you. We were..."

"Don't start glossing over things," put in Jeb.

"We were stationed inland from Doggone for several years. Came here for vacations. Zacchaeus and his twin, Ezekial..." Corinne covered her eyes with a hand and could not continue.

"Ezekial?" Chippo queried in great surprise.

"Zeke."

Stan returned with a half bottle of Beefeaters, Schweppes Tonic and a tumbler with some ice. Lotus mixed Corrine a drink and she gulped it down, together with a pill from her purse.

"You couldn't know," sobbed Corinne, "but one year, Zeke himself nearly died after being bitten by one of the horrible snakes here. It forever weakened his nervous system."

Jeb took up the story. "Zeke just loved Tlula. To this day we don't know what went on out there, Zach being so unable, or unwilling to talk about it." Jeb stopped, glanced at Corrine drying her eyes, began again. "They surfboarded to that nasty island and Zeke never came back. Great swimmers both of them, but one drowned and the other didn't. We never found Zeke's body."

"Our beloved son. We like to think he was chosen by the Lord for a higher calling." There was a sudden fierceness in Corinne's voice. "Elevated to glory.

"A terrible tragedy," said Jeb. "We gave up our Ministry in Bomzawe immediately and returned to Omaha. Within a month of getting back Zach tried to drown himself in a local swimming hole. He tried it other times. There always seemed to be someone around to rescue him, but he deteriorated. He even began calling himself Zeke or imagining others were Zeke. Poor Zach some people said, he's lost half of himself. To me it looked like guilt for whatever he did to Ezekial out there. Yes, they were identical twins but that is no excuse. There was no alternative but to have him medicated and put away. It was for his own salvation, but I don't think he ever saw it that way. We could never get him to talk honestly about what he was going through. Every year he became more devious. As I said, guilt written all over him."

"Hush, Jeb," said Corrine, resting a hand on his arm.

Jeb persisted. "The boys did not always see eye to eye. They had become susceptible to ungodly influences. I blame it on a renegade teacher at their school and a poor choice of literature. We and other parents tried unsuccessfully to have that man removed. Zach in particular had developed a blasphemous streak. I always knew if anything happened it would be Ezekial who..."

"Jeb!"

"We were left with a devil. A devil with the name of an angel."

"Honey, please! Zach did well. He majored in the social sciences at Nebraska State but he did have bad years. The psychiatrists did their best, but only succeeded in turning him even further away from God."

"Frankly," said Jeb, "I was ready to wash my hands of him, but Pastor Swingle telephoned and insisted we come and collect him before he did himself real harm."

Corinne poured herself a few more inches. A splash of Schweppes.

"Too big a journey as far as I was concerned, certainly for Corinne, with her drinking problems, look at her, and with him so ungrateful for all we had done for him over the years, the financial burden, but the Pastor put it in the context of a pilgrimage. He is hosting a reunion of old friends up country at the mission next week, so it was two birds with one stone. That allowed me to feel I was spending on something worthwhile."

There was a long silence before Corinne said, "Pastor Swingle made me ashamed to even think of not doing my duty as a mother." Reptilio was in a yogic posture in front of her. She held out a hand and he clasped it to his chest, closed his eyes. Corinne took another gulp or two.

"Zach always had – problems. It was not just guilt for whatever murderous thing happened out there on the island."

"Jeb!" said Corrine warningly. Jeb raised a protective arm clearly expecting her to throw her drink or even her tumbler at him. The moment passed and he continued. "You may not have noticed. I myself had no idea, it is only a mother who can know such things, but when it was confirmed in that most satanic way, even I..."

"Honey, will you just shut it! I say hate the sin but not the sinner and leave it at that. The Saviour's way." Corinne turned from her husband, and in a determined tone said. "Dr Reptilio, we'll have the body exhumed and returned to the States. Jeb is not going to stop me having Zacchaeus back where he belongs and that's that. I'm happy to have him in the family plot."

Chippo wanted Zach to come down from his room, reveal himself, be reconciled with his parents, let them know that Reptilio was succeeding where everyone else had failed. How could the Carnival really be a Final Healing for Zach if his parents were prevented from sharing his release from his demons?

"I recommend you stay for our performances tonight," Chippo said. "It will be Dr Reptilio's Supreme Triumphs for us. And tomorrow there will be a spectacular flotilla of canoes sailing to the Sacred Crocodile Pond, a Sports Jamboree, a Regatta..."

"I think that Mr and Mrs Shaler would like to be on their way," Reptilio interrupted, frowning. "In any case, there is nowhere to stay." He turned to the Shalers with a smile. "You see, this is a very African occasion. We are here merely on hire, poor white people, third rate entertainers, getting away with some amateur cabaret."

"We never came to the Carnival in the old days," said Corinne, "but it had the reputation of being a nice occasion. Very English in flavour with strong Christian touches. The Liberator was known to be an upstanding gentleman. Always got an excellent press." She took another drink and a faraway look came to her eyes. "Hey, honey, we could take a nostalgic walk on the beach, eat here. The menu looks good. And I don't mind after dinner cabaret if it's a special occasion. Let's do it for Zach."

Jeb was momentarily at a loss. "Do it for Zach?" he queried. "Zach!"

"And Zeke of course. Our true angel."

Jeb was up and putting on his jacket.

"Where's Stan with that tea," demanded Cerisia.

Jeb sat down again. "Okay, if you insist. We're not too far away. That big hotel in Doggone. I like the sound of the crocodile pond event tomorrow."

Reptilio and Cerisia exchanged a look.

"I'm so glad you have decided to stay," said Chippo. There was still that thought in his head that Zach would want to see them. He decided to go to his room and encourage him. The second he stood up, Reptilio thundered, "Sit down!"

Stan brought out the 'tea' – a glass jug of sweetened pineapple and lime juice, patiently frappeed with a rotary egg-beater. "Pretty drink."

"Oo," said Corinne, reaching once more for the Beefeaters.

At that moment, Chipman saw Zach's face peering through the heliconias planted along the old palisade. His parents' backs were to him.

"Zach! Come and be reconciled!" Chippo motioned him with an arm. "Zach!" Cerisia gave his ankle a well-aimed kick. "Ow!" Jeb and Corrine turned to see, but Zach had ducked.

"Yes indeed, Stan. Thank you." said Reptilio. "This is Stan. We are all so happy with Stanford's increasing ability to articulate."

Lotus appeared with a tray of her coconut cookies and a set of glasses that went with the jug. Stan poured the frappes and they all sipped.

"To the memory of Zach," said Reptilio.

"Zeke," said Jeb.

"It's a lovely ceremony, don't you think, Corrine?" murmured Lotus. "A little something my darling Stan and I learned in the Haight-Ashbury. In the good old days."

"And now we will sip three times more," said Reptilio. "The first will be subtle, like truth, the second, strong, like love, and the third, enduring, like life."

THIRTY EIGHT: *Are you being served?*

As the sun fell below the forested hills behind the old slave castle, the Director of the Bomzawe National Museum made a speech. The trumpeter and trombonist from the *Uhuru Contemporary Dance Orchestra* duelled a fanfare. The Great Liberator pulled a cord and the legendary Bomzawe Bronzes were revealed. Applause reverberated through the grounds of the Hornbill Palace Hotel.

Thirty gleaming Bronzes were affixed to the wall or displayed on a couple of trestles covered in tablecloths from Liberty London. Cleaned and polished by hard-working school girls from the village, the Bronzes were not large objets d'art but their Presence certainly was. They had been cast in the Okidoki foundries over three hundred years before. "By the 'lost wax' method," said Cerisia, her information gleaned during that high tea with Mr Ichoko and Sir Henry and Lady Kmango. Plaques and plates, masks and figurines, decorative, delicate, bejewelled, the finest achievements of master craftsmen, mostly seeming to convey aspects of an aristocratic culture devoted to sex and violence, taken to the most sophisticatedly blasé of extremes. The consummately-cicadaed head, given pride of place on a plinth put together by Billy Carpenter, glowed with an aura of almost supernatural intensity.

"To prove there's no hard feelings, Chippo, I'll get your cicada bust to you if it's the last thing I do. The Cherrynose totem." Drift, aware that the guards had special instructions to watch out for him, had not wanted to be present. He had gone to Kassini Junction to arrange for a truck. The *Star of Casablanca* was scheduled to leave for Southampton early on Tuesday. "Don't skimp on the sandpaper, Chippo. We are looking for perfection here. And make sure they are keeping Fangga well away. Back by sunset. I sure don't intend to be late."

With darkness settling, the Liberator segued easily from the ceremony of Unveiling to that of Consumption. Much help had been provided by Sir Henry's chef and assistants who had been seconded from the Kmango mansion in Okidoki, but undoubtedly it was Attah the Punjabi's finest moment with much for the discerning omnivore to enjoy: Lalwani's Iced Lobster and Shrimp Swill, Lady Chompia's Lancashire Hotpot, Royal Balmoral Bangers and Mash, and the giant Oratorio Squids and Pork Platter for Two.

Moon Looking Down (a seasonal snapper-like fish) grilled whole and served with hearts of palm salad and plantain chips fried in peanut oil extracted from Sir Henry's own nuts, was a particular Tlula specialty. A last minute addition were juicy seared steaks cut from a manatee detonated in the seagrass lagoons by the Ivory Coast border. A young steer from the vast Kmango cattle ranch in the drought-depleted savannah lands of the far north west had arrived in the back of a lorry and been butchered behind the kitchen, sending Old Idi and his flock into a frenzy. It had been roasting most of the day on a spit out on the beach below the sea wall. Word was that even the worst cuts were not only tender but tasty, and the beast was going fast.

For dessert there were offerings like Gracie Field's Bread Pudding and Duchess of Windsor's Dorchester Delight, which was a tinned plum duff served with Bird's Eye Custard.

All in all, nothing too fancy or inaccessible, and more or less in the bland English tradition favoured at the hotel.

At the circular official tables, The Great Liberator and the Kmangos were entertaining an insanely rich group of entrepreneurs, financiers and embezzlers which included Sir Henry's eldest son, who was governor of The National Bank of Bomzawe. The Chief Executive Officer of the Fanta Bottling Plant sat next to a geologist advising Sir Henry on a newly discovered seam of ore in his gold mine. Nearby were Darryl and Dotty Brewster from the Bluestone Tyre and Rubber Company. Samuel Ichoko was also prominent. Five years ago, he had been The Great Liberator's Chief of Staff. He had departed in disgrace shortly before the time of the coup but after a period in the wilderness, had re-emerged as Director of the Museum.

Close by the *Westminster Dance Theatre's* table was a wooden crate stocked with baby crocodiles caught by the massive Qaddo and the indefatigable Drift at the ponds up the Wawa River. Of the twenty, six had already been barbecued. Attah had asked if it was possible to get more, or even eggs, which were regarded as a local delicacy. The shells would be ripped open and the about-to-hatch youngsters thrown straight on the embers.

With Drift absent in Kassini Junction, Tophphi was at her most beguiling, radiating a boundless desirability that had everyone downing their utensils as, like a thoroughbred filly, she breezed through the dining room. She was sweet sixteen again she said, on school vacation at Jacksonville Beach on the Florida coast. She had a jar of fireflies, or lightning bugs as she called them, captured from the wet sand.

Qofia, bare-naveled in a neon-orange crepe top, and matching crimplene mini-skirt, sat with Seamus who wore freshly laundered beatnik black and had his greying pony tail caught in a tortoise shell clasp. Chippo was most admiring of the ease with which Seamus had established a close relationship with the coquettish Qofia.

"Why is it so out of reach for me, Seamus, with someone like say, Zach, and so easy for you? Love, I mean."

"I'm a lusty Dubliner raised on Joyce. I keeps me head down and follows me heart's desire, matey." Seamus winked. "It's a knack." What was it about knacks? Tibor had had a knack.

Around them sat those who were, after dinner, going to be made aware of their capitalistic bourgeois sexual hang-ups and brought to joy. The women favoured world-weary postures and wore creations which represented the latest in urban smart. There was the opulent gleam of gold and platinum jewellery, pearl chokers, Tiffany watches, tanzanite rings, a tiara or two and a lot of other Okidokian flash. Samuel Ichoko's *filles de joie* in concert with other ladies of the night occupied two whole trestle tables. There was a rambunctious, rhinestone air about them. They were all made up in the manner of Qofia, with skin whiteners, pale lipsticks, lengthy eyelashes and heavy perfumes, but Qofia herself clearly felt more at home with the cynical society wives who parried her giddy overtures for hand mirrors and cigarettes as though she was an irritating horse-fly.

"The cheeky slut! You give her one good smack, Englishman," came an authoritative cry from a matron kitted out for some catwalk beyond her ken. There was a chorus of laughter, causing Seamus to squirm behind his mutton chop whiskers and shades as he tucked into his prime manatee filet.

"I trouble you wit my fun?" Qofia queried.

"No, no, doll, not at all."

"You look good at dat vulgar man dere," said Qofia indicating Samuel Ichoko who had left the official tables and joined his *filles de joie* who were clamouring for more Dorchester Delight. "And do not be embarrass on my account." Even at that moment, Ichoko took out the breasts of one of them and began rubbing them with a piece of papaya. His open mouth began to slobber as he bent forward. Corinne Shaler put her hands over Jeb's eyes.

Zach was spending the night secreted in his room. Chippo had already taken him a bowl of the delicious Swill and some cicada brochettes. Plus a helping of the Bread Pudding. "Zoe?" he had to ask. "Zach, who was that in the photo you showed me?" The Nebraskan was at his most enigmatic and looked away. Chippo sighed.

Back in the dining room, open to the beauty of starlit sky and reflecting sea, there was festiveness on every side. Chippo gave himself to appreciative musing. "Who will benefit the more from our consciousness-raising exercises," he wondered. "Mr Ichoko or Corrine and Jebediah Shaler?" How happy he was that this beau monde was about to experience *The Pygmy Head Rushes* and the land bound version of the *Afro-Esthers*, all in the context of spiritual African ritual as Reptilio interpreted it, or English theatrical tradition if you looked at it through Sir Henry's eyes. Yes, the decadent materialistic ethos so apparent around the elite tables would be stripped away, a more compassionate and egalitarian humanity for Bomzawe would emerge. In time, a true democracy even. It would be worth it. Today Bomzawe, tomorrow the world. Yes! Yes! It would be so very worth it.

Sir Henry stopped by, drawn like a moth to Tophphi's incandescence, certainly, but more particularly to advise Cerisia on a last minute change of plans. "Please do not think that I am censoring your artistry, my dear Lady Reptilio. With the President's – how do you say it – killjoys here from Okidoki, we must not get dear Ulysses over-excited too early." Cerisia's belly dance with scimitar and tray of filled champagne glasses would be performed to better advantage later with the *Uhuru Contemporary Dance Orchestra* rather than as part of the performance of the *Westminster Dance Theatre*.

Cerisia blew a pretty Gitaned smoke ring for him and bowed her head in acquiescence. She had pencilled in a diabolical crook to her eyebrows especially for the evening. A royal red chenille robe covered the diaphaneity of her baladi costume, the fabled depth of her décolletage. Two young hornbills and a plastic pail of cicadas for them were secured into her headdress. "Very Covent Garden, very Joan Sutherland, my most esteemed Madame, if I might say so, your outfit. And you, Dr Reptilio, in mau mau mode."

Lotus had quartered Reptilio's freshly shaven head and face into the national colours of the Democratic People's Republic of Bomzawe – with the red star within the black on both his cheeks. A dozen painted-up lizard skulls hung down from the rays of a copper circlet. He presented an appearance of uncompromising theatricality, but in fact, was not at his best.

Reptilio had enjoyed a substantial meal (the Lancashire Hot Pot) but for dessert was road testing Adolf's DMT. Earlier, he had consulted from a list in front of him. "The Professor calls this one *Destiny, Miracles, Travail.* He says that the only thing worse than smoking too much, is not smoking enough." He had Lotus roll up joints of the impregnated parsley flakes. "Floralee," Cerisia had said, "it's every trip you've ever taken telescoped into fifteen minutes." Lotus added, "Of infamy. None for Stan, thank you very much."

Reptilio had decreed that they take it all together to prime them for the evening's performance, but everyone, even Floralee, declined the opportunity, and Reptilio was left to do his experimenting alone. At the moment Sir Henry appeared, he was seven minutes into his trip, and quite unable to speak or do anything but be rigid in his chair and stare askew through sanpaku irises. Lotus poked his tongue back in, wiped away some dribble with a napkin.

"The Liberator is looking forward to your turns so much, Dr Reptilio. Particularly the..." He peered helplessly at the leaflet that Stan had lettered for him. He looked up. "Doctor?"

"*Piccadilly Promenade*," said Cerisia coming to the rescue. This was the re-titled *Non-Verbal Communication Work-Out*, a name which Sir Henry had rejected as sounding "too American, too scientific."

"Exactly. So evocative of London! What a way with rubrics you all have. Already I can picture the *Okidoki Post* headlines."

"I'm eager to be on stage tonight," Chippo enthused, also coming to the rescue. "It means a lot to me, Sir Henry. My official coming out as a gay man. A new beginning."

Sir Henry smiled politely if blankly. "Ah, the eccentric Mr Cherrynose! Performing – he peered once again at the program- "*Chippo's Grand Efflorescence*. Ha Ha! This evening you and your friends will be stars of the limelight. Shine as radiantly as you wish. Shine like the fireflies in Miss Tophphi's jar. And of course, Ulysses my dearest friend is also a star, and tonight, he will shine right back for you."

He flapped a hand in front of Reptilio's glazed eyes. "Hello...?"

"Meditating," said Cerisia. A viscous bubble blew to the size of a watermelon. She pressed her husband's lips together tightly and blew. Cut off at its source, the bubble floated off into the night.

Sir Henry shouted in an ear. "I wish you all the best, Dr Reptilio." He straightened, gestured expansively. "My happy band of players. Play, play, play! And afterwards, dance, dance, dance. And stroll the hotel grounds, serpent-free now, like Elizabethan troubadours of olden times. Oh, what a night we are having. My people's carnival. How Tlula looks forward once more to my little event. So respectable and civilised." He patted his forehead with a handkerchief he pulled from the appliqued central front pocket of his silver-threaded saffron robe.

"Henry!" came Lady Chompia's yell from the Liberator's table, which was close to the moonlit pasture by the sea, where the maypole was already positioned for the great ritual dance the following afternoon. Picturesque indeed, the very best of transposed English bucolic, the maypole's looping, multi-coloured cotton streamers were tied in a Bo-Peep bow at the bottom.

"Excuse me, ladies and gentlemen." Sir Henry ushered himself away. "Matrimony summons."

"What a sweet man," Corinne cooed, coming over from her table, much taken with the hotelier's old fashioned courtesies. "Sometimes these African types can really surprise you. Oh dear! Is Dr Reptilio not well?"

THIRTY NINE: *When continents collide*

Dr Reptilio was feeling better. Precisely on fifteen minutes as ordained by Sandoz and Adolf, he came to. "The New Siegfriediana is doggerel," he burbled, "Super glycaemic, nuclear white. Orgasmic fuck on stage tonight." It was as though he had not been away.

"On stage in ten with all your stuff!" cried Cerisia, dismissing the players. "You douched, Chippo?" she queried with almost motherly concern as she began slapping Reptilio into shape.

Chippo was douched and had all his stuff. Stan and Lotus had everything all arranged – the carpets, the trapeze, Reptilio's huge gong hanging between two palm trees, the musical instruments in their cases, the masks hidden on their rack, Chippo's transparent cicada wings costume all ready to slip into, a chopping block, a vulture in a bag, the cutlass for the *Daddy Dance* razor sharp, the diamond python in a basket. Tophphi had managed to persuade Drift to allow Cerisia to dance with the python which had proved adept and intelligent. Rehearsals had gone well.

The forecourt was flanked with flambeaux furnished by Sir Henry. Already dipped in a gasoline-mix, they were to be lit as the performances began. The big banner – WESTMINSTER DANCE THEATRE *presents* REPTILIOZONE, A PSYCHOTHERAPEUTIC SALUTE TO OUR SACRED TESTAMENT – OFFICIALLY SANCTIONED BY THE BRITISH MEDICAL ASSOCIATION – FROM THE CHRISTIAN PEOPLES OF ENGLAND TO THE DEMOCRATIC PEOPLE'S REPUBLIC OF BOMZAWE – was up for all to see and for the photographer-in-chief from the *Okidoki Post* to record. In the gentle southerly night breeze, a Union Jack flapped desultorily beside the national flag. There had been a short tussle with Sir Henry about words like 'psychotherapeutic' and 'testament'. "They give our show gravitas," argued the hotelier. "Considering the sensitivity of circumstance this time, making use of the imprimatur of the BMA is an inspired touch, don't you think, Doctor? There is also the required hint of both Hippocratic and Biblical values." Reptilio had given way.

Cerisia had arranged to be carried on stage in the palanquin. A covey of school girls from the village would be kneeling beside her on the cushions, plying whirrers and whirligigs.

Desperate for yet another last minute drink, Chippo pushed his way towards the bar which was awash with Red Star and Guinness, cream-foamed, ice cold for once. Ntank was nearby, imbibing with the security guards, close to the Bronzes and keeping an eagle eye on them. The heavily-armed guards in their Black and Tan inspired uniforms were remarkably similar in appearance to Ntank. By himself, the oblong chauffeur had always exuded a tantalising air of thespian menace, those teeth, but in concert with the others, he looked like nothing so much as one of a posse of over-dressed ruffians.

Qwami and his assistants at the bar and a second drink station were being overwhelmed. Chippo went to his room, and after chugalugging from his bottle of Bailey's Irish Cream, took a moment to heighten the metalline redness of his nose from a tube of rose madder liberated from Lotus's paint box. For extra emphasis he gave his nipples a touch-up also. He dashed out again only to see approaching along the verandah an elegant fiftyish-looking gentleman. His long, ruling class nose went well with a mousey moustache and a rumpled cream linen suit. An artificial red carnation adorned his lapel and he carried a cane. "I say, Room 5, do you by any chance, know a Chipman Smith?"

"Yes," he laughed. "I mean, I used to be Chipman Smith. Still am. Sort of."

"Good Lord!" He proffered his hand. "William Oates." The voice was clipped, assured. "Consular Attaché, British Embassy in Okidoki."

"Well. After all this time." Chippo shook hands vigorously. "What a delightful surprise."

"We've just arrived. Had dinner in Doggone. That ghastly white elephant of a hotel above the bay. Wally insisted on popping in on you. He was worried about your well-being. Charging on all cylinders sort of thing. Some tinkly little card you sent that arrived just before he left Sydney."

"Wally Whitbread is here?"

"He blew in early. The Lagos shindig isn't for a few days, so he thought..."

"Well, how marvellous."

"Sir Henry organised a nice little table for us." Oates twirled his cane. "Care to join us for a quick one?"

Wally's backward step and blink at Chippo's g-string and painted tits did not prevent the former lawyer from joyfully flinging his arms around his boss. He found himself shoved backwards with some force.

It was Chippo's turn to blink. With saucered eyes, he assessed this substantial apparition from his recent Sydney past. Chalk-white sharkskin suit, now imprinted with the mark of Chippo's rose-maddered nipples, deep blue shirt with his familiar black opal cufflinks; thinking-man's large head, horn-rimmed glasses clamped on well-textured, bloodless, agreeably run-of-the-mill nose surmounting the well-trimmed, otherwise would-be walrus moustache. A man of considerable responsibilities, Deputy Clerk of the Peace, a senior bureaucrat privately working for many years on a doctorate in forensic jurisprudence, a family man who had dedicated his entire life to criminology and public service, still awaiting a probably never-to-be-fulfilled ambition to be actual Clerk. Occasional prosecutor extraordinaire. He sat there under his marcelled mane of thick silvery hair, fingers of left hand pulling nervously at his equally silvered eyebrows. Chippo had forgotten that familiar, endearing gesture. He smiled. Yes, it really was him, his handsome boss, a Sydney scion, a sometime player of tennis with Bob Askin, the NSW Premier, keynote speaker on the second day of the conference on *Law and Order in an Increasingly Lawless and Disorderly World* at Lagos University in Nigeria. His mentor. He had always striven to emulate him, practised the smooth dignitas of his manner, the studied modulations of his voice. The nonchalance of his sartorial savoir faire had been blatantly imitated. Yes, what admiration, what deference. What strangled lust! He was sorry he had overwhelmed him with the effusion of his greeting, smeared his suit. Chippo was after all, a different man now, an openly gay man, beyond all stigmas, perhaps overly flushed with newly-won sexual minority freedom. After the performance, when Wally had had a few and was more relaxed, he would tell him all about his emotional, mental and physical catharses, take him gently by the arm, introduce him to everyone. The smooth Wally Whitbread and the suave Sir Henry Q. Kmango would be sure to get along. A meeting with the exalted Great Liberator himself was not out of the question.

Chippo was not prepared for what happened next.

"Do you know that absurd, painted creature in front of us, Chipman?" Wally asked, pointing to Reptilio, cavorting at that moment by the stage.

"Why yes, that's Dr Reptilio himself, the producer and undoubted prima donna of our show tonight."

"Not the psychotherapy dance stuff Kmango's cooked up this time, I hope," put in William Oates. His eye had a little tic. "Sounds a trifle boring."

"Oh, yes indeed."

"Sorry," said William Oates. "No offence meant."

"I didn't know you had enthusiasm for any sort of dance, Smith." Wally paused. "Do you think the Waverton Musical Society will be able to place you in future?"

"I have a prominent role. I kick in the chorus lines. I..."

"Prepare yourself, Chipman Smith. That man is Raymond Vincent Grable, a Houdini wanted on felony charges of rape and kidnapping in association with the West Wahroonga Psychiatric Clinic scandal. Surely you remember! In your youthful presence as our Clerk of Arraigns in Justice Carruthers' courtroom, I might remind you, Grable jumped out of the dock and disappeared. He was last seen outside the Quarter Sessions at Taylor Square, getting into a waiting van. It was all prearranged with his underworld connections."

Chippo was disbelieving, but he did remember. He had taken the jury's verdict for the judge, but Carruthers, rather than remanding the accused, had sentenced him on the spot to six years hard labour. The fact that Grable had a previous conviction for Public Indecency – streaking as it is often called – had been partly responsible for Carruthers' irate attitude. In that earlier case, the sentencing magistrate had called him a National Disgrace but had put him on a two year good behaviour bond. The Clerk of the Peace Office appealed unsuccessfully against the leniency. What the naked Grable had done, was urinate in the Pool of Remembrance in Canberra at the ANZAC Day Dawn Service. The only known photograph of the prank was published in *Honi Soit* (for which Grable occasionally wrote when he was at Sydney University), a photo taken from behind as he was about to jump into the Pool. Grable's downy bum.

Reptilio went flaunting by again and Chippo still did not recognize him.

"Are you sure it's Ray Grable, Wally ? It can't be."

"Smith, of course I'm sure. You know I never forget a face, tarted up or not."

Chippo went from dumbfounded to flabbergasted as he stared back at Wally. Had eagle-eyed Starry Sanguini suspected who Chippo was from the very first day he had arrived at Tlula Beach? That was why he had sounded him out about the Attorney General's Department? The former lawyer's mouth opened to deliver a string of self-justifications; that before the Makeover here, Grable had a Ned Kelly beard, crazy hair and was never without dark glasses... but Chippo became overwhelmed by feelings of total inadequacy and a shudder passed through his body. Surely he would have remembered a snaggle tooth. Grable, had been in grinning mode throughout his brief magistrate's hearing and even more so when he vaulted out of that dock. Chippo's knees began a weakening tremble which did not stop and in his sudden panic he reached for a pillar in support. His spasm loomed.

"It would be wise, Smith, to distance yourself from this man immediately. He is not one of our ex-patriates who is making good."

No sooner had Chippo's boss paused to take a gulp of his drink, than another Whitbread fuselage began, this time on the subject of the Liberator, about whom Chippo had assumed he knew everything he needed to know.

The way Wally told it, the Liberator's illustrious reputation was a chimera, a carefully controlled facade behind which there was the life of one of the scumbags of the dark continent. Opprobrium not only worthy of the worst of the emperors of ancient Rome but those of the worst of post-colonial Africa. Unconscionable behaviours involving prepubescent girls and boys, even tots, in his pool and palace bedrooms had recently come to light. Righteous-thinking people around the world were justifiably shocked. The Bomzaweans, more concerned with polishing their reputation on the international stage than with publicly exposing their revered Liberator, had covered up excesses so foul as to beggar description.

"Amnesty International has produced a definitive and damning report on his secret tribunals and torture chambers. He is now *persona non grata* everywhere. Even Haiti, I am assured, will not have him back. Willy, William, will be asking for transfer to a more salubrious posting if the Liberator remains in the country."

"Reptilio told me about the goosing of Pat Nixon on the trip to Washington D.C. There was a King Farouk-like rampage on The Croisette with those good-time giddy starlets at the Cannes Film Festival, that unfortunate squashing of the Queen's favourite corgi, but Wally, these seem to be merely light-hearted escapades that..."

"Reptilio, Raymond Vincent Grable, this new friend of yours?" asked Wally. "The man with the wonderful wonderful magic bus, the cosmic guru. I presume, in your wilful ignorance, that you find him – nourishing?"

Chippo, unable to fully absorb the shock of Wally's revelations, had trouble getting his words out, but he finally summoned up the impetus to make a stand. It was an appeal to Wally's understanding nature.

"Reptilio may well be the Grable you want him to be, but ten years on, he is a completely different man, has earned redemption for past errors. In a few moments you will see for yourself how much he has accomplished."

"No newspapers here? No radio? No television? It's criminality of enormous dimensions. Interpol is again involved. The Siegfried sex and drug commune in Verbier? Illegal manufacture. Zombie House of Horrors. In the walls. We have one recent report, as yet unverified, that Raymond Vincent Grable was recognized there in August last year, but disappeared before he could be apprehended. Houdini again, but this time, the miscreant Grable will be brought to justice at least for what he did a decade ago to poor Jane Coolidge. I have to add, Mr Chipman Smith, those crimes against innocent fourteen year-old Jane pale into insignificance compared to what he was getting up to in Switzerland."

William intervened. "Now, now, Wally, be kind. You're going to put the blinders on Mr Smith's performance tonight."

"Yes, I must go," Chippo managed to blurt out. "The djembe drums have started, Reptilio will be looking for me." Experiencing yet more unparalleled agitations, he stepped away and almost fell, as though a rug had been wrenched from under his feet.

His boss signalled for another drink. "We'll be watching for you, Chipman Smith. Don't do anything I wouldn't do."

"Ha ha ha!" went William Oates.

"I want you here, front and centre when it's all over," said Wally Whitbread. "Cleaned up and presentable."

FORTY: *A man of wealth and taste*

Ulysses Q. Oratorio, The Great Liberator, resplendent in a voluminous robe, woven in a shimmering pattern of tiny rectangles, pink and purple, apple green and periwinkle blue, sat on his gilded throne of beak and bones. Terminal illness or not, he was a truly imperatorial presence. In the Caravaggiesque light from a nearby flare, his pitted moon face was like the treacle and suet pudding that Matilda sometimes served up on cold winter nights.

The Liberator's hands clutched a ceremonial cane, the head of which was a human skull, that of a favoured child bride, long gone.

On his right sat Sir Henry Kmango, attentive to his every need. On his left, Lady Chompia, a bella donna in vintage, floor-length Schiaparelli shantung. Ntank and various courtiers, sycophants and minders milled about. Dr Imensah, armed with a nitrolingual spray and perched precariously on a camp stool, took the Liberator's pulse from time to time and dabbed when necessary at his calf liver lips which tended to trickle copiously from both sides. Chunkia agitated Ulysses' fan, one of tail feathers from an albino peacock, set in the hide of an infant white rhino, an object of great sentimental value to him. He had it with him when he had made his hair-raising seaplane escape from Tlula five years earlier.

Chippo had been looking forward to this occasion as one of the most exciting and challenging in his life; yes, The Great Liberator was actually there front row centre, seated on his wonderfully macabre throne, but Wally Whitbread's revelations had set in motion such an unravelling of the Cherrynose persona that there was nothing left to look forward to at all. He was unable to prevent himself from relaying to Reptilio all that Wally had said.

"So you really are Ray Grable?"

"At your service. I will tell you the true story of me and Jane Coolidge in due course. Wrongfully accused, wrongfully sentenced. I knew what was coming from Carruthers and had worked out how to get out of that dock. Floralee and I had the whole scenario planned down to the last detail. Chippo, enough! I have atoned and more. I am no longer Ray Grable."

"What about the Siegfried clinic?"

"There is no truth in your boss's remarks. It's the usual persecutory nonsense from the Swiss Nazis. It never stops. Ask Seamus. In any case, Adolf is well able to deal with it. He's too big for anything as tawdry as arrest warrants."

"I didn't care for what Wally said about the Liberator either."

"Like me, Ulysses has atoned for past sins. If that is what they are," said Reptilio. "His people have certainly forgiven him. This evening, we are continuing the healing of the land of Bomzawe with our humble redemptive tribute."

Lotus was making a round of the audience with the programme. *PART ONE – HEALING ARTS* and after an intermission, *PART TWO – CULTURE AND EDUCATION*.

The cabaret line-up was provoking wild amusement and expectations among the Okidokians. Lotus handed a programme to Jeb and Corrine Shaler who were sitting a little way back, looking quietly engaged. Apart from the antics of Mr Ichoko, they had enjoyed their dinner very much; every last morsel of their generous Giant Squids and Pork Platter for Two had been consumed and the Dorchester Delight had indeed been a delight, home-style cooking so far from home.

When a barely-clad Lotus approached Wally and William, seated in their prominent position in the second row, much closer to the improvised stage than the monitors from the Morals Squad and the Amnesty International representatives (who had complained bitterly to no avail about their distant seating), Chippo collapsed under the unprecedented proportions of the crisis that had descended. He would not have been surprised to see Interpol agents arriving any moment to arrest Reptilio and the Liberator both.

Head in hands, he tramped in circles around the hessian bag in which the vulture for Tophphi's exorcism protestingly flapped. There was a childish desire to hide in a closet. "Oh, Lotus dear, the revelations about the Liberator and Reptilio are one thing, but I have surely lost all modesty as well. What I am about to do is conduct unbecoming. Indecent, to say the least. Even obscene."

"Oh, stop this!" said Lotus. "You dumbo!"

Praying was something that Alfie steered his wife and children well clear of, but later, with Melody exhorting and leading by example (even insisting on with the aid of that nasty little rod he could employ), praying was a daily practice to which Chippo had dutifully succumbed. Now he went down on his knees and looked up to the heavens. Where was one of the Reverend Melody Motherwell's hassocks when it was most needed? "Dear Lord, please let me have the courage of Reptilio's convictions. And mine." The cocopalm tops, the nightly home of the big lizards, ever an inspiration for Reptilio, and now a safe haven above the mayhem below, seemed to be blocking his plea. "Or just get me out of here."

"Reptilio," cried Lotus in sudden panic. "Chippo's got stage fright. A moment of doubt and pain."

Reptilio drew him up. "This is no time for faintness of heart. Believe in our cause. Individual salvation for you, a healing for the world and all its Whitbreads and Oatesians. What more could you ever ask for?"

"I'm about to be publicly humiliated. And in front of my boss who has already accused me of incompetence. Don't the Geneva Conventions specifically forbid the sort of thing we're about to do?"

"You should have smoked the DMT and scoured your head. Never mind. These will do the trick." Reptilio thrust into Chippo's hand a couple of Avalanches, "a new generation of drug, the most finely engineered yet of all the Siegfried solutions to psychic emergency." Reptilio had been talking up the sled-shaped lozenges ever since Seamus's arrival. "They are designed to slalom you off your feet. They're interactive, they're whatever you want them to be. Over here with the gin, Lotus." Reptilio watched Chippo wash the first one down.

"I'm not a degenerate? You're not worried about Interpol?"

"They're strong. The second one only if you absolutely have to."

Sir Henry Kmango was at the microphone, making the introductions. "...truly multi-cultural, inter-tribal... affirmation of English Old Money and the latest in Christian family values... the ancestral traditions of the village healers and medicine men of the Democratic People's Republic of Bomzawe... our noble African heritage... how lucky we all are to have the world famous animal spirit dancer Dr Reptilio of London West End fame, here at the carnival for the first time with his sensible English theatrical interpretations and contemporary psycho-educational stuff..."

Stan sounded the gong. There was a drum roll. Just as Floralee lit the flambeaux, Chippo felt the Avalanche sweeping him away with surgical precision to clarity and pleasure, right on time, right on target. He gave a huge sigh of relief.

"Oh, how wonderful it all is," he whispered to himself, as their cabaret program unfolded. *The Happy Go London Conga* (the renamed *Neural Pathways Programming*), for example, was as arousing a mass healing construct as ever. "Boop boop a choo, boop boop a choo," they all chanted, improvidently casting wide the pounds of glitter Sir Henry had supplied. As Reptilio and Cerisia led them in a syncopated chorus line into the thick of the crowd they handed out rattles and shakers. Stan kept everyone's consciousness well expanded by randomly tossing bangers that exploded on impact, and strings of fizzing crackers.

There they were, Whitbread and Oates, declining Sir Henry's urging to participate, fanning themselves with their programmes, smoking cigarillos, sipping their cocktails, coughing on the sulphurous smoke and acrid fumes. Chippo kept both of them in his sights as he danced and he saw plenty of laughter, if more from William than Wally, as Floralee shimmied for the two of them, shook her pompons in their faces. There was neither shock nor derision but Reptilio was right. That career of his with the Office of the Clerk of the Peace belonged to Chipman Smith, that earlier identity, gone for good and good riddance. Smith had been Reptilioed, had moved on. He was a different breed of lawyer now. More an educator. Times they had indeed a-changed. He was Chippo, Chippo Cherrynose. And ever so happy to be so.

Whitbread and Oates didn't even know what the phrase "consciousness raising" meant. They were the ones who had created the need for this message, Establishment types who in fact needed it the most. Their aplomb and impeccable manners, their stuffy diplomacy, were virtual euphemisms for hypocrisy and bureaucratic deceit. Chippo didn't believe for a second that wild story about the Adolf Siegfried clinic. And Grable? Well, Chippo had never had a good memory for faces. Incompetence? It was Wally himself who had told him to leave his work behind on his 'holiday'!

"Oh, Oh, Oh, Oratorio," the Westminster choristers sang out appreciatively. Led by the rampaging Reptilio as The Great Lizard-God, they made a special effort as they danced their way past Ulysses. Lotus had slaved over Reptilio's ambitious dragon-spined spandex costume into the midnight hours but had run out of time. With the lovely Lotus in tears, Reptilio had graciously settled for what was possible. From the small of his back hung a long spring wired tail with an authentic looking orange knob.

At that moment, the Liberator did look, Chippo conceded, like some dark blob of plutonium, a picture of malignity, chewing at something, spitting a tooth and some blood into a plastic cup; but stop it at once, he admonished himself, giving his wrist a slap. So unfair to judge merely by appearances.

Mistress Tophphi's Soho Solutions was a scene of great hyperactivity, with Samuel Ichoko and many other volunteers undressing and donning the brightly patterned togas provided for them, all of them more than eager to be intimately handled, 'flown away' and healed. It wasn't quite the instructional and emotional purgations Chippo felt they had achieved out by the banyan grove and the palm shelter, but the feeling in the night was ribald and enthused, with lusty guffaws filling the air. Yes, lit up by the flaming phosphorescence of a liberated Tophphi, the Solutions was hot and sexy, fiendish and fun; Reptilio's cosmic erotic frenzy at its intoxicating, evangelical, de-wowsering best.

Not wanting to take any chances with the cover, lead feature and centrefold for *Thug*, Reptilio had hired his own professional photographer from Doggone and more than one set of flash bulbs was festively popping. Chippo did have the passing thought that it was lucky that Drift had not been present. He could be a damper on all things Tophphi sometimes, could he not? And where, after all, was he?

Apart from such scattershot thoughts, Chippo was enjoying himself so very much that their first intermission came far too quickly, but then, as they were recovering in the pavilion dressing room, the particular civil magic attached to the Avalanche abandoned him. Without warning, in mid-laugh.

He found himself engulfed by an Iguassu Falls of unwillingness to prepare for his Maiden Voyage, his Coming Out. A nightmarish slime coated everything he looked at. A welter of whimperings was coming from his throat. He had been abducted by an abject terror.

"Get a move on," cried Reptilio, rushing by, his orange knobbed tail waving wildly.

"Reptilio, I absolutely have to take the second one."

"Whatever it takes."

The second sled-shaped lozenge was swallowed. He guzzled akpeteshie until he gagged. In the dark behind the pavilion he closed his eyes and smelled the fear and shame that now had his body in a vice. Reptilio being revealed as Raymond Vincent Grable, now a man with nothing to lose, what on earth might he do?

With his temperature close to immolation level, he staggered a few steps towards the sound of the surf, looked out to sea and the island. Zach had the right sort of idea after all. "I am denying everything I have learned at Tlula Leisure Beach," he told himself loudly. This retro mode, this denial of primal self, is pathetic. Naked and screaming in public view, vomiting, yes, penetration by a man, yes, but...

"Viva la revolucion, Chippo!" the lovely Lotus trilled from the pavilion.

He began to suspect that the second infallible Avalanche was also failing him. Interactive, Reptilio had said. He began talking to himself, reiterating the context. Freedom. Accommodation of that side of his persona that Reptilio's therapies had awakened, a Coming Out that would be the envy of every queer man in the world, hullo to the love of his life. African spiritual tradition, time-honoured mysteries paralleling the latest in Western psycho-therapeutic techniques, the urgent need to put the Bomzawean Anglophiles back in touch with their heritage; cultural terrorism, if you like, of the most cultivated nature. It was educational, cross-cultural, multi-ethnic, Wally Whitbread would be eager to inform the delegates about it in Lagos. More modestly, he thought of it in terms of commitment to performance and audience. "I made a solemn promise to Reptilio and the Family. His African dream could depend on me."

"There's a breathless hush in the close tonight, something something, the match to win, a bumping pitch and a blinding light, an hour to play and the last man in..." How did it go? The old Henry Newbolt poem from his Manly Boys High School days came welling up. *Play up, play up and play the game!* The game, in fact, was over. The fact that Reptilio was Grable merely nailed down the lid of the coffin? Calumny! He had to resign himself to fate, like Ronald Ryan to the gallows. Like Marie Antoinette to the guillotine.

Lotus grabbed Chippo from behind. "Hey, no more whining boy! We need you now!" She gave him a shove.

"Lotus dear, want to do it instead of me?" he pleaded. "I'll pay you anything you want. Hundred dollars?"

"Hey, it's your healing. Who else is going to let themselves get fucked stupid on stage?"

"Five hundred. For Stan." Everyone has their price.

Lotus shook her head. "Not my Stan, boy. Stop exuding. Your paint's running."

"Chippo's Grand Efflorescence," came Reptilio's voice, blaring through the megaphone. "An entertainment, a dance exorcism,

starring our famous Australian, the one and only Mr Cherrynose, the former Chipman Smith of the New South Wales Office of The Clerk of the Peace. Wally Whitbread, give your man a big hand, the man who watched your naked bedroom exploits from a tree outside your window!" To which he added, lowering the megaphone, "And fuck you!"

Chippo roused himself one last time. Enough of self-pitying. A simple sexual act, what was the big deal ? Context was all. "Let my naked gay self be healed. I'll be proud, Lotus. I'll walk tall!"

"Yes, your moment," giggled Lotus, giving a last minute extra rouging to his cheeks and a painting to his lips. "You star!"

As the music swelled, and The Tlularettes, a trio of dancers from the village withdrew to their role as terpsichorean backdrop, Chippo walked out, looking like a tart, and lay down on the raised platform. "No mask, dump the cicada wings (symbolising joyous flight into his true sexuality), not sexy enough." At the last minute, Reptilio had settled on travesty, much to the annoyance of Lotus, who had worked hard on his insectoid costuming. "Euro-trash make-up. Frilly brassiere. Tape the dick. Paper panties. Big blond wig. Ulysses likes lots of Nordic hair. Nothing's changed, Chippo. It's just show business. Pancake and powder the proboscis, Lotus."

The Humours, led by Cerisia in her hornbill headdress, banged him about in the usual places, got serious with the deep tissue massage. Smoke from Floralee's fresh set of flares stung his eyes. There was a spot fire in the front row, put out by a couple of distinguished looking gentlemen who took out their dicks and pissed on it as though it was a normal thing to do at a Hornbill Palace Easter Carnival.

The minutes went by. Reptilio exhorted everyone to dig deeper, scream louder. "Buck about, Chippo, give them some of your great moves."

From the corner of his eye, he saw the Liberator on the edge of his seat, eager to participate. In his hand he held a meat chopper, an item extracted from a pocket in his robe. He made a sudden move forward and Sir Henry, glancing behind with alarm to the Morals Squad, pulled him back. Ntank prised the chopper out of his hand. Lady Kmango yelled in his ear, banged a shoe down on his head. Dr Imensah prepared a hypodermic.

Chippo knew he should have been revelling in his power as cynosure of all eyes, at least calling for Cerisia to hurry up with the vomit inducement, but any resolve was evaporating, resistance was beginning to reign. The drums were now drills, perpetrators of pain. His good intentions faded, a paralysis took over, and soon became so profound it achieved something akin to catatonia, a state far beyond what Starry would have described as embarrassmentia. It was as though he was trying to deny his very existence to Whitbread and Oates in the second row there. He was subjecting himself to all this for Raymond Vincent Grable? There was the crack of a whip. What was that all about? Oh God, there was a grinning Ntank with his persuader. What was he doing on the stage? There it went again, practically by his ear. Chippo's vulnerable colon twisted spastically, causing him to double up in agony. Professor Siegfried's sled-shaped lozenge had failed again, but his own body had decided to save him. "Reptilio, I'm ill," he gasped. "I – I can't continue. I have the most terrible cramps."

Crack! Crack! Crack!

"Keep your wits about you, Cherrynose," hissed Cerisia. "Cramps will work! We have to give them what they expect."

What on earth was she talking about? "I need a doctor! Not a Dancedoctor. Ow! Ouch!" he shrieked as the leather streaked his torso, stung his calves. "Dr Imensah, help!" No joy there. "Drift!" Not back of course. Chillumed out somewhere on the road.

Reptilio was throwing himself around the stage. He glared at Chippo from the top of one of the leaps. Through his lizard mask, his eyes were those of a famished beast, ready to sink incisors into its prey. Chippo grabbed for that swinging red-knobbed tail but failed. He made a sharp crab-like movement towards the darkness. Once more, Ntank's leather slashed him across the buttocks. Reptilio pounced, slammed him to the boards, tore off the panties, threw the shreds into the front row. Reptilio unzipped. Ntank withdrew. Cerisia held Chippo down.

"No, Reptilio, no! To work it has to be a loving act. You have always said... Aargh!" His sphincter was in lock down.

"Make it look good!" Cerisia was yelling. "Relax! Twist and shout! Scream! Earn your keep."

Reptilio singsonged into his ear, "Chippo, Chippo bad, bad boy. Legs in the air, and be my toy." It was doggerel time.

"Reptilio dear, love's turned to hate," Chippo singsonged back, "You've gone through the zombie gate." The dank smell of blood, his blood, filled Chippo's nostrils. Had it become a question of survival itself?

"By the hairs of my chinny chin chin, let the doctor in, boy, let him in!"

The pain of the colonic cramps was reaching a new pitch. Reptilio spat and then holding Chippo's legs high by the ankles, pushed brutally. He felt his tender virgin flesh ripping. Consciousness was slipping away.

"Your Tibor says to let me in!"

"Reptilio, no! I love you. Aaargh! Tibor never..."

"Here's the grease," shrieked Lotus. "Reptilio, I forgot the grease."

A vision of the ravished Jane Coolidge and the West Wahroonga Psychiatric Centre common room filled Chippo's head. Jane's deposition had left little to the imagination. In extremis, he appealed to the only Higher Power he now knew; there had to be compassion somewhere in her heart. "Cerisia, stop him!" he gargled.

"Reptilio! TOOTS!!"

Reptilio stopped abruptly. Chippo's head hit the ground. The wig fell off. The photographers moved in for yet more close-ups. Flash! Flash Flash!

"Encore! Encore!" came from a hundred throats. Feet stamped in appreciation. How could they be so insensitive? Chippo did not understand. His body was on fire, he scarcely knew where he was.

"We did it, Chippo, we as good as did it," exulted Reptilio.

"Timing was perfect." Cerisia yelled as he crawled away.

"Don't leave now!" came Reptilio's voice, in clear surprise. "You have to do your spin. Cerisia, grab the little fucker."

"Your cicada wings, Chippo" cried Lotus. "They're here! Your mask!"

Yes, the segue into his dervish dance on the table top, the hook and pulley that would fly him into the starry starry night, but he was off into the safety of the dark. Even as he collapsed behind a clump of pandanus, his colon began untwisting, and a rapturous relief suffused his whole body. He Avalanched out and down.

Water being sloshed in Chippo's face was the next thing he knew. Qofia, in gold fishnet stockings, spangled bustier and spiked heels, towered above him with a bucket. "I very sad for you." Qofia sluiced him down, helped him get clean and dried.

"Dat fat turd Cerisia, and Mr Reptilio dey do terrible tings to you."

Seamus appeared. He was wearing a silky deep purple track suit. Brass bells tinkled in his beard. Sir Henry was following.

"The new improved Sanguini," Seamus remarked drily.

"Yes, indeed," said Sir Henry in buoyant mood. He twirled his champagne glass. "Congratulations are in order, Mr Cherrynose. I am sad that we cannot allow Ulysses to participate, but look at him – he is in eighth heaven, as you say. So well behaved." He waved towards the Liberator, being swabbed and mopped. One of his minders had sledgehammered an iron stake into the hard ground by his throne. Another was chaining one of the Liberator's ankles to the stake. His meat chopper went back to Attah's kitchen. At the back, the monitors from the Morals Squad were yawning, so too were the representatives from Amnesty International. There was no sign of Interpol. "Your turn was close to the bone but we are definitely getting away with it."

"Getting away with what?"

But Sir Henry had gone. Qofia gave Chippo a foul-tasting swig from a bottle labelled BLOOD TONIC that Seamus had bought for her in the village. Lotus Band-Aided his bleeding face, up-ended him and applied one of her analgesic creams. "Hey, I was a little late with the grease. You could have waited."

"What did he get up to next?"

"Oh, this and that. He did your wings thing for you on the table. Threw up all over Jeb's slacks. The Lancashire Hotpot. Tore Corinne's dress. Accidentally knocked her over with his tail. Cerisia had to yell again." Lotus was giggling heartlessly. "He was making sure that was a couple who would not be back. Now we can trot Zach out for the *Daddy Dance*."

"Oh my God, did he do anything to Wally? Did they confront each other?"

"Don't ask."

Chippo queried her about Sir Henry's mysterious remark.

"Well, Reptilio and Sir Henry worked it out together. What would be beyond the pale, what wouldn't. I mean, give Ulysses a taste of the show he's used to but avoid getting busted by the local FBI or whoever those goons are out there."

As Chippo breathed in the murk of the equatorial air, he started thinking anew about Reptilio. What he always presented convincingly to challenged Chippo Cherrynose as the cutting edge of sexual freedom, the Dionysian breakthrough, the Final Healing for his patients, putting the Anglophiles back in touch with their African spiritual traditions, what he and Sir Henry were packaging as English theatrical variations on traditional voodoo ritual as practised by cultured hill tribes in the interior of Bomzawe, was being indulgently received by the audience as something else entirely. Chippo suspected that what he was experiencing as real was being experienced indulgently by the fat cats as simulation in the light of the changed circumstances of the Ulysses return. Simulation of what, he asked himself? Where was love and tenderness in all this? Reptilio felt himself to be his new Tibor, but in fact he was behaving, in his wish to utterly control him and everyone else for that matter, more like a monster of another sort, someone like Reverend Melody Motherwell. Chippo saw himself for the first time as a hapless brainwashed pawn in ambitions beyond the merely despotic into the idealistically and ideologically depraved. "You mean the Shakespeare, the entertainment, the Carnival itself, were always a cover-up?"

Lotus became evasive. "I make it my business not to know too much about it." She paused. "Yes, for what they used to call The Customs."

"How long has Reptilio known this?"

"You'll have to ask our Fuhrer."

"Reptilio..." Chippo called, as the Dancedoctor went springing by.

"Blood should flow," he shouted, not missing a stride. He ripped off the Band-Aids, smacked Chippo across the face. "Now you've got the look!"

Stan's atonal music, a satyric suite specially composed for the occasion, began.

"The Westminster Company is proud to present..." came Reptilio's voice.

Was Chippo really going to continue to perform for the fat cats who liked the blood to flow? For Ray Grable, forever the profane Pisser in the Pool, the iconoclastic Streaker, the raper/kidnapper of vulnerable youth at the West Wahroonga Psychiatric Centre? The illicit Adolf Siegfried collaborator and guinea pig?

"Nobody can play that thing like my Stan," noted Lotus fondly as the erratic notes of the ghaita imposed themselves.

Was he going to run out on Lotus? "Stan's new music is not as bad as it might be," he managed to say graciously, licking his blood as it trickled down to his mouth.

"Chippo, I'm so disappointed. You sound like you did when you first arrived here." Lotus made a final adjustment to his sequinned jockstrap, his dried sea grass chaps.

"Lotus, why can't you see that..."

"Oh, give us all a break! In Reptiliozone we only applaud. You know that. Come on, let's sock it to them!"

He allowed himself to be led into the light of the flares for the *Sacred Vulture Daddy Dance*, his mentor's *piece de resistance*.

FORTY ONE: *Plight of the Condor*

Reptilio and Tophphi had shed their clothes and had already been ceremoniously covered with fresh clay from a large stoneware pot; white for Tophphi, ochre for Reptilio. He was labelled *HEALER*. Tophphi was holding up a placard saying *INNOCENCE*. The vulture's sack read *TURPITUDE*. When Floralee, as handmaiden, fastened their masks, Tophphi became the serenely beautiful Virgin Child, Reptilio the all-powerful Farisha who was going to present her with the vile Daddy Fuck, sitting there trussed in its sack. Cerisia was an imposing creation, some kind of Gloriana, crowned as she was with her headdress of honking hornbills and wrapped in the Union Jack flag which had been flapping above in the night breeze not half an hour before. She held a familiar object from the back room of *Whatever Forever*; its large gold silk covered cushion, on which now rested Reptilio's cutlass, resharpened once more by Attah Lalwani.

Tophphi's exorcism proceeded through its various stages. Ulysses Oratorio, that steamy smoke thickened night, may not have been the Fount, the blasphemic, antique Lord of Harmattan and Half Moon of his Customs, as he had been at the previous carnival, five years before, but he was on the edge of his throne, agitating his death's head cane, desperate for that even closer view. Dr Imensah pushed a tranquilliser between his lips. The solicitous fan-wielding Chunkia kept him cooled. Sir Henry Kmango had his hands clasped high in front of him, a sure sign of pleasure. Lady Chompia had a forbearing look, almost as though she had been through this sort of thing far too many times before. The vulture, sensing correctly that something hideous was about to happen, flapped about wildly inside its prison.

"Grab the bag and run with it. Save the poor creature," Chippo exhorted himself, but Lotus had already untied the bright red cord.

Tophphi had reached her writhing sequence. What Chippo once understood as a necessary step in her cure, he now saw as no more than sex club bump and grind, with Reptilio's convulsions in front of her a barely controlled libidinous frenzy.

Stan's charivari moved into an explosive rhythm. "Stravinski inspired," hissed Lotus. "My Stan's *Rite of Spring Variations!*"

Chippo stomped on a flare, as though by accident, and sent the lighting down a notch. Floralee slapped his wrist and had it re-ignited in a trice. Reptilio hauled out the vulture and began spinning, holding it high for all to see.

"Oh no! It's Old Idi," Chippo cried. That bird had shared its breakfasts with him. The hoarse sighs of the Seamus Shamrock saxophone joined the symphony of Stan's balafon, the gourd rattles, the village boys' drums and bamboo clackers, the marimbas and the tintinnabulations of cow bells. Cerisia stepped closer with the cutlass and cushion. An inflamed Liberator stood up, rattled his chain.

Floralee was backflipping in her monokini through the billows of pink smoke. A bespangled Lotus swung upside down and dangerously close on the low trapeze. Chippo remembered he was supposed to be cancanning again, Reptilio's simple but unforgiving choreography. If Zach, kicking away beside him, could do it, so could he. "You bastard," Chippo said in intimate fashion, "I strongly suspect you're not the regular bloke you make out to be. If we can do things like this together, you might yet turn out to be a new Tibor Radovan."

"Can't hear." Zach's eyes caught his but were glazed and indifferent, even zombified, Chippo thought, with more than a trace of alarm. Well, just say he seemed to have other things on his mind. Confidently, Chippo put his arm through Zach's with no objection. Kick, two, three, spin, two three. Chippo gave him a kiss on an unshaven cheek, again with no objection.

Yes, handsome Zach, obviously Reptilioed (or at least as drunk as a Shameless Seamus on St Patrick's Day), was, like Chippo, fulfilling the demands of the Dancedoctor. Chippo of course, could sympathise with that, but really his mind was moving ahead rapidly. He was already seeing the blood spurting, the Old Idi neck thrusting, the ogling audience being drenched in a climactic, participatory shower. Reptilio may have become something akin to a local shaman in a trance or even a revolutionary Shiva, Lord of the Dance, but to Chippo at that moment he was a showman out for sensation and porno-shocks, base thrills for Ulysses and his followers, public humiliation for his victims, getting paid very large sums for a showstopping finale. Reptilio and Sir Henry Kmango were mountebanks, scoundrels, blackguards both, each with a nefarious past, each as bad as the other. He heard Sir Henry's voice coming from earlier days. "Perhaps, Dr Sanguini, we are well met."

The noise of a rapidly approaching diesel engine at full throttle cut through the escalating fervour of the drumming. Headlights flashed briefly from the grove over the scene, a squeal of brakes, then the motor cut. The slamming of the vehicle's door.

Old Idi was no pushover. Daddy Fuck and Reptilio were engaged in a battle royal for mastery. Outraged cries came from the venerable bird's throat as he was forced into position for decapitation – and Tophphi's salvation. Reptilio had him well trussed. His left foot was holding down the long scrawny neck on the chopping block, but Cerisia was a trifle late as she swept forward with the cutlass on the gold cushion and in that little window of opportunity Old Idi managed to extricate a wing. So powerfully did he beat his wing for freedom, that Chippo felt a liberating wave of cooler air flood his body and in that same moment, there came from somewhere in the audience, a fierce shout. "Stop!" A tall, bare-torsoed figure, long dark hair, monkey-masked and wearing tattered pineapple patterned Bermudas was pushing through. The crowd parted, applauded. The figure jumped on to the platform and straight-armed Reptilio in the face.

Reptilio's head hit the boards. Dazed, he still managed to keep Old Idi's legs in a tight grasp and his clay-covered self on the point of ejaculation. The vulture's wings, both now released, flapped furiously in a pantomime of flight.

"Get up, Tophphi." Drift had her by the hair. "We're outta here!"

"Ow! Drift, you promised," Tophphi cried, resisting fiercely.

"Honeybucket, I wore a mask. Just for you."

"Chippo! Cerisia!" Reptilio gasped, still stunned and unable to rise. "Stop him."

The Great Liberator reached the end of his chain, was jerked back. He gave a frustrated roar, a fearsome sound that rose above all others. He tried again, and the stake holding the chain gave way. He dodged his handlers, clanked to the platform and began raining his stick down on Drift's bare back. When he drew blood, he started squealing like a pig. The audience leaped to its feet. This was more like it. "Go Ulysses, go!"

"Let me be," Tophphi screamed at Drift. "Save yourself!"

Old Idi, flapping in Reptilio's unslackened grasp, twisted his neck around, began a savage assault on his captor. Peck! Gouge! Peck!

The Morals Squad woke up and were soon nodding their heads significantly. As were the representatives of Amnesty International. The reporters from Sir Henry's *Okidoki Post* began penning notes for the spin that would be their story. The professional photographer from Doggone moved in close. Flash! Flash!

Dr Imensah emptied one of the fire extinguishers on the Liberator to no avail. Tittering and dripping with foam, Ulysses picked Drift up and flung him to one side like a piece of flotsam. He tore the cutlass from Cerisia's grasp and began swinging it wildly. His supporters surged forward, cheering him on. Chippo was shocked to see that William Oates was one of them. Missing Old Idi by a wide margin, the Liberator focussed on Cerisia. A mighty slash burst the golden cushion she had raised to protect herself. Goose down exploded in a snowy shower, sending the Liberator into a paroxysm of sneezing. Boldly, Cerisia took advantage and advanced, kicking and imprecating, but the Liberator would not be denied. His sneezes not withstanding, he steamrollered forward, and the two smashed into each other. Cerisia fell flat on her back.

The Liberator raised the cutlass in both hands and would have butchered her if Drift, having picked himself up, had not got him in a hammer lock. Swinging the superheated old sadist to one side, Drift tripped him with a foot, crashing him to the platform. As the cutlass fell from his grasp he let out a series of unholy bellows. Belatedly his handlers moved in. He was dragged back to his throne and the stake once more pounded in. A chorus of jolly boos came from the audience. A chant began. "More, more, more!"

"Do I still owe you that 200 quid?" Drift knelt and checked Cerisia for broken bones; but Cerisia, noticing that Reptilio was recovering and that Tophphi had scrambled for the cutlass, dragged Drift down and held him on top of her in a captive embrace. Drift's hair fell all over her face. "Go, Toots go! Go Tophphi! Do it, do it now!"

Reptilio smacked away Old Idi's jabbing beak, and finally managing to get the great bird retrussed, he lurched up. Tophphi got into position, Reptilio knelt like a supplicant and presented the huge bird to her for dispatch so he could set in motion his sanguinary finale. Drift was squirming violently in attempts to free himself from Cerisia. "Ungrateful bitch," he swore, and attempted to take a bite out of her. "Chippo, give her a whack!"

Chippo had other plans. His vocal chords had long since ceased their chirring, but he knew the joyous cicada spirits still lived within him. Now they were activated and at full throttle, sooling him on, perhaps with the delayed help of that second Avalanche. "Okay okay, I know exactly what your advice is. Watch me," and so saying, he picked up the big stoneware pot left on the stage. Reptilio's back was to him. "Don't you dare!" Cerisia screeched. "My buddy," Drift cried.

Steadying himself, Chippo brought the heavy artefact down hard on Reptilio's head. The pot shattered, the pieces and the liquid clay exploding in every direction. Reptilio slumped like a dead man. Chippo felt the most wonderful feeling of exaltation, as though ever since he had been Sound of Musicked on the beach that Full Moon Makeover day, he had been building up to this point. "Surrender to the Dionysian, the deepest, the darkest," Reptilio had said. "Do whatever those noises in your head want you to do." Yes, he had found the formula, the fiend, and the fun within. Shot the Buddha on the road, avenged his rape, saved Old Idi.

The king of the vultures shook his pink, wrinkled neck, beat his ragged pinions, hopped a few feet and was airborne. He flew over everyone's head in a circle, faltered when Mr Ichoko got him with an empty champagne bottle, but flapped off through the palm trees in the direction of freedom, even if that meant his usual roost on the roof of the hotel.

Drift picked up Tophphi in his arms, covered her white clayed breasts and face with kisses. Cerisia rolled over to Reptilio who had not moved.

"Oh my goodness," Chippo gasped, hands to his head, "what have I done?"

Cerisia removed Reptilio's mask. "If you've killed him, Chipman Smith, I'll shred you into tiny pieces." Her voice rose into an engulfing yell. "Why don't you go back to Sydney where you belong? Jump off your stupid Harbour Bridge or something."

"For Christ's sake, Cerisia," Drift said, "Have a heart! We're lucky to be alive."

"If you hadn't come barging in, everything would have gone as planned." She lashed out with a slippered foot. " Septic tank Yank! Twiddle off."

Tenderly, Cerisia kissed Reptilio. His eyes opened. "Oh, toots!"

The crowd were whooping for encores. The performers, those that were able, finally took their bows.

FORTY TWO: *Sweet William (and other flowers)*

The *Uhuru Contemporary Dance Orchestra* struck up, bang on schedule and The High Society Easter Ball got going. Sir Henry and his wife, together with a hand-picked few, waltzed several circuits of the floor to a version of *Norwegian Wood*, a particular favourite of Lady Chompia. Later there was a clever transition into the belly dancing, as arranged. Cerisia appeared first, samite-clad arms on high, flashing her scimitars provocatively, secure in the knowledge that the Liberator was well-corralled but equally well-prepared to take him on if he were not. Lotus and Tophphi joined her and the women swayed into their triple baladi. Clash! went the finger cymbals, jingle went their ankle bells. Stan had the ghaita wailing. At the climax, the hips of all three were whirring like rotary whisks. It was unfortunate that five minutes into the second sequence, Cerisia was overwhelmed by Drift's undertrained and overly-pumped python, which came close to squeezing the life out of her. With Cerisia locked in a Laocoon-like struggle, and the crowd barracking for the snake, it was almost too much excitement to bear to have Tophphi's shoulder collide with the tray of champagne glasses balanced on the head of Lotus, and cause everything to go flying. There was no time to clear away the broken glass. The well-shod dancers happily stomped it to fine powder. The python made its own way back to its cage.

It was outside on the beach, under the palms and the ever expanding universe of stars that the real Easter Ball took place. The drums thundered. Some age-old, anarchic message was telegraphed through the night to Tlula, for more and more of its inhabitants began to appear, many against their better judgment, but Forgiveness was in the air, or at least a great Forgetting, even at the highest level. Fangga and Blossom, both in belligerent mood, circled the outskirts, spiralled in.

Charged with a fervid excitement, Ulysses Oratorio, all unshackled magnificence once more, was on his feet. Friends milled around, spurring him on. Wheezing and squirting, the wanton behemoth began a beguine, a heavy-footed version learned in the night clubs of Port-au-Prince. The unwary and the weak had their toes squashed or were caught by his savagely lashing cane. Yes, The Great Liberator was among his people, back from his lonely Caribbean exile, once more doing his thing. He had suffered enough, they were saying. The horror of those last worthless years of his long reign, with their unspeakable deeds, when he had abandoned the responsibilities of governance for the depravity of his private pleasures, had no relevance for the moment.

Ulysses moved towards the main pavilion, waving in imperial fashion. At the top of the three steps, he turned, and exuding foul gases for the special delight of his laughing, singing, dancing, inhaling supporters, he gave a long held Hitlerian salute. From the bar to the beach, the night was awash with emotion. Any ill feelings still pent up until that point of the carnival, were finally subdued. As Reptilio would have said, exorcism had taken place, ecstasy was now possible.

There was Floralee Bush, doing her wound-up-forever grandmomma doll dance, melded with her 'bine and her latest beau, a man of polished boot blackness, who had been instructed to keep her satiated. She had begun a public flirtation with Qaddo, even climbing naked into his custom-built, oversized bed when he was taking an afternoon nap beside his diminutive wife. Floralee's 'bine high, easing off as it was, was still too hot to handle. Qaddo's wife had doused her with a bucket of sea water, tied her to a rail and put her to work pounding fufu. Qaddo contacted Qiddo, his much in demand cousin, known as the Kassini Junction Candy Man, and pleaded and paid for his assistance.

"I wish my old Mum could see me now," Floralee cried as they jiggety-jigged into the dark. In her paisley peasant skirt and hand-painted, patchouli impregnated scoop neck top, bottle-blond bangs, bougainvillea bunched above each ear, the old rouee smelled and looked exactly what she imagined herself to be that night, an irresistibly desirable teenage flower child left over from Woodstock.

The fabulous noise lifted everyone effortlessly through the risen dust, above the palms and the poincianas into the empyrean cool. *Oh, Africa, happy, happy Africa,* sang the fat cats from Okidoki, the men from the Morals Squad, Amnesty International, the reporters from the *Okidoki Post* and Reptilio's paparazzo from Doggone. Yes, everyone was chorusing and living it up by the luminous, carnival sea. Africa has no memory, said someone. Africa obliterates.

And there were Samuel Ichoko and Sir Henry's guards carefully taking down and wrapping the Bronzes. Each piece was placed inside two large trunks, which were then locked and carried to The Great Liberator's high-security, iron-barred chalet. The trunks were of ebony hardwood with exquisite copper fittings that had high antique value in themselves. Ulysses was reportedly looking forward to spending one last night in the Bronzes' presence. Chippo and Drift stood in the shadows watching the entire operation.

"Short of armed robbery, what can you do?"

"There has to be a way. I'm gonna smoke a chillum and work on it."

Washed and repaired, Reptilio and Cerisia were in the main pavilion, exchanging greetings with The Great Liberator, the Kmangos and Chief Akwa. Old Idi's beak had certainly exacted an unsightly retribution, but Reptilio seemed none the worse or wiser for Chippo's assault with the stoneware. Zach was with them, a wide band stamped with the national flag around his forehead, looking translucent, even saintly rather than his merely under-fed, over-liquored, intensely attractive, Rocky Mountains self. Chippo watched in continued surprise as Reptilio introduced him first to the Liberator, then to Kraka, the Crocodile Fetish Priest.

Zach and Chippo had high-kicked together for the *Vulture Daddy Dance*, but there had been no chance to unravel the mystery Chippo was determined to clarify and Zach determined to conceal.

Accompanied by Seamus and Qofia, Chippo pushed through the throng towards the tricky Nebraskan, but at a table by the seawall, they came upon William Oates who was entwined with Riki Steam, one of Samuel Ichoko's filles de joie. The rich smell of the still roasting bullock – with Attah himself and a sous-chef down there basting and slicing away – was wafting up.

"Well, you know," William said affably, apologising a touch for Riki, "it's nice to get away from Eileen now and again." Chippo looked at him blankly. "Eileen. My wife. Your boss's little sister."

"Oh. I was supposed to present myself front and centre." Chippo scratched his head. "I even took a shower. Where is he?"

William waved vaguely. "I sent him into the surf to cool off. Trouble with old Wally, he wouldn't know a good time if one sat on his face."

"Hullo, Mr Willy," said Qofia.

William Oates stared for a moment, then smiled. "Qofia. I didn't recognise you."

"I still hab dat nice blouse you gib me."

"Blouse? Ah, yes, the blouse. The mules. Ha ha! How's the Bottoms Up these days?"

"I disco dere ebery night, Mr Willy. Why I no see you dese days? You no like de pussy boys no more?"

Pussy boy? Chippo looked with fresh eyes at Qofia. And Seamus. He could not stop staring in amazement. He had had no idea.

William waggled a finger at Qofia and turned to Chippo. "I say, Chipman Smith, I rather enjoyed that performance your little gang came up with. Confusing with the dim lighting, smoke and all, but bravo indeed. Kmango endlessly apologising, of course, for it all having to be so tame and silly, no sex and so on, but he asked us to be patient and humour him. For Ulysses' sake. I was here for the last carnival, you know, five years ago. Hush, hush, naturally. Tlula and its Customs were strictly off-limits for the Embassy."

Having noticed William Oates's enthusiasm for the Liberator's antics during the performances, Chippo found nothing was now surprising him about William Oates.

"Isn't it strange how the wheel turns? Here we are censoring ourselves!" William sighed. "Oh for the good old days."

"What do you mean?"

"Well, how can I put it? More gladiatorial. You know, the Roman Colosseum or something. Jacobean drama. Ulysses was quite a boy in his declining years. He got hold of that good old fetishistic religious stuff and used it to justify his blood-lettings."

"Blood-lettings?"

"Supposed to be criminals, but a few political opponents usually got creamed as well. Cutting through some of those awkward tribal knots. Keeping the ship of state together. Bit of a charnel house, really. Drawing and quartering, heads on poles, things like that. Amputations. Ha ha! You should have seen Kmango's production of *Titus Andronicus*. They gave old Ulysses an axe and just let him loose. So much more visceral excitement, back then. All that delight in savagery and excess. Top hole!" William paused, cleared his throat. "Don't get me wrong. You put on a jolly good show, considering it was absolutely verboten this time to have even a suggestion of what went on before. Clever of Kmango to hire you, all your fluorescent therapy masks and things. That blond wig was a nice touch. Actually, your buggery number was bang-on as a substitute for some of the less barbarous routines Sir Henry used to conjure up for the Liberator. With his failing eyesight the old ogre probably didn't even know that it was all mime and masquerade. He wasn't chuffed by half. Ha! Ha! Ha!" William wiped his eyes. "Pity that damn bird got away. Ulysses likes that animal sex stuff."

"Wally didn't seem to..."

"Don't worry about him," said William. "I knew Kmango had been told to clean up his act, but frankly I still wouldn't have had him along. What could I do? Some tiny letter you sent. Had to use a magnifying glass to read it. Was in a tizzy about you."

"Not surprising, I..."

"And don't feel too down about not recognizing Ray Grable. We have had an Interpol wanted poster of him on the wall at the Embassy for years. His face always on file. When Sanguini turned up at our cocktail party last year, I didn't recognize him either."

Lotus swanned up, Stan hugging her from behind. "You probably will hate to hear this, Chippo, but the old buffoon wants an exclusive re-enactment of the *Daddy Dance* at midnight. Money no object. If I don't find Tophphi, Reptilio will start looking for her. They're not in their room."

Chippo's nostrils took in the expertly distributed perfumery of the utterly lovely Lotus. As usual she seemed to have a different fragrance for every part of her body, particularly the moister areas. In the midst of her gush, he detected a sadness and wondered if she had finally become aware that that she had sold herself and Stan up the river and to the devil. "Are you sure you and Stan want to continue with those two after tonight?"

Lotus's eyes strayed to the pavilion where Reptilio and Cerisia were still socialising with the official party. "They're my family. I owe them a lot. They provide the framework within which I do my designs, make my costumes. Cerisia's taught me this wonderful baladi. One day I'll be able to hit the country fairs in Oregon and cash in. Reptilio has repaired Stan's brain lesions. Really developed him as a musician, don't you think? He won't be crashing the bus too much any more. In fact, he's a whiz. He can get a job driving school kids or something. Sing and play for them." Lotus slipped her arm into Chippo's. "The year Stanford freaked out in San Francisco was the worst of my life. It took me a long time to adjust to someone in a vegetative state, my wonderful boy as a flatliner. Until he discovered the healing joy of playing the spoons, I didn't think there was any hope at all." She paused, moved a little closer and lowering her voice said. "Chippo, we've decided we're going to make babies."

"Oh, that's fabulous, Lotus," Chippo said even as he wondered about all these confidences.

"Are you coming with us tomorrow? We've upped our departure time, hitting the road right after the Regatta."

He was not surprised that Reptilio was now taking flight.

"Reptilio leaves at the flood. Don't say you're not coming after all. It will be more fun than you can possibly imagine. The next reality." She paused momentarily. "You know he got us to trash the trotro that night because he loved you. Couldn't bear the thought of you leaving us, all fucked up as you were."

"I can't believe that Cerisia would ever really want me along. What about Zach?"

"Zach? Oh, your dilemmas." Lotus thrust her face into Chippo's and sent her teapot earrings shaking. "You think too much. It's in the cards. I did the Family's Tarot. I threw the Ching as well, to check." And she and Stan ricocheted away into the fiery dark.

"Not returning to Australia just yet?" asked William Oates, who had managed to completely remove Riki Steam's skirt.

"No, no, I'm going back."

"Oh, Chippo," cried Qofia, "buy me passport and I go wit you. Seamus he cheap fucker. All he dash me is de nasty blood tonic." Seamus looked affronted. He took his sax out of its case.

"Wally's got a pole up his arse but he's okay." William continued. "I suppose the old fellow was giving you a hard time back in the office? He's fond of throwing his weight around."

" It was probably me who was giving him a hard time."

"Yes, Chipman Smith, you were, and not just in the office apparently, if our disreputable Mr Grable can be believed. I had no idea it was you in my tree," said Wally, coming up at that moment. "But I was heartened to witness you giving Grable a hard time just now. Maybe there is hope for you yet. Not too hard I am pleased to add. Certainly a well-deserved comeuppance, but we need Raymond Vincent Grable alive and back in Sydney to face the Coolidge family. Not a family to be taken lightly, I have to remind you. In concert with the British government we have an extradition treaty with Bomzawe. I'm putting everything in motion immediately."

Wally was dripping wet, his portly frame at odds with his sportingly brief pair of swimming trunks. Chippo had not seen Wally's nipples since that calamitous life-changing night outside his bedroom window. A remarkably bright pink, they rose from a sea of silvery chest hair, nubbly promontories he had distantly longed to caress and suck. As he stared, they now acquired a certain grotesquery.

"Sorry about this," Wally said, as he towelled down. "Obviously butting in on a side of you you'd prefer to keep private. Tried to telephone, but you're off the radar here. I presume you didn't get my telegram."

"Sea lice bite you?" Chippo asked. "They can be bad at night."

From beneath his knitted brow, Wally sensed impertinence and fixed his one time junior colleague with the judgmental glare that once made Chipman Smith quiver with fear, respect and an ill-concealed lunatic lust.

"I'm sorry about my voyeurism, Wally. But it's all behind me now."

"And there I was thinking you were just a badly behaved drunk. I must confess to shock, Smith. And now this!" Wally put a hand inside his swimmers and made a slow adjustment. "I have no objection to pursuit of an interest in the theatre or even dance. I have been a leading performer with the Waverton Musical Society for many years, as you know, but what you have got into here smacks of criminal debauchery. If you plead insanity, I would not object."

Qofia tugged at Chippo's arm. "Come wit us, handsome man, away from dis ugly one."

"There are less pagan avenues to pursue. Think of *Annie Get Your Gun. The King and I.* Clothes."

"Now then, Wally," said William Oates, as Riki Steam gave him a slap. "Get into the swing of things." He drew Riki up, handed back her skirt. "Excuse-moi, ma petite vicieuse."

Whitbread reached for a brandy bottle. "You're imbibing, of course, Smith?" The liquor tumbled into the glasses.

"Is there any sugar?"

"I beg your pardon?"

"I must have been crazy to have fallen in love with you. You almost had me spending the rest of my life, my one time around life, in Macquarie Street."

Screwing up his face, Wally cupped a hand to his ear. "Can't hear!" You'll have to stop these tomtoms, they're driving me bananas." He coughed on the smoke from the fetish fires, swallowed his brandy, poured more. "About Lagos." Whitbread raised his voice to make himself heard. "Accommodations there are very tight. I think it would be best if you didn't, after all..."

"Tomorrow," Chippo shouted, as a blast from the Seamus saxophone hit his ear. "Let's talk about it tomorrow."

One of the black and white goats that had arrived in Lady Kmango's Humber Super Snipe was carried forward. With far less ceremony than Reptilio had planned for Old Idi, Kraka made an incision, drained the blood from its garlanded neck into a calabash, offered it to the Liberator. Ho! Ho! Ho! shrieked the multitude, as the former power in the land drank. Acolytes draped the goat, alive but subdued, around Kraka's neck. He proceeded to do a cabbalistic dance, sucking from time to time at the goat's wound and each time, he spat the blood into Ulysses, who opened his huge mouth for the offerings, like a baby bird in its nest. In the darkness it took a while for Chippo to realise that Kraka was attired in his old safari suit, transformed for the aesthetic better by a paint job and an accumulation of bells and whistles. The goat grew weaker. Ho! Ho! Ho! The crowd screamed again, stomping about in some fierce zarabanda, entrained in a miasmic conjunction of movement and sound. It was an ancient and atavistic world that belonged to them alone.

"I'm not sure about Reptilio's involvement in all this," yelled William Oates. "Deep waters these, Chipman. Can be foolhardy, dipping one's toe into this sort of stuff." He cast a look over to The Great Liberator's pavilion. "I don't want to alarm you, young man, but your lovely friend Lotus has the right idea. I'd get out of here as soon as possible. I managed to ring Okidoki earlier this evening. Ulysses Oratorio is behaving himself, but Sir Henry Kmango has certainly misread the country's mood. Something's up. I noticed a lot of movement by the Army barracks in Doggone when we came through."

It was hard to tell from the blithe tone how serious he was. "Things are coming to a head," William went on. "I'd give it forty eight hours at most. Check in with the Embassy just to be safe. You may be on the wrong side of the equation here."

FORTY THREE: *Up the lazy river*

Early the next morning, Chippo was hastening along the track to the village and the Wawa River when a red MG roadster pulled up in front of him. Beside William Oates in the driving seat was a smiling Riki Steam. In the back was Wally Whitbread, with a similarly smiling young woman. The Morals Squad roared by in a shiny Toyota Corolla, heading back to the city. Amnesty International's observers followed in their Jeep. A trotro laden with journalists completed the convoy.

"In a hurry," Oates remarked. "Do they know something I don't? Very likely. Kmango refused access to the ponds to Amnesty and everyone else. Can't say I have much sympathy. They've hounded poor Ulysses for years. Why give them more grist to their mill? Anyway, had our fun." He jerked a thumb back at Wally and his companion.

"Please, Willy, no discourse," said Wally, as his ebony beauty's hand attempted to unzip his fly.

William gave Chippo a wink. "Is that a joint?" It was handed to him. "Thanks. Don't mind if I do." Oates took a couple of tokes. "Hmmm. Damn good weed. Makes me sorry to be missing the maypole this afternoon. That can be pretty wild." He offered the joint to Wally who rejected it with great irritation. "Ah yes, the maypole. You don't have any to sell, by any chance?" Oates asked, toking again.

"Chipman," said Wally, "I'm feeling more charitable towards you this morning. We can make room if you want to pack up and come with us. There's a dicky seat."

"A squeeze," said William, "but these dusky trollops get dumped on the docks in Doggone."

"I can't miss the crocodile ponds."

"I appreciate that you have feelings for Grable," said Wally, "but Chipman, whatever you say he has achieved, he is clearly beyond any redemption. He will be in the hands of the appropriate authorities within days. There's no future for you with him. Loyalty is one thing, but there is also guilt by association, if you remember anything at all about the law."

Chippo knew this was a serious moment, a veritable crossroads in his life.

"You have fallen in with the lowest of the low, Smith. Chippo if you insist. You are taking downward mobility to Dickensian extremes. I am still in shock at your confession to voyeuristic inclinations. You clearly need integrative professional help and more. But the Department, I suggest, may be sympathetic."

"Thanks for the offer, Wally. I'll think about it. Really I will. But I may have a future as a cabinetmaker. A carpenter. Or a photographer. I'm thinking about the Peace Corps. The British Council. Maybe you would approve of that."

Wally gave Chippo one last magisterial glare. "Be it on your own head, Smith. Ouch, you black bitch, be gentle," he said in the next second, giving his companion's probing fingers a little slap. "Perhaps it's best that this has all come to light now rather than later. To be honest, the question of competency aside, with your sexual tendencies, criminal as you must surely know, you are hardly someone who should be in a position of authority within the Department at all. It is, when everything is said and done, the law-loving people of New South Wales for whom you would have been making policy decisions. I somehow knew I was making a mistake propping you up all these years."

William revved the engine.

"Happy trails, Wally," Chippo sang as he pulled out his camera. "toooo yooouu." He knew he was being insouciant, even insolent, but all he could think of really, was that Zach was already on the river heading for the crocodile pond festivities. Click, click, click! Too late, Wally shielded his face with his right arm, his erection and the black fingers around it, with his left.

"Give me picture. I want picture," cried Wally's dusky trollop, reaching out her free hand.

"Don't forget to check in with the Embassy." William Oates accelerated, the tyres spun and the Roadster shot off in a billow of orange dust.

Sir Henry Kmango's Grand Flotilla set off for the Sacred Crocodile Ponds from beneath the shadow of Castle Vinkenoog. The Great Liberator led the way in his canopied pirogue, a vessel of almost barge-like proportions. Close behind, in a supply boat, sat Kraka and several acolytes, accompanied by clucking from a crate of unsuspecting chickens.

Following were ten other decorated pirogues, each with six guests. There was not room for everyone in the fleet, and only the more generous benefactors to the war chest of Ulysses' Rehabilitation Committee had been invited. The well-funded and festive Mr Ichoko had a whole canoe for himself and his girls. As principal members of the *Westminster Dance Theatre*, which had brought such discreet joy to Ulysses the night before, Reptilio and Cerisia floated in a smaller pirogue carved with suns and crescent moons. There had been three spare places. Democratically, straws had been drawn. Lotus, Stan and Zach had secured them.

"Rigged," said the irrepressible Floralee, who had no intention of missing the 'diles, as she called them. She pumped up her red rubber dinghy, one of the many items of sporting equipment, like surf boards, she carried in her Kombi van.

Over ablutions that morning, Reptilio had been airy about Chippo's Efflorescence. He said that worrying about what others (i.e. William Oates, Wally Whitbread and various colleagues at the Attorney General's Department) might think, Chippo had lost focus, no longer able to experience himself as part of a glorious, subversive tableau for which the *Westminster Dance Theatre* was even getting handsomely paid. If he hadn't achieved the full fairytale, thank Cerisia for making it so brief. As for the interruption to the *Vulture Daddy Dance*; "Never mind. I forgave you before you even thought to do it. And look what has come out of it. No longer betrayal of the performers' integrity, but an additional layer of meaning to the ritual. You have opened up the flood-gates to fresh realities, enabled me to move onwards and upwards yet again. I thank you. You are my good luck charm."

Reptilio had rested his dark eyes softly upon the estranged lawyer. He presented his patched-up cheeks to Chippo for a kiss, and gave him a feel of the horribly crusted lump on the Reptilio skull. "Another notch on my healing gun."

"How much did you know of what used to go on here at Tlula, Reptilio. The Customs."

"All I know is I don't want you adding new layers of meaning to any more rituals. As the famous Artaud himself said, if you can't stand the heat, stay out of the kitchen."

"You and that twinkie Drift with your RSPCA twaddle," said Cerisia. "You're either with us or against us."

"Oh, I'm with you," Chippo lied. "I admit to being troubled by carnage and cruelty in the name of art, even in the name of catharsis and ritual, and I am disillusioned about other aspects, particularly the commercial ones, and things like corruption of ideals and values, but please don't think me ungrateful for..."

"Insect!" said Cerisia, cutting him off.

Even though in the mood for clemency, Reptilio still firmly denied Chippo permission to attend the ceremonials at the Pond - whether he drew the right straw or not.

Disillusioned as he was with the Dancedoctor, disobedience for Chippo was a snap, and he immediately took up Floralee's invitation to travel in her dinghy.

All was quiet but for the dip of the paddles and the muffled beat of the ceremonial drums coming from the lead canoes. Once they were out of sight of Castle Vinkenoog, the river tunnelled in, running murky, deep and narrow, with mangroves thickly lining the banks, and behind the mangroves, clusters of palms and impenetrable vegetation. As the hills began to rise more steeply, the palms gave way to grey-boled mahogany and teak, obeche and the other great trees of the rain forest. Trunks near the water provided homes to masses of freshwater sponges and lividly coloured fungi.

Epiphytes clung to the mighty limbs of their hosts, proliferated in the forks of the larger boughs. Clouds of butterflies and other insects were visiting the flowering vines on the sunny side of the bank. As the river took an eastern turn, the Tlula Escarpment appeared, jaggedly dropping from the road far above. Fishing eagles glided high across the rock face.

The water level was down, the current slight. The streamlined pirogues skimmed up the river with the greatest of ease, and the rubber dinghy fell further and further behind. Chippo experienced a momentary concern that they would miss the ceremonies altogether, but a dream-like state soon enveloped him.

Trailing his fingers in the water he let his mind drift back to the previous evening; to an encounter with Zach he had had on the dance floor, immediately in front of the *Uhuru Contemporary Dance Orchestra.*

"What a night! Making it through?" Zach yelled in his ear.

"What's with this kamikaze band around your head?" Chippo was stoned and drunk, and unrestainedly grinning, the cicadas in his brain zing-a-zing zinging. Should he stop himself from being so ecstatically happy to be with Zach? And from being, in every fibre and inch of his brain and body, so very – aroused? And in love.

Zach gazed out towards the blackness that was the midnight sea. The dancers shouted and spun around them. He looked back into Chippo's eyes and his lips parted but no words came. He smiled, almost sorrowfully, shook his head. There was a luminescence about him that more than matched Chippo's own at that moment.

Nice, nice, nice
Tlula nice like sugar and spice,
We is livin' in Paradise...

sang the leader of the Orchestra in chorus with his four indefatigable dancers, who could shake their tits and bottoms, knock their knees, wave their hands and harmonise all at the same time.

"You got Reptilioed? You're in love?" Chippo's lips were a hair's breadth away from the shell of Zach's ear. He was shouting above the noise, drinking in the wonderful smell of his skin. He sensed something, something entirely erotic. Queerotic. It had to be coming from the Nebraskan as much as from him. Zach was in love with Chippo, there was no longer any doubt about it! All he had to do was reach out, and he would be received. Their arms would go around each other, they would be entwined, finally confessing to a loving and limitless desire. Chippo kept close and, more fervently than earlier that evening as they performed for Reptilio, he kissed Zach on the cheek and then the neck, only to have the man slip away without returning any such affection. He looked back to give no more than a belated wave. There was a regret in that wave and Chippo, left stranded as he had been, was convinced that both love and desire were there. Something else, something utterly compelling, was in the way.

"You paddle and I'll bail," came Floralee's voice. The dinghy had sprung a leak.

The landscape changed. The forested hills on the right bank fell back, the mangroves split into islands, and a swampy savannah, with dense copses of raffia palms, appeared. The Great Liberator's pirogue, far ahead by now, left the river for the swamp, with the rest of the flotilla following. Chippo and Floralee were alone on the dark green water. The sound of a large fish breaking the surface startled them. Yellow frogs with red spots plopped from logs. There was a distant rumble of thunder.

Long before Chippo pulled into the backwaters, the official party had debarked at an old wooden jetty which protruded from an island higher than the rest of the swamp. It was covered with grasses and clumps of tall bamboo. Mosquitoes, midges and swarms of gnats as well as the sinking dinghy kept both of them busy. All around were fallen trees and decayed vegetation. Slower and slower they went, with patches of purple-flowered water lilies clogging their progress. Cormorants, sitting in rows on the dead branches, dried their wings in the sun. A lone heron waited unconcernedly on a log as a flock of pygmy kingfishers skimmed low, uttering their reedy cries. The diurnal frog choir was louder than the stridulations of all the insects. Chippo listened for the shimmering song of the cicadas. It was strangely absent.

The closer they drew to the island, the shallower and more stygian became the water. Strange low-bellied barks and whines came from far and near. Ripe cloacal odours hung in the air. These marshy stretches were Tlula's infamous crocodile ponds, this steamy primordial stew was their domain, the foetid smells were their smells. Floralee pointed out bones and human skulls, half buried in the mud of the shoreline. Chippo thought of the bodies washed up on the beach all those weeks ago and of Kraka's role in disposal. Of Zach's scrap of faded blue denim.

By the time they hauled out, drums were beating, the ceremonials well under way. They ran to the far side of the island. A parasol, grandiose and polka-dotted, under which Ulysses Oratorio, The Great Liberator, was sitting, dominated the spectacle. Kraka the fetish priest, withered and stooped, was nearby on a raised platform, an incongruous figure in a fresh outfit: stove pipe hat, granny glasses, and a braided matador jacket but otherwise close to naked, his chest and abdomen cabbalistically marked in red and white. He was in the process of finishing his prayers and invocation. He had called the crocodiles by having his acolytes spear the chickens in their sides, then throw them bleeding, squawking and in their death throes, into the pond. In rapid motion and to one side below his platform were the drummers and a small but energetic troupe of male teenage dancers. They wore skirts of what looked like narrow strips of crocodile leather and their torsoes were glistening with sweat. Chippo was happy to see the voice-unbroken Qojo allowed to be amongst them.

The water was alive, churning with reptilian thrashes. A pair of wide open jaws clamped down on a bird, the crocodile disappearing into the depths with a twist of its serrated tail. Feathers floated to the top. Convulsing poultry continued to be thrown in. "Yes, set those chookies free," Floralee cried merrily.

The crocodiles were as fast as they were agile, as muddy coloured as their milieu; corrugated backs, ferocious teeth and bulbous eyes passing back and forth in a blur. Chippo struggled for a better view and his eyes were soon on the crowd clustered by the Liberator. Reptilio and Cerisia were there, decked out in their oversize papier-mache heads as the Father and Mother of all Crocodiles, Lotus's greatest triumph. Each head had a vicious looking snout, toothed with shards of glass, the sprung jaws operable by pulling a string. As Reptilio and Cerisia danced through the crowd in a vigorous duet, Chippo saw they were not alone. Right behind them was Zach, who was naked but for a garland of variegated flowers on his head similar to that on the sacrificial goat the night before. Always it seemed, the last to know, Chippo's shock was so great he almost fainted. Now he realised why Reptilio had forbidden him to come – he wouldn't approve. And of course, he didn't. He watched as Cerisia wound a skein of leaves around Zach's loins.

"Well, I'll be buggered," Floralee exclaimed. "The old witch cut a deal with Kmango. I bet they're raking it in for this one."

Zach stopped in front of Kraka who swiftly made incisions in the Nebraskan's wrists and ankles, causing small jets of arterial blood to spurt from him. Kraka took hold of two ceremonial spears and brandished them over Zach but did not strike. Reptilio and Cerisia, with Zach tightly hemmed between them, approached the water's edge. The drummers settled into their most blistering tempo.

"Whoopee!" came a callous cry from Floralee, "Where's Seamus? He could play *The Last Post*."

At last Chippo understood Zach's recent beatific moods. Reptilio had probably been working on him for days and Zach had come to terms with it. How could Chippo have been so obtuse? *The Siamese Re-joining*. Zach and Zeke. But now, now that his moment had finally come, Zach seemed unwilling.

"Zach, don't," Chippo's shout was as loud a shout as he had ever uttered. He was pushing his way rapidly through the crowd when Ntank wrapped his arms around him from behind.. He struggled and would have escaped had Ntank not sunk his incisors into Chippo's shoulder, just above the scapula, close to his neck. He gasped in pain. The pointed teeth went deeper. Ntank, who had that morning slotted a large bone through a hole in his septum, was breathing stertorously. Chippo felt moist nasal exhalations hot on his skin. Saliva gushed from the chauffeur's rank mouth.

The teenage dancers parted and Kraka moved swiftly forward, making some arcane gestures with his spears. Soon Zach was up to his waist in the foul water. He turned around, a look in his eyes both pleading and confused. Cerisia grabbed one of Kraka's spears and prodded Zach with it. "Darling," cried Reptilio, "there's no need..."

Members of Ulysses Oratorio's retinue, lined up on the bank, began shouting. "Go white man, go." Cerisia prodded again, and Zach lost his balance. He came up covered in slime, tried to get back. Cerisia repulsed him with a resounding whap with the blade of the spear. Zach yelled something at her, swore, then set out diagonally for a clump of mangroves on the far bank.

Kraka stood dispassionately, slowly beating a small drum which had been smeared with blood from both Zach and the chooks. At the Liberator's feet were Zach's chinos, his cowboy hat and the Camelot t-shirt along with a scattering of chicken feathers. Ulysses drained a goblet, dabbed his lips. The napkin came away stained red. Zach's blood. He leaned forward in his sese-wood chair and belched in anticipation of the inevitable.

Zach had gone but a few strokes when there was a mighty crack of thunder directly above. Simultaneously a flash of lightning illumined the scene with a blare of ballooning purplish light. A warm deluge followed, soaking everyone to the skin. The surface of the water calmed, merged with the rain. Miraculously not a single crocodile made a move, and Zach continued to swim undisturbed. He approached the other bank, found his feet, and waist deep in the water, his arms flailing, he began to wade out.

There was another sharp report. It was no drum, no thunderclap, no divine intervention. Ulysses had drawn an automatic from his robes and had fired a shot at Zach. He fired another and another. Like the first, they missed. Not even close. Zach clambered though a gap in the mangroves, squelched in the mud to firmer ground. Baby crocodiles, almost invisible in the heavy rain, scattered. A mother, hidden nearby, lumbered forward, her jaws open. Reaching for a branch, Zach swung himself up, hooked his legs around another branch, and ended up lying across a tangle of foliage. His limbs hung limply, barely beyond the reptile's lunges and snapping jaws. He rested his head in the leaves and closed his eyes, his face drained of colour. Blood dripped down.

Ntank's teeth had loosened their bite. Chippo tore free and ran to the water's edge. Ulysses was grinning idiotically. He fired one more shot which went into the centre of the pond before Dr Imensah wrenched away the automatic. Cerisia gave her mask's snout a final glass-shattering snap of fury and disappointment.

The heavenly inundation ceased as quickly as it had begun. The clouds rolled away and the sun came out. A wash of pale lightning momentarily over-exposed the whole scene. There was another rumble of thunder. Distant this time.

Kmango, Kraka and Chief Akwa engaged each other in vituperative discourse. The crowd dispersed towards the pirogues, almost as though to disassociate themselves from a ritual that had undoubtedly failed.

"This is terrible! He's bleeding to death!"

"There is no need for all this hysteria, Mr Cherrynose." Sir Henry appeared, delicately flattening fingers to his ears. "Chief Akwa has already organised a canoe for his rescue. And goodness me, look, there is your Floralee already paddling across the waters. What other little old lady would have such intrepidity!"

Long before Chief Akwa's capacious canoe, trailed by Floralee, had brought back Zach (already given urgent on the spot treatment by Dr Imensah with sutures and bandages), the crocodiles had returned to their logs and lairs, their daily routines. One lay on a distant mudbank, its jaws wide open, an egret picking at its teeth. Others floated at ease on the surface of the water, eyes closed, their legs spread like sky divers, seemingly taking the sun. The pond was just another docile stretch of water, as though the frenzy had never been.

"Are you comfortable there, Mr Cherrynose?" asked Sir Henry as everyone made their way back to where the flotilla had drawn up. His shoulder, with its double row of oozing perforations, had also received attention from Dr Imensah. "Please do not judge us, good sir."

Zach was being carried by Ntank and his colleagues on a hastily constructed stretcher. "Don't trust these ratbags, Zach," Floralee was yelling through cupped hands from her dingy. "Come back with me." Zach was well-bandaged, but chalkfaced and wan. His dulled eyes briefly met those of Chippo. One arm hung limply over the edge of the stretcher and Chippo could not resist a squeeze of his hand. The answering squeeze that came from Zach seemed to contain, for the first time, a sexuality, causing a flush of intense pleasure to suffuse Chippo's face and body. He reeled slightly even as the man drifted into insensibility. Chippo remembered a similar Whitmanesque connection between injury and Eros when Zach had lain stricken in his hotel room. Had Florence Nightingale in the Crimea been similarly able to keep going by putting to good use transcendent aspects of the power of sexuality? Chippo momentarily wondered what this arousal said about his capabilities for a loving relationship as opposed to serial lust. He tucked himself away, adjusted his shorts and giving Zach's slackened hand a final caress, he placed the Nebraskan's arm across his stomach, gave a lingering kiss on his forehead.

"There was every indication," Sir Henry was saying, "that until the last second this was an appropriate sacrifice. To all intents and purposes, Zacchaeus Gabriel Shaler no longer existed, and Mr Zach was more than willing. I have no idea what caused his change of heart. The ambience was all we could wish for, but I respect his decision. My well-stocked dispensary with its selection of world class antibiotics is at his disposal. The excellent Nurse Lanfal is on duty this very moment."

"You said that offerings were now appropriate," Chippo could not help reminding him. "No more sacrifices."

Sir Henry closed his eyes. "So I did. But I have the utmost regard for the old ways, despite what I might have indicated on earlier occasions. This sacrifice was needed to correct the unforgiveable incident a year ago today. President Mguavas has been demanding redress ever since. Kraka was a sorcerer, disobeying regulation and sending his devilish soul into the crocodiles who ambushed the entire Gucci delegation. The luxury goods market was for the taking. A great business opportunity was lost for the nation." Sir Henry paused to have the ever-attentive Ntank mop his brow. "Mr Shaler, it seems, was lucky. The crocodiles were possessed by the sorcerer, as before, but had already been propitiated by an overly large quantity of chickens. To think we had to stoop to using domesticated fowl in the first place! Excuse me." He collected himself. "Or perhaps," he continued, looking round lest he be overheard, "the old fool is losing his grip. I rather hope that is the case. For he is the epitome of evil."

"Zach was being taken advantage of."

"You could say, my dear sir, that Mr Zach was the one taking advantage. Exploiting both Dr Reptilio and the Rehabilitation Committee to make his much desired final exit. Kraka is, at this very moment, consumed by a most righteous rage. I am humiliated in the extreme, at having failed to deliver for our benefactors. And dear Ulysses, of course, has been deprived of an intensely anticipated pleasure." Sir Henry wiped his face with a bandanna. Casting a sideways glance at Chippo, he continued in a more conciliatory tone. "In times past, the ponds were a traditional way of dealing with troublesome rivalry. You must forgive Ulysses. And as a Christian, it was you who reminded me that God himself sacrificed his Son for the greater good. I am sure we can find a way for you to review us favourably in that notebook of yours."

The muddy debarkation point was reached. Ulysses, pouting and mouthing to himself, had already been deposited beneath his crimson canopy. Dr Imensah was fussing about, preparing to bottle-feed him something to draw him out of what was clearly a funk of Napoleonic proportions. Zach was placed in the pirogue's stern, along with the polka dotted parasol. Dr Imensah and the fishermen were unable to stop Ulysses from lashing at him with his cane. The wildly rocking royal pirogue was not where Chippo wanted to see Zach laid down.

"Tah rah!" cried Sir Henry, indicating Zach with an outstretched hand as the pirogue's stability was re-established. "Presidential Care." The hotelier was all smiles as he clambered aboard. "We will see you, I hope, at the festivities this afternoon, Mr Cherrynose? The Maypole Dance for one, is not to be missed. Nor the Regatta, around which also swirl the symbols of the old religion, not just my fond memories of Henley-on-Thames."

Sir Henry waved from the motorised vessel as it surged, loaded to the gunnel, across the swamp and away. Zach had not opened his eyes once.

A cloudlet of black insects, large as humming birds, broke from the reeds and droned by. The morning was advancing, humidity was taking its toll. Chippo scooped water and cooled his brow, doused his regrowing blond curls.

"How much did that man pay you?" he asked bitterly as Reptilio and Cerisia arrived.

"Like total twits," Cerisia interjected as she clambered into their pirogue, "we didn't get cash in advance. If Kmango tries to renege on the deal, I'm going to kick up one fuck of a stink."

"You coming, Chippo?" Floralee called. "I've repaired the boat."

"Forget Floralee, travel with me in my five star canoe. We gods of the revolution must stick together." Reptilio gave his shaved head the usual vigorous two-handed scratching, this time ripping off his scab. Concerned with placation of Chippo, he scarcely noticed. "Zach's whole life is a propulsion to re-join his dead twin. To ease his suffering, an end to which, in my humble opinion, there is no possibility, I offered a loving reunion, a Twinsome Re-joining. What he was actually getting, of course, was not only a much longed-for death, and with dignity, but an unselfish one, in the context of art and ceremonial rite, of immense spiritual value to the village which has harboured him these several weeks. Did it not remind you of the Gallipoli Anzacs, the nobility of sacrifice for a common good?"

Reptilio's gathering smirk made it easy to recall Ray Grable's antics, and dismiss such self-serving talk. "We found out the true story of Zach and you still went ahead."

"The true story of Zach has yet to be told."

"What true story?"

"Treat me like a force for evil if you wish, Chippo, call me Dr Death, but you cannot say that I am not on the side of our better angels. Tophphi is well, you are extremely well. Two out of three ain't bad. Or is it?" Reptilio's pupils were mere pinpoints. He made an effort with his most winning grin which, as ever, included that misshapen tooth on the upper left. His hand was trembling as it made a grab for Chippo's arm. "She's become my greatest challenge," he whispered hoarsely. "She's up to no good. We have to get to work on her."

"Cerisia?" Chippo's brow creased.

Gitane in the corner of her mouth, Cerisia was busy with the chipped green lacquer on her toe nails, but Chippo knew that her ears were always well-wired for sound.

Reptilio motioned to the pirogue. "Don't let her scare you. Get in."

Chippo put one foot in the canoe then stopped dead. Cerisia's smile was not a believable welcome. She was not a pretty sight, nor meant to be, in her swamp grass wig. The hinges of the Siegfried shades, stuck now with bloodied chicken feathers, did not help, nor did the smudged third eye. There were purple bruises on her upper arms from her bouts with the Liberator and Drift the night before.

After making an adjustment to the loops of lurid fungi that concealed her punctured veins, Cerisia leaned forward, patted a flat cushion on the seat opposite her. "VIP seat for you." She dragged on the last of her cigarette, flicked it into the water. Jets of smoke from her nostrils were laden with murderous intent, but Chippo sat. No sooner was the canoe moving than she screeched, "I knew I was right about you from the start."

"Darling, this is Chippo Cherrynose. A nemesis from my distant past if you like, but now a trusted lieutenant."

"You've dragged Reptilio down to your level."

"Bubbie, I'm giving you the deaf ear from now on. Do you hear that, the deaf ear!"

"He's never going to look after you like I do. He's a twat and a twank." With both feet, Cerisia made a determined effort to push Chippo out of the pirogue which began rocking dangerously. "The crocodiles for you!"

A babble of scoldings came from the paddlers. The bank was but a few yards away. Floralee was readying to embark.

"Reptilio, I'll see you back at the dispensary."

Chippo dived in the direction of Floralee's dinghy, leaving Reptilio to his wife's Reign of Love and Terror.

FORTY FOUR: *Ray (also known as Betty) Grable comes clean*

"Oh Irish Man, he love me good,
Handsome man, he gib me present..."
Seamus and Qofia had just finished taking a 'baf' as Qofia called the shower. Chippo had lent them his room for the morning. She was crooning in Seamus' ear, plaiting his pony tail.

"Mr Reptilio, he next door with Mr Zach."

The dinghy had sprung another leak and Floralee and Chippo were lucky to get back at all. When they did, they found the dispensary deserted. Ripped from the door, crumpled and cast aside, was a page torn from a school exercise book.

> *we protest, mr kmango. you is giving*
> *us no new proper medicine like you promise.*
> *we is shut until further notice*
> *when you replenish us.*

"Mr Zach, he like me."

"Oh, I don't think so, Qofia. You're a – drag queen."

"I very experience in dese tings. Many married men like me. Mr Zach tell me he is married man. Mr Zach like me very much. We do plenty tings last night at dance."

"You don't count," Chippo joked, rather desperately, looking at Seamus who shrugged.

"Why you rude wit me. I better dan girl. I got back pussy. I got pretty dick."

"What did you do to him?"

Qofia fluttered her eyelashes and looked coy. "I give him plenty drink. Mr Zach he big. Very sexy man. I sorry for Mr Zach he get hurt."

Chippo didn't want to listen a single second longer to the lying, treacherous tart and went outside. Qofia's story of Zach as a married sexual philanderer was certainly utter nonsense. Zach was

just a bloke, vulnerable, a forever bereaved identical twin, a fragile
hold on life, vainly looking for a heart. He could not help dwelling,
however, on Qofia's choice of words. Chippo too had a 'back
pussy.' And his dick was certainly 'pretty' enough. Zach and he had
seen each other's dicks plenty of times. They were both
circumcised, both much the same.

It was already approaching midday. Tubas, trombones,
trumpets, an English hunting horn, snare drums, bass drums. The
Kassini Junction Brass Band, kitted out in topees and cotton khakis,
and assembling right below the back verandah, struck up the
Bomzawean national anthem. A procession of local dignitaries and
elders appeared from the interior of the Hornbill, where they had
been enjoying an official early luncheon. The band led them across
the field to an awninged dais by the rickety bridge that led over the
tidal swamp. Two government issue umbrellas, made of brilliantly
coloured fabric and each large enough to shelter twenty people,
had been set up close by.

In the centre of the procession were the bullocky bearers of
Ulysses, splayed at ease in his litter, which had been decorated for
the occasion with plastic flowers and children's stuffed toys. The
Liberator had changed from his blood-encrusted clothes. Chippo
could not see him as anything but a fat and entirely loathsome
toad, his baby blue stretch jumpsuit and snazzy summer-weight
sombrero notwithstanding. Beside him walked Ntank and the
Kmangos, Samuel Ichoko with a trio of his simpering girls, and
Chief Akwa, almost unrecognisable in a velveteen robe, mauve and
worn off the shoulder. On his head was a parchment crown and a
gold fillet. His arms, riveleted with sweat, were circled with wood
and ivory bracelets and on his feet was a pair of fine Gucci sandals,
souvenired a year earlier.

Reptilio came out of Zach's room and closed the door. Chippo
noticed he had filched a couple of books, had them under his arm.

"How is he?" He had to make sense of Qofia's remarks. "I have
to see him."

"Zach's recuperative powers are astounding. You'll find him a
man risen from the tomb. It is after all, Easter Sunday." This was

accompanied by a leer. Reptilio, determined to keep Chippo away from the man, grabbed his arm, pulled him towards the stairs. Finding his former patient unwilling, he added in a more serious tone, "As your longtime Dr Feel-Good adviser, I advise you to allow dear Zacchaeus Gabriel Shaler a further hour or so."

At the bottom of the stairs he paused. "Resist me at your peril, my dear Chippo. Do I have to reiterate, yet again, that I am no longer your old adversary, Ray Grable?"

Chippo lit a Pioneer, motioned Reptilio towards a couple of chairs and a table outside a nearby bungalow. "Now that Wally has revealed you as Grable, it is impossible for me to forget that. I am chiding myself every minute of every hour that I did not have the perspicacity to recognize you at any stage over the past weeks."

"That's right, you didn't. Amazing. Even though you stared at me for a day and a half at my trial. But Chippo, forget that kangaroo court. What about my finest moment? In a complacent society, I spear-headed a long overdue re-think of the old Anzac Day glorifications."

"I'm not sure that a wake up call was needed at that time."

"What a sacrifice I made. It was freezing that day. My unit was never so small. An object of derision for the soldiers who pulled me out. Brutes!" He gave a smirk full of his old swagger. Came the snaggletoothed grin. "Yes, my proudest achievement and also the beginning of my downfall. My life of societal dedication has always been at least a redemption for my leap into the Pool of Remembrance."

"Within six months, Reptilio, you went from Aussie larrikin to convicted felon. You had been sneaking into Jane Coolidge's room at the West Wahroonga Psychiatric Centre and rooting her – her word – all summer. One night, you even had sex on a sofa in the Common Room. According to her, anal sex. Sodomy. And you gave her drugs."

"You heard my side of the story at the trial. Unfairly discounted by that judge for hire. We were in love. We decided to run away together. There was no coercion, no kidnap."

"Well, you denied everything when the police transported you back to Central Police Station from Coffs Harbour. From her we knew you took her out one Sunday afternoon for fish and chips and an ice cream, you had a two hour permit to do that but you never came back. Not only were you a clinical psychologist, a man in a position of authority, but she was mentally vulnerable and under age. Legally, it was a kidnap.

"Thus began my life as a fugitive. Wally Whitbread didn't make it easier, getting that international bench warrant going, working with Interpol. Maybe you can tell me a few things. What has happened to Jane over the years? Floralee had no information."

"She recovered from her mental problems and went back to her parents in Point Piper. They are the ones keeping your case alive, still baying for your blood."

"I bet she's not. Crazy Jane. I didn't fuck her much. I was gentle. I mostly went down on her. My speciality. What could be less aberrant than that."

"She was jailbait, Starry." Chippo did not intend to say that word. Maybe his use of the illicit 'anal' had him over-excited.

"Chippo, she was an experienced girl, mature for her age. The nympho thing was the reason her bloody parents committed her to begin with. She hated West Wahroonga. They weren't good to her there at all. They sedated her heavily, told her parents she was schizophrenic. Shall I keep talking? Perhaps Jane gave me a taste of what I could do to heal this world. My first light bulb moment. Our love affair, and it was love, provided Jane with her first steps back to sanity. That's what I stated in the courtroom. Dismissed without a thought by that odious prosecutor. Need I remind you it was Wally Whitbread? As you must know, my youthful beliefs have now been confirmed in my mind. I've become a Reichian. Good sex, and with Jane it was good sex, is essential for a stable society."

"If that's remorse, it will be a nice line in your mitigation plea when you are flown back. Who knows, Reptilio, it might work now, that line, even in Australia."

Chippo took a deep drag on his cigarette, blew out the smoke, kept Reptilio waiting a second or two. "There's something I can tell you. She had a child. She swears it's yours. He's ten years old now."

"Oh, for fuck's sake!" Reptilio did his jack-in-a-box spring, swirled around, stamped a foot. A minor tantrum, similar to the one Chippo had witnessed his very first day at Tlula. "What's the kid's name? Is that in your bloody files too?"

"She tried to get rid of it and was prevented. He was christened Vincent. In your honour. The one thing her parents allowed her. They call him Vinny. Vinny Coolidge."

"Enough! Why the fuck didn't I take Cerisias's advice and let you piss off back to Okidoki. Well, I know why."

"A fateful decision. For both of us."

"Fate is always kicking in. I recognized you from almost the first moment you turned up. Well, I wasn't entirely sure but after I raided your room I was. Your adolescent just-out-of-school face, sitting in that black robe beneath the judge." He rummaged in his shoulder bag. "Let's have a look at the Carnival. Want one of these? Get you through the day."

"No."

As they walked, he popped one of his Siegfrieds. "Where's real justice when it's needed? If there's one thing I have always hated, never had any respect for, Chippo, it's the legal system. And all its hypocritical minions. I'm glad you, or some improved replica of you, has seen the light. Thanks to me of course."

Sunday was the day Tlula villagers attended the carnival. They thronged the grass and the low sand dunes, or tempted disaster by promenading en masse across the tottery bridge. Hamid and Hamou strolled hand in hand by the seawall in their white djellabas and turbans. It was a rare sight to see them together. There was the equally rare sight of Tlulans actually swimming, or playing in the shallow water at the sea edge. The tide was low, and on a broad expanse of wet sand mirroring the sky, mothers sheltered their toddlers with parasols.

In the deep shadow under the mango trees on the forest side of the field there did not seem to be a single centimetre of room. Drift's sensimilla-growing friend Qaddo (but no friend of the Bomwaze Bronzes), was there with his family; a baby in a cloth sling was on his minute wife's front, and with them was Floralee, arm in arm with Qiddo, the exhausted candy man cousin from the Junction. Floralee had got herself into a traditional outfit. Lilibet and Josiah Lanfal sat beneath a striped canopy where was arrayed a selection of free soft drinks stacked in buckets of rapidly melting ice. All the village factions were present. Even Blossom, less than hostile in fuchsia pedal pushers and slingbacks was there with Scarlet the Harlot, her sometime girlfriend. Supporters of Ulysses, who tended to flock together, had hauled out dashikis or dresses printed with large grainy images of the face of a healthier, leaner looking Liberator.

The ocean going dugouts, which were going to participate in the Regatta towards the end of the day, were lined up on the sand in front of the Hornbill. The fishermen from the various villages along the coast to east and west were already in their commemorative t-shirts, provided for them by Sir Henry. Cerisia was eating kippers from a tin beside the official dais, above which fluttered lines of patriotically coloured bunting and oriflammes patterned with the red stars of the national flag. Old Idi was perched on top of the maypole.

Reptilio had his arm tucked into Chippo's and together, their eyes roamed over the spectacle, which had to be described as gorgeous, but the Dancedoctor was searching for someone that Chippo was not. Suddenly she was spotted.

Chippo watched him bound off and thread his way expertly through the crowd. There was an embrace but almost immediately, a squabble. He left them to it and ran back to try his luck with the Nebraskan.

FORTY FIVE: *Excuse me while I kiss this guy*

Chippo approached Zach's bed. The same bed on which he had been lying, his head bandaged, when he had had his first sight of him two months before. Then he was a stranger, his interest aroused only by a passing resemblance to a boyhood love, but now… every restraining virtue (if virtue it was) in Chippo was about to be abolished. Not immediately flinging himself on top of him, translucent blood-drained body, opaque-white bandages and all, was too much to bear. There was nothing else on earth he wished to do more. Fear had flown. Excitement gripped him. Yes, he was going to cover him with kisses, make love to every inch of his body. Make love to him ever more! The room smelled of swamp, carbolic and crocodile.

At that very second, Zach's eyes opened, and lit up at the sight of Chippo so vibrantly – and voyeuristically – close. He smiled, and when Chippo, ever so gently flung his arms around him, Zach embraced him in return. A first real kiss. A shockingly lovely thing. Not since Tibor Radovan an eon before had Chippo been so kissed by another man. Soon he was as naked as Zach. Nakeder. Even though the New South Welshman had more bruises, the Nebraskan had more bandages.

"They never understood what a gruesome thing they made of my life. The Alpine House funny farm in Idaho, with them insisting on lithium, even wanting a transorbital. That Walter Freeman guy and his lobotomobile was around back then. The ice pick through the tear ducts into the frontal lobe. You know about that?"

Chippo shook his head.

"Somatic intervention?"

"No."

They were lying together, as close as two men could be side by side on a single bed. For Chippo, it had been amazing, that first time. It was all the boy-doings that he had shared with Tibor Radovan rolled up into one. It was also a reverential, holy thing and he felt utterly happy. Happy to just lie there and let Zach talk at will.

"That's another name for electroconvulsive therapy. Ostensibly it was all about getting my life going after Zeke, getting rid of my objectionable taste in literature, but that wasn't the real reason they had me done over, again and again. Zapped."

"There's a real reason?"

Zach lit a Pioneer, offered Chippo one. "I've got three older siblings, all happily married, the apples of Jeb and Corrine's eyes. There's a rabble of nieces and nephews I'm not allowed to see. And there's Joshua, my younger brother. I was the queer and he was the quickie Mom was just young enough to squeeze out. The Zeke replacement. Joshua's already got a full-scale teenage hetero romance going. There's no black sheep in the Shaler family except us. Me. Sorry about that pronoun."

Zach raised himself on one elbow, looked down at Chippo. "You're such an innocent. I don't know that you are ready for what I am going to tell you next. Close your eyes." Chippo did so and there came a kiss on the eyelids, causing the eyes to open again and smile at a serious face.

"As far as my parents were concerned Zeke and I were out of control even before the missionary deployment in Bomzawe. To coin a phrase, we had become beat generation bozos and they hated it. But the big thing they found out about the two of us happened here at Tlula, and it was something they couldn't even begin to handle. They had suspected for weeks and finally decided to put a stop to it. Such an aberration in their conservative Christian set-up could not be tolerated. They snooped and waited and then one night they burst into our bungalow. He tore us apart. She screamed until she fainted. When she came to, she insisted it was assault and rape. Her darling Zeke would never allow something like that. Me up him to the hilt. Pop scourged our butts until we bled. We had to swear never to touch each other again. Separation was the answer. I was to be sent home immediately."

Zach put his Pioneer to Chippo's lips. "I know, it freaks everyone out. I'm sorry. That's when we decided on the island. We loved each other so much. Too much. I didn't understand it then of course, but it was that love beyond boundaries and reason when you get completely lost. In each other and to the world around you. If we couldn't have each other, they wouldn't have us either. That's how we were thinking back then. We drank and stoned ourselves for the final ride, intending to swim out to sea and oblivion. But were too stoned to realise the full chaos of those waves on the south side. It wasn't quite like the story I told you but it was the same rock that did us both in. Well, I told you and Reptilio what happened after that."

"When did Reptilio find out about you and Zeke?"

"I kept it back, resisting that greed of his to have everyone exposed and at his mercy. I had never been able to confess what really happened anyway. The disgrace of having failed Zeke in death. Guilt. I was the older. The stronger. The one that got us both reading all those doomy romantic books." He paused. "It got worse over the years, not better. The Nurse Ratcheds in the madhouse were no help, dragging me from the ward, tying me down, the psychos periodically shocking the shit out of me. The oestrogen injections. Not only had I failed Zeke in our pact, but over the years I became ashamed of my sexuality. Much more than you. Infinitely more."

"Whose photo was that?"

"Ah, Zoe. Name means abundant life. Named after a Greek saint who was martyred by the Emperor Diocletian. Sorry about that." Zach gave Chippo a sad little kiss. "She's my wife. The daughter of friends of my parents. I married to make them all happy. It worked for a while. Yes, all those shock treatments had their effect, creating in me a state of total homosexual denial. Pathetic really. Zoe moved on of course. Reptilio did drag the subterfuge out of me. But not until after the Makeover. When you were gaga up in the trees."

"So Reptilio deceived me. He knew you were a young gay blade but always insisted to me you were straight; straight as a father of six he said one time."

"Hey, no more straight than a penis of those pigs around here." Zach laughed. "Oh yeah, he knew. He wanted to keep me isolated. Particularly from you. He told me to be kind but not to encourage you by showing too much affection. To give him his due, he was trying to protect you from mad suicidal me. You could do better." He laughed again. "Wasn't long before he and Cerisia worked out how to make a buck out of me. That crazy African Dream of theirs. They sure kept me loaded. The green and orange caps. He give you those ?"

"*The Siamese Re-joining.*"

" I bought it, I guess. Neat idea actually."

The sound of the Kassini Junction Brass Band was coming through the heated air of the late morning.

"You know those stories of guys who've lost a leg but can still feel it. The phantom limb. I'm the opposite. I know my heart is in here but it feels like some Aztec ripped it out and threw it into the sea. Every day is a search for a heart. Was. I think I'm finally over it. I hate to think I should be on my knees thanking Reptilio. And Cerisia."

"That's what you were doing when you let the mamba bite you?"

"To sleep, perchance to dream and all that. Yeah! Find that heart. Sounds crazy now, doesn't it, lying here with you? It wasn't until then that Reptilio worked out that he could manipulate that urge. He programmed me to surrender to it on cue."

"In the context of altruistic ritual."

"I was ready. All the way down to the wire. Then Cerisia gave me one poke too many with that spear." He smiled ruefully. "Blunt, thank God. What I really can't believe, Chippo, is that I have actually survived all these years. I guess I'm more of a coward than a true believer. Or a true lover." He stubbed his cigarette into the ashtray, lit another one. "I'm bitter about what Mom and Pop did to Zeke and me, but not that bitter. I've never told them what Zeke and I were really going to do out there on the island. Mom is better than she used to be, she's discovered compassion, but Pop has never changed. I've let them think we had a lovers' quarrel and I killed him, stuffed his body under a rock or ate him or something. They're well educated, but they're trapped in the Old Testament darkness, trapped by the bondage of their faith. In those fundamentalist minds of theirs that's what people like us do. They've never shown any signs of regret for the way they have dealt with me. Convinced they have done the right thing. They're proud of their family loyalty in not telling anyone what they saw in the bungalow."

Chippo accepted another puff of Zach's cigarette.

"The lawyer in you probably agrees about the proscriptions in just about every society against incest, but I can't see how it's any big deal, when it comes to identical twins having a full and loving sex life with each other. It's not as though any genetically compromised offspring are going to be produced."

Chippo gave an assenting half-laugh. "Zach, the lawyer in me has been well and truly effaced. As Reptilio says, everything that happens is a beginning."

"A death is a good start," Zach parodied, "if not an end in itself. Jesus, we're still quoting the dickhead. He is a dickhead, isn't he?"

"We can go forward together. We..."

"We, white man? Whoa, there. You've found your freedom. Let me find mine."

Found freedom? Chippo knew that something definitive had been happening ever since he crashed the clay pot down on the fiendish Reptilio's head. Only that morning, before the crocodile ponds, he had climbed one of those favoured poinciana trees shading the hotel, sent Bonnie & Clyde and some other hornbills flapping off, rescued the half-awake cicadas that they had been tossing into each others' mouths. He had examined the insects' singing snare drums, examined those vibrating tymbals, those organs whose sound had filled Tibor and him with a mad sexual joy. As he watched the beautiful creatures wake up to their daily existence, a deep gratitude towards them erupted. He murmured thanks for the part they had played in a coming to his senses about his true nature. Yes, there was freedom in that somewhere. Certainly the boldness to say whatever was on his mind.

"Come with me to Okidoki, Zach. You have been suffering here in Tlula too long. We both have, if I have to tell the truth about myself too. We can go travelling. You're a free spirit now. Your new identity." Zach was silent. "We could go to Douala. Climb Mt. Cameroun like Mary Kingsley. Play in the cascades at Cribi with Floralee."

"Hey, what about that British Council? We could get a job with them." Zach's enthusiasm was accompanied by a healthy colour infusing his body. "We could find all sorts of ways to stay in Africa. We could go north and help with famine relief in Chad or Mali. There's groups working up there right now. I already have a bit of French. Never go back. To hell with that Motherwell monster your Matilda married. You know now the extent to which he fucked you over. Do you really want to ever have anything more to do with that level of bigotry?"

"Melody certainly had a bee in his bonnet about Alfie, but Matilda's more fulfilled with him than she was with Dad." The two men both chuckled. "Hey, I'm in no hurry. Africa with you sounds good."

Chippo became aware that he needed to rein himself in a shade. The idea of not seeing his mother again was in fact, quite unsettling. In the long run, would the presence of Zach as companion make up for disconnection from family, no matter how dysfunctional?

"Are we in love?" Chippo asked. "Is this love?"

"You keep using that word, Chippo," Zach was behind him, pressing his body up against him, speaking softly into his perforated shoulder. "Dangerous word. I wouldn't want to say I was if I wasn't." His lips were playing on Chippo's skin. "I'm sorry for everything. Don't count on me. Ever. I know you don't want to hear that, but I took advantage of you just now. You were a way to complete my escape from those stinking ponds. You came to me Chippo, and I just ate you up."

"We're both celebrating, Zach, are we not? An on-going celebration of a new freedom for both of us. It's perfect."

"As perfect as matters. My peacekeeper is all ready to explode again. Chippo. I was so happy it was you when you woke me up, but if it wasn't you it might have been someone else. I'm no monogamous denier of simple bodily pleasures. Even though I was always emotionally married to Zeke and his spirit, I certainly did the rounds for a while. Before the treatments got to me. Alpine House had some sexy nut cases in there."

"I don't care," Chippo lied. "Starry always says that lust decried is life denied. Zach, this is all new territory for me."

Zach ground himself even closer. The crocodile swamp and the remembrance of its ritualised savagery was all around them in that humid hotel room. It was seeping from the stinking muddy streaks in Zach's hair, it was in the shreds of river weed that had fallen to the floor along with his discarded Peace Corpse t-shirt. And then there were the sobs he was almost choking on. Zach's hot tears were all over the back of Chippo's neck.

"No, no. It's relief. He's gone gone gone. It's over." In Chippo's ear he whispered, "I'm going to fuck you. I'm good at it."

Yes, Zach knew what he was up to. He was gentle, he took his time, had his way. Shouts and cheers coming from the sports field to the right, the drums from the grove and the tuba and trombone sounds from beyond the kitchen, the ever present cicadas, were the music to their ears. There was the touch of the brute as well, as Zach's excitement grew. Which Chippo did not mind at all. Nothing even of the other hurt, the first time pain of penetration that he had expected. The hymen breaking sort of thing. It was in fact, merely a marvellous efflorescence of sensual pleasure unlike anything he had known before. Zach induced in him a sweet delirium, provoking words of love and endearment he never knew he was capable of. They poured from Chippo's throat, as fluidly and shamelessly uttered as the old ecstatic cicadan vocalisations.

Was he now, finally, a whole man, Crown Jewelled, as Reptilio would have put it? Were the ignorant and reactionary forces in the world now morphogenetically shaking in their boots?

"We did it. How about that?"

"Not half bad," Chippo said with smirky deprecation.

"Zeke, oh Zeke! What do I do about Zeke?" Zach murmured as they lay about afterwards.

"Dear, oh dear," Chippo silently responded. But really, by this time, he was prepared for anything. He took it as Zach's usual summer storm of ambivalence and sure enough, a few minutes later, the survivor twin was on his feet, hauling Chippo up. "Time for a shower and out. Out of this stinking room."

"Together through life?"

"Whatever you want."

"Whatever Forever?"

"Right!" and they laughed, gave each other a high five. Their mood was buoyant as they made their way through the deserted hotel. The telephone in Attah's office began to ring. Zach went in to pick it up.

"Better not," Chippo said for some reason.

"Could be Zeke," he joked, his hand just above the receiver.

"It's none of our business," Chippo said, even as he picked it up himself. "Hello?" The line went dead.

FORTY SIX: *The sporting life*

The afternoon was well under way. Kassini Junction Local
Authority Mixed School, Mbutu to the east and other villages along
the coast were competing as well as Tlula. Events had begun with
the kindergartens and worked their way up to the teenagers.
Throughout, the brass band continued to play. Reverend Adomako
and two of the school teachers took turns making announcements
over a megaphone.

"Final of Boys' 6th grade 100 yards."

"Final of Girls' 7th grade 75 yard dash."

On one side a high jump was in progress, on another, a broad
jump. There was a sense that the sports were being well-managed,
although the organisers were the only ones who wanted to keep
things moving. The equatorial sun was so hot, the air so vaporous
after the morning rainstorm, that to Chippo the whole shebang
looked like yet more delight in cruelty, particularly for events like
the mile and the cross-country to Mbutu and back. Competitors
were slow to accumulate at the starting line, and once in motion,
seemed to move at a lackadaisical pace. If it were not for the small
amounts of cash that were distributed along with the pretty
rosettes, it was doubtful that anyone would have competed at all.
To specially favoured winners, the Liberator was handing out his
stuffed toys and exposing himself. Dr Imensah and the minders
were kept busy maintaining yet another cover-up in order to
perpetuate the illusion of respectability so dear to the heart of Sir
Henry Kmango. If heart there was.

Tophphi lay in the crook of Drift's arm, the shade of a young
banyan protecting them from the sun. Seamus and Qofia had also
settled there. The latter had discarded her drag that afternoon for

singlet, shorts and bare feet and looked exactly like all the other Tlula lads. Seamus seemed less than happy about it, clearly preferring her in slap and stilettoes. Drift's left cheek had a long scratch down it. Tophphi's right eye was slightly puffed. Was it inevitable, Chippo wondered, that woundings, physical as well as psychological, were part of the give and take of many an otherwise worthwhile loving partnership? With Zach, there were certainly affinities, but he was well aware that there had to be many things about the man as yet of which he knew nothing. And of course, Zach knew practically nothing about Chippo. Did all relationships entail leaps into the unknown, and a hope for the best? Were they really 'prepared for anything'?

Drift cooled Tophphi with sweeps of a palmetto fan. They were wearing matching Hawaiian shirts. The Beautiful Couple, Chippo thought, battered but reconciled. He could smell the chillum they had shared earlier. Drift's Arthurian knight on a white charger rescue, even if unwelcome, must have certainly touched something deep in Tophphi's soul. If only Drift had been able to get the Bronzes back as well, his troubles with Tophphi might have been over once and for all. Chippo had noticed as he went past The Great Liberator's chalet that all was secure, the guards lunching on the verandah, chatting amiably with Mr. Ichoko and that afternoon's preferred young ladies.

Hamid and Hamou came by, and bowed. "I didn't know there were two of them," said Drift.

A minute later, one of the reluctant schoolboy athletes appeared in front of them, trying to sell Tophphi a juvenile Black Colobus.

"Are you about to exchange the skeletons in your closet for another monkey on your back?" Chippo queried with a smile.

"There were never any skeletons in her closet," said Drift.

"Chippo, I love it when you're being funny." Tophphi's gaze focussed on him. "Your nose has lost its colour," she cried. "That metally thing. What happened?" Her eyes skittered from Chippo to Zach and back again. "Hey, Reptilio was right. All it needed was a good fuck. Zach, I always knew you were a macho man really."

"Dis de only ting dat I is lackin'." Qofia reached with both hands and tested Tophphi's tits for tautness and lift. "Bosom like dis."

"Now you're ready for *Vogue*," said Drift. "Torments, wart, burns, all air brushed away."

"That crazy wart. It must have finally sloughed off during the performance. The clay probably. Something Reptilio did."

Drift tapped her with the fan. The petulant gesture caught Chippo's attention. He realised only then that the bliss beneath the banyan was merely fancy on his part. There was both despair and desperation in Drift's voice.

"This is our farewell." Drift looked down at her still resting form and added, almost choking on the words. "Tophphi's leaving first thing tomorrow with Reptilio and Cerisia. After all the irresponsible, dangerous, despicable things those two cheap thugs have done, it's way, way beyond my comprehension."

"Oh, honey, please quit all that crap. They're family to me. Cerisia's my Mom. Mother Bub. How can you deny me this? We are going further into Africa, my spiritual home. You know you can come on the bus if you want to."

"I'll do them both in first."

"Drift, you made a vow." Tophphi sat up and took both his hands in hers. "You're not going to do anyone in. You're not going to cry again. We had this all out earlier."

"Nothing good will come from it. You heard what they tried to do to Zach! Look at him! Cerisia's a deathwife. She buries people."

"I don't judge Reptilio and Cerisia. I like people who can make the big moves, even if they are wrong. And they love me so much." Tophphi gave him a kiss.

"Our ranch doesn't have to be in Hawaii. It can be California. You loved those hills in back of Big Sur."

"I'm wicked. I don't deserve you, Drift."

"We can settle in Brazil. Bahia. That's a part of the African diaspora. I made the biggest move of all last night. For you and you alone. What more can a man do?"

"You mean the Vulture Dance?" Chippo asked, knowing it had to be something else.

"Yeah, how about that." Drift flicked his hair back and avoided Chippo's eyes.

Shrieks came from where the Married Women's Thread the Needle was ending in hysteria, but with Lilibet Lanfal a popular winner. Cerisia was waiting her chance in the Women's Egg and Spoon. Sir Henry was nearby supervising the sharpening of cutlasses for the Men's Coconut Eating, a contest in which ferocity was all, and apart from the Maypole Dance, the event that everyone was waiting for. The sportive Mr. Ichoko had insisted on being a contestant.

Reptilio, gaily popping MDA (Moonlight Dreams Amnesia) from his new supply into waiting mouths, came loping over and proved a complete distraction. His fresh head bandage was soaked from a plunge into the sea, and oozing blood. His face was heavily stubbled. Lotus's grenadine lipstick brightened his lips.

"Aha, the Crown Jewelling! You did it!" Reptilio cried, his eyes sweeping knowingly over Zach and Chippo. "Didn't I promise Supreme Triumphs all round?"

There was no guilt attached to what he and Cerisia had attempted that morning at the crocodile ponds. The only sign of anything coming from Zach was a conciliatory if rueful smile he gave as Reptilio lifted him up by the elbows from behind and displayed him. Zach had never looked more – well, what Chippo always fondly imagined was Nebraskan. His happiness about everything to do with him was, like the universe, continuing to expand. Despite those forthright words of warning back in his room.

"Three out of three, Chippo, can't do better than that. Unless I can manufacture something for Ulysses. We hors d'oeuvred him last night. Fucked it up this morning, I admit. Can we make amends and Supreme Triumph him this afternoon?"

Reptilio dropped Zach down, pushed him and Chippo together, and to the oompah-pah of the brass band, proceeded to bedazzle with every trick in his book – gliding chassés, grand jetées, pointy-toe pirouettes, arching arabesques, dervish deviations, cossack kicks, baboon bounds, Barnum & Bailey bounces of amazing grace, even a leisurely levitation. Drift refused to watch, but the rest of them were seduced by Reptilio all over again. Supremely Entertained. Chippo understood how Tophphi remained in his thrall, understood how they were all still there at Tlula, two months on, enjoying what he was at that moment thinking of as entrancement rather than entrapment. Even after the purgations of the previous night, the monstrosities of the morning.

Reptilio, the Dancedoctor – a bare-torsoed superstar in a pair of shoddy Turkish pants with a dark shine that matched the umber of his eyes – had finally put it all together. Chippo waited for him to top it with some crassly-worded doggerel, but the exquisitely timed climax came in eloquent silence. Reptilio gave a low and elegant bow. "That was for the world, but particularly for you, my Chippo Cherrynose. For you and Zacchaeus Shaler."

While he had everyone's full attention Reptilio seized the moment to outline a few possibilities. "Sir Henry's generosity may yet enable the Eighth Chakrans to penetrate the heart of this ravishing and ravaged continent. Cerisia, accomplished negotiator, is working on him. We will incorporate the best of totem and taboo into our communications and embracements. For Tophphi we will delve into the archives in the Ashanti palaces of Kumasi, achieve spiritual enlightenment again in the fetish convents in Abomey, join Floralee in the sacred rainbow dances of the Bwiti Cult in the remote villages of Gabon. Gyrate with the gorillas in the Ruwenzoris. Danny high Dudgeon will disseminate our message for us."

Reptilio was flushed and laughing-eyed, his baritone delivery well-buttered by both the bastardry and passion of his beliefs, his body still functioning in fervid, psychedelically stimulated motion.

"Lord Wittering's heart will soften when he hears of our triumphs. Cerisia will be second favourite daughter once more. We will jet our African circus around the world, blast away centuries of Christian puritanism and Islamic medievalism with our brilliant aberrations. Our joyful misrule! The Bauls of Bengal! Bombay! Broadway! Even back home. A season at the Opera House if it's ever finished. That mysterious Mr. Whitlam you mentioned, Chippo, will welcome us all. He will declare the National Disgrace a National Treasure!" He paused and bowed his head, almost as though he had shocked himself into a moment of modesty. "Drift, I invite you on board with all my heart and being. Send those serpents off by themselves." Dr Dance was unaware of, or took no notice of, the intensity of the disaffection in Drift's returning gaze.

"The Carnival is climaxing. Ulysses will travel up the Wawa and die in the arms of his sainted mother. Sir Henry Kmango will return in glory to the capital. We will leave tomorrow morning at first light. Yes, Chippo? Will you and Zach be the icing on my cake? I offer you both my unconditional gift. Reptiliolove! "

At that moment, Chippo did not see the canker in the soul of Reptilio any more than Reptilio himself could see it. The Dancedoctor's fantabulous dreams still had an appeal. Deeper and deeper into Africa. Divining the sacred secrets of civilisation's savage womb, involvement in a rich world of consciousness-expanding group interactions. A revolutionary, pedagogic, peripatetic terpsichorean theatre, a community of loving beings in which, as the man was always saying, nothing was rejected, everything was permitted. Chippo recalled the signed edition of Mary Kingsley he had seen in *The Beautiful Afreakans* bus, his very first night at Tlula. Mary Kingsley, the intrepid Englisher, a feminist before her time, living with the Fang, a woman learning to liberate herself from the stultifying strictures of the Victorian age, having an awakening to life and lust in Libreville.

A temperate, down-to-earth voice admonished him that Reptilio's vision was nothing but an impractical, head-bandaged fantasy, a piece of drug-induced vainglory, but the admonition was overwhelmed by a retro shirring erupting from his throat. He had assumed that sound, indicative in him of trance and euphoria, but undeniably received by others with irritation, had gone forever. In this moment, it represented a song of successful Sydney return, not with Wally Whitbread, but with Reptilio and the all-conquering Chakrans. The return of Chippo Cherrynose, a man of power, conviction and sexual sophistication, just like Reptilio. Still a drinker, but not a drunk with a problem.

For once no-one slapped him into silence. In fact, Chippo could see the patience in everyone's demeanour as they waited for him to come back to himself from his personal Ecstasy in the Extreme. For the first time he was able to take charge and in a considerate gesture, cut it off. For once and for all! "It sounds wonderful," Chippo said. "What about you, Zach?"

Zach's eyes went to Cerisia, tacking up, breathing stertorously after being soundly trounced by the better conditioned and brawnier Blossom in the Egg and Spoon. She had missed Reptilio's stirring oration.

"The bus is not already overcrowded?" he queried.

FORTY SEVEN: *What goes up must come down*

The maypole dancers were assembling. Calf-length frocks of fine white net over pink slips, ankle socks and white shoes with buckled straps showed the girls off to dainty advantage. Their hair was straightened and plaited with even pinker ribbons. Village mothers were milling around, making final adjustments.

Floralee Bush came in from the surf with her board and her boot black Qiddo. "I didn't want to miss the maypole, Reptilio, after what you were telling me earlier. I had thought it was just a pretty dance that Kmango had ripped off from the Anglo-Celts like he ripped off the Wheelbarrow Race."

"In old Europe it started off as a fertility ritual," Zach put in. "To ensure successful crops. The ones I saw back home as a kid were kinda cute. Sunday school girls all in white."

"But not like this one, Zach," said Reptilio, sinking to a more sober sensibility. "It's a different kind of fertility. When the girls have finished winding in the ribbons, the energy spiralling in has nowhere to go. Someone has to shoot up the pole to release it, like sperm. The whole dance is one long fantastic trip towards orgasm. The pole is the big phallus. In his prime, Ulysses got to fuck all the girls. Nine months later he got to ritually eat any female offspring. This time, in view of the changing moral climate, he gets to fuck just one. Qumqwat."

"Why can't we get this sort of thing going in Australia," cried Floralee. "Not even in Byron Bay."

Qofia had listened with great interest. "When I was young boy, dere not enough girl and I dance de maypole. Ulysses he like me but my mudder she trow his money back to him." Qofia was continuing to surprise them all. "I tink Qumqwat she run away." Qofia sped off to investigate. "I's coming."

"Last night, the great Reptilio did Africa," cried Reptilio, a boastful tone resuming in his voice. "This afternoon we are getting to see the great Sir Henry Kmango do England."

The Men's Coconut Eating was over. The Director of the National Museum had been the surprising victor. To quell accusations by cutlass waving contestants of cheating, cash prizes were quickly awarded to everyone. Even so, several well-aimed nuts bounced off Mr. Ichoko's skull as he fled. The Great Liberator invited his old Chief of Staff onto the litter and the bearers bore the pair with fear-laden rapidity across the field.

Beyond the maypole, the sea was a harsh blue, crinkling with bellicosity in the afternoon light. The tide was coming in, sending foam surging towards the bleached driftwood and the creeping heliotrope leaves, glossy on the low dunes on the far side of the rickety foot bridge. There was a wonderfully fresh smell of brine in the air. Oratorio and Ichoko were safely lowered into a place of honour. They had the sun behind them, their view of the maypole close up and unimpeded.

The Kassini Junction Brass Band, which had already taken up its position, was coming to the end of their Ivor Novello medley. The strips of cloth had been unfurled and the girls were in position, each standing as far from the centre as the stretch of her ribbon would allow, forming a delicate, rippling Big Top. "My friend Zach," Chippo murmured to himself, "my buddy" (to borrow a word from Drift), enjoying the proximity of the crowd as it pressed them closer together. Their bare arms touched and remained so. Their fingers became entwined. Their lips met.

The band swung into a medley of Old English folk songs, and the dancers began to circle, weaving in and out of each other in the meticulous choreography that they had been rehearsing with Sir Henry and Reptilio. As they danced, the girls spiralled inexorably closer and closer to the centre, continuing to sweetly sing as they did so. On the pole, their streamers gradually created a descending lattice in the national colours.

"Where's your camera?" demanded Reptilio, his face florid, eyes fulminous. "This is what big bad Danny wants. More ethnic. More rooty toot toot." He waved his left arm, ajangle with bracelets, wrist to elbow, towards the hotel. "Now if not sooner. Go!!"

Chippo ran back. As he was returning, camera in hand, the phone once more began ringing in the empty office. "Hullo?"

A crackle answered him. Then a distant voice. African language, panic stricken. He identified Kmango's name. "You want to speak to Sir Henry Kmango?"

"Where is everybody there? We bin ringin' and ringin'. I tell you this is most urgent. I will inform you because the telephone will be cut off any minute. Now they have taken over the radio station. Turn on your beam this minute and you will hear it all. They say the presidential guard dive into the sea, and Bnana Mguavas is dead in his palace. The traitorous General took unfair advantage of the siesta period this afternoon, and it has been proceedin' now for two hour. There is resistance, but all is lost. Englishman, I trust you to tell Henry to get movin', for the General will be sendin' cohorts from the barracks at Doggone to Tlula. They may be already arrivin'. Tell him it is Regulator Qweku Ronson, his good friend ringin'. He will know that Ulysses Oratorio is in grave danger." There was a strangled scream. A gunshot. Then the voice continued, somewhat choked. "Tell him this change our plan for the Bronzes. He and Samuel must now…"

There was another scream, the phone went dead.

Chippo ran to the field. The girls were continuing their spiral inwards. "*Jacky boy, master, sing you all, very well. Hey down, Ho down, derry derry down, among the leaves so green oh,*" they sang with the band. "*With a hey down down, and a ho down down…*"

As he closed in on Sir Henry, standing there with Reptilio and Cerisia, Samuel Ichoko and Chief Akwa, Chippo noticed a taller, older girl among the dancers, a white ribbon tied around her forehead. And when he reached the space in front of The Great Liberator, cleared by Ntank with his whip to ensure the great man's uninterrupted view, he saw that it was Qofia. The frock designed for Qumqwat was short on her long thighs, but she was doing the dance with a maturity not yet available to any of the local girls, who tended to run to the plumpish plainness of early pubescence. Beside them, Qofia had the radiance of a Bollywood starlet.

"Not what they call a virgin back in Australia," said Floralee, giving Seamus a wink and a dig.

Chippo could not resist taking a hurried picture or two, and a few more for Reptilio and Danny Dudgeon, but then turned to Sir Henry, who was standing in his posture of rapture, a smile on his lips, his manicured hands clasped high, level with his chin. Beside him, Samuel Ichoko and several others were loudly serenading the dancing girls. The music was reaching greater and greater heights of improvised festiveness. Further back, Dr Imensah was administering an injection into The Great Liberator's rump.

"My methamphetamine," shouted Floralee proudly in Chippo's ear. "He's going to climb."

"The maypole?"

"He goes up, explodes at the top like orgasm. Waves and smiles, grabs the bouquet, comes down again. Traditionally he had a severed head stuck up there, chucked it down. Some poor galah." Qiddo, the source of her surely dubious information, was nodding vigorously.

Would it be wise for him to interrupt the Maypole Dance, this most sacred and maybe profane of rituals with the worst of all possible news? He was among an alien, debased clique of people, in an unfamiliar country far from home. Potentates like Oratorio put to death bearers of bad tidings. Why be the Wicked Messenger, another poor galah? His sympathies were certainly not with The Great Liberator, but...

It had to be. Chippo went over and whispered into the ear of Sir Henry, who stiffened, nodded mutely, looked over to Ulysses, his old school pal.

"Thank you, Mr. Cherrynose. Keep it for the moment between us." He checked his Rolex. "We will complete the ritual, then put the situation into perspective." Behind his hand, he confided softly. "All is not lost. We already have asylum granted with Sylvanus Olimpio in Togo. The motorised pirogue is right there by the new chalet."

The Great Liberator was on his feet. Lotus helped straighten out his baby blue jumpsuit. Chompia raked him close with the infant rhino-hide fan. A smile began to beam on his face. The rolls of flesh around his collar seemed to lift up along with the wet livery lips. As he stood in front of the litter, pulling in his girth, straightening his spine, gathering his strength, Chippo could see, practically see, the methamphetamine surging like a river of life through his sclerotic arteries.

"Ulysses himself began the custom," Floralee was relaying, "Now of course, it's a bit pathetic. A 300 pound dumpster climbing a pole. He had trouble even in the old days. They had a team of presidential pushers for when he got stuck. He wasn't going to do it at all, him being in his terminal condition, but Reptilio got some pushers together and talked the dirty old bugger into it."

Chippo noticed for the first time, two long sturdy poles each with a broad, doubly-supported cross-beam at the top.

As the dancers finished, almost as one, they tied the last inches of their streamers to the pole, and then turned prettily outwards to face the spectators. They curtsied towards the immense bulk of the advancing Ulysses. He was styrofoam light on his feet now, bouncing along, his rheumy eyes darting here and there, taking in all the dancers. Particularly Qofia, the only one with the eyes bold enough to not adopt a downcast gaze. She was flushed with the dance, a stunning head and shoulders above the others. Ulysses' wandering eyes came back and fixated on her.

The Great Liberator took hold of the maypole. Reptilio was there, others too, all eager for the privilege of giving Ulysses the first shove on his journey skywards. The band broke into a stirring Bomzawean something, which sounded very much like the *Tara Theme* from *Gone With the Wind*.

Up Ulysses went. In a moment or two he was free of the helping hands, and amazingly, he began to haul himself unaided, like a plump little boy climbing a coconut palm all over again. The crowd crushed in, eager to press palms to the pole.

Higher and higher he rose. Then his ascent began to falter. He looked towards the top, gave one more valiant effort and then was stuck, his belly squashed into the pole.

"Go, go, go, Ulysses," chorused his supporters, punching the air. The music blared.

"The pushers," shouted Reptilio and Sir Henry, "the pushers." Ntank and a hulky colleague moved in with the cross-beamed poles and with their help Ulysses struggled higher, two feet more, three. His face was grey and sweating, his eyes cloudy. He began gasping for breath. His mouth fell open and a torrent of drool fell to his shirt. His jumpsuit was soaked with sweat and it seemed that the seat of the pants was becoming unstitched. He was a lump of grease about to melt in the sun. Tophphi caught his falling sombrero.

"Get in here, Chippo," cried Reptilio in a delirium of delight. "These are our centrefold shots."

Chippo got in there. He got right underneath with Reptilio, Samuel Ichoko, his girls, Drift and Tophphi, Ntank and the beefy bodyguards. Everyone was gazing skywards.

Twenty five feet up, with the bouquet at the top (tucked with Bomzawean bank notes for distribution to the dancers) just out of reach, Ulysses looked down helplessly, a look that was utterly lost. One eye seemed to slide out to sea, the other to the green forested hills of his birthplace. The huge head lolled to the side. One beringed hand let go the pole, then the other.

"Look out," Chippo yelled, along with many others.

The knees parted, and backwards, Ulysses Oratorio fell to earth with a bone shattering crash. He was dead on arrival.

Only Reptilio failed to get out of the way. He had stayed put until the last possible second, his arms raised wide as if to catch The Great Liberator in an all-enveloping, healing embrace, Reptilio in his eighth, moving on to a ninth, chakra mode. "Take a picture," he had shouted. Chippo took a picture, at the same time as had come Cerisia's voice, her Divine Intervention, accurate as an eye surgeon's laser, right on cue. "BACK, TOOTS, BACK!!!" But instead of responding – as once he would have – and leaping nimbly away from the path of the plummeting Oratorio, Reptilio stayed put. When Chippo realised what was happening, he grabbed the doctor's arm and would have hauled him out of danger (and his trance), if Chippo had not been impeded by Drift who seemed to have placed himself somewhat in the way.

THUDDD! CRACCK! SPLATTT!

The Brass Band stopped abruptly and there was a great silence. Into that silence came the full-bodied sound of the surf at high tide, the single scream of Cerisia, and the click of an Instamatic as someone caught the moment.

Reptilio's lower body was free, but the rest of him was trapped. Chippo let go the arm he had grabbed. Reptilio waved the arm and bicycled his legs, almost as though he did not know he was immobilised. As they tried to roll the Liberator's tonnage off him, there came the sound of automatic rifle fire, and the first platoon from the Army barracks at Doggone swarmed into the Hornbill grounds, firing their weapons in the air.

There was Qojo pointing to the transistor radio held to his ear and crying out the first news of General Kporpor's coup. Three Jeeps roared onto the soccer field and headed towards the maypole. Most of the crowd, particularly those wearing the Liberator's face, but including the more timid of the Okidoki cosmopoles and the Zandra Rhodes-clad Chunkia with the fan, had already taken to their heels along the beach.

Samuel Ichoko had been the first to flee. Pistol in hand, he had run to the chalet, forced the guards to bring out the antique trunks. Commandeering the motorised pirogue, he had the trunks loaded up, and ordered the crew to speed him out to sea.

FORTY EIGHT: *Viva la revolucion!*

Lieutenant-Colonel Osei Q. Bonsai, as he introduced himself, was young, petite and of a cheerful disposition. He was deferential to Chief Akwa, curt to Sir Henry Kmango, and listened with close attention when Dr Imensah, rising from where he had been trying in vain to restore life to the Liberator, confirmed that the former great power in the land had well and truly departed.

Bonsai gave only the briefest glance at the distraught white people clustered about Reptilio. Seamus, making use of medical knowledge long discarded for another drug-soaked career, was doing his best to assess his condition; probable concussion, broken shoulder blades he thought, several crushed ribs, something internal. Reptilio was breathing with difficulty. There was blood. Tophphi was in tears. Angrily pushing Drift away from her, she knelt with Cerisia.

Lieutenant-Colonel Bonsai's mission had been simple enough – to arrest Ulysses Oratorio, and escort him back to Okidoki to be tried for various heinous crimes against The Democratic People's Republic of Bomzawe; to bring with him the long-lost Bomzawe Bronzes; to arrest Samuel Ichoko on charges of misappropriation of public funds and multiple murder during his period as President Oratorio's Justice Minister. Tlula village was to be treated with the utmost respect. As for Sir Henry Q. Kmango, the Lieutenant-Colonel had been given a free hand.

He barked orders, and the two platoons of soldiers spread out exuberantly through the hotel grounds, firing at random. They were neatly dressed in well-worn green fatigues, dark glasses, Chinese cloth caps, and armed with oddly assorted rifles and axes. There was an occasional substitution of thongs or bare feet for boots. They checked the stream of departing vehicles for known criminals, and then began kicking in the bungalow doors, smashing windows.

If Sir Henry was saddened by the sudden passing of his friend, Ulysses K. Oratorio, he did not show it. He ordered Attah to open up the bar to the Lieutenant-Colonel and his men, so that a celebration of the new order could begin. "The Bronzes are safe, Lieutenant, I assure you. Mr. Ichoko, the esteemed Director of the Museum, unfortunately not here at the moment, will have them for your inspection in a trice." He laughed, he joked, he played for time. Pointing to the canoes still lined up on the beach he proposed that it was possible to lift everyone's spirits even higher by holding the Regatta as scheduled, if postponed for a minute or two. "What about passing the time with a friendly tug of war between Tlula and your men?"

Cerisia was hysterical (Lieutenant-Colonel Bonsai threatened to have her shot) and made it difficult for Dr Imensah as he did his best with Reptilio, who was carried, along with the body of the Liberator, into the new chalet. Imensah was hampered by the absence of supplies in the Kmango clinic, and recommended that Reptilio be driven the ten miles to the hospital at Doggone. Josiah Lanfal put himself at Cerisia's service and, shortly, the Dancedoctor was loaded into his trotro. Cerisia began screaming "assassin!" at Drift. His response was to turn to Tophphi. "Honeycomb, I swear..."

"I weep for Dr Reptilio, even as I weep for Ulysses." Sir Henry held Cerisia's hands as she took a seat. "Great forces in life, both of them. Every year, God and President Kporpor willing, I will return and remember Dr Reptilio. His famous friends from Europe and America will visit. Our pretty chapel will become a place of pilgrimage. Maybe a special memorial..."

"He's not dead, you little twerp," Cerisia snarled, cutting him off. It was not surprising that Sir Henry was copping a serve. The tycoon had refused to pay even a reduced sum for Zach's *Siamese Re-joining*.

"My dear, of course he will live. But if there is a slip between the cup and the lip, please feel free to bring him back for burial here, where he has contributed so much. Men from the village will dig the grave, Reverend Adomako will perform the necessary obsequies. It will help heal differences between the hotel and the village."

Sir Henry motioned to where a table was being laid for Bonsai on the chalet's patio. "Join us in a repast, my dear friends. The living must eat, the better to mourn the dead."

Attah Lalwani soon had a cloth spread with the treats originally intended for the delectation of Ulysses – a jumbo-sized tin of Beluga caviar, rich pates and terrines, smoked oysters, packages of savoury crackers, a fruit cake, some Highland shortbread and licorice all-sorts in a crystal container from Harrods. Sir Henry's dear friend, President Kporpor, was toasted in Drambuie, imported lagers and a selection of Kmango's Nwalabi Hills wines. Lieutenant-Colonel Bonsai settled for a Red Star beer.

The toasting didn't do much good. Nor did the reappearance of Samuel Ichoko. When the motorised pirogue bypassed Oratorio Island and turned west, the crew realised that Ichoko was heading for the Togo border. They muttered amongst themselves and then mutinied. The Director of the National Museum was overpowered and returned to justice.

When Lieutenant-Colonel Bonsai ordered Ichoko to unlock the antique trunks, all that was revealed were cinder blocks. The priceless Bomzawe Bronzes were gone.

The Lieutenant-Colonel, his fellow officers and the soldiers prepared to leave. Sir Henry Kmango found himself a prisoner of war. When Ntank, covered by weapons wielded by two soldiers in the back seat, drove the Silver Cloud convertible out of the Hornbill grounds, his boss, barefoot, stripped to his underpants, hands lashed in front of him, was at the end of a rope tied to the back bumper. Ichoko, similarly humiliated, was beside him.

"Is such treatment really necessary?" Cocooned by a love beyond limerance, Chippo was feeling nothing but benignity for all mankind.

"How dare you!" cried Lady Chompia to the Lieutenant-Colonel. "He's a Knight of the Realm."

Bonsai gave a surprising chortle. "I run them like curs for the satisfaction of the people of Tlula, who have over the years suffered much at the hands of your Henry Kmango. But unlike the Liberator, I am no barbarian, Lady Kmango. After we leave the village, I assure you he will be transferred to the safety of the boot."

"Where's Amnesty International when we need them?"

A phone call to Okidoki had ascertained that General, now President Kporpor, wished to view personally the body of The Great Liberator, whatever its condition. The Mercedes, with the disembowelled cadaver propped up in the back seat for all to see, his organs (and the last of the Hornbill's ice) in a plastic bag beside him, was driven off under guard. Ulysses' other two limousines, loaded with his luggage, followed, along with Dr Ali Imensah and the small staff that had accompanied him on his arrival. Outside Ichoko's bungalow, his women giggled around the chrome-encrusted Cadillac, debating whether any of them had the ability to drive it.

The Lieutenant-Colonel mounted the bonnet of his jeep, slapped his palm with a swagger stick and began a short peroration. He gestured towards Kmango and Ichoko in the near distance, jogging off through a gauntlet of hornbills and jeering villagers. "There goes the pollution of the old colonial order. Our brave revolution is for the well-being and maintenance of our tribal cultures, for sanitation, health care, housing, education and environment. Food production, no more famines. Regeneration of our country's infrastructure for the equal benefit of all. Roads, telephones, railways, reservoirs. Economic planning, sovereign control of our resources, respect for Bomzawe's international obligations. Law and order by day and night. President Kporpor's National Salvation Committee will end the state of emergency and call for democratic elections."

A lump rose in Chippo's throat. He clapped excitedly, wiped away a tear.

"Get real, kiddo," said Floralee. "Nothing's gonna change."

"Don't be cynical, Floralee. Noble ideals. It's what the world needs more of."

"Down the drain in six months max."

"These once fine men fought bravely against the English occupation, but were debased by the seductive surface of its legacy." Lieutenant-Colonel Bonsai threw a glance towards the abandoned maypole, raised his stick high. "To the end of corruption and madness. To the end of these sorry dregs of Empire. Soon, everything will be okey dokey in Okidoki. We are a beacon for the New Africa."

He leaped nimbly into his seat, put on his shades. His driver stepped on the gas. "White peoples, enjoy the remainder of your stay in our esteemed Democratic People's Republic of Bomzawe!"

Bonsai's second-in-command and a complement of soldiers were left behind to continue the search for the Bronzes.

Lady Kmango showed scant emotion. She had spoken out strongly on behalf of her husband, but had no fears for her own safety and prepared to leave for the capital. While Qofia loaded up her bags and beauty cases, she fumed to anyone who would listen.

"I will use my influence to make sure that Henry is treated with the respect that a great man deserves. I do not trust the new President to observe the decencies. Those hideous Bronzes. They've always been more trouble than they are worth. Their curse will accrue to the traitor who has taken them. And onto the unfortunate fools who find them." As she stepped into her Snipe, she spat on the ground. "I have nothing but contempt for the tiny Mr. Bonsai and his ilk. Ulysses had his faults but should have remained here with his people. At least his heart and testicles. One day Henry will build a monument to Ulysses' glory. The Hornbill Palace will live again. Qofia, get in. No, he can't come with us." She slammed her door in Seamus's face, lowered the window.

"Mr. Cherrynose, if you see that tramp, Chunkia, tell her to toss the fan, that fucking fan, and take the trotro."

FORTY NINE: *Sleepy time down south*

Early evening, Cerisia returned with Reptilio. The downed Dancedoctor was carried into *Whatever Forever* and placed in the inner sanctum at the back. From the waist up he was bandaged and plastered like a mummy. "So brilliantly bright," he whispered, of the dim lamplight. Cerisia placed his old designer Siegfrieds over his eyes. "The maypole was a good start today, Chippo," he continued in the same tremulous voice, "if not an end in itself. We can incorporate it into our show. The Maypole Miracle. I will climb. Suddenly I have this longing for home."

"Give Chippo a break, toots. You're rambling."

"Chippo, we will go back to Sydney, you and I. Floralee too. Where's Floralee? We will belt Wally to billyo, out of the cricket ground for six of the best. Find Vinny, my Vincent, son of the starry starry night. How could I have not known that I had a son. It can't be hard for a father to track down a son. I thank you for that, Chippo. We will have reconciliations all round. Chippo Cherrynose with his Mum and the melodious Mister Motherwell. Reptilio with his fascistic Mum and Dad. They could all use a Reichian massage or two. Poetry lessons. *Doctor Dance just loves a two step, Benito's gone and so's his Goose Step.* Chippo, is a seventeen syllable haiku allowed to rhyme?"

"Twiddle off, the lot of you. He needs rest. Look at this itemisation. A broken nose. Cheek bones. Six ribs, collar bones. Hairline skull fracture. Concussion. Critical bruising of the heart, lungs and diaphragm. Suspected internal bleeding. Oh toots!"

"A stay in hospital might have been a better bet."

"You know what Reptilio thought of that abattoir. Those twerps tried to stop me but I couldn't leave him there." She snuggled up to him. "My poor tootsie. My wootsie."

It seemed the hotel was deserted. Neither Attah, his kitchen staff, nor the watchmen had been seen for hours. The soldiers had been thorough but had abandoned their search for the night and joined the wild festivities in Blossom's. Dark figures flitted through the hotel shrubbery and its shadows.

Drift's truck was arriving on the morrow and he intended to spend this last night in the Polynesian Long House, guarding the mamba cages. Qaddo had been hired to help keep watch.

"How on earth did you manage it?" Chippo wanted to know, when he had the chance to get him and Tophphi alone. "I mean, beat Ichoko and Kmango to them?"

Drift flicked his hair back. "The guards sat at the front door, getting ripped, staring out to sea. One was singing to a ukulele. There was nothing I could do about them. I checked the back windows, the side windows. All locked, barred. But the little bathroom window had no bars. You know what a rush it was to get the job finished. Well, Billy Carpenter's stoned workers must have just overlooked it, or thought it was too small to worry about. That side of the chalet was in shadow, overhung by those bushes they planted. I managed to squeeze through and went to work. It was mayhem at that time outside, everyone dancing around, drunk and drum crazy. It took me half an hour and my only worry was that the Liberator would peg out and his handlers would decide it was time for him to go to bed. Apart from that it was all too easy. Even for me. Those antique chests had heavy padlocks, but the back hinges just unscrewed. Ichoko had gift-wrapped those little Bronzes so very neatly and all for Drift and Tophphi. I was handing them out to her in the shrubbery, one by one. The workmen had left a few cinder blocks along the outside wall. I knew what to do with those. After re-screwing the hinges, I closed the window and that was that. Tophphi and I were watching when the Liberator was wheeled back in just after ten. I was in luck. He was comatose, definitely in no shape to have another look at the Bronzes."

"No problem with my cages? Loading up."

"The fake panels? Slid like a dream, Chippo. My chillum had already taken care of Kmango's menagerie guards. They were out there at the party, bouncing their nuts off. No sign of Fangga." Chippo was about to ask if he had set aside his promised cicada head but Zach – not privy to the whereabouts of the Bronzes – arrived at that very moment and distracted Chippo with a kiss.

Drift carried mattresses from one of the deserted bungalows and packed the useful chillum. Tophphi had a tray of cookies and nightcaps. There was a steaming mug for Qaddo, one for Drift. "Drifty, by all means smoke a little with Qaddo before bedding down. But not too much. Play it safe."

"Sweet cakes, you're right." Drift put the apparatus to one side, took a sip of his drink. "This chocolate tastes a little bitter."

"It's cocoa. More sugar?"

"Thanks. You sure you don't want to bunk with us here?"

Tophphi shook her head. "You know how they freak me out. I would never get to sleep."

Even then, the snakes were restless, coiling around. The occasional hiss. The colobus monkeys too were unsettled. The sound of drumming came from the village. Loud, insistent rhythms, talking drums, fractured cries. A foreboding in the air.

"Tophphi, sweet pea, this has to make a difference. Reptilio out of action for weeks, months even. You have to be coming with me now."

"Drift, honey, you know I don't care about the fortune you will be making. I'll always be grateful for everything you've done for me. Wonderful things. Been there for me in every way. But you drive me batshit, and you know it. I've told you a thousand times." Tophphi leaned over and kissed him warmly, hugged him, lay in his arms.

"Every kiss you give me now is a stab in the back."

"I'm truly sorry it has to end this way, Drift. I'm one of Reptilio's success stories. Like Chippo and Zach. We're not going to abandon him now when he needs us most. I know you think he's a monster but it's a price we're prepared to pay. For what he gives. His vision."

"You still think I deliberately got in the way don't you?"

She paused, looked down at the mattress. "Finish your cocoa. The bus is leaving before dawn but I'll come by to make sure you are both awake and everything is ready for your truck."

Chippo told himself that the former Chipman Smith had, by his transformational experiences, been lifted above such things as crass materialism, and the desire for possessions but nevertheless, he was hurt that Drift still seemed to have forgotten about his cicada head. Not that he would know what to do with it. Perhaps it was just a matter of asserting honour among thieves before letting it go. With Zach giving his arm a tug, he decided not to take Drift aside, but to bring the matter up in the morning. They were going to spend the night on the far beach – in the palm hut.

FIFTY: *The back of the night, the beyond of the day*

It had been Zach's idea to go to the palm hut. Not a place Chipman associated with romance, but the far beach at night had its eerie appeal. On moonlit walks with the Family, they had sometimes seen Fangga scuttling about out there like a hobgoblin or some Cocos Island crab.

Reptilio was foremost in their minds. The sight of a man who had always seemed impregnable as well as imperious but now immobilised and entirely vulnerable, had been sobering. As had been the maddening smell of patchouli with which Lotus had doused him.

There was no denying Reptilio had affected Chippo's life profoundly (and for the better) and Zach's too, but their passages had been perilous. They both had the scars to prove it. Good luck had certainly played a part in their survival. As for the Dancedoctor, he may have long left the streaker/jailbaiter/rapist identity behind yet essentially he was the same. Reptilio was a man who flirted with the civil in his nature, but in his truer moments, one who would go for the savage.

Of Reptilio's misadventure by the maypole, Chippo mused that the man had been hoist on his own petard, downed while indulging in one of the more outrageous whims of his fourth dimensional fantasies. It was hubris that had gotten him flattened.

Reptiliolove? Now that Chippo had Zach by his side, light pouring down from the wash of stars and the waning moon, the nightjars hovering, the sea glittering darkly, the air balmy, close to divine, he knew Reptiliolove was not really a love at all. Or at least a love he had to firmly reject. The Dancedoctor would recover, but neither he nor Zach had any desire to accompany him and Cerisia to the Ruwenzoris or anywhere else in Africa for that matter. Nor would they be pursuing money and fame with the dubious Family along the world's Great White Ways. There was also the not insignificant factor of Interpol, once more hot on Reptilio's trail. Wally Whitbread would be making sure of that, but the Dancedoctor might yet find another way to disappear. He too had a knack.

Chippo gazed at Zach, who was staring out into the emptiness of the gulf. With him, Chippo was on the threshold of something entirely new in his life. Adventure and misadventure would all come. Threat and opportunity. True love? He was wary of that four letter word now, wary too of the construct he had yet to experience in his adult life, a – dare he say it – relationship. The very word vaulted him into an ecstatic shiver. Perhaps the time had come. What was that other saying of Reptilio's – everything is for the very first time, always.

"Qofia and Seamus," Chippo uttered by way of ending their friendly silence.

"Yeah, how about that!"

"She has invited him to stay at the Kmango mansion in Okidoki."

"The heart of the beast."

And that was that. Zach, after pouring out his true story in his room, was back to his usual taciturnity. Now, blessed with love and empathy (surely its soul mate), Chippo felt he had no need of discourse either. He took Zach's hand and kissed it. They looked out to the palm-clad island, the progenitor of his troubles and listened to the benevolent crash of the waves, the click and clack of the breeze in the coconut grove, the soft hoot of a jungle owl and the occasional shriek from some invisible jungle pixie. The fireflies went back and forth in their silent swooping flights. A sheet of white lightning lit up the horizon. The wet season was on its way.

Zach lit a joint and they each took a toke. The minutes passed and Chippo couldn't help himself. "The Ezekial spirit has not been calling you?"

"I've never told you, have I, how it happens. What he looks like." As Reptilio often said, there would always be more to Zach's 'true' story. Zach arched a piece of driftwood into the surf. "I've never told anyone. Certainly not Reptilio. At odd moments, when I get really stoned, that's when he appears. Like on Makeover day when we were out there on the island. I feel something emerge from my chest and there he is. A classic homunculus, dome for a head, he's shining and glowing, all silvery fluorescence, sometimes with a cap. He can cling to me like a baby, ride on my back, sit on a chair, more often he slides away and looks back at me. I can just make out Zeke's features, on his face, or mine like a mirror. Sometimes he gestures for me to follow him, an irresistible beckoning – as you must know. Mostly he fades before I am lured to a point of no return. Sometimes he climbs back inside me. Through my navel." Zach's head lowered a little and he gave Chippo a nervous look. "Now you know how crazy I am."

"Did your little Zeke man appear when you let the mamba bite you?

"No, that was some kind of opportunistic moment I seized all by myself. I had smoked a whole joint at breakfast that morning though. Qaddo's. We should never smoke more than a couple of tokes of that shit."

"Perhaps we're both getting stoned too much."

"Like now." Zach gave a short laugh. "Come here." They toked no more, talked no more, lay down on the sand and dozed in each other's arms.

Forty minutes later they were awoken by a freak wave from the peaking tide. It engulfed them, bringing with it something that at first looked like a manatee or an elephant seal. As they spluttered in the phosphorescent wash, it rose on two legs and became an Aphrodite flecked with foam, a woman. Zach and Chippo found themselves astonished at the sight of The Honourable Cerisia Twitchley, the one time toast of Swinging London. "What's so fucking funny, you faggots? I swam out to my island. He named that for me. ME!"

"How is he doing?"

"Everything is tickety-boo. Tweedledum and Tweedledee are on watch while I took a twiddly. And a widdly." She gave a mad laugh and padded off in the direction of the Hornbilll.

"There's no way she swam out to the island," said Zach.

Mother Bub the Divine was not the only one they encountered on the far sands that night. No sooner had Cerisia disappeared into the darkness than they heard approaching, the sounds of a saxophone. Mournful and slow. Seamus Shamrock.

"A pavane for Starryo – I mean Reptilio," said Seamus shaking spit out of his sax. "Came all the way down here to get his mojo going again and let the worst of Africa fall on him like a ton of shite. Almost winds up an organ donor."

Seamus blew a few preparatory notes, sat down beside them. "There was nothing original or African, by the way, about that cute vulture exorcism of his. That was pure Amsterdam Wet Dream Festival and Otto Meuhl." He paused. "Well, re-contextualised. I'll give Reptilio that. But he had become obsessed about doing it somehow, somewhere. He had a girl, a gander and a hatchet lined up for the Munich gig, but Otto never gave him the go-ahead."

"Seamus, how did Reptilio get that scar across his chest?"

"Well, as you know, he has never really found himself as a performer. Never met the right people to utilise his unique energies, to channel his ambitions productively. Always playing second fiddle to wankers like Otto. When his career bottomed out, he decided to up the ante." Seamus blew a few more tentative notes. "He went for the ultimate auto-mutilation, the final closing of the gap between art and action. In some flea-pit on the Lower East Side, trying to upstage someone else's performance. He slashed himself with a carving knife."

"His Mishima moment?" Zach asked.

"More like his Murphy's Law moment. Heh heh! Nah, he wasn't in the seppuku league. He was out there. His trashy Angel Dust days. It's one thing he never talks about. They patched him up, badly, shipped him back and he wound up in the clutches of Adolf Siegfried, the Bavarian Jew. No one else would take him on."

So that was it. Chippo closed his eyes and shuddered.

"He's lucky to have made it to thirty five. Guinea pigging for Siegfried doesn't help. But I don't put Adolf down. He knows how to mix a martini. Respects Hoffman. Works with Sandoz. Turned me away from the IRA into a lovin' spoonful."

Seamus stood up and riffed for a minute or so before stopping again. "Reptilio's as corrupted as the old *Accra Queen* rusting away over there on the rocks, but there's also a blindness that keeps him unbowed and bearable. He will always soldier on. Just don't get entangled in what he calls his sense of fun. Or his wife. You might die." Seamus stood up. "I reckon I'll go see how he is. They're giving me a lift to Okidoki, dawn tomorrow. Qofia is calling." He readied himself for a proper tune. "Any requests, Chippo?"

"Anything, Seamus. I trust you to make the perfect choice. *Galway Bay?*"

"No more Bing Crosby," said Zach. "How about *Shenandoah.*"

Seamus meandered off, back towards the hotel, blowing something stirring. Zach started gouging a hole in the sand with his heel.

"*Moondance?*"

"*You'll Never Walk Alone.* From *Carousel.* Seamus can't help himself."

They slept on coconut matting in the palm shelter. "This is the first time in my adult life," Chippo murmured as they drowsed into a dreamworld, "that I have spent the night in the arms of another man."

"It's my turn to be shocked. Are you sure you're going to make it through the night, Chippo?" There was a touch of sarcasm. "Are you content?"

"Much more than content. Happy."

"If you say so. Me too. As happy as matters." He gave Chippo a kiss, the first of several.

There was a rare chill in the air that woke them well before dawn. They swam and surfed in the starlit dark, then began a stroll back towards the hotel. They could shower. Together. Attah would have returned and they would order the Full Breakfast.

The waves flopped onto the beach, and withdrew, whispering assent. An early morning breeze woke up the coco-palms and set them creaking. In the gathering light, seagulls began a squawking.

It was then that the Hornbill Palace Hotel, a quarter mile away along the shore, burst into flames.

PART FOUR
Various Departing Gestures

FIFTY ONE: *Smoke gets in your eyes*

Clouds of black smoke trailed into the sky as the gable of the central building went up. Urged on by Blossom, in tin hat and battle fatigues, Ulysses' chalet had been the first that the villagers had looted and lit. The bungalows had soon followed. The conflagration seemed to have a mind and a sound of its own, a cracking, roaring dragon, dancing, exploding, along the waterfront, reflecting red in the surf, dispelling the pre-dawn darkness. The imported plantings, philodendrons, heliconias, poincianas, brugmansias and various palms and palmettoes, were twisting in the heat draughts, shrivelling, dying.

Running figures, dousing more and more petrol from the bowser opposite the Chophouse, were silhouetted against the inferno. The rejoicing Tlulan villagers were drumming and drinking. It was clear that Qwami's bar had been well and truly 'liberated'.

"The Kmango era is over," Chippo called back to Zach as they raced over the rickety bridge. "More than over."

"We'll be okay but watch out for Blossom and the blunderbuss."

The back of the hotel had not yet been set alight. Hastily packing their belongings, they headed for the Menagerie. The monkeys were undisturbed by the smoke and fires, but the Great Blue Turaco pair and the African Grey parrots were flapping and biting at their wire mesh. Drift lay curled up under a sheet on his mattress, sound asleep. Qaddo was nowhere to be seen.

Tophphi arrived at the same time. "The fire won't get this far, but I was just checking he was okay."

"We should wake him."

Tophphi looked down at Drift. "He's so out of it. Why don't we just let him sleep? I said my goodbyes last night. Over and over." There was something frantic in her demeanour, not so much to do with the fires, something else. "The bus is leaving. You gotta come and say good bye to Reptilio." She was off, then stopped. "Come on, leave him be."

Once she had them following her she ran ahead. Smoke from the bungalows was drifting closer. There was a scream in the near distance. But Chippo knew there was something amiss back at the Menagerie.

"Catch her up," Chippo said to Zach. "It's not safe for her." And returned to check. It didn't take him long to discover that despite the cage doors being closed, the mambas were all gone. "Oh dear", he said to himself. "I've got to tell him."

He slapped Drift awake, got him to focus. "What's all this smoke?" He verified for himself, sank to his haunches. "Fucking Fangga. Kmango gave me the green light. I should have taken him up on his offer and blown him away."

Chippo put an arm around him.

"We'll catch more. I'll get a team together. You can help, Chippo. We've got the python. The monkeys. I still have my permits." In his own way, Drift was as unflagging as Reptilio. "I'll book another boat. A week. Ten days, tops."

Chippo noticed the chillum beside Drift's mattress. It had been smoked to the bottom.

"Qaddo and I took a little toke to nod us off. We must have got carried away. He looked around . "Hey, where's Qaddo?"

An insidious drizzle, fine and hot, had begun to fall. The sun, a murky globe low over a glaucous sea, was now shining through the smoke. The waves were full of ash.

"Maybe Fangga got the Bronzes too," said Chippo. "Kmango always said he had an eye for them."

"Don't say that. The compartments are undetectable. Your masterpieces." But he went to the closest cage, pressed the first catch, then the second, pulled open the divided back and revealed the secret area. Empty. They opened up every cage. Not a single Bronze. All that was left was a metallic whiff.

"I had your cicada head all ready to give you this morning."

Chippo was sorry to have doubted Drift would keep to his side of the bargain, but no covetous feeling for the cicada head came flooding back. "Maybe one of Ichoko's or Kmango's lackeys has taken them. What about Bonsai's soldiers? Can you trust Qaddo?"

"They're in the bus!"

Chippo's reaction was one of disbelief.

"You know what's been going on between Cerisia and me. She's not scared of snakes, knows about antique stuff like the Bronzes. She's dead broke and desperate. She's convinced Reptilio will dump her if she can't support him. Got Lotus and Stan to help with the dirty work. The Mother fucking Bub fingerprints are all over this. Clever old cunt. Pretending to be distraught with grief. Tending her man. It's revenge for everything. She always resented Wittering giving me the snake deal. The maypole." At this, Drift's tirade came to a sudden halt. His head sank and that shifty look Chippo knew from early days came into his eyes. "Why the fuck didn't I settle that *Twiddlers'* bill!"

"Drift, she was out on the far beach. She swam all the way to the island last night."

"Like hell she did. Alibis, alibis, I'm not interested. What a fool I was. Pity my python didn't strangle her when it had the chance." Drift checked his revolver and demanded Chippo accompany him to *Whatever Forever*. "Back me up."

"No gun," Chippo said.

"I've never fired this thing in anger. Do you think I'm going to start now?"

"Drift, whatever Cerisia is, she's family. She would never do such a thing."

"This is my ranch that she's taken. I've seen her talking to Fangga. I bet she gave him some of her bullshit twittery about me, paid him to let the snakes out. That front latch is easy enough. Then she could come by and take the Bronzes."

"But she didn't know the Bronzes were ever going to be in the cages."

"I don't give a fuck. Maybe she saw me last night in the dark, loading up. Somehow she found out."

Chippo sucked in a breath. Even if she had seen Drift doing the transfer – most unlikely – Cerisia could not possibly have known the secret of how to open his compartments. Unless...

As Drift headed for the bus, Chippo lingered and let out the beautiful turaco pair and the distressed parrots. Watching their flight into the trees, he noticed Fangga, almost invisible at the jungle verge. Eyes closed, new boots, a spotted bowtie, flowers in his hair and shadowed by thick foliage, he was crooning his sacred song. Two silvery black mambas had coiled themselves up his stave and around his neck. Neither the cries of the departing birds, nor the fiercely cursing Drift, had awoken the Snake Fetish Priest from his trance.

FIFTY TWO: *A bridge too far*

Chippo found himself coughing on the smoke and fumes as he ran the length of the bungalow area. In his path, and seemingly impervious to the fires, Bonnie & Clyde and a troupe of hornbills were regurgitating pips and pulp. "Ork! Hic! Ork!" They were all voluptuously drunk on a fruit fermenting under a nearby tree. Floralee was outside a bungalow about to be torched. She was helping villagers throw bedding and other contents out before it went up. "My farewell good deed," she shouted when she saw Chippo coming. A bottle of vodka from Qwami's smashed-up bar was being passed around.

"Looking for Zacho?" Floralee asked. "He's inside having a bit of a loot." Yes, Floralee had already intimated that her dream of settling down with a local man, becoming a village mammy, pounding fufu to sell in the street with hot sauce, had been just that. The sort of dream, Chippo realised, that she must always be having on her travels, the prelude to moving on to the next country, the next cousin. The next naturally growing hallucinogen.

Chippo pushed his way through the scorched bamboos and past the opulent Brugmansia trees which were letting off a mind-bending odour as they burned. The palanquin was in flames, and there was Drift on his knees, banging his head into the ground. The bus was gone.

"What did I tell you," Drift yelled as Chippo went to him.

Floralee, loaded down with pillows and a coverlet, Zach a short distance behind carrying some kind of juju, came in sight. "Bus is on the other side of St Bede's. Cerisia and Reptilio were on their way, but the villagers had chopped a couple of Kmango's exotics down earlier in the night and the track was blocked. Stan tried to drive around and got bogged in the sand. The worst possible place. Really soft. They're still digging out. Didn't Tophphi tell you?"

Whatever Forever was well stuck. Lotus, Stan and Tophphi were shovelling briskly. Planks and dry coconut fronds were ready to be laid. Inebriated villagers laughed and jeered. Reverend Adomako, on the other hand, in true Christian fashion, was on his knees, placing rocks around the back wheels. St. Bede's had been spared the torch, but the sacristy had been plundered. The pastor's clerical vestments were to be seen on several of those flitting back and forth through the fires.

Drift went straight to the engine, lifted the hood and removed something.

Cerisia sat at the dining table, playing tiddlywinks with Shameless Seamus. She hadn't showered since her swim. Matted with salt, her hennaed spikes were standing straight up, or plastered over her forehead. Her eyes were wild and set in wrinkled nests of purple. Kohl had trickled down her cheeks. The *embonpoint* that lately she had been carrying as lightly as a soufflé, had succumbed to something of dough and shapelessness. There was a gin-filled jeroboam beside her, and she was well soused. Drift made his accusation.

"You came in while I was asleep and you would have gotten clear away if the road hadn't been blocked. Circumstance got the better of you."

"We were always set to leave at dawn. But Reptilio's taken a turn for the worse. He's raving, has no recollection of what happened. Thinks Adolf sent him a bad batch. Wants to sue. We are heading back to the hospital." Cerisia had roused herself. Her response was weary, but dignified.

"Bullshit. A few broken bones." Drift was derisive, but Chippo, who had followed Drift inside, was ready to believe her.

Seamus said, "Twitch, I'm sure you and your *bandido* chum here can sort this one out with no help from me." He left the bus.

"Drift, you demean Reptilio by dishing up this rubbish." Cerisia picked up a pack of playing cards and began a rhythmic shuffling. "Tootle off, and take your friend the faggot with you."

"Fuck you, Cerisia." It was the first time Chippo had ever uttered the word.

"Fuck you too. Cherrynose! Ha ha ha!"

"Cerisia, you've been too clever by half and now you're busted. I'm ripping this bus apart."

"Go ahead, there's nothing to find. As soon as Stan finishes digging us out, we're on our way. Why don't you lend him a hand?"

"You're not going anywhere." Drift moved towards the back of the bus.

Cerisia stopped her shuffling, lit a Gitane. She threw a glance at Drift's revolver as he went by and began to lay out a game of Patience.

Tophphi came in, took a seat beside Cerisia, gently drew a strand of hair away from her eyes. Cerisia's face softened. "Love you, babe. Love you like my own daughters." She gave Tophphi a friendly jounce with her hip. "Go talk some sense into your snakecatcher weirdo back there." She returned to her cards and Tophphi went along to Reptilio's sanctuary.

Drift was going through the huge compartment under Reptilio and Cerisia's honeymoon bed. Reptilio lay on his back, deathly still. Lotus, who had also come in from her digging, was giving him some liquid. Chippo could scarcely bear to look at him or at the hypodermic with which he had been morphined. At least he would be feeling no pain. Tophphi was smoothing away tears, gave him a kiss. Chippo gave Reptilio's hand a squeeze.

"Quit that gay shit, Chippo," said Drift at his narkiest. "Go start on the rest of the bus. The bunkhouse area."

Stan came in, announced the way was ready and he was going to give it a go. He sat in the driver's seat. The bus wouldn't start.

"Drift removed something. Find out what he took."

Stan went outside again. The hood went up. Lotus sat down at the table opposite Cerisia who remained fixated on her cards. Lotus pushed the jeroboam out of her reach and kept avoiding Chippo's eyes. His mind flashed back to his first night at Tlula, back to carefree remarks about secret panels, about all the things that Reptilio and Cerisia had smuggled across borders.

Floralee popped her head in. "Cerisia, doll, I just checked the Kombi. Someone's ripped off my 'bine. There was six months supply I was going to flog. No one except you..."

"Go take a twiddly, grandma."

"Well, excuse me, fatso, but..."

"Fuck off!"

The others hung about on the sand, hushed and confused. Chippo caught Zach's eye momentarily. He had not wanted to enter the bus. He shrugged, took a seat under a palm tree. After lighting a Pioneer, he pushed back his hat and stared phlegmatically out to sea. Seamus had borrowed Stan's tin whistle and was playing it over by the front door of St Bede's. Something mournful. Improvisations, in fact, on *"Danny Boy."* Oh, Starryo, you reckless evil fucker, the pipes, the pipes are calling, from glen to glen, and down the mountain side...

Increasingly frustrated, Drift began ripping masks and drapes aside. He did in fact, locate a few ingeniously concealed cavities. He pried them open, only to find them either empty or stuffed with some other contraband.

Drift held up a plastic garbage bag and a brown envelope. "Floralee's yohimbine. Zach's money. What's left of it." Drift threw everything at Chippo. "Get it back to them." Chippo tucked Zach's envelope into his waistband. "Vulture video of Tophphi. Hang onto that for me. Here's your fucking watch." Chippo caught the Girard Perregaux.

"They're under the floor!" Drift pulled up the linoleum beneath the sink. "I'll take a pick axe to it, Cerisia", he shouted maniacally, "so you might as well come clean."

"Drift," said Lotus, "let Tophphi and I do a healing for you." She knelt beside him, put her hands on his shoulders and began a soothing hum. Even Tophphi's arms around his waist were insufficient to deflect him. Drift shook them off angrily, smashed the lock on a low, narrow cupboard which ran along one of the walls..

Cerisia swept up her cards, reshuffled and laid out a new spread.

A group of boys approached from the hotel, hauling a booty-laden cart. Qojo was among them. "Mr. Chippo," he called up to a window of the bus, "my mudder, my fader, dey say you and Mr. Zach come shelter at our house until you go big city. Our house small small, but Qwami he gone this morning for soldier, and we gib longtime room foh you."

Happy thoughts set Chippo tingling. The village would soon be calm. It would be wonderful for both of them to get to know Josiah and Lilibet Lanfal better. Qojo and Aqosua would love to be taught how to improve their reading and writing. They could start up a whole school. More wild dreams of lifelong partnership swept through him. Chippo did not see what he could do to further assist Drift. His future was outside the bus, not inside. He was still not convinced that Cerisia, even Cerisia, could be so treasonous. "I'm going out to sit with Zach, Drift. Maybe Attah or someone took them. Hamid and Hamou. Qaddo. That cousin of his."

"First sensible thing you've ever said," Cerisia growled.

"Stand by me, Chippo. I know you want your cicada head."

"What's the point of us stealing them?" Cerisia's voice had gained an edge of hysteria. "We're heading back to Abomey, then central Africa. There's no market for them there. Junk, I call it!"

She and Drift glared at each other, two gunslingers whose high noon had arrived. In a sudden fury, Cerisia picked up her cup of plastic tiddlywinks and sent them scattering like confetti at Drift. "If they were here, Drift," she shouted, "you would have found them by now."

"Tea?" asked Lotus with a despairing chirpiness. "It's in the pot."

"Yes, tea," shouted Cerisia. "Put some 'ludes in Mr. Paranoid's here. The twerp's gone round the twist." She pulled open the table drawer.

There was a shriek from Lotus. "No, Cerisia!"

"Shut up, Lotus," said Cerisia, levelling the revolver at Drift. She rose and moved to a position where she could command the entire bus. There was a long silence.

"So," said Drift finally. "You pulled a gun on me."

"Reptilio loves this bus. I'm not letting you destroy it. Get out. Scram! "

"This proves it."

"Every householder has a right to protect their property from vandals. And I want my money."

The sight of the levelled gun produced that gripe in Chippo's intestines that the soldiers' semi-automatics had the previous day. He backed away towards the front door. Cerisia's eyes flicked at him. He reached the door only to be blocked by Stan coming in.

"Oh," said Stan, brought up short by the sight of Cerisia. He pulled at an earlobe. "This dipshit motherfucker Drift here, took the distributor rotor." It was the most complex speech Chippo had ever heard him make.

"Drift, let's get out of here." Chippo's wish to join Zach was becoming ever more acute, but somehow he again wanted to help extricate his former fuck buddy from an increasingly dangerous situation.

"Nobody's going anywhere until he hands over the part." Cerisia was immense, majestic, the full Mother Bub the Divine. "I warn you, Drift, if you don't stop messing with my bus, I'll shoot you. Put your hands up."

Slowly, Drift did so.

"Stan, frisk him."

The first thing Stan did was cleverly snatch away Drift's gun. Stan stepped back, released the safety catch, pointed it. From the first pocket of Drift's shorts Stan put his hand into, he pulled a couple of hundred dollar notes.

"They'll do," said Cerisia. "I'm not greedy." Stan tossed them onto the table.

"Now I've paid your fucking restaurant bill, hand over the Bronzes."

Stan's hand went into Drift's other pocket and came out with the missing part. It was a little thing, no more than a couple of inches long. He moved back quickly, out of Drift's reach. "It'll take me just a moment to put it back."

As Stan backed away down the aisle, Drift lunged for his gun and missed. Cerisia fired a warning shot, a shot which ripped into the painted ceiling, Lotus's blue firmament with Van Gogh stars and swirls, Chagallian angels. The sound in the enclosed space was deafening. Lotus and Tophphi screamed. Chippo dived for the floor. Cerisia had the gun in both hands, and was focussed on Drift once more.

"Darling," came Reptilio's muffled voice, "did you say something?"

"I'm dealing with it, toots. Go back to sleep."

"Jesus, Cerisia." Drift had his hands up. "We're not going to shoot each other. We're all family. I never believed you'd fire that thing."

Stan stepped over Chippo on the floor, and out the front door. He fiddled briefly with the engine, came back inside, sat at the wheel and started up the bus without difficulty. He rested Drift's gun on his lap.

"Let's go," cried Cerisia.

"What about Seamus?"

"Now!"

Stan pulled the lever that closed the front door. He put the bus into gear, the tires briefly spun then engaged. Reverend Adomako directed the heavy vehicle as it ground slowly along the planks to firmer sand and the track that led from the church to the village. Chippo looked despairingly out at the boys loping along beside. Zach was on his feet, looking up, his forehead furrowed. "Chippo, get out here."

"Zach, this is yours!" he threw the envelope out of the window at him.

"You leave us?" came Qojo's voice.

"My sax," cried Seamus. "My backpack!"

"Floralee! Your 'bine."

"I'll take that." Cerisia had the gun on Chippo, who put the yohimbine down and his hands up.

"Reptilio wants to do good in this world. He brought happiness to you. Even your stupid nose looks normal again. You distort his legacy, you write so much as a negative word, I swear I will hunt you down like a dog and shoot you dead. Dead, I tell you. You don't even know what that means!" Her voice rose to a shriek. "It was you made him give me the deaf ear! I should kill you now!"

The bus rapidly approached the junction where the road left the village for Doggone.

"Twiddle off, the pair of you." She pointed the gun at Chippo, then Drift. "Get out!"

"What if I refuse?"

"You and your stupid python!"

"Drift, you've made a terrible mistake," said Tophphi.

"Sugar bowl, I'm doing this for you."

The bus reached the junction. Josiah Lanfal had just fuelled up at the bowser across from Blossom's Leisurely Chop House. A rumpled, cheesed-off Chunkia (Chippo hadn't got round to telling her to toss the fucking fan) and three other passengers were waiting by the trotro. The bus made the corner awkwardly, the tyres squealing. It began the climb up the slope towards the Tlula Escarpment.

"Jump!" Cerisia held the gun in both hands, motioned with it.

Chippo moved to the step above the door. "Stan, open the door. Slow down a bit."

"Faster!" shrieked Cerisia at Stan. "Get out!" she shrieked again.

Stan pulled the lever that opened the door.

Madness. Chippo had to get back to Zach, the man he had come to love. The man who loved him, even if he mostly thought he was loving his long dead Zeke. Reptilio, or an apparition of Reptilio appeared from the passageway to the inner sanctum.

"Lubricio falls have done no harms, let maypoles be my call to arms, " he recited as he swayed. Another haiku. "Darling, it's dark. Are we on our way?"

"Be with you, toots. As soon as I get rid of these scum. Take off your shades."

"Okay, Cerisia, we're leaving," said Drift. "But you're not getting away with this. I'll chase you across Africa if I have to."

"They're not in the fucking bus," Cerisia hissed through clenched teeth. She tossed her head agitatedly from side to side, an anti-personnel mine set to explode if there was just one more provocation.

Drift stood behind Chippo at the front steps.

"Good bye, Drift. I'll always love you." Tophphi gave him a farewell kiss, then a little shove to get him moving.

The bus was coming to the top of the slope, gathering even more speed as the road levelled off approaching the corner. To the right, over the edge of the Escarpment, the coastal plain appeared far below, the very first view Chippo had had of Tlula Leisure Beach, two months earlier. He moved to the bottom step and contemplated the jump, trying to figure if he could make it without falling flat on his face in Sir Henry's fresh gravel.

"Die, you twank!" Cerisia fired. The bullet missed him, put a neat hole through the front window. The shot startled Stan and the bus veered. Drift plucked Seamus' saxophone case from the floor and flung it at Cerisia, knocking her sideways. He made a dive for the gun on Stan's lap. Stan jerked his knee and the weapon fell to the floor in front of his seat.

Cerisia fired at Drift. She was off balance and the bullet went into the back of Stan's head. Lotus gave a scream as he slumped. She rushed past Cerisia towards him.

"Oh no! Oh Stanford!"

Stan's foot jammed down on the accelerator and the bus charged for the 300 foot drop. Chippo jumped out, landed running and stumbling. Drift grabbed Tophphi, pushed her hard and she fell out onto the roadway. Lotus was cradling Stan's head. Drift applied the handbrake. It didn't work. He tried to pull Stan's foot off the accelerator, had a go at redirecting the speeding bus, but it was all too late. He dived out the door and the next second *Whatever Forever* went into the blue. Drift's momentum had him heading towards the final edge also. He scrabbled desperately for holds in the rocks and vegetation.

The engine continued to race as the bus fell. There were two more shots. The bus caroomed off a ledge half way down and began a slow motion somersault. A mudguard detached and fell separately. There was a tremendous crash as the bus hit the boulders at the bottom of the cliff. It bounced, skidded off the trunk of a massive tree, and smashed into the mud and mangroves at the edge of the Wawa River. There was a momentary silence, and then it blew up. A plume of flames and smoke rose skywards.

Josiah Lanfal's trotro came chugging up the hill.

FIFTY THREE: *A case of do or die*

Chippo had been roused by Zach stirring in the dawn dark, felt his arms strongly around him. A rub of long unshaven cheek against long unshaven cheek, a kiss, and then he had once more fallen asleep.

When Chippo awoke a short time later, Zach was gone.

Beside the bed was his new passport, Wilbur John Fedoroff, and his envelope of money, along with his shades. There was a feeling of relief until Chippo remembered the surfboard missing from the top of Floralee's Kombi van the day before. She had searched everywhere, blamed the looters, and left without it. The saxophoneless Seamus Shamrock had gone with her.

Chippo feared the worst. His loving had brought into his life a strength of feeling that he had never known before, uncharted depths way beyond his comprehension. An entanglement with a heart. And what about his soul? Had he given that to Zach as well, with the 'true' story of the man, another country yet, if ever to be, discovered?

He flung Zach's essential stuff, including the never-taken medications, his long discarded Rimbaud, his old Dylan tapes and his newly acquired passport, into the all-purposes Chippo satchel. He had paid Floralee Bush a lot of money for that passport. Too bad about Wilbur, who was ever called Wilbur, for heaven's sake? At the last second he grabbed his binoculars and ran from the Lanfal compound to the beach. Zach could not have gone far.

That Easter Monday had been busy with many visitors, both official and unofficial, who had come in the aftermath of the Hornbill fire and the early morning disaster with *Whatever Forever*. It was a long, fraught day. Chippo had plenty of tears. The site of the crash was not easily accessible. Human remains had been brought downriver and identified. Representatives from Interpol who had turned up with a warrant for Reptilio's arrest, left satisfied to some extent but disappointed more. Attah Lalwani had been found in the bushes behind the kitchen with his throat and his genitals cut. Old Idi and his gang had been at him. Yes, it had been the most difficult and devastating of times.

"They're in the ceiling. The Bronzes are in the ceiling," Lotus had screamed at the very last second. The odd twisted or damaged Bronze may have sunk to the bottom of the murky Wawa. Drift did some diving in vain. "Dredging's not out of the question," he had shouted as he grubbed about in the mangroves. Chippo didn't care whether any Bronzes were found or not.

Drift was not entirely defeated. He collected from Qaddo the sensimilla for which Chippo had helped fund purchase, and packed it into the secret compartments of those cages he decided he still needed; these cages were occupied by the python, the rare Colobus monkeys and four, slow moving mambas (suffering from smoke inhalation) that Drift had actually snared that day.

Qaddo had proved allergic to Tophphi's bitter chocolate. It had him waking, ill and vomiting, in the middle of the night. At that hour, all was quiet in the Menagerie, except for Drift's heavy breathing, so he made it home and had himself looked after by his loving wife.

By the time of the arrival of the truck booked for the journey to the *Star of Casablanca*, Drift and Tophphi were ready to ride. "I've had it with Wittering," said Drift. "He can join his second favourite daughter in hell." Apparently there was some stoned-out animal park in Wiltshire that would like what he still had to offer.

"Tophphi, do you want Cerisia's video of the *Vulture Daddy Dance* rehearsal?" Chippo queried. She shook her head.

"Hand it over,'" said Drift. "I'll throw it into the lagoon."

"Keep it for the archives, Chippo," said the one time runner-up to Miss Georgia Peach.

"You're the boss, pumpkin."

Late afternoon, the bodies scarcely taken care of, they were gone. Tophphi, a caramel ice cream flash, not quite as gold as she was dark, silken skin, cream halter top, semi-straightened hair scraped back into a bun with ribbons and raffia, free as a breeze, running Drift's show. She had kissed Zach, kissed just about everyone, including the distraught out-of-work Hamid and Hamou. Those she didn't were very grateful to get a handshake, or a glance from those large, unforgettable eyes. When the Range Rover followed the old Ford truck onto which the remaining cages had been loaded, and left the coconut grove, those eyes were fixed on the road ahead, and unlike Drift, she did not look back. It was good bye to Tlula Leisure Beach, with no regrets or time for grief.

When Tophphi had kissed Chippo, she looked coolly and unrepentant into his face. She was telling him what he already knew – that she had been complicit with Cerisia, that she had told Mother Bub that the Bronzes were in the cages, and how to get them. Had told the 'death-wife' that Drift would surely be chillumed out for the night, and even if he wasn't, Seconal in his and Qaddo's chocolate would have done the trick. Chippo hazarded a guess at the deal that must have gone down; Cerisia would have wanted to put an end to Drift as he slept. Tophphi would have argued against it. Cerisia had certainly contracted with Fangga to release the snakes, making it that much easier and the more complete a revenge.

Tophphi smiled, and kissed him a second time. He expected that kiss to be bitter, with a saccharine aftertaste, but no, it was sugarcane sweet, through and through.

"Be nice to him," Chippo said. "If you can't be good."

"I'm always good. Even when I'm wicked."

Chippo immediately lost the piece of paper Tophphi had given him with a forwarding address. Well, better a clean break than a connection that could only bring catastrophe. Tophphi's arrant duplicity made him wonder if he would ever trust anyone again. Drift was wilfully ignorant, of course, of any betrayal by Tophphi.

He had mixed feelings about the dropped-out smuggler. The sexual pleasure attached to the clandestine blowjobs already seemed cemented into Chippo's better memories of Tlula, and he was grateful to him of course for having saved Zach's life. Enlightenment for Drift about Tophphi's treachery was pointless and it was hard to forget his obstructive behaviour at the Maypole.

"Hasta la vista, Chippo." Drift had enfolded him in a hearty bear hug, kissed him defiantly on the lips, swivelled his hips against him. He had firmly cupped Chippo's balls, given his dick a brief massage. "This is instead of that fuck we never had. If only you had put the hard word on me." Chippo had suppressed Drift's stupid grin with a kiss in return, also with a touch of defiance, but warm enough, for it was because of their different sexual orientations (rather than in spite of), that they had forged some kind of friendship.

"I'll get you next time, Chippo buddy. For sure. Pity about that cicada head. Your totem."

"Another totem will find its way to me one day, Drift. Go easy on those chillums."

Zach and Chippo waved until the Range Rover and the truck were out of sight and then went to the village, where they had already been set up in Qwami's old room. To replace the former bartender's humble stretcher, Lilibet Lanfal had moved in something bigger, a real and rather splendid bed, liberated from the Oratorio chalet.

They toked some of Qaddo's excellent jambo and Zach, after murmuring a few circumspect professions of love without the name of Zeke once passing his lips, or the homunculus spirit being activated, had fallen asleep. Chippo sat nearby, absorbing the profound intimacy and pleasure of his presence and thinking of the remarkable Lanfal family, of the decadent William Oates and the less-than-perfect Wally Whitbread, of the uninspiring architecture of the Department in Macquarie Street, and of the future as an infinite number of possibilities and points of view.

He wondered about the extent of Reptilio's complicity in the decision to steal the Bronzes from Drift, and when that decision had been made. He found he was missing him intensely anyway, weepy about all of them, particularly the talented, industrious and not to mention ditzy Lotus. Even Cerisia. He just couldn't help having a soft spot for the perfidious. Like he had for Sir Henry Kmango.

The hooting and clown clack of a couple of hornbills came from the Lanfal courtyard. Bonnie & Clyde, sober now, put their heads inquiringly around the open door. "Come in," and put a finger to his lips lest they waken Zach. He laughed in some relief for he had been concerned for their safety. Bonnie & Clyde. Another example of Reptilio's light hearted gift for taxonomy or at least, a way with a name.

The bushy eyelashed hornbills settled on an occasional table in front of a looted full length mirror and lit up the room with their cabaret presence. Gaily, Chippo put a piece of paper in the Olivetti which by chance, had been in his room rather than in the bus at the time of Reptilio and Cerisia's ill-fated departure. Not the Leisure Beach Story Reptilio always had in mind, nor the seriously subversive feature article that Danny Dudgeon was awaiting, but something disreputable enough. *STARRY SANGUINI'S LAST HURRAH – Reptilio, The Streaker come Dancedoctor* he typed. A stirring excerpt from the letter that Dudgeon had sent Starry appeared in his head, autocue clear.

…Saturate me with bare breasted ETHNIC and FULL FRONTAL vaginal ROOTY TOOT TOOT. Into the PSYCHODRAMA, the LUSTODRAMA. Generally more SEXFILTH and ATROCITIES, more LOTUS, much more TOFFEE, less ZACH and DRIFT. No more environmental ENCHANTMENT crap. No more spiritual. Let's go for CLITORAL. Think ENGORGED and ERECT. Think WET DREAMS, WET LIPS and SPREAD SHOTS. Think SENSATION and SHOCK. Let's rewrite the SUCK AND FUCK MANIFESTO. Let's get LOOSE, let's get LEISURELY!!! Do I have to descend time's greasy pole and JACK OFF for you?

In half an hour, Chippo had banged out quite a few pages. He didn't know if he could claim the high ground of "just the facts" nor did he know what it was that drove him on. Maybe the wilful distortion of a legacy, maybe letting Danny 'high' Dudgeon know *"who the hell is Chipman Smith anyway."* More likely it was the cicadas shrilling encouragement from the trees in the village square, and those vamps the hornbills, squatting on the table like pelicans, those Wagnerian eyelashes making their frequent slow blinks look both Tristan and Isolde.

Yes, *Thug*, the brain child of Danny, the renegade media magnate of the 'new journalism'. There were many reports about what happened to Cerisia Twitchley and Starry Sanguini at Tlula, not to mention young Lotus and even younger Stan, *Whatever Forever* and the Bomzawe Bronzes. The London tabloids had a front-page field day with Cerisia and got themselves sued by an irate Lord Wittering – unsuccessfully – little had he known. The projected AFRICATASTROPHE *Thug* never appeared, but the teaser in the June 1972 issue, written in the promotional and scabrous Dudgeon style, did.

ALL THE HI HO AND WACKO THE DIDDLE O YOU CAN HANDLE O.

Yes, we will SPREAD the LEGS of the rotting REMAINS in our REQUIEM for one DISASTER after ANOTHER in our alimentary AFRICA issue. Read about the plummeting DEMISE of our dead as a dodo DANCE MAN, the rootin' tootin' REPTILIO, and former LONDON mafioso Medusa, MOTHER BUB who both MET their MAKER, GOT the CHOP in the WHATEVER FOREVER bus SHOOT-OUT and DROP-OFF on the WHITE MAN'S GRAVE coast of the ENGULF of GUINEA. Yes INDEEDY all you NEEDY, we will have you ORGASMING one more time when we feature our DAREDEVIL DUOPOLY in the CHERRYNOSE report on their showbiz SWANSONG, the PSYCHO-TORTURE and COMING-OUT carnival at Tlula Leisure Beach, the UBER-NOTORIOUS and turbo-charged HIPPIE HANG-OUT and HOTSPOT. Our EGREGIOUS couple were destined for this, the most OUTRE and EQUATORIAL of all their SEXPLOITS the moment they CRASH LANDED on the DARKEST and DROUGHTEST continent these many HOODOO VOODOO months ago.

We have the jigs UP and the low DOWN on those TERMINAL days, when Auntie ANARCHY and cousin CHAOS came A-CALLING, and the bane of BUTCHERY dealt the delight of DEBAUCHERY a bad hand.

Danny Dudgeon had an epiphany of epochal proportions on
Halloween Night the same year, and quit publishing shortly
thereafter. His spirit of adventure survived and subsequently, he
made a considerable fortune as a grain-trading baron. He, Wanda
and their seven children lived a full life, plying the warm waters of
the world's torrid zone in his sailing yacht *Thugmosis* until Cyclone
Cerisia (wouldn't you know it) put an end to them and their crew
in 2013. Danny lives on in infamy, as does Reptilio, as secure a
place in history as any other.

Chippo put his pages, the video of Tophphi and the very best of
his less-than-adequate photographic documentation of events at
Tlula, in a big envelope, and addressed it to *Thug*.

He thought briefly of his mother. And glanced at Zach. Did he
want to see Matilda again or not? His mother already suspected
that the best efforts of Melody at the elimination of any goodness in
either Alfie or Tibor's existence and the brutal reorientation of
Chipman's life, had come to naught but should he not tell her about
his Bomzawean sexual and emotional awakenings? Chippo could
hear her voice. "That's all very well, but you'll have to find your
own place to live. It can't be with Mel and me in the rectory.

Somewhere far far away." Chippo put another piece of paper in the Olivetti.

Dear Matilda and Melody,

My time here in Bomzawe is coming to an end. Extraordinary things have happened. It has not been easy, I have never been happier. Never. This is because I have come to terms with my true nature and become a modern man. I am in love, truly in love, with Zach. Another man. One day you may meet him. He is an American. From Nebraska. I am no longer a fool for everlasting love, nor the lesser loveydovey. As my late friend and mentor Starry Sanguini used to say, man is not built for monogamy alone. But we will love each other until thick and thin no longer works. Zach (short for the biblical Zacchaeus) ...

He added a photo, one of several that Lotus had taken with her Polaroid, of unshaven Zach and unshaven Chippo kissing. He hoped that wasn't rubbing it in too much for her, although he did hope it was too much for Melody. Then he lay down on the Liberator's sumptuous bed and put his arms around the sleeping American. From Nebraska. He let his passion and deeper longings carry him away once more. The love that may come just once in a lifetime. Tibor Radovan, oh so long ago and far away, had been a warm-up, a truncated pre-dawn run. Alfie? Well, that was just his happy go lucky Dad, an adolescent Peter Pan perhaps, behind the man of his lovable if carefully constructed façade of conventionality. Many sublime and tender minutes flowed by. There was a sound from the compound, and through the door came a grinning Qojo "You is sleepin?" The boy had suddenly grown three inches taller and his voice had acquired a young man's baritone leak. At last.

Qojo had the Toshiba radio. He turned up the volume. Bomzawean High Life filled the room. Zach woke up and the three of them began to dance. Bonnie & Clyde shook their feathers, rolled their eyes at each other, took one last look at themselves in the full-length mirror and stalked out, uttering their wild magical cries. They swished back to the trees, their wing beats the transcendent sound of a steam engine at full speed.

HORNBILL HOTEL

FIFTY FOUR: *The price of one*

The tide was out. The lemon green mist was thick that morning. It hovered close to the water, clung in curling wreaths to the sand. The early sun was lost behind a bank of heavy monsoonal cloud. Chippo raced to the pirogues drawn up on the beach. Not a single fisherman, but Qojo was there. Yes, he had seen Mr. Zach. He had gone out on a surf board not twenty minutes before. "I tink he go to island."

"Where is everyone, Qojo?'

"Dey is on strike. Is holiday always now. Everyone up all de night and party. In Doggone, big big problem. Peoples dead in street. Dere is petrol bomb."

"Qojo, I have to go out to the island. Round up the fishermen and I will pay them good good money."

"Mr. Zach he in trouble?"

"Go go! Now. It will be too late."

"I's comin'."

"Run!"

Chippo paced up and down on the wet sand. The mist didn't rise. He leaped up the steps two at a time to Castle Vinkenoog. At the top, he gathered his breath, waved away the first flies of the morning. The mist had retreated as far as the island and he focussed there with the glasses. As he watched, the promontory, then its palms drifted into view. Zach's last place. There was no sign of him, but Chippo wasn't about to believe the spirit of Zeke had already lured him into that treacherous sea off the south shore.

Two fishermen arrived below. From behind came the excited converse of monkeys. It was a troupe of black colobus arriving to feast on a purple fruit, ripening on a tree which grew on the saddle of land connecting Castle Vinkenoog to the jungled slopes behind. The crumbling edifice had long been favoured by monkeys. Their scat was in the thick grey dust, along with the prints of many feet from the villagers who had fled Lieutenant-Colonel Bonsai's soldiers. From the roofless centre, steps led down to the dungeons, the sharply odorous bat caves in the deepest recesses of which Drift had stumbled upon the Bronzes. Chippo closed his eyes and let the querulous simian squeals and chatter fill his skull. It seemed he could also hear the old stone of the battlements crumbling all around him, amid the cries of the Fanta, sold into slavery by the Ashanti , their old enemies.

Perhaps in response to Chippo's impatience, the residues of mist cleared and then dissipated entirely. No sign of Zach on the island. The sea was flat and pewter grey. He searched further, taking in the entirety of the wide bay. It was then that he saw him. Far out, beyond the shipping lane, heading south. He was naked, not even his cowboy hat. Chippo was slammed in his gut with an empty, stricken feeling.

He recalled the heat and smell of his body. The long kisses. The sadness in the warm embraces. The tough unsentimental talk. Even that initial coming together in Zach's room had had its elements of farewell. The never-ending repercussions from that pact with Zeke. The fluctuating fear that always prevented him from quite fulfilling that pact, from assuaging his guilt once and for all.

He gazed down at the pirogues. There was Qojo, waving. More fishermen had arrived. In five minutes they would be ready. He began the descent.

"You've found your freedom, Chippo," Zach had said. "Let me find mine." His recalling those words brought him to an abrupt stop. Leave him to his fate?

He found himself rooted to the spot, watching Zach until the sun rose above the clouds on the horizon, and shone wanly in a humid, tumescent sky. The ocean gleamed dully, the pewter turning slowly to a blue. The clouds would burst, torrential rain would fall. Zach was a silhouette in the silver, heading out to sea, executing the final farewell to his sorrows.

Chippo's vigil became a torture. His resolve began to falter. He suspected the imminent onset of the Starry Sanguini-induced spasm and that was shock enough for him to change his mind. He bounded down the steep steps of Castle Vinkenoog sure-footed as a Barbary ape. "Let Lanfal, come," he insisted when the fishermen kicked Qojo out. "His voice has broken."

Twenty minutes later, Chippo rose from where he sat in the prow and challenged the still distant surfboard paddler. "Zach, this is madness!" The man certainly was not able to either hear the shout or see him – or even want to – but it was only a matter of time before the pirogue caught up with him.

It was then that Chippo noticed the ship. It was no big affair like the *Star of Casablanca*, on which Drift and Tophphi would travel across the bay that afternoon, but a creakier coastal vessel, travelling west, trading between places like Ouida and Accra, Cotonou and Conakry. Dakar. Okidoki too. It was beyond the usual sea lane, but not as far out as Zach.

It was difficult to know at the distance, with the occasional curlicue of mist still lingering, whether Zach had seen the pirogue, but it became clear he had seen the freighter, for he began scooting the surfboard back towards the north west, a direction that would take him across its bow.

"Faster," Chippo ordered the fishermen. "Zach!" he yelled across the water, frantically waving. A high slow swell blocked sight of him but at two hundred yards he was in the binocular's view again. Chippo saw him signal the vessel with both arms. The vessel changed course slightly and began to reduce speed. The surfboard disappeared behind the ship's superstructure.

He accepted what Zach had done. He had saved himself, chosen to live and face once more whatever was to come. He wanted no part of Tlula Leisure Beach and his twin brother's memories ever again.

Telling the rowers to stop, Chippo regarded the becalmed freighter and raised his right hand high in a gesture of farewell. Only then did he begin to cry. Stinging tears of sorrow that Zach had left him as well as Tlula; sorrow yes, but there was an overflow of relief and thankfulness that he had made a wiser choice. Love is freedom, if nothing else. All the rest is desire.

The pirogue and the coastal freighter both rocked gently, close by each other out there in the troughs and crests of the blue-green Atlantic. A bundle, roughly wrapped in sacking, was tossed from the bow. Weighted with something, it sank quickly. Chippo hated to think that it was a body. The fishermen pointed excitedly. A shark's fin appeared. The first Chippo had ever seen in the sea around Tlula. Figures came into sight above the pirogue, looking towards them. He scanned the lines of black faces for a white one. He changed his mind again. After all, he did have Zach's passport with him. He told the fishermen to start paddling even closer to the yellow hulled freighter.

"Zach!" he called. "I'm here. I've got your passport." Yes, he was once more hoping against hope. Talk him into coming back. "Hey, Wilbur!"

A man in dark glasses, shabby braided jacket and cap appeared. He looked Syrian or Turkish. A moustache and beard. Young, not much older than Chippo, but the captain.

"You want surfboard man? We gave him some water. And a hat."

"You let him go?"

The man shrugged. "It is not our business. On a journey somewhere. Maybe he go to Fernando Po. Or San Tome. Paradise! Many virgins. Ha ha! You lose your – buddy?"

It was almost as if he was playing with him. Chippo found his clear amusement somewhat cruel. "Where are you going?" He had the wild idea he could get the ship to chase after Zach.

In easy, French-accented English, the captain explained. The ship was crowded with refugees. There was sickness on board. Everything was not okey dokey in Okidoki. A breakdown of law and order. Anarchy. Chaos. Jackals tearing at bodies in the street.

Suddenly the Democratic People's Republic of Bomzawe was not where Chippo wanted to be either. "I'm a refugee," he cried. "Take me."

"Who are you, white boy, for me to take you? You are a doctor? You have medical knowledge? What can you do for us?"

He wasn't going to say he was a lawyer. "I'm an educator. Ah – in the school of life." What would Zach have said? "Peace Corps."

"Educator? That is good." He laughed. Again, Chippo had the distinct fear he was making mock. It was almost enough to make him change his mind again, but a rope ladder was already being lowered. He unzipped his money belt, paid the fishermen. And something for Qojo and his family. With the pirogue scraping up against the hull, he grasped the ladder firmly and started to climb.

"Good bye, Qojo. Take the typewriter. The Girard Perregaux. The clothes. Take everything. It's all yours. Some day I'll see you again. There's a big envelope on the table for Danny Dudgeon. And a little one to Australia. It's for my Mum. Make sure you post them for me."

The yellow freighter gathered speed once more and headed for the far cape. The Tlula fishermen in their sea-going pirogue turned back to begin a working day in the rich hunting grounds around the palm-clad island. Lobster, prawns, tuna, sometimes turtle. Moon Looking Down.

"You still cry for your friend?" The Captain was beside him at an upper rail. Chippo had been looking south for the retreating figure of Zach on his surf board but he could not see him. Even with his binoculars. It was over. He bowed his head. The Captain put an arm around his shoulder. "I think you love him." He offered a cigarette. "Please don't cry." It was a fine black tobacco, like one of Cerisia's Gitanes. "I have something to cheer you up."

There was much more than kindness in his remark. Chippo regarded the captain more closely. He was tough and compact. A fine, almost Levantine nose. The moustache and beard were well-barbered. Skin leathered with salt and sun. A heavy gold earring. An attractive sailor smell. Something about him made him wonder about the eyes behind those concealing shades. He could not help smiling at the man, who smiled in response. They both laughed, rather shyly. At the fact that they had made an immediate and strong connection. Chippo realised the captain was a man who liked sex with men. And open about it. Like he was.

"Yes," the captain said. "But I have something to show you."

He took Chippo down a companionway to a lower deck. Goods and chattels, life possessions. It was a crowded scene but clean, not chaotic. There were people dozing, others hanging over the rail, watching the forested shore. The mood was buoyant, conversation animated. Men, women, children, families glad to be out of danger, on their way somewhere. Anywhere but Okidoki. A small group of musicians, a guitarist desultorily picking out a tune, a balafon player. From a mother breastfeeding her baby came a crooning. And beyond them, under an awning, sound asleep, and sharing with several others, were Drift and Tophphi. Stacked further off, were six of Chippo's ever-so-carefully constructed cages. One of the monkeys was chikkering. In the warmth of the morning sun, the diamond python was awake, moving very slowly.

"Americains, comme toi. You will make friends with them. He is handsome enough. She is very, very beautiful."

"They were supposed to be on the *Star of Casablanca*."

"You know them?"

"I know them only too well."

"Ah, the *Casablanca*. That is a sad story. It will not sail again. At midnight, they close the port. I was smart. I go quickly. He had been robbed of his money but made me a good deal. So I take them on board with their little zoo."

They went back to the Captain's quarters. Leaning against a wall, half-hidden by his desk, was the good deal. It was a Bomzawe Bronze. One of the wall plaques. Hardly damaged at all.

"It is okay. It has value. I have a connection in Dakar who knows about these things. Your friends have two or three others. A head, magnifique, with many pretty insects. But this is the one I like."

He drew Chippo towards him and kissed him on both cheeks. Then, after a moment's hesitation from both of them, on the lips.

"My name is Lateef," he said.

"Chippo."

As he continued to hold him in that gentle hug, he continued, "Chippo, I have something else to show you. We play a little trick."

He was led to an alcove. There was a bunk inside, partially concealed by a ragged curtain. He pulled it back. "Voila!" And there was Zach. He was wearing a pair of borrowed shorts. Chippo could see that he had been crying but he was also sporting the biggest of grins. As Zach stood up to greet him, there was an urgent shout from somewhere. A small explosion. Lateef went out. They heard him descending the companion way, issuing instructions.

Zach tasted of salt and deep water. There was something overpoweringly strange, even euphoric about him. He pulled away, grasped Chippo by the arms, started crying again. "It's Zeke," he said in a choked voice.

"The spirit form came again?"

"The captain. Zeke!"

Chippo stared at him in disbelief. He too was beginning to feel strange, filled with a torrent of mixed emotions. Of being cheated of his sorrow.

"He looks older than you. Not the same at all."

"Fifteen years have gone by but nothing has changed."

Chippo had to sit down.

"I couldn't sleep last night," Zach went on. "I got up, toked some of that jambo and my old guilt overwhelmed me. He beckoned me, yes the spirit form. I was sad to leave and kissed you farewell. Everything I had, I had to leave behind. Naked as I was born. I was at peace paddling out there. Accepting my fate. But when that yellow ship hove into view, something momentous occurred. Again the spirit form appeared, and it drew me with inexorable force towards the ship."

Chippo was silent. Sanguini was fond of saying "Everything is at least coincidence," but if it had taken yet another turn of the screw in Zach's brain to save himself so be it. He was very happy to be back with him again. Just to have him close. His chest began surging with warmth and a not-so-rare cicadan joy. Tears begin to course down his cheeks. Chippo held Zach's hand in his, not humouring him, but accepting him in his heart of hearts.

"I told you before about the Makeover, Chippo. It must have been this same ship that sailed by that day. My spirit was activated by Zeke being so near. I tried to swim to it. If it had not been for Floralee…" his voice trailed off.

Chippo had been with Drift in the hills above the bay that day and remembered a ship passing beyond the island, but had it been a yellow hulled freighter?

"Zeke must have told you just now what happened to him back there on the island fifteen years ago."

"He was plucked out of the sea by a fishing trawler. Bleeding, semi-conscious and near death. He was in a coma for some weeks and woke in Abidjan, being looked after in a hospital. His benefactor was a Syrian Frenchman, owner of a fleet of ships. He adopted him. He learned to be a sailor. They became lovers. It took years for him to recall just who he was. He was not even sure of what had happened on the island. He had no clear memory of me but came to believe I had drowned. His new life has much greater significance than his old."

It seemed to Chippo that Zach had had this kind of scenario in his mind for a long time. It sounded rehearsed.

"I saw you chasing me in the pirogue." Zach went to a porthole, looked down at the sea. "I suppose I knew you would do that."

When Lateef returned, Chippo drew him aside. "Are you really Zeke Shaler, his twin brother?"

For a moment, he held Chippo's hands in his. "I am Lateef." He glanced over at Zach whose eyes were fixated on the passing ocean, and twirled his finger around his ear. Chippo remembered Attah Lalwani having made the same gesture that very first day he had seen Zach through a jalousie. Chippo Cherrynose had fallen in love with a madman. Well, there are madmen and there are madmen.

Lateef removed his dark glasses and rubbed his eyes with a weary palm, blinked them clear. "I have urgent matters to attend to. It is a difficult morning for me, as it has been for you. Now the moment calls. I will arrange a cabin for you both and there will be time on our voyage to be happy in each other's company." Lateef smiled at him, glanced over at Zach, put his shades back on and left. His eyes were a deep green with a gold fleck. Zach's eyes.

Zach came over from the porthole. "Happy on our voyage through life, he meant. Zach and Zeke together again. Chippo, you get two for the price of one." He grinned and drew Chippo towards him.

Now that you have finished reading *Chipman's African Adventure,*
Valentine Press and Jim Anderson would appreciate your
feedback. There is a Reader's Comments page on the Valentine
Press website: **http://valentinepress.com.au/?page_id=1866**